To: Warren Kingsley

Best Wishes

CODE

NAME

ANTIDOTE

A NOVEL

CODE NAME
ANTIDOTE

Paul T. McHenry III

BROADMAN
& HOLMAN
PUBLISHERS

Nashville, Tennesee

0-8054-2083-5

Published by Broadman & Holman Publishers
Nashville, Tennessee

Dewey Decimal Classification: 813
Subject Heading: FICTION

Unless otherwise noted, Scripture quotations are from the Holy Bible, New International Version, copyright © 1973, 1978, 1984 by International Bible Society.

Library of Congress Cataloging-in-Publication Data

McHenry, Paul T., 1952-
    Code name—antidote : a novel / by Paul T. McHenry, III.
        p. cm.
    ISBN 0-8054-2083-5
    1. United States. Navy—Officers—Fiction. 2. Biological weapons—Fiction. I. Title.

    PS3563.C36845 C63   2000
    813'.54—dc21

                                    99-087462
                                    CIP

1 2 3 4 5 04 03 02 01 00

ACKNOWLEDGMENTS

First and foremost, to my wife Patricia for her editorial help and emotional support. After the sixth rewrite she affectionately dubbed it the "novel from Hades." Her critical insight helped me to round out my feminine characters.

To my son Paul for his editorial input.

To my Georgia Writers, Inc., novelist workgroup. Y'all kept me from adducing any effluvium. (They'll know what I mean.) If you are a writer in the Southeast, you need to be a part of this organization.

To Rush Limbaugh, the individual who provided the initial inspiration prompting me to seize upon a dream. Rush's underlying world-in-life view shapes the presuppositional foundation regarding his political comments and comes across clearly to anyone willing to listen with an open mind. His belief that America is a great nation full of opportunity for those who envision success and who vigorously pursue their dream is the warp and woof of what drives his political commentary. That message incited me to attempt the novel I always wanted to write.

Landlubber's Glossary of Navy Terms and Acronyms

1-MC	General announcement system, which can be heard throughout the ship.
AMIDSHIPS	Literally, "in the middle." (1) A relative location. (2) A rudder command.
ASROC	AntiSubmarine ROCket. A rocket-launched torpedo. Nuclear or conventional payloads available.
ASW	AntiSubmarine Warfare.
ATTACK BOAT	Nuclear submarine that does not carry strategic ballistic missiles.
AYE	Yes.
AYE AYE	Yes and I will comply.
BLACK SHOE	A term referring to surface warfare officers. The term has its origin in the early days of steam power when coal was the primary fuel. It is primarily used antithetically to the term "brown shoe."
BOAT	Any vessel that can be hauled aboard a ship. Submarines are called boats, which is a tradition that dates back to the time when a submarine could be hauled aboard a tender or other vessel.
BOATSWAINMATE	A rating or subspecialty. Handles small boats and most deck functions. Stands a bridge watch as the boatswainmate of the watch. Responsible for passing messages to the crew from the officers controlling the ship.
BOATSWAIN'S PIPE	A small musical instrument with a high-pitched shrill used in the old sailing days to give orders to the crew. Still used to sound attention, to announce chow, and to signal the crew to sweep down the decks. Also used in ceremonial functions.

BOOMERS	Nickname for strategic missile submarines.
BROW	A metal gangway that leads from a ship's deck to the pier or to a platform situated on the pier.
BROWN SHOES	Aviation officers wear brown shoes with khaki uniforms.
BUG JUICE	Navy Kool-Aide®.
BULKHEAD	Wall.
CAT	Short for catapult. Machinery used to launch fixed-wing aircraft.
CO	Commanding officer. Ship's captain. May, or may not, hold the rank of captain (0-6).
COVER	A hat. Something worn on the head.
CIC	Combat Information Center.
CINCLANT	Commander-in-Chief Atlantic.
CLOSED UP	Flag hoisted to the top of a yardarm.
CON	Term to describe which officer is giving maneuvering commands on the bridge. That officer is said to "have the con."
DAVEY JONES LOCKER	The place reserved for deceased mariners. Heaven or hell depending on the context of usage.
DECK	(1) Floor. (2) A term that describes which officer is in immediate control of all functions regarding the ship. The OOD usually maintains the "deck" while he will occasionally relinquish the "con" to a subordinate.
DIP	Flag halfway up a yardarm.
DOD	Department of Defense.
DZ	Drop Zone. Prearranged location where a combat vehicle or aircraft will insert or recover personnel.
ECM	Electronic Counter Measures.
ENSIGN	The American flag or a rank. The lowest ranking commissioned officer.
FIRST LIEUTENANT	(1) American Navy—a job title given to the officer responsible for deck operations. He is

usually the division officer for the boatswainmates on a small ship. On a large ship, he is usually a department head. (2) Royal Navy—equivalent to the XO.

FLAG OFFICERS' COUNTRY
: Area reserved for admiral's staterooms, head, mess, and office.

FLANK
: A speed command. The fastest speed possible.

FLASH TRAFFIC
: Flash is the highest priority. Traffic refers to any transmitted communication.

FORECASTLE
: Main weather deck area at the foremost part of the ship.

GERTRUDE
: Equipment used in underwater voice communication.

HEAD
: Toilet.

HF NET
: High-frequency radio net. Used for long distances.

ICBM
: Intercontinental Ballistic Missile.

JCS
: Joint Chiefs of Staff.

JG
: Shorthand for Lieutenant JG (LTJG).

JOOD
: Junior Officer of the Deck.

LADDER
: Metal staircase.

LAMPS
: Small helicopter used in ASW.

LZ
: Shorthand for Landing Zone.

MAD
: Magnetic Anomaly Detection. Measures disruptions in the magnetic signature of the earth indicating a large metallic presence such as a submerged vessel. Normally associated with a towed array used by LAMPS and other ASW aircraft.

Author's Note: In another novel, I have a fictional satellite MAD. I have no idea if such a capability exists. However, we can measure a number of geological conditions from space, and if I were planning defense weapons, I would certainly have developed a satellite-based MAD system by now. MAD was used in ASW when I served in the navy during the middle 1970s.

MAST — A ceremonial place, or formal event. A commanding officer conducts a nonjudicial punishment hearing at "captain's mast." If the crew is ordered to "lay before the mast," it is the nomenclature that indicates a formal ceremony is to take place.

MESS — An area used for eating.

MESS DECK — The enlisted crewman's mess.

OBA — Oxygen Breathing Apparatus.

OFFICERS' COUNTRY — Area reserved for commissioned officers' staterooms, head, and the wardroom.

OVERHEAD — Ceiling.

PCS — Permanent Change of Station.

PLANK OWNERS — Original crew of a ship at the time of its commissioning. According to tradition, each crewman owns a plank of the ship's deck. The author is a plank owner of the USS *Spruance*, DD-963.

PORT — Left.

QUARTERDECK — Place of ceremony. Where the OOD stands his watch when the ship is in port or at anchor. On smaller ships it is the place where one embarks or disembarks the ship.

QUARTERMASTER — Navy—Navigation associated subspecialty. Army—Supply subspecialty.

READY ROOM — Briefing room usually associated with aviation squadrons.

RIO — Radar Intercept Officer. A naval flight officer who is not the pilot.

ROMEO — "R" flag. Used during underway replenishment maneuvers.

SS-N-19 (24 or 26) — SS-N is the nomenclature used regarding Russian shipboard missiles. The 19, with later versions 24 and 26, are submarine-launched multistage ICBMs with multiple reentry vehicle (MRV) capability. Each missile is capable of delivering 8–10 nuclear warheads to individual targets. The Typhoon class SSBN with twenty launching tubes could theoretically strike up to two hundred cities. Because these submarines patrol within a few hundred miles of the American coast, the flight time of an ICBM would be drastically shortened, compared to a land-based missile, making detection and defense extremely difficult.

SAM	Surface-to-Air missile.
SEAL	Sea-Air-Land. Navy special forces.
SHOOT	A command that means "fire." In the navy the word *fire* is reserved for something burning uncontrolled.
SPECIAL SEA & ANCHOR DETAIL	An underway manning condition used in restricted waters where additional personnel are needed to get a ship in or out of port.
SPLASH	A command to shoot down.
STARBOARD	Right.
TAD	Temporarily Assigned Duty.
TAO	Tactical Action Officer. Usually in CIC. Has written "weapons release" authority. Needed for swift reaction to a modern threat environment when the commanding officer is not physically present in CIC.
TACTICAL NET	Radio net used between ships or aircraft.
WARDROOM	Commissioned officers' mess and lounge.
WHEEL BOOK	A green-bound, standard-issue notepad. Officers and chief petty officers usually carry them (i.e., the "big wheels").
XO	Executive Officer. Second in the line of command.
YOKE	A manning condition where most hatches are closed; however, some along main passageways remain open to allow the crew to move freely about the ship. The standard condition set while a ship is underway.
ZEBRA	A manning condition where all watertight hatches are closed. Used during general quarters.

PROLOGUE

0200, September 1, 1980.

DRY AIR TORMENTED EACH MAN. AFTER VIRTUALLY NO RAIN IN JULY and August, the dog days of summer along the Tigris and Euphrates river basin were brutal. Punishing temperatures of up to 125 degrees were not uncommon, even at night. Not a single pilot in Saddam Hussein's Revolutionary Guard could sleep. Each man tossed, turned, and worried. Every mind contemplated 0700 and the call to the flight line.

Ever so gently, Lieutenant JG David Egan slid a handheld, night-vision periscope above the surface of the water.

Four minutes behind schedule. I hope these Iranians sleep soundly. The air in our rebreathers will be exhausted soon.

David needed to get his SEAL team ashore quickly. The last thing he wanted now was an aborted mission. No new officer wants to look bad while leading seasoned men.

It'd be just my luck to fall on my sword the first time out.

He took a quick glance at the four other team members and the two small submarines below him. They were busy positioning the spare rebreathers necessary for their escape. Each apparatus lasted only forty-five minutes. David knew that he needed most of that time to get the team out of the harbor and back to the USS *Baton Rouge.*

The Iranians were using two of their Vosper Mark 5 class frigates to aggressively patrol the area. The skipper of the *Baton Rouge* made it clear that he'd stay within range for half an hour. Everything had to go according to the scheduled time sequence. Since the maximum speed for each of the Perry Oceanographic scuba submarines was 5 1/2 knots, David knew he would need a full forty minutes to reach the rendezvous.

The first thing he saw was a freighter alongside one of the piers.

Rats! Too many lights—even the boom's lit up. Must have every deck light on the ship turned on.

He saw no activity around the deck. Next, he panned slowly to the right along the empty pier; at its head he sighted the guard shack and a solitary soldier. Scanning further right along the shoreline, he saw a couple of run-down buildings and warehouses.

Good. All's quiet and dark.

Along the shore itself he could see the pipeline that ran from the refinery to the holding tanks and the utility lines just above. If the Iranians hadn't changed anything, this should be the only telephone line out of the port area. David continued panning to the right. He spotted the targets of the mission— the storage tanks.

David paused a moment. His stomach churned fire into his throat. It wasn't the mission itself that made him so apprehensive. It was the wisdom behind it. No matter how much he tried, he couldn't suppress his feelings. The whole mission annoyed him.

Who am I to question the wisdom of my orders? I'm barely a JG.

He knew that Iran and Iraq had been rattling sabers over the oil-rich province of Khuzistan for several years. Just because Hussein declared the 1975 agreement with Iran null and void and planned to recover the disputed Shatt al-Arab estuary, Washington had no reason to take sides.

Look what happened to the Shah. Who's to say Hussein will last any longer?

Did Washington really believe that allowing Hussein to take over these oil fields would diminish the fervor of the Iranian Moslems to export their brand of Islam?

Too late for questions now.

Hussein's major offensive was planned for 0900.

According to the information he'd received in the mission briefing, the fuel was piped from the nearby Abadan refinery to the storage tanks used by an Iranian air base. Hussein planned a major offensive, including an attack on the refinery. The team mission was to set a timed charge that would explode at 0800, an hour before the offensive was scheduled to begin. It would destroy the fuel supply of this air base and create confusion.

0200. *Only forty minutes to accomplish the mission and head out toward our rendezvous.*

It would take twenty-four minutes to set the charges and an additional five minutes to return to the subs and change equipment. He was already four minutes behind schedule. That only left seven minutes for any contingency that might arise.

David pulled the periscope down and swam back toward his team. Using prearranged signals and a waterproof sketch pad, he ordered Harper to take care of the single guard and take his predetermined position as the team's rear guard. It was also his responsibility to cut the telephone leading out of the pier area. Harper nodded agreement, then swam away. The rest of the team swam toward the tanks.

Once again, David raised the periscope and took a quick look around.

No hostiles.

The four men stood up and moved out of the water as quickly as possible, depositing their gear along the shore. Torrez, Kahn, and Jennings were assigned to set the charges. They took the explosives out of waterproof bags and moved away toward the tanks. The explosive experts who planned the mission had determined the pattern for setting the explosives so that all the surrounding tanks would also explode.

As the three moved to set the charges, David pulled out a set of night vision goggles and a Scorpion Model 61 with silencer. He took his position as cover for the demolition team.

Tiny waves breaking at the water's edge rhythmically soothed his nerves. The only other sounds David could hear were the occasional buzz of a mosquito and the hum of the ship across the estuary. An occasional light breeze delivered the pungency of the ship's sewage discharge. Each minute seemed like an eternity.

They've got this timed to the second. Besides, they've handled this sort of thing before.

Fifteen minutes later, Kahn came into sight and went toward the equipment on the shoreline. He entered the water and dove under. Seven minutes later, Jennings emerged and also entered the water. The plan called for Torrez to arrive in two minutes. Harper was scheduled to reenter the water from his position at the same time Torrez was scheduled to return.

Two minutes went by, and Torrez appeared right on time.

Shots rang out.

David motioned for Torrez to take the gear and get into the water and then turned. Harper was down. An Iranian had a gun trained on him. David started moving carefully toward them along the water's edge.

The Iranian used his foot to turn Harper's body. As Harper rolled over, he gave the Iranian a burst from his Beretta. The Iranian stumbled backward and fell.

Now, almost two-thirds of the way to Harper, David stood up so Harper could see him. Harper didn't move.

Come on Harper, get up.

When he didn't, David broke into a run for several hundred yards. Then he slowed and approached the two men carefully.

Blood covered the Iranian's body from multiple chest and stomach wounds. David checked the soldier for a pulse. Then he threw the enemy's weapon into the water.

Harper was conscious but disoriented. Two of the wounds were in the abdomen, and the other through his upper left leg.

David drew his knife and carefully cut the wet suit near the leg wounds.

I need to keep his wet suit functional.

On the leg he could see a clear entry and exit wound. David tore strips of the dead Iranian's clothing and used them to pack the wound. Then he tied the packing in place with another strip. He used the wet suit as a cover to keep the bandage in place.

David lifted the top of Harper's wet suit and repeated the process of packing the stomach wounds. Then he pulled the wet suit down over the bandages, took a few of the military pins from the uniform of the Iranian soldier, and pinned the leg of the wet suit together.

That should keep it closed.

The other three team members emerged from the water, fitted Harper's rebreather and mask, and moved him into the water. While the team got Harper secured, David dragged the dead Iranian into the water. He tied the body to a rock on the bottom of the estuary using a strap from one of the expended rebreathers.

Guard's not likely to change for several hours. Hope they have a lazy sergeant-of-the-guard.

Forty-five minutes later.

The skipper of the *Baton Rouge* secured the hatch behind him. "Diving stations," he commanded. "Make your depth one hundred and fifty feet."

"Aye aye, sir," the officer of the deck responded. "All ahead two-thirds, five degrees on the down-bubble. . . ."

David sipped coffee while he watched the activity. He replayed every detail of the mission in his mind.

Don't know if it was worth it. At least I got Harper back alive.

ONE

September, 1995.

THE SEAS CHURNED WITH INTENSE FURY. COMMANDER DAVID EGAN breathed through his mouth so as to avoid smelling the rank air.

Will this storm ever end? Half the crew's sick.

Sickness was evident from the stench in the combat information center. It was strong enough to give the hardiest old salt a queasy stomach. David didn't linger long in the CIC. He quickly got to the top of the metal ladder. As he emerged onto the bridge, his vision fixed on a wall of green water about to slam into the superstructure. Considering that the bridge was over sixty feet above the waterline, it was a dreadful sight.

Everyone on the bridge reached to hold onto anything bolted down as the swell slammed into the ship. First, there was the thunderous crash. Then, as the bow was forced underwater, the enormous bow-mounted sonar dome caused the ship to shimmy. As the shimmy grew more intense, the ship began to groan. The groan started out as a deep guttural sound vibrating through the steel of the ship. As the bow was forced deeper and the stress from the shimmy became greater, the pitch of the groan went up. It grew in intensity until David was sure that a witch from the deep was screaming in his ears. The sound and the intense vibration would make anyone wonder if the ship was tearing apart.

David looked at the bridge crew. He caught a glimpse of the expression on the face of the messenger of the watch. It was sheer terror.

Same expression I had.

David remembered his first mission into Iraq fifteen years earlier. He recalled spending most of the hour prior to embarkation hugging the toilet.

Performance while terrified builds character. He'll get his sea legs after this.

A reassuring smile spread across David's face. "Good morning, Johnson."

"Captain's on the bridge," the boatswainmate of the watch sung out as Johnson returned the captain's greeting with a weak smile.

Lieutenant Ian Ferguson, the officer of the deck, turned toward David. "Good morning, Captain. I trust you had a good night?" He grinned.

"Morning, Ian." David walked from the centerline ladder to the starboard side captain's chair. The messenger from radio entered the bridge and walked up to David's chair.

"Mornin' Captain, here's your traffic," he said as he handed David a stack of messages.

"Morning, Plarady."

Everyone on the bridge grabbed hold of something as another swell slammed into the ship. This time the swell only came to the top of the forecastle. Ian Ferguson approached David and started his report.

"Captain, we're steaming independently until this front moves by. According to Tom, we should start to see calmer seas within the next—"

"Great. I'll be glad to get things back to normal and cleaned up. You ought to get a whiff of the stench in CIC. I didn't realize we had so many fresh crewmen."

"I'm not so sure they're all new. I've been feeling a little green myself, and I'm sure some of the old salts down in the chief's mess are packing away the saltines."

"What else do you have to report?"

Ian continued his report while David began to sift through more of the message traffic.

"Thanks Ian."

David read on, message after message, all very routine until one caught his attention. It reminded him of the bad publicity the navy had received regarding the Tailhook incident. He turned to Ian. "I see the secretary of the navy announced plans to have women on every major combatant. Including subs."

"Doesn't surprise me."

"Boats, blonde and sweet," David said looking at the boatswainmate.

"Aye, sir."

"I wonder how some hard-nosed feminist would react to the way I order my coffee."

The boatswainmate brought David his coffee. While making a boorish obscene gesture, he said in a heavy New Jersey accent, "Ah, don't youse guys worry the captain, we'll get 'em straightened out."

Most of the bridge crew chuckled.

"That's what we're worried about, Boats," Ian said. "I can see the headlines now, DESTROYER GATE, SEXUAL HARASSMENT ABOARD THE *PETERSON*. . . ."

As they continued to kid with each other, David drifted off, thinking about all of the changes that had occurred over the past ten years. Ships had always been a coarse, rude environment where men didn't have to worry about the conventions of mixed society.

I can't believe how much things have changed.

David's daydreaming was interrupted by the scratching sound of a voice coming over the radio net.

"Charlie Delta, this is Xray Foxtrot. I am prepared to authenticate, over."

Ian picked up the handset as the quartermaster of the watch scrambled to find the authentication table. The quartermaster found the table and threw it to Ian as Ian began to respond. "Xray Foxtrot, this is Charlie Delta, authenticate Delta Delta Alpha November, over." Five seconds later, "Charlie Delta, this is Xray Foxtrot, I authenticate Alpha Alpha, immediate execute. . . ."

Everyone scrambled to get the code although David recognized it as being rendezvous instructions. Tom Warren, the navigator, had just come onto the bridge from the chart room and began to plot the rendezvous point.

"That's odd," Tom said. "Captain, the rendezvous is nowhere near the task group. It's well to the west of our present position."

"Mr. Ferguson, what are you waiting for, an engraved invitation? That was an immediate execute."

"Aye, sir," he responded. "Left standard rudder."

"Left standard rudder, aye, sir," sounded the helmsman. "My rudder is left standard, passing zero two zero."

"Belay your headings," Ian said.

"Belay my heading, aye, sir."

"Set new course two seven zero," Ian commanded.

"New course two seven . . ."

"Two nine zero, Ian," David blurted out.

"Belay my last, set new course two nine zero," Ian said.

"Aye, sir, new course two nine zero."

David looked over toward both Ian and Tom. "Any traffic over the net today?"

"No, sir."

Ian picked up the shipboard telephone. "Wilson, this is Mr. Ferguson on the bridge. Would you look up today's call signs and confirm that Xray Foxtrot's the commodore?" After about thirty seconds, he said, "Are you sure?" Turning to David with a puzzled look, he said, "Captain, Xray Foxtrot is CINCLANT."

"What's he doing out here?" Tom blurted out.

"Permission to pipe down chow?" the boatswainmate of the watch asked.

"Very well," Ian said. "I'll bet there aren't many takers."

Everyone chuckled, including David.

The boatswainmate began to pipe attention followed by chow call. David got up and walked to the chart table. Looking out at the rain, he realized that the ship hadn't taken many major swells since the first one that greeted him as he came to the bridge over a half-hour ago. "Get me a weather report," he said.

"Aye, sir," the quartermaster responded.

"Tom, where's the rendezvous?" David asked as he looked at the chart.

Tom pointed to a spot west northwest of the ship's present position. "Right here, Captain."

"Time to rendezvous?"

"About one and three quarters hours at this speed, sir."

"Let's run north for about twenty minutes at this speed," David said. "The seas'll be better for those hardy souls up for a good breakfast. Turn west and set whatever speed is necessary to be on time. Have the first lieutenant make preparations to go alongside. We need to top off this morning."

"Yes, sir."

"I'll be in the wardroom," David said as he headed for the starboard hatch.

"Captain's off the bridge," the boatswainmate called out as David went through the hatch toward his sea cabin.

The captain's sea cabin was only five steps from the bridge. David could hear Tom and Ian as they began to speculate about the rendezvous with CINCLANT. They knew, just as David did, that CINCLANT rarely left Norfolk, certainly not to participate in a routine NATO operation in the North Atlantic.

David stepped into his cabin. He had a queasy feeling in his stomach. To have the *Peterson* leave its present task group to join the *Kennedy* probably meant that Admiral Bill Hopkins wanted him to leave his command and return to some kind of staff intelligence position. After having only been in command for a little over a year, he enjoyed being back in the navy. He appreciated the fact that Bill was looking out for his career.

It'd be nice if it could last a full tour.

David took out his razor and began to lather up. It struck him as being a little odd for Bill Hopkins to come all this way to tell him he was about to receive orders.

Certainly he'd have told me in Norfolk—or waited until the *Peterson* returned in three weeks. CINCLANT doesn't travel halfway across the world to tell a commander he has orders, even if that commander's a friend.

David washed away the residue from the shaving cream. He felt the coffee he had consumed a little earlier boil up into his throat. Reaching into the cabinet beside the basin, he wondered if his upset stomach was related to the weather or the rendezvous. With a sigh he took two Tums and then headed out of the cabin toward the wardroom.

"Good morning, Captain," Lieutenant Commander Miles Landrum said as David entered. A chorus of good mornings from the five other officers seated at the table followed.

"Good morning, gentlemen. I trust you're all well rested and ready for a busy day."

Miles Landrum was the *Peterson's* executive officer. David and most of the other officers didn't really care much for Miles. In the six months since he had arrived, David had come to realize that he was an arrogant brownnoser with limited competence. David knew he had to work with him, and so he kept his feelings about Miles hidden from the other officers.

The sound of the phone reserved for the captain's use interrupted the conversation.

"Captain," David said.

"New tactical commander, sir."

"The *Kennedy?*"

"Yes, sir."

"Thanks, Ian," David said. He turned to Miles. "We've been assigned to the *Kennedy*. Get with Ron and make sure we have worked out all the replenishment details. I'd like to top off this morning. I want a smooth operation."

"Yes, sir."

After ordering grits and toast, David turned to Jack Pearson, the wardroom's resident Dallas fan. "Hey, Jack, quite a game!"

Jack knew David was a Miami fan. David knew Jack would be smarting from last weekend's matchup between the two teams.

"Dallas had the game won—'til they made that boneheaded move," David said.

"Oh, that's a low blow, Captain."

"Seconds left to play and that blockhead had to go and touch the ball on the two-yard line. Whoo-ee, now that's chokin'."

"I've got twenty that says Dallas'll be in the Super Bowl."

The other officers at the table couldn't leave this conversation alone. They all jumped in, championing their favorite teams and arguing vigorously the strengths and weaknesses of each NFL team. For the next five minutes, David ate his breakfast while being entertained by a colloquy of male verbosity regarding that most noble of all preoccupations, football.

The captain's telephone interrupted. It was Ian reporting a planned course change.

"Good. I'll be in my in-port cabin if you need me."

David stood. "You know, Jack, Dallas might have a chance against Philadelphia if they can get back to basics this week—like which way to the goal."

"Philadelphia, they're no good. Dallas'll—"

"Gentlemen, if you'll excuse me." David motioned to Lieutenant Frank Baron, the operations officer, to join him. They walked from the wardroom to David's in-port cabin.

David offered Frank a seat. "Frank, we've changed task groups. We're to join the *Kennedy*. Get together with the XO and the department heads as soon as you receive operational instructions for today's exercises. I've asked Miles and Ron to arrange a fill-up as soon as possible."

"Yes sir. Captain, any idea why such an abrupt change?"

"Don't know yet."

"Oh, regarding the night war game scheduled for tomorrow . . ." The two men continued to discuss the scheduled operations for several minutes. "I'll take care of it," Frank concluded as he got up and left the room.

David looked down at the mound of paperwork that had accumulated in nicely color-coded folders arranged before him. He decided to dive into some of the paperwork for the next half hour while the ship proceeded to join the *Kennedy*. There, on the top of the stack, he saw the fitness reports. Jack Pearson's evaluation was on the top. David smiled.

Let's see, top 1 percent for loyalty, toward the Cowboys, that is.

The phone rang.

"Captain," David answered.

"Captain, flash message from Gabriel's coming over the HF NET," Ian said with a slight crack in his voice.

David was stunned. A rare feeling of anxiety shot through his body. He sat staring at the picture of his two sons for a few moments. "I'll be in combat."

After he hung up the phone, he ran to the CIC faster than he had ever run there before.

What in the world's going on? Flash traffic from the Joint Chiefs of Staff? Have I missed some important news developments regarding Russia? Have the communists overthrown the government? JCS wouldn't send flash traffic unless an ICBM's about to be launched!

David entered the hatch leading into CIC. The tactical action officer moved out of the center command chair and handed David the message. It stated that within the last twenty-four hours, two Russian attack submarines, together with a boomer, and most of their northern naval surface units had entered the North Atlantic. In addition, a flight of TU-16 Badger and TU-105 Blinder aircraft had been detected leaving Russian airspace heading toward the two task groups involved in the NATO exercise. The final sentence said that the Russian government had not responded to NATO inquiries. A coup d'etat could be in progress.

David quickly glanced around to get a tactical picture. Because of the weather, the task group was independently steaming, and the Naval Tactical Data Systems (NTDS) Net was down. All the ship had for information was derived from its own sensors.

That's just great.

"ECM," he said loudly.

"Aye, sir."

"Any contacts?"

"Not really, sir."

"What do you mean, not really?"

"Sir, about fifteen minutes ago I thought I detected an 'I' band emission. It only lasted a second. I assumed it was a phantom."

"What bearing?"

"Wasn't able to get a bearing, sir. It came from the east northeast."

"Air tactical, any contacts?" David shouted.

"None, sir."

David reached down to the communication console and keyed the microphone. "Sonar, Captain. Any contacts?"

"No, sir."

Where's the blasted NTDS when you need it? Hundreds of millions of dollars for state-of-the-art equipment, and I'm a blind sitting duck.

The old task group was well to the south, and the *Kennedy* was still well to the west. That would make the *Peterson* the northeast picket.

I'd better play this one safe.

"Bridge, Captain. Sound general quarters," he ordered over the communication console.

"Aye, sir."

The boatswain's pipe shrilled attention over the 1-MC. "General quarters, general quarters, all hands man your battle stations, now general quarters."

The general quarters alarm started to sound, and a flurry of activity resulted. David got up and put his inflatable life vest on. He tucked his trousers into his socks and sat back down. A messenger handed him a grey helmet with CO painted on the front and back. Within just a few moments the status boards were manned and condition reports were flowing in. It must have been a record for this crew. Within seven minutes the ship was battened down, tight as a drum.

As abruptly as the activity began, it ended. Dead silence in CIC. The nets were quiet. There was no message traffic from radio or the bridge.

Shattering the silence, Petty Officer Flint, the ECM console operator, shouted, "Contact bearing zero five two."

"What'd you have?" Tony Scappecchi, the *Peterson's* CIC officer, demanded.

"Fifty-four forty megahertz, sir. That's a 'C' band radar, sir."

Several seconds passed. "ECM, give me a report!" Tony said.

"It's a WXR-seven hundred weather radar, sir. They're generally found on Airbus and Boeing commercial aircraft. It looks like it could be a Russian or Scandinavian airliner."

"Contact, zero five four," the air tracker called out.

"What do you have?" Tony asked.

"Eighty to one hundred miles, sir, contact bearing zero five four. I'm designating it bogey alpha. It's squawking, sir."

After a short pause, the air tracker called out again. "It's squawking a commercial aviation IFF, sir."

"Thank God," Tony said.

"Flint, what radars operate in the 'I' band?" David asked in a loud voice.

"Well, sir, the major radar we'd see is a surveillance system called the Puff Ball."

"Isn't that the radar the Soviets use on their Bear aircraft?"

"Yeah, ah, I mean yes, Captain. That radar's been around a while, but it's a good system. It's also the surveillance system for the TU-sixteen Badger. Oh, and the TU-one forty-two Bear."

The message from Gabriel referenced Badgers.

"What fire control radar would a Badger have?"

"They carry the 'Short Horn' radar system that operates in the 'J' band, which is about fourteen hundred to fifteen hundred megahertz, sir."

"Flint, I don't care what's going on, if you see even a moment of 'J' band emission, you make sure I get that word immediately! Do you understand? Immediately."

"Aye, sir."

"Air tactical," David called out.

"Aye, sir."

"If this is a Badger or Bear trying to look like a commercial airliner, we're already in range of an air-to-surface missile. Let me know if you see any splits moving at a high rate of speed. Immediately."

"Aye aye, sir."

David leaned over and keyed the microphone for the communication system. "Bridge, Captain. Get a message off to the *Kennedy*. Tell 'em we've an unidentified bogey bearing zero five zero our position, sixty miles out. Possible Badger flight. Make sure you give them our position."

"Aye, sir."

Russian military aircraft are equipped with electronic counter measures. If I paint the Russian with our fire control radar, the pilot'll get an immediate warning.

"Tony," David said. "Time to find out if they're friendly. Assign bogey alpha to the missile fire control system. I want 'em to see our target acquisition radar. Let's make them realize their disguise didn't work."

"Yes sir," Tony said.

With general quarters set, the captain now had all of the voice and data net operators located around him in CIC. Messages and a frenzy of activity took over.

"Message from the *Kennedy*, sir," the air controller called out. "Two Tomcats inbound. On top in five."

"Message from the task group commander," the tactical net messenger called out. "NTDS net's being reestablished. E-2's airborne."

David was glad to hear that news. NTDS would allow the ship to see all the contacts that all local NATO ships and aircraft were tracking. The E-2, an airborne radar platform, can see three hundred miles in all directions.

David sat looking at the *Peterson's* new contact display system. It gave him a wide area geographic display of surface and air contacts using holographic images projected on clear Plexiglas. When the NTDS link was established, the *Peterson's* CIC would have a full tactical picture of just what was going on.

In the meantime, I'm almost blind.

"I have the two Tomcats," the air controller called out.

"Assign intercept vectors to bogey alpha," Tony ordered.

"Aye, sir."

"I've lost contact," the ECM operator called out.

Almost in the same instant, air control reported that bogey alpha had stopped squawking IFF.

"Time to intercept?" Tony asked.

"Six to eight minutes."

"Tell 'em to floor it," Tony said.

"They are, sir."

"'I' band contact zero six zero," ECM reported. A second later, "'I' band contact zero five five. . . . 'I' band contact zero five zero, . . . 'I' band contact zero four five. . . . Captain, I've got 'I' band contacts all over the northeast, sir."

"Very well, Flint. Let me know the moment you see 'J' band, or any other emission."

"Aye, sir."

"Tony, let's get our players on the headsets; there's too much noise in here," David said as Tony approached his chair. Everyone overheard David's order, and all of the console operators put on their headsets.

"Assign bogey alpha to missiles," David said.

Tony, standing beside David at the command tactical control console, highlighted bogey alpha and pressed the assignment button.

The missile control console operator responded. "I have acquired bogey alpha. Bogey alpha's not in range; I do not have a firing solution at this time."

"Captain, it doesn't look like bogey alpha's on an intercept to us, or the *Kennedy*," Tony said as they both watched the console monitor.

"*Kennedy* has launched ready aircraft," air traffic control reported.

Over the dull drone of console operators chattering, David heard, "Link's up."

The Plexiglas displays in front of David lit up. In an instant the officers could see the track of every ship and aircraft for hundreds of miles around. And there, at even intervals over the whole quadrant, was the flight of Russian badgers. The historical track for each aircraft was a semicircle starting from the northwest and moving south, then up toward the northeast.

"Tony, put the air distress frequency in this speaker," David said pointing to a speaker box above his head. "Oh, and put the *Kennedy's* air boss on the speaker next to it. I want to hear what's going on."

"Yes, sir," he responded as he picked up the telephone to call radio.

"Time to intercept?"

"Three minutes, Captain."

"ECM, any changes?"

"No, sir."

David sat back in his seat and surveyed the tactical picture. He wondered why the Russian high command would set about to attack a NATO exercise shortly after overthrowing the democratic government—assuming an overthrow had actually occurred.

Certainly, they'd be much more concerned with subduing local opposition rather than picking a fight with the West. Even Hitler wasn't that stupid! Why would they use that odd tactical pattern?

With the bulk of the NATO fleet well to the south, it seemed clear that the Russian commander wasn't interested in the NATO forces. There hadn't been a major flight of aircraft leaving Russian air space since the fall of the Soviet Union.

Suddenly they put seventy-five aircraft in the air? It's surprising they have the fuel. What's going on?

"Tomcats have taken up wing positions on bogey alpha," the air controller said.

"Assign bogey alpha to surveillance," David said to Tony.

Tony reached to the appropriate buttons on the tactical control console and reassigned bogey alpha from fire control to surveillance.

David was puzzled as he tried to make sense out of the tactical picture.

Submarines, seventy-five aircraft. They don't seem to be coming after us. It must be a rogue Russian they're after. And with all that firepower, it'll be a ship or an aircraft with nuclear capability. I wonder if this has anything to do with . . .

"Captain."

The voice startled David. Miles Landrum was standing beside his chair.

"Yes, Miles."

"We're scheduled to go alongside at thirteen forty-five. You're due aboard the *Kennedy* at fifteen thirty for the meeting with CINCLANT. You're also expected for dinner at seventeen hundred."

David nodded acknowledgment toward Miles. Then he returned his attention to the status boards and the tactical situation. Tony's air of confidence and command of the situation had settled the CIC. The men were functioning with superb professionalism. It pleased David to know that his crew could really pull together and perform when the situation was potentially critical. Of course, most of them were laboring under the assumption that the Russians were about to engage the NATO fleet. If so, the *Peterson* would be the first ship engaged.

It was clear to David that if the Russians were interested in the NATO task group, they'd have taken a more aggressive posture already.

The aviation distress frequency crackled as the pilot of one of the Tomcats began talking to the pilot of the Badger designated bogey alpha. In broken English, the Russian was indicating that they were looking for a freighter that was supposedly in distress. They were requesting that NATO provide information from its E-2 regarding the freighter's position.

"Tony, what do you think? Think they turned out the whole Russian navy and Air Force for a search and rescue mission?" David asked.

Tony shrugged his shoulders. "Who knows what they're up to?"

"Captain, the third Tomcat's on top. Where do you want him?" air control asked.

"Five miles inside bogey alpha's present position."

"Aye, sir. Captain, the *Kennedy* is launching four more F-14's."

"Very well."

"Tony, how many targets can the F-14s missile computer handle at one time?"

"I don't keep up with all the changes, Captain. I seem to recall that it can handle six at one time."

"Yeah, that's the number I had in mind."

"Seven Tomcats could do a lot of damage," Tony said.

With our surface-to-air missiles as a backup, the task force would have time to get other aircraft airborne if the Russians did turn south. With this strange tactical layout, the Russians only have eighteen aircraft that could be a threat. The others are too far away.

"Bridge, time to rendezvous?" David asked.

"Half an hour, sir."

"Have the first lieutenant report to me in combat."

"Aye, sir."

Moments later, the shrill of the boatswain's pipe wailed over the 1-MC. The first lieutenant was paged to CIC.

"Captain, looks like our Russian friends are continuing to sweep back toward the northeast. Toward home," Tony said.

"Yeah, looks that way. Air Control, have you been able to make out the gist of the conversation between the pilot and the Russian?"

"Well, sir, the Russian continued to talk about the missing Russian freighter. You know, kept asking for help from our E-2. The air boss had the F-14 tell the Ru¯ski that we'd accounted for all shipping south and west of his position. The missing freighter hadn't been sighted. When our pilot relayed that information, the Ru¯ski acted grateful. Kind'a like he seemed to accept what he was told. Anyhow, it worked. They've turned toward the northeast."

"Interesting."

"Captain, I'll bet they knew we'd kick their butts. They turned yellow," the air controller said.

David knew better. They may be a little out of practice, but this was the same military that used to taunt American and NATO forces in the North Atlantic regularly. No, he was sure that they weren't interested in a fight with NATO.

"Bridge, Captain."

"Bridge, aye."

"Have the crew stand relaxed at their stations."

"Aye, sir."

Moments later the boatswain's pipe was sounding attention on the 1-MC. "Now relax general quarters. Set condition yoke above the main deck. Make reports of open hatches below the main deck to damage control central. All hands stand easy on station."

"Captain, bridge. Main engineering wants to know if you want all mains and all generators on line."

"Set standard steaming conditions."

"Aye, sir."

"You sent for me, Captain?" Ron Pearson, the first lieutenant, said as he approached David.

"Yes, Ron. We're scheduled to go alongside shortly after we secure from general quarters. I don't want a delay on our part."

"I'll pull the chief and two others out of repair five. Petty Officer Stanton is qualified to act as the repair party leader," Ron replied.

"Very well. Find out from Frank how long it will take him to line up the fuel systems."

"Yes, sir."

Once again, a voice could be heard over the tactical radio net. "Charlie Delta, this is Delta Alpha, I am prepared to authenticate, over."

"Delta Alpha, this is Charlie Delta, authenticate November November Xray, November, over," the OOD on the bridge responded.

"Charlie Delta this is Delta Alpha, I authenticate Bravo Alpha, immediate execute, . . ."

Delta Alpha was the *Kennedy* task group commander. Given the present air show being given by the Russians, proper procedure would be for the *Kennedy* to take tactical command and to order the *Peterson* to a station as a picket ship. David expected the task group commander to order the *Peterson* to a picket station several miles north of the carrier.

"Captain, the *Kennedy* has taken tactical command and has ordered us to a station," the OOD said.

"Proceed. Where is our station?"

"Plane guard fifteen hundred yards off the port quarter."

"Are you sure?"

"Yes, sir."

"Very well, proceed at twenty-five knots."

"Aye, sir."

"The E-2's taken over CAP control," the air controller said.

"Very well," Tony responded. "Captain, the Russians are definitely heading toward home. I wonder what they're up to?"

"Tony, we know that several submarines sailed in the past few days. Get your best operators on the sonar plot. Have them report any anomalies," David ordered.

"Yes, sir. Captain, do you think they will be able to detect much? You know, considering how rough the seas have been?"

"How did you get through ASW school?" David asked in a stern tone.

David was six feet two inches tall, weighed two hundred and twenty pounds, and didn't have an ounce of fat on his body. With a strong set jaw and steely blue eyes, he could look awfully imposing when he was angry or stern.

"Just get Chief Baril on it. He'll spot 'em if they're not under the thermal layer."

"Combat, Sonar, request you clear the baffles."

"Combat, aye. Stand by," Tony said.

"Bridge, Captain. Left full rudder, all stop."

"Aye, sir."

As David waited for sonar to tell him they had cleared the baffles, he had a sinking feeling about the events that had transpired. Something was up, and he knew it had to do with the rendezvous with CINCLANT. If you took things as they appeared, it was clear that something important had gotten away from the Russians. Given the economic collapse of the country since the fall of the Soviet Union, it was surprising that they even had the ability to pull off such a major air exercise.

"Combat, Sonar. Baffles clear. Request permission to go active."

David nodded approval. Tony responded, "Sonar, Combat. Permission granted."

"Bridge, Captain. Proceed to station."

"Aye, sir."

"Secure from general quarters," David continued.

"Aye, sir."

The shrill of the boatswain's pipe sounded over the 1-MC. "Now secure from general quarters, set condition yoke throughout the ship. Make reports to Damage Control Central."

When standard steaming conditions were set, David ordered flight quarters. He left the CIC and went to the flight deck.

Several minutes later.

The 1-MC sounded attention and was followed by four bells. David couldn't hear the message because of the noise from the helicopter. He knew they were announcing his departure. The pilot gave a thumbs up. David crossed to the aircraft. The crewman sat David down and made sure he was strapped in. David felt a jolt and then the sensation of the aircraft rising above the ship. The pilot banked to the right, and David found himself looking straight down at the *Peterson* with nothing between him and the ship except the nylon seat belt. He could feel his stomach tighten. As the aircraft leveled up, he could see the *Kennedy*. It doesn't take long to fly four thousand yards.

The landing on the carrier was smooth. The crewman helped release David's seat belts while the pilot shut down the rotors. He sat for a few moments while the rotors stopped.

David stepped out of the aircraft. He could hear the *Kennedy's* 1-MC. Four bells sounded, followed by "*Peterson* arriving." Then, another single bell sounded.

A chief petty officer, with a flagstaff epaulet and gold piping, met him. David followed the chief through an endless maze of passageways until they finally arrived at a door marked "Flag Officers' Country." A marine guard snapped to attention.

"At ease."

A man in civilian clothes was about to enter when David approached. "Commander Egan," the civilian said as soon as he saw David. He extended his hand. "I'm Bob Reese from London."

"Bob, I must say, you have me at a disadvantage. Have we met before?"

"No, sir. I know you from your file."

"Oh, I see. Well, I guess I'm about to find out what's going on."

They both signed the security log and received badges from a second guard.

TWO

**Earlier, in a small town north of
St. Petersburg, Russia.**

F RESH SNOW POWDERED THE TREES AND BUILDINGS. THE A–FRAME
sporting lodge was located in a remote, wooded crest of
hills overlooking a deep ravine. The landscape was rough, yet
majestic. An occasional stand of evergreen trees punctuated
the scenery. Smoke billowed from the chimney with a sporadic
flash of tiny hot embers.

Inside, the center of the main room was dominated by a
circular fireplace with a massive black wrought-iron hood suspended from the ceiling. A raging fire gave warmth to a broad
area while casting a yellow hue on the dimly lighted room. The
smell of hickory masked the lingering odor of burned tobacco.

To one side was a small kitchen. Beside the kitchen a
woman and two men sat at a large, round oak table playing
cards. On the other side of the room, Severny Iourtchak sat
reading a magazine while listening to Mozart's Clarinet Concerto in A major playing softly on a CD player near him. Beds
were located in a loft near the back of the structure.

The door flew open and Mikhail Kruzanshtern stepped in
quickly, shut the door, and began to knock the snow off his

coat and trousers. He removed his fur hat and slapped it against the door frame to remove some of the snow and ice.

"Such a cold night," Alexander Andreyev said as he looked up from his cards.

"Are you going to play?" Leonid Vodokanal asked with a demanding tone. Leonid was nervously tapping his knee with his left hand. The clenching and unclenching of his teeth caused the veins in his temples to slightly protrude. It was obvious he didn't like waiting.

"Come, Mikhail. Sit, drink. We have much to celebrate," Alexander said while ignoring Leonid. "A little vodka to warm you."

"It's too early to celebrate," Leonid said. "Cards?"

Mikhail didn't respond. His pronounced movements, as he removed his cold weather garments, combined with a preoccupied stare were out of character for this normally jovial man. As he took a seat, the others noticed that he was out of breath and sweating.

"You look like you've just wrestled a bear," Alexander said.

"More likely that new redhead," Dasha said with a smile.

"Da, Da. The redhead." Alexander laughed.

"How many cards?" Leonid said in a slightly raised tone of voice.

Severny Iourtchak smiled as he listened to the others tease Mikhail. While there were a number of fair-haired women in northwestern Russia, Severny didn't know many women with red hair.

At least not any good-looking ones.

Alexander certainly didn't have many in his brothels, only one. She had a darker shade of hair, almost auburn in color. Her skin, while very fair, had no freckles. Her sky-blue eyes and delicate nose enhanced her beauty.

Mikhail was smitten by her, and everyone knew it. He sometimes appeared peeved when she didn't show deference toward him. As a top lieutenant in Alexander's organization, he acted like Alexander's brothels were his private harem.

My, my, how he would get agitated.

It frustrated him and provided his companions with an endless source of material for teasing. But this time Dasha's words had no apparent impact on Mikhail. He didn't wink or change expression. In fact, he had a distant look about him, almost as if he weren't aware of the joke being made at his expense.

"Two," Alexander responded as he took two cards out of his hand and discarded them. "If not the redhead, then what's bothering you, Mikhail?"

"Rostislav called from Moscow," Mikhail said in a quiet tone.

"And?"

"He said the Ministry of Security has issued an arrest order for us."

Leonid stopped thumping his leg. Everyone looked at Mikhail. The only sounds were the roar of the fire and the soft music playing in the background. Severny reached over and turned off the music.

"They know about Ilya," Mikhail continued. "Rostislav says that there is a crisis atmosphere in the Kremlin and the president has directed the military to use all means possible to find Ilya."

"How could they know so quickly?" Leonid said as he got out of his chair. "Ilya reported himself sick. It should have taken several days for them to suspect." He paused, punched the wall, then turned to Alexander. The light color of his face turned red. "Ilya's always been a security risk. I warned you not to use him! He was not able to keep his mouth shut in Spain. I told you he could not do this. He has raised suspicions."

Alexander turned his face away from Mikhail and looked directly into Leonid's eyes. He stared at him for almost ten seconds without blinking.

Severny closed the magazine he was reading. "Choose your words carefully, Leonid." He spoke slowly, in a low-pitched tone.

"Who asked you? Prima donna." Leonid clenched his fists.

"*Nyet,* Leonid," Dasha said. "If Ilya tipped them off, they would have reacted sooner. He's been gone for almost two days."

"She speaks wisely," Severny said as he walked over to the table where the others were seated. "Wisdom and beauty. Such a melodious combination."

Dasha blushed slightly as she looked into Severny's eyes. "Is everything music to you?"

"Enough," Alexander broke in. He turned to Mikhail. "Did Rostislav know how they found out?"

"*Nyet.*"

"Maybe they found the weapon missing," Dasha said.

"Doubtful," Severny said. "Two of Ilya's scientists have defected to America. No one but Ilya would have suited up to make a routine inspection of the virus. Indeed, most of them would not know what they were looking for. No one in his right mind would expose himself to that bug."

"Da," Alexander responded. "The how is not important. If they are looking for us, they will surely go after the Vasily Ukraina. Where is it? Under way or in port?"

"Berthed in Stockholm," Mikhail said.

"Stockholm? It was not scheduled for a stop in Stockholm."

"I rerouted it there. I had an opportunity to obtain two hundred Glock .40 calibers that were untraceable."

"I've always said you were the best quartermaster in Europe. You may have saved our butts." Alexander paused. Then he looked at Severny. "Do you think the Americans know?"

"Da. It's possible."

"I fear them much more than our own intelligence service and military. Can you still activate Communications Technologies?"

"Da. Rostislav has kept us updated on changes."

"Good. Do it. Any possible mission is to be reported."

Alexander turned toward Mikhail. "Contact the Master of the Vasily Ukraina. Have him put Ilya ashore. Give instructions for

Ilya to proceed to Oslo and wait there. If we do not contact him within two days, he should proceed to Spain."

"Da."

Alexander turned to Dasha. "Get the plane ready."

"Won't that be dangerous?"

"We will stay low and fly to Helsinki. Once we fly out of Russian air space, the coastal watch is likely to see us. But they usually do not care much about outbound planes."

"Unless Moscow has alerted them already," Severny said.

"Given what Rostislav said about the state of confusion in the Kremlin, I doubt they notified the civil border watch. They will be arguing about who is to blame and plotting coupes for the next—"

"But what about the military?" Mikhail said. "They are not bureaucratic idiots!"

"Da! A problem," Alexander said. "Their radars are set up to search low altitude approaches toward Russia. They depend on the civil authorities for domestic radar air control." He paused and thought a moment. "We could fly from Sestroretsk to Vyborg at treetop altitude virtually undetected. They may see us cross the border, but by then it would be too late to scramble interceptors."

"Da, Da," all three responded almost at once.

"What then?" Dasha asked.

"I have a contact in Lappeenranta. We can switch aircraft there and fly to Helsinki. I have an old friend who can get us to Turku and arrange a boat to take us to Stockholm."

"Then?" Mikhail asked.

"We find Ilya," Alexander responded with a scowl on his face. He paused staring at Mikhail. After a few moments, his scowl turned into a smile. "If I know Ilya, we just need to find the ladies."

"We have to assume that Russian intelligence agents will come after us," Dasha said. "Sooner or later the Americans too. They know who we are—Who Ilya is—How do we get out of Norway?"

"Good point." Alexander said. "I have always said you are as bright as you are beautiful." He stared at her for a moment and then shifted his eyes to Mikhail. "Do you have sources for supplies in Helsinki?"

"Da."

"We need controllable sport parachutes for each of us."

"That should not be a problem."

"Your plan?" Dasha asked.

"Commercial aviation will be the last thing the authorities will shut down. We will take a flight heading for France and then go overland to Spain."

"And the parachutes?"

"Back-up plan. If we get in a bind, we can hijack the plane and fly to France. We leave the plane before it lands."

Ten minutes later.

"Good evening, Resources International. How may I serve you?"

"Extension 23689," Severny said.

"Thank you." There was a pause.

"Please enter your six digit access code."

Severny entered 830669.

"Thank you. One moment."

"Communications, Decker."

"Oh. This is not personnel? I'm sorry. I was trying to find out about my health coverage."

"No. This is a communications staff office."

"My mistake. I was about to travel overseas for the first time, and I needed to know what to do if I got sick or in an accident."

"Sorry, can't help you."

Severny hung up and waited. It would take at least a half hour for Decker to leave Langley and get to a phone.

Forty minutes later.

"Hello," Severny said.

"This is the AT&T international operator. I have a person-to-person call from Mr. Johnson of Communications

Technologies in Alexandria, Virginia for Mr. Pavel Krylov. Is Mr. Krylov available?"

"Da. This is Krylov."

"I can't believe that after all these years . . ."

"I need to know if there are any priority shipments of equipment to northern Europe," Severny interrupted in a low-pitched voice. "Can you e-mail that to our Edinburgh office?"

"You'll have it within two hours." There was a click, and the phone went silent.

The cold war's over. Why do they need me now?

Ivan Krupsky, also known as Robert Decker, had only been activated twice in the late 80s, both times by the standard approach.

Must be something serious to call directly into Langley.

After obtaining the required information, Ivan's standing orders required him to make his way back to Russia.

No way. I like America.

He'd been hoping that the end of the cold war would have brought an end to his special intelligence unit. However, the Communications Technologies office in Alexandria remained open. Ivan had no idea who used the company office. If the office closed, he planned to quit his job with the CIA, change his identity, and move to New Orleans. But now his past had caught up to him.

He hadn't seen anything in the news or through the communications center that was serious enough to warrant the possibility of exposing his identity.

Why now? Why were they asking about covert operations in the northern European area? Even during the height of the cold war, very little happened in Sweden, Denmark, or Norway.

As one of five senior communications watch officers, Ivan had access to the names of every mission. He also knew who had access to mission information. Depending upon the stations involved, he could usually figure out where a covert operation was focused.

As he drove back to Langley, he knew he had to deliver the information.

I can't ignore the order. All the Russians need to do is tip off the CIA, and I could spend the rest of my life in jail. No, they'd just sanction me.

But what about going back to Russia? He could just disappear by faking his death and taking on a new identity. He could do that.

Two hours later.

By the time Alexander and his associates arrived in Vyborg, he had decided that they would cross the border overland. It would take a little longer to get to Helsinki, but security was important. They checked on a rental car. The attendant said it would take ten or fifteen minutes, so the group decided to wait in a nearby restaurant. Severny had the waiter bring him a phone. He plugged a laptop computer into the phone and accessed the Edinburgh Internet provider that would have the anticipated e-mail message.

The message read:

> Per your request, the only shipments are medical supplies labeled antidote. For more information contact: William B. Leighton, William C. Hopkins, Robert L. Reese, Dr. Catherine F. Evans, Steven M. Hsieh, James B. Washington, Richard A. McReynolds. Government approval for the shipment was granted by James Dillon at the White House at the urging of Senator Tidwell and Congressman Winston. The Salesman responsible for this order is David E. Egan.

Severny saved the message and unplugged the phone. He turned the computer screen around to where Alexander could see it. Alexander read the message. He stopped at every name and thought a moment.

"The Americans are onto us," Alexander said. "They cannot resist cute names that have some meaning relating to the mission." He paused and started to scratch his head as he pondered the message. "This female doctor is undoubtedly their biological expert."

"Da," Severny said. "I doubt the Americans have carried out a covert mission in northern Europe in years."

"I recognize several of the names. Military officers of high rank."

"Da."

"David Egan? Is that name familiar?"

"Da," Severny said. "Madrid. GRAPO."

"Da! Da. The intelligence officer who shut down GRAPO."

"And killed Grigori! I would take great delight in meeting him again," Severny said.

"Mikhail, contact Rostislav," Alexander ordered. "I want to know all about David Egan. Also, get me a file on the doctor."

Mikhail nodded his head.

THREE

FLAG OFFICERS' COUNTRY WAS THE ONLY PLACE IN THE NAVY'S SEA OF grey paint that looked like a suite of executive offices. In fact, it was one of the few places on a ship where wood paneling was still allowed. The bulkheads were finished with cherry wainscoting. Above the wainscoting was a vinyl covering with a striped pattern of forest green and burgundy accented with gold. The door handles and other fixtures were brass. A suspended ceiling concealed the cable runs in the overhead. Two marines stood guard at the door of the flag briefing room. One of the marines opened the door to admit David and Bob.

The room was laid out like the wardroom on the *Peterson*. As David entered from the passageway, he saw a conference table to the left. An elaborate audiovisual setup occupied the bulkhead at the end of the table. To his right a rear admiral sat on a couch beside a male and a female civilian. A glass of bug juice rested on a small coffee table in front of the woman. Admiral Bill Hopkins and a navy captain stood to David's left next to the audiovisual equipment.

"Ah, David, it's good of you to join us," Admiral Bill Hopkins said.

The individuals on the couch stood as he spoke. The rear admiral, an aviator, was closest to Bob and David.

Possibly the Kennedy task group commander?

David's eyes were drawn to the stunning woman who looked to be no older than thirty. It was all David could do to pull his eyes away from her and focus on the others in the room. Across from him was a civilian of Asian descent.

"What could I say to such a gracious invitation?" David said.

"And this must be Bob Reese with you."

"Yes, Admiral," Bob shook his hand.

"Well, gentlemen, let me make the introductions. Commander David Egan, Bob Reese, this is Admiral Mike Newton."

They shook the admiral's hand while Bill continued. "This is Captain Oscar Collier, Mike's chief of staff. Mike and Oscar have been gracious enough to lend us this space for our meeting. They've also invited us to the flag mess for dinner."

"I look forward to an improvement over the seven-way beef cuisine we get on destroyers," David said smiling.

Oscar grinned. "Legends of our culinary exploits are vastly overrated, my dear sir," he said in a deliberate drawl.

Admiral Newton turned to Bill. "Admiral, I know you've got a lot to discuss this afternoon, so, with your permission, Oscar and I'll take our leave and let you get to your meeting."

"Thanks, Mike," Bill said. Mike and Oscar left the room.

"Let me introduce you to our other players," Bill continued. "Gentlemen, this is Dr. Catherine Evans. Dr. Evans is on loan to the CIA from the Centers for Disease Control in Atlanta."

David extended his hand to her. He studied her face, feature by feature. The alabaster hue of her skin was soft and radiant. It was highlighted by her high peachy cheekbones, which delicately accented her sensual mouth. Her lips were full and perfectly shaped. Indeed, they were almost pouty. Her nose was delicately arched. She looked back with wide, clear blue eyes that shone like cobalt. She met the hand that was offered with an infectious, arresting smile.

Suddenly, the image of his deceased wife, Rebecca, flashed across his consciousness. The prickly feeling he associated with guilt washed across the back of his neck and shoulders.

"Dr. Evans," he said.

"Commander," she responded with an adventurous toss of her head.

"Gentlemen, let me introduce you to Steve Hsieh," Bill said. "Steve's the officer in charge of the CIA's Armageddon Group."

I can't say I'm happy to meet you.

David extended his hand to Steve. "What'd you know, there really is an Armageddon Group."

David had heard the rumors. Allegedly comprising the most elite agents in the business, they were an antiterrorist hybrid of the Delta Force concept, literally America's exceptional agents of last resort.

"Let's get started," Bill said as he motioned toward the conference table.

Everyone walked to the table and sat down. The door to the room opened. Oscar Collier entered. Several aids, carrying boxes of printed material, followed. Two mess specialists also entered with fresh coffee and bug juice. They quickly deposited what they had and left the room.

Bill walked over to the door and called the guard inside. "Sergeant, no one's to enter this room until further notice."

"Yes, sir."

Steve began to distribute the printed material. On the cover of the sealed briefing folder was the large "TOP SECRET" stamp along with the title: Antidote. As David broke the seal and opened the folder, he could see a letter written on White House stationery and signed by the president.

TO: Director CIA & Chairman JCS,
            CDR David E. Egan, USN
SUBJECT: Letter of Finding

IAW the National Securities Act, I have determined that recent theft of biological weapons grade material from a Northwestern Russian weapons facility poses a clear and present danger to the security of the United States. I do hereby exercise the powers granted me in the Act, to wit:

1. I authorize a covert intelligence operation code named: Antidote. I appoint CDR David E. Egan, USN, as the officer in charge.

2. I authorize the Special Operations Group CIA, code named: Armageddon Group, to support Operation Antidote. Extreme measures, including preemptive executions, may be employed to ensure the success of Operation Antidote.

3. JCS shall give full and unconditional support to this operation.

The following persons shall have knowledge of this operation. All other information will be on a need-to-know basis.

The Chairmen of the House & Senate Oversight Committees
The National Security Advisor
GEN William B. Leighton, USAF, Chairman JCS
ADM William C. Hopkins, USN, CINCLANT
CDR David E. Egan, USN
Mr. Robert L. Reese, CIA Special Operations
Dr. Catherine F. Evans, CIA Special Operations
Mr. Steven M. Hsieh, CIA Special Operations-
       Armageddon Group
Mr. James B. Washington, CIA Northwestern Russian Desk
Mr. Richard A. McReynolds, CIA Quartermaster Division-
       London

CDR Egan, you are ordered to locate and recover the stolen biological elements. In so doing, you are authorized to take any action you deem necessary.

Bill opened his sealed folder. "Dr. Evans. Gentlemen. Four days ago, a Russian biological weapons scientist, Doctor Ilya Choutov, didn't report for work. He'd been a surveillance target of the Mossad for over a year, and the Mossad immediately called on the CIA for assistance."

"Choutov?" Catherine looked surprised.

"You know Doctor Choutov?" Bill asked.

"Yes, well, as a professional acquaintance. We were introduced several years ago in Brussels."

"Is that so?"

"Yeah. It was a world health symposium on AIDs. Choutov was a featured speaker. His specialty is the process of mutations in viruses. He's one of the world's leading experts. I had no idea he was involved."

"I'm afraid so. According to the information we received from the Mossad, Choutov became a primary surveillance target when he was seen in Madrid eating with a known operative of the First of October Antifascist Resistance Group, GRAPO. In the navy everything has an acronym."

"GRAPO. You're kidding." David grimaced.

"Thought you'd find that interesting." Bill paused. "Commander Egan already knows all about GRAPO. David, why don't you enlighten us a little about this group?"

"I didn't know I'd be put on the spot. Let's see, they're a small Maoist urban terrorist group with fewer than a dozen known operatives. Loosely associated with the Spanish Communist Party, their activities have been focused on removing the United States military presence from Spain. In the early eighties, GRAPO carried out small-scale bombings on U.S. and NATO facilities. In 1985 the Spanish government pretty much shut 'em down. Or so I thought."

"They did. Aided by the CIA and our own Commander Egan," Bill said. "They made substantial arrests which, for the most part, shut down the activities of GRAPO. With the exceptions of a rail bombing outside of Madrid and the bombing of segments of a NATO pipeline in Spain in 1991, we've not seen much from them."

"Is that why I got tagged for this mission?" David asked.

"Partially. You're certainly our best expert on GRAPO. But with Alexander Andreyev's shipping connections and his military background, we felt we needed some expertise in that area."

"Andreyev? The same Andreyev I know from the eighties?"

"You bet. We'll get to him in time." Bill paused. "I know you want to keep your command. We all live for the chance to have a command at sea. But David, you're an experienced field operative, a naval officer, and you're here. It'd take several days to get someone else here. Plus, I doubt anyone at CIA would have your unique combination of experience." Bill shifted his notes.

"Glad to hear you've had some field experience, Commander," Steve said. He didn't smile. In fact, David couldn't recall seeing him smile the whole time he'd been in the room.

Must be a real fun-loving guy.

"The reason Mossad has this group under surveillance is the development of a disturbing relationship between GRAPO and certain members of the Fatah," Bill said. He looked at David. "Since you and Steve have some familiarity with terrorist organizations, you may recall the Fifteenth May Organization. It was formed in the seventies from remnants of Wadi Haddad's Front for the Liberation of Palestine-Special Operations Group. The group's leader is Muhammad al-Umari. He's known as Abu Ibrahim, which translated means "the bomb man." This group claimed credit for several bombings in the early eighties. The bombings included a hotel in London as well as El Al's Rome and Istanbul offices. They also hit the Israeli Embassies in Athens and Vienna. U.S. targets included an attempted bombing of a Pan Am airliner in Rio and the actual bombing of a Pan Am flight from Tokyo to Honolulu in 1982. The Fifteenth May Organization disbanded when several key members joined the Fatah. Two of those same members were seen meeting with members of GRAPO a little over a year and a half ago in La Rochelle. That's on the coast of France. The Mossad became quite concerned because GRAPO was known to have ties to the French Action Directè as well as the Italian Red Brigades. So, let me ask, what does this suggest to you?"

Everyone looked around at each other in silence. Finally Bob spoke up. "It's uncharacteristic, I mean, not very typical for these groups to have any intercommunication. Don't they operate in small uncoordinated cells? You know, to avoid detection."

"What would a Communist European group have in common with Abu Nidal?" David asked.

"Good observations," Bill said. "Bob, you're correct in your assumptions about how these groups tend to operate. That's one of the things that worries our analysts. David, I see you're still up on your knowledge of Middle East terrorism. For the benefit of the others, let me explain. Abu Nidal, also known as the Fatah, is actually a very large organization made up of several hundred militia. Over the years they've assimilated the Fatah Revolutionary Council, the Arab Revolutionary Council, the Arab Revolutionary Brigades, Black September, and the Revolutionary Organization of Socialist Muslims. Since 1974 they've been credited with over ninety terrorist attacks in more than twenty countries, killing or injuring almost nine hundred people. While they do operate in cells, they also have the most structured organization of any of the major terrorist organizations. They were headquartered in Iraq from 1974 to 1983 and in Syria from 1983 to 1987. Since 1987 they've been headquartered in Libya. With the fall of the Soviet Union, there's been an increase in the number of reported interactions between these Mid East groups and European groups such as GRAPO. Most experts believe this unholy alliance is developing because the European Marxist organizations have so many contacts within the old Soviet KGB. It's believed that the effort is focused on obtaining weapons of mass destruction. With all that ordnance up for grabs in Russia, it's only a matter of time until they succeed in obtaining something nasty."

After pausing for a drink, Bill continued. "It would appear that a number of the old Soviet spooks have found a new profession in the growing ranks of Russian organized crime. Until now, our intelligence evaluations have concluded that these were loyal Russian nationalists who were content with making money off of drugs, prostitution, and protection rackets. Similar to organized crime in the West, these enterprising individuals have branched out into a number of legitimate businesses, which include high technology, transportation, and some manufacturing. Of particular interest to us is Alexander Andreyev. He's based in St. Petersburg and has built one of the first private shipping companies in Russia. He has thirteen freighters that cover routes throughout the world. An old Soviet spook, he has an ongoing relationship with Doctor Choutov. While serving with the KGB, Alexander was posted in both France and Spain. Choutov was involved in a joint research project with the French while Alexander was posted in Paris. You'll find his dossier in your package."

The group members began to shuffle through their papers until they found the CIA dossier folder. On the left corner inside the cover was a current picture.

Bill Hopkins continued. "Alexander Andreyev was the leading KGB contact for a number of the groups, including the French Action Directè and GRAPO. Mossad is convinced that the Libyans have offered a huge sum of money for him to smuggle a weapon out of Russia on board one of his ships. Our experts are not sure the Libyans are the bankers. Iranian, Libyan, it really doesn't matter."

"Why a biological weapon?" Bob asked. "Several Arab countries already have biological weapons."

"Good observation, but you're just a little ahead of me," Bill answered. He took another drink of the bug juice and then continued. "Our best guess is that the original prize for Abu Nidal was a nuclear device. With several good friends, including our Doctor Choutov, Alexander Andreyev had access to a variety of weapons. Abu Nidal's focus has apparently changed from dirty nuclear devices to biological agents. Dr. Evans is going to tell us why and answer your question, Bob. Catherine."

Catherine stood and arranged her notes.

"Gentlemen, please refer to your folder labeled 'Viruses.'" She paused while they shuffled through their briefing material. "We have reason to believe that the missing weapon contains a hemorrhagic-type virus similar to the Ebola virus. In the past, both the United States and the Soviet Union have experimented with the possible use of a mutated form of yellow fever for biological weapons. The research was abandoned in the late seventies. In 1989 research resumed briefly when an Ebola-type virus was discovered in Reston, Virginia. As you know, these viruses are extremely deadly to humans. They tend to spread very rapidly. The renewed weapons research focused on controlling the way a virus spreads by developing a hybrid strain of the Ebola virus—one that would mutate in a predictable manner. This super virus would also have a much shorter lifespan. If such a strain could be developed, the theory went, a weapon could be used to wipe out life in a specific area. Subsequently, the area would be reclaimed by vaccinated troops. The theory also held that the virus could be localized. It didn't take our folks long to realize the folly of that research. The weapons angle was dropped."

"We can't be assured of what a simple flu virus is going to do," Bill said.

Catherine smiled and nodded. "Our sources tell us that the Soviets never dropped their research. In 1976 and again in 1979, Ebola had spread through N'zara and Maridi in the Sudan's grasslands. The Soviets obtained cultures from one or both of those outbreaks, which they used in testing right up until the summer of 1990. Here's the kicker. The researchers involved in the Soviet project manipulated the test data to induce the government in Moscow to continue funding."

"Where have I heard that story before?" Bob asked.

Catherine continued. "It was assumed by key leaders in the Russian intelligence and military communities that Russia had actually developed such a weapon. Moscow couldn't keep that kind of information in check, and it became well known among senior officers in international intelligence circles. The

CIA and DIA both picked up on this information and eventually concluded that no such weapon had been developed."

She shifted her note page. "After the fall of the Soviet Union, we were able to interview two of the Russian project scientists. That's how we learned about the false reports to Moscow. Since Andreyev was a senior intelligence officer up to the early nineties, we believe he convinced the Arabs that they could actually defeat Israel using such a weapon. After destroying Israel, they could move in to occupy without any damage to the infrastructure."

"That explains the Mossad's interest," Steve said.

"What about the Palestinians in Israel? Wouldn't that kill most of them?" David asked.

"We don't know if Israel was the intended target for this weapon," Catherine responded. "It could have been the United States. However, the theory held that a shortened lifespan of the virus would help to localize its reach. If it were released during a Moslem high holy day, say Ramadan, good Moslems would be abstaining from food or drink during the day. Their special evening meal would be with other Moslems. Human contact is the assumed method of transmission. Since they wouldn't be working, contact with Jews would be minimized. Key people would be vaccinated. Other Palestinians might die, but their deaths would be a glorious sacrifice to Allah in the defeat of Israel."

Catherine flashed a slide onto the screen. "Now, gentlemen, if you will give your attention to this slide, I will try to give you a little more detail as to what we are up against. Hemorrhagic viruses can be divided into several families. First, we have the flaviviruses, which we've known about for a while. This family includes the Amaril virus that causes yellow fever. It's transmitted by mosquito. Recently, we've identified three other families called arenaviruses, bunyaviruses, and filoviruses. All of the known arenaviruses and bunyaviruses are responsible for hemorrhagic fevers. These viruses occur naturally in certain populations of animals. Rodents seem to be the most common. These rodents shed viral particles in their feces and in their urine. A trace amount in the air or in your water supply is all that's needed."

"The filoviruses, including Ebola, are still a mystery. We don't know how they're transmitted. They have a short incubation period, less than a week. They cause a diminution in the number of blood platelets, which are the cells used by the body for blood clotting. Superficial bleeding through the skin and appearance of bruises are characteristic of these viruses. Cardiovascular, digestive, renal, and neurological complications quickly follow, and the patient usually dies of massive hemorrhages. Sometimes multiple organ failure occurs."

She changed slides and continued. "Hemorrhagic viruses change and adapt faster than anything we have ever seen. These viruses have genes consisting of ribonucleic acid (RNA) rather than the DNA found in the genes of most living things. This RNA is what biochemists call 'negative stranded.' Before the virus can make viral proteins in an infected cell, the gene must be converted into a 'positive strand' by an enzyme. This particular enzyme frequently causes errors. That gives rise to new viruses as the mutations accumulate. Some viruses adapt to invertebrates, others to vertebrates. They adapt so quickly that they confound the immune systems of their hosts."

Catherine clicked another slide. For the next ten minutes she gave a detailed history of all the known outbreaks of the virus. Then she showed a slide depicting an actual Ebola virus. "The Ebola is an example of a filovirus. It is so named because of its filamentous appearance."

The group sat in silence. David couldn't take his eyes off the deadly virus.

My Lord, what am I getting into?

If they didn't succeed, tens of thousands, maybe millions, would die.

After a few moments of silence, Catherine asked if there were any questions.

"What claims did the Russian scientists make to Moscow that caused them to believe they had a controllable weapon?" Steve asked.

"They knew their superiors had a grasp of the theory but no real microbiological understanding of the life cycle of viruses. I'm sure they had some success in their research, just not the kind that would produce a useful weapon. The key was to keep the research going in the lab."

"Yeah, but knowing the destructive capability, how could they even consider misrepresenting the truth?" Steve asked.

"Well, gentlemen, do we have any more technical questions for Dr. Evans?" Bill said as he stood to rescue Catherine.

"Yes, I do," Bob said. "How is this virus supposed to be dispersed?"

Catherine's face brightened at the question. She seemed relieved to return to a more technical discussion. "Remember, I told you that we don't know much about the transmission of this type of virus. Virtually any contact with humans is deadly. Tears, blood, saliva, even touching a contaminated area can be deadly. Dried contaminate in a fine dust can be breathed or introduced to a water supply. It's assumed that it could be introduced into an area by several means. In an urban setting, a water supply would be a likely target. We also suspect that airborne dust in ventilation systems may be possible."

"Did the Russians succeed in altering the genetic composition of this virus?" David asked.

"Yes, they did. They claimed to have developed a mutated strain with a shorter incubation period."

"Are their claims plausible?"

"We don't know. Doubt it. Ebola has been a major concern to the CDC for several years now. We've done as much work as anyone on it. I hate to say, but we really know very little about it. One thing I'm sure of. If this viral agent is disseminated in any significant quantity, humankind could join the dinosaurs."

"How is it contained? Is it in one container or several?"

"It can be contained in anything that's airtight and nonporous. Glass would make an excellent liner. I'm sure that anyone with any sanity would encase the glass in something that would prevent breakage. As to the amount or number of containers removed from the Russian lab, our source of information regarding the theft is a Mossad operative. We just don't know."

Silence filled the room.

Everyone sat looking up at the Ebola virus slide. David began to think about his two sons. Rebecca, his wife, had been killed in a car accident a little over five years ago. They had two great kids who were now grown. Edward was the oldest. He had graduated from Georgia Tech with a degree in computer science and was working for Bell South in Atlanta. John was in his third year at George Washington University. Both were full of life, and David was sure they had the world by the tail. It had only been a few weeks ago when they had all been together. Ed had brought his girlfriend.

Such a great weekend.

He could hear the three of them laughing and cutting up around the table.

"Thanks, Catherine," Bill said, prompting David back to the present. "I want to wind up this briefing before dinner, so let's continue. David, you'll have PCS orders when you return to the *Peterson*. You will be directed to turn over command in Oslo, and you'll be authorized thirty days leave before reporting to your new assignment as the Senior U.S. Naval Adjutant to the United Nations in the Hague. I hope we can wind up this awful business in just a few days. However, if it takes longer than expected, the leave cover will fit with your need for extra time. David, if you pull this mission off, the president will give you any command you want, and I'll buy you a pair of brown shoes and give you this carrier if you want it!"

David smiled politely in response. "I'll stick to being a black shoe."

Bill chuckled. "Oh, and congratulations. You've been promoted to captain. The UN job calls for an O-6, and no one deserves the promotion more than you."

"Ah, thanks," David responded. Promotions were usually something to get very excited about. Not this time. He just felt empty, almost in a state of shock. Making rank just didn't matter.

"Since the UN job is just a cover, do I get to keep the rank?" David asked in a casual, jesting way.

"Keep it? Son, they're likely to make you an admiral. We want to keep the questions at your hotel to a minimum. Catherine will pose as your wife, although you'll have a suite of rooms."

"Wife?" David swiveled slowly to face her.

A smile crept across his face. Catherine cast her eyes downward and then slowly lifted them.

"Well," David responded as he looked back over toward Bill. "That's the only pleasant thing you've said all afternoon."

Bill ignored his comment and went on. "David, you'll have to brief your XO and officers since they know you're not married. The *Peterson* will be ordered to sea after the change of command, thereby reducing the chance of exposing your cover. The cover's not all that important, you know, enlightened Norwegians and all. But that's the way the boys in Langley have set up the passports. Nobody's likely to question a couple on vacation."

Bill turned toward Bob and continued. "Bob, you'll be known as 'Mother' on this mission. The *Peterson* will follow any movements David makes. Stay within communications range. After dinner, return here for a special equipment briefing. The *Peterson's* being fitted with equipment as we speak. We're replacing the helicopter and the helicopter detachment with our own gun ship and personnel. You'll also have a second helicopter for troop and utility needs.

In addition, you will have a squad of marines and a squad of SEALs attached if needed. The *Kennedy* will take position eight degrees east longitude and fifty-eight point five degrees north latitude, which is in the Skagerrak north of Thisted, Denmark, and south of Kristlansand, Norway. She'll have two destroyers and three attack boats in her task group. That should be sufficient to cut off any escape by sea."

Moving toward the audiovisual screen, Bill put up a slide of a map of the region.

"Three days ago," he continued, "a Russian-flagged container ship owned by Alexander Andreyev left St. Petersburg and made a short port call in Stockholm. It then proceeded out of the Baltic, through the Skagerrak, and turned south heading toward Lisbon. Late yesterday, it departed from its posted itinerary and made an unscheduled port call in Rotterdam. In the meantime, Moscow got wind of the stolen virus and pulled out all the stops in order to look for this ship. Had the ship stayed on its published schedule, the track would have brought it near our NATO task group by this morning. One name on the crew manifest reported in St. Petersburg was not on the crew manifest reported to authorities in either Sweden or the Netherlands. This may have been our Doctor Choutov."

"Do we know where the crewman got off?" Bob asked.

"No. We assume Stockholm. We know that when Moscow got wind of this situation, the authorities tried to find Alexander Andreyev. To no avail."

"Not surprising," Steve said.

Bill continued. "We have one report from a less than reliable source that puts him in Helsinki two days ago. Our own DEA has followed some of his operatives to Oslo. His ships routinely call there, and we suspect he is using a UN conference in Oslo as cover for a rendezvous with Doctor Choutov. It would be easy to slip in undetected with so many foreign visitors arriving at the same time."

"Do the Russians have this information?" David asked.

"Don't know for sure. Our lead to Oslo came via DEA. We have to assume that the Russians have the information, though, since they work together on Russian mob activities. You can expect Oslo to be crawling with Mossad and Russian intelligence operatives."

"What about our Arab friends?" Bob asked. "Should we expect to see them?"

"Don't think so," Bill responded. "It's very hard to track these cells. Our best guess is that the exchange will not occur in northern Europe. The shipping angle's a good one, but you have to remember that this virus and its containers can fit into a small overnight bag. Easy to transport by air. It's imperative to get to Doctor Choutov before he has a chance to meet up with Andreyev."

Bill changed slides again. "Steve and his group will be your muscle. His operatives will take over surveillance of Andreyev's men from the DEA and will provide cleaners if needed." He walked over to the projected image of Doctor Choutov. "We've sanctioned Doctor Choutov. David, you may choose the time and place to carry out the sanction once you've recovered the virus. We've also sanctioned Andreyev. Again David, you call the shots.

"You may need Andreyev to lead you to Choutov. You're authorized to use any preemptive military strike you deem appropriate without seeking higher authority. The *Kennedy* will keep an F-14 available to move you anywhere you need to go."

Admiral Hopkins returned to his place at the table and sat down. He continued. "Now, a few final details. David, Catherine, you have a suite at the Inter Nor Hotel Bristol. Steve'll be in the adjoining room. We have rooms in the Hotel Continental for Steve's team. David, you'll also have available several long-standing Norwegian operatives who are not part of the Armageddon group. The chief wine steward at Engebret Cafe will be your contact for the firm in Norway. They expect your contact, David; however, they'll not be aware of Steve's presence. They've been assigned to use existing mob contacts to obtain any leads to Andreyev's operatives. Since they have several agents deep in the Norwegian underworld, we're likely to get our first bead on Andreyev or Choutov from them."

The sound of the 1-MC could be heard through the outside bulkhead as the boatswain's pipe announced dinner to the crew. Almost as the pipe stopped, David heard the dinner chimes for the flag mess in the passageway outside.

"OK," Bill said as he stood up. "We will reconvene here at nineteen thirty for an equipment briefing. At that time we can tie up any loose ends. Leave your briefing materials here. After dinner you'll have some time to return and read through the files."

The group stood up and in a relaxed manner began to move toward the door.

A chief mess specialist was waiting in the passageway outside to lead the group to dinner.

"Gentlemen, ma'am, we have a special treat for you this evening. Please follow me," he said. He turned and started walking toward the flag mess.

FOUR

Forty minutes later.

DAVID FOLDED HIS LINEN NAPKIN AND SET IT BESIDE HIS PLATE. THE meal had been elaborate, especially when he compared it to the typical fare served by Navy messes. The stewards served broiled stuffed mushrooms for an appetizer, and the next course was gazpacho. To David, the only soup worse than gazpacho was vichyssoise.

I hate cold soup.

After removing the soup course, the stewards brought tarragon marinated vegetables for the salad course. For the main course, haddock fillets with cucumber sauce were served. Three vegetables accompanied the main course: asparagus au gratin, gingered carrots, and kohlrabi parmesan. Since David hated brussels sprouts, cabbage, or anything similar, he passed on the kohlrabi. He was convinced that some demented supply corps admiral had purchased all the brussels sprouts futures lasting well into the next millennium. By forcing the navy to serve brussels sprouts at every other meal, that admiral was punishing the surface line for some perceived injustice.

Following the main course, David savored a frozen lemon torte and coffee. Several individual conversations were going on at the same time. Oscar and Bob were talking college football. Oscar was a Notre Dame graduate, while Bob was from UCLA.

The XO of the *Kennedy* had joined the group for dinner, and he was talking with Steve about flight operations. Steve had been on the bridge earlier during flight operations. He was fascinated by every detail of the process.

Bill, Mike, and Catherine were deeply involved in a discussion regarding good seafood restaurants they had each enjoyed along the Gulf Coast. Bill and Catherine thought Skopelo's in Pensacola had the best seafood, while Mike favored The Boat in Fort Walton Beach.

David didn't feel like chitchat. His mind kept wandering back to the briefing. As far as he was concerned, he'd rather get on with it. But, it was Bill's show. He excused himself and walked to the other side of the room, which had been set up with couches and leather high-back chairs. He sat down in one of the chairs and reached onto a nearby table for a copy of the *Naval Proceedings.* He wasn't much interested in the magazine but thought it might provide a moment's distraction. As he began to thumb through the pages, his thoughts were drawn to his mission.

Andreyev had been reported in Helsinki, and it was only several hours by air to Stockholm or Oslo.

Andreyev could have already joined up with Choutov, and the team would be too late.

However, if intelligence reports were correct, Andreyev was not likely to take regular commercial routes. Choutov was most likely to travel by air. He could already be in Oslo, assuming they were going to Oslo. A boat trip for Andreyev would take much longer.

If I were Andreyev, I would try to fly noncommercial from Helsinki to Stockholm. In fact, I'd fly all the way to Oslo.

If Choutov went ashore in Stockholm, what would prevent them from meeting there?

We have a lot of assumptions at work here. That doesn't give us much time to find them.

David got to the end of the magazine. He hadn't read a word, so he decided to go back to the flag briefing room and look over his briefing notes. The others were still chattering away. As David opened the door and stepped out, a marine guard snapped to attention.

"Good evening," David said as he turned to proceed toward the briefing room.

"Good evening, sir."

Inside the briefing room, he saw three men. One was a lieutenant commander with a medical corps insignia, and the other two were civilians.

"Good evening, gentlemen, I'm David Egan."

"Good evening, Commander, I'm Dr. Fred Garvey," the lieutenant commander said.

"Good evening, Commander, I'm Richard McReynolds, your logistics and material specialist," the civilian said from across the room. He didn't move over to shake hands but continued to work on something sitting on the conference table.

"Good evening, Commander, I'm Jim Washington," a rather large, muscular black man said as he approached David with his hand extended.

"Jim," David said as he shook hands. "What's your role in our mission?"

"Well, Commander, I break things and kill people."

"You must be a marine," David said with a slight smile.

Jim broke into a big grin and gave a little chuckle. "Sometimes I wish I were in the Marine Corps. Actually, I'm on the Russian desk, Northwestern European section."

"St. Petersburg?"

"Yes, sir. We cover the territory from the White Sea up north to the southern part of the Russian Baltic."

"How did you get that assignment?"

Jim smiled again. "Commander, you don't think I would fit in with all those blonde northern Europeans?"

"It must make the undercover work interesting."

"True, but it's almost expected for a mule."

"Oh, I see, you have a subspecialty."

"Yes, sir. I know most of the players in St. Petersburg."

"Outstanding! I'm sure glad to have you aboard."

"Thanks, Commander. If any of them show up in Oslo, I'll be able to finger them."

The door to the briefing room opened, and Bill and Catherine entered the room.

"Well, gentlemen, Catherine, let's get this briefing going," Bill said motioning toward the table.

"Let me start off with the *Kennedy's* chief surgeon, Dr. Garvey. Dr. Garvey's going to implant a tiny transmitter in your scalps. After we've concluded here, David and Catherine will need to report to him in sick bay. I've asked him to be here this evening to answer any questions you may have." He paused and looked around.

"If there are no questions, Admiral, I'll take my leave and let you continue with your meeting," Dr. Garvey said to Bill.

"Thanks, Doc."

"Well," Bill said, "let's get to the reason for our meeting this evening. Richard, you're up."

"Thanks, Admiral. I have several standard issue items and a couple of special order items for this mission. First, distress homing beacons. Gentlemen, each of you will be issued a black belt such as this one." He held a standard man's leather belt with a simple brass buckle up so everyone could see it. "You will notice three rivets holding the leather together here. The rivet closest to the buckle should be pressed together. We set the pressure tolerance high enough not to be set off by accident, so you'll need to use a little force. It will activate the beacon in the belt telling Mother you're in trouble."

Richard then took a small jewelry box out and looked at Catherine. He opened it in front of her. Inside were two diamond earrings in a simple setting.

"We've just met," she said as she raised one eyebrow and broke into an open, friendly smile.

"Right. Uh, these both contain beacons. Pinch either one as hard as you can, and we'll know you're in trouble. Be sure to wear these if you venture away from David or Steve. I know your job is to deal with the weapon once it's located, but things have a nasty habit of changing in the field. Remember, diamonds are a girl's best friend."

Richard lifted a one-cubic-foot container from the deck and set it on the table. He opened it and passed each person a Smith & Wesson 442 Airweight. "This .38 caliber weapon is a small and lightweight five-round revolver. It'll fit inside a pocket or lady's handbag."

Next he took out three Heckler & Kock model USP .40 calibers and handed them to David, Jim, and Steve. Then he reached for a briefcase beside him and took out what appeared to be a silver cigarette case.

"OK, if I could have your attention here, please. This cigarette case is our latest stun gun. Simply open the case, then press this top edge into your victim. Because of the shape and size, it has only one charge, but it is sufficient to drop a horse."

Opening the cigarette case, he held it up so the cigarettes could be seen. "Notice the cigarette nearest the hinge. It is actually a small metal tube containing a simple firing device and a tube with our newest sleep aid. Hold the cigarette as you normally would and press the filter in toward the front like so. Make sure you are close and you aim toward the target's face. The detonation will crush the ampule and spray it up to two feet. It takes from ten to thirty seconds to work. Once the drug hits the brain, the target is out cold for hours."

"Secondhand smoke is more dangerous than you'd guess," Steve said with a grin. Catherine smiled in response.

The comment caught David's attention.

What'd you know, he cracked a joke.

Reaching into the briefcase again, Richard pulled out what looked like a common cellular phone. "When you press the pound key and then the star key, the internal computer chip will use the local cellular network to access a satellite. Mother'll answer."

"Not very secure," Jim said.

"True, but given the short duration of the mission, it really doesn't matter. Just use the cellular link for short conversations."

He set the equipment down on the table. Looking at David, he said, "Remember, all cell phones have a trace signal when they are on. Your position can be pinpointed. The trace signal is on whenever the phone is on."

Richard continued to speak as he reached into the briefcase and pulled out a Mont Blanc pen. "Standard issue pens. The black pen has a highly concentrated solution of acid that should dissolve most metals."

He released some of the acid into a dish on the table. He then dropped a ball bearing into the solution. With a fizz and some noxious fumes, the acid dissolved the ball bearing in a matter of seconds.

He reached into the briefcase and pulled out a burgundy Mont Blanc pen.

"Burgundy is your spring-loaded dart injector with nerve agent. Press the gold clip while aiming the white top at the victim's body. The dart will accurately strike a target within ten feet. It takes thirty seconds to a minute and a half for the agent to reach the brain."

Turning toward Bill, Richard said, "Well, Admiral, that about sums up my portion. Oh, one last item. I'll be located at the Comfort Hotel Majorstuen, room 109. Commander, if you need anything, I can have it to you in a matter of hours. Most of our inventory items are located in London. We will have pilots and aircraft ready to transport anything you request."

Bill stood up. "Bob, if you'd accompany Richard, he's going to give you a detailed briefing of the electronics being installed aboard the *Peterson*."

Bob stood as Richard gathered several items. They both exited the room.

"Jim, you're up," Bill said.

Jim stood up and walked around the table toward the audiovisual control equipment. He dimmed the lights. A picture appeared on the screen. The subject was a man in his mid-fifties with a round face. His eyes were average in size and set. Dense, dark eyebrows looked as if they had grown together. The bone structure along the top of the eyes predominated the upper part of the head, making him look like the Java man with a round face. He had a full head of dark hair with only a few grey highlights. Although David could only see him from the shoulder up, he could tell that this was a husky man.

"Alexander Andreyev," Jim said. "Former colonel in the KGB, now retired. Andreyev's pretty much the godfather for the rackets, prostitution, and drugs in the northwestern region of Russia. He's based in St. Petersburg where. . . . If there are no other questions about Andreyev, I'll move on."

Jim paused and flashed another picture on the screen. Everyone recognized this picture from the earlier briefing.

"Doctor Ilya Choutov," Jim said. "Head of research at the Central Weapons Laboratory located near Arkhangeisk on the White Sea. This is a secret facility that doesn't exist on any map. We've known about it since the cold war days. Research and development on every kind of biological and chemical agent known to humankind are conducted here. In spite of treaties and the fall of the old Soviet state, this facility seems to carry on, unaffected by current events. Of course, the Russians will deny its existence."

Jim stepped over to the table and took the silver coffee decanter and poured himself a cup. "Choutov. According to our information, he's something of a strange bird. Never married, he lacked any of the social skills necessary to advance beyond the laboratory. They'll let him supervise pure research but not much more. He doesn't socialize with any of his work associates. However, he is known to have an obsession with pornography and prostitution. He frequents several brothels in St. Petersburg that are known to belong to Andreyev."

"How could someone involved in such debauchery get the job as head of research for Russia's most sensitive weapons development facility?" David asked. His face drew into a frown.

"He's brilliant," Catherine said in a tone filled with awe and respect. "Besides, it's not all that uncommon for guys who are capable of doing that kind of scientific work to be a little awkward socially."

"We don't really know," Jim continued. "Russians don't necessarily recognize scientific brilliance. They put a high premium on social conformity. Our guess is that Andreyev knew of Choutov's weaknesses and wished to exploit them. We surmise that Andreyev used his contacts within the Kremlin to have Choutov appointed to this post."

Jim took a sip of water. He flashed another picture on the screen. It was a blond man in his late thirties. He looked well built. Obviously a Northern European, he had blue eyes and light skin color.

"Severny Iourtchak."

"I can't believe it," David said, barely able to control his gasp of surprise. His eyes narrowed, and his back became ramrod straight.

"You know this man?"

"I can't believe my eyes. They must have been twins! Ah, sorry," David said as he noted the questioning look he was receiving from the others. "I ran into his brother, Grigori Iourtchak."

"Do enlighten us," Bill said.

"Well, Grigori Iourtchak was a KGB operative back in Spain. He provided technical support for the anti-NATO activities of groups like GRAPO. I ran up against him while I was in Madrid."

"Oh?"

"He had a most interesting cover. I didn't figure out his role until it was almost—"

"Cover?" Catherine asked.

"Yeah. He was a soloist for the Madrid symphony. A really accomplished pianist. I heard him perform several of Debussy's classics once. Really moving performer."

"And?" she said.

"We were making a mass arrest with the Madrid authorities. We followed several of the GRAPO operatives to a studio near the concert hall. I thought they were taking Grigori hostage—until he almost killed me."

"Go on."

"Well, let's just say he was better at the piano than he was at karate. Small world, isn't it?"

"Yeah," Jim replied as he jumped in to take control of the briefing. "Back to Severny. Considered second in command in Andreyev's organization. He's also an ex-KGB operative who speaks English and French flawlessly. By the way, Catherine, he's considered quite the ladies' man."

"I can see why." She winked at Bill.

Bill chuckled, and David smiled.

"He's some piece of work," Jim responded. "When he was working for the KGB, he was known as one of Russia's best assassins. One of his little eccentricities is that he has been known to seduce the wife or girlfriend of his victim. Then he taunts the victim before he eliminates him. The KGB felt that this aberration presented too much risk of exposure. They eventually stopped using him. That's when Andreyev seems to have recruited Severny. Watch out for him. He's very bright and a most formidable foe."

Jim changed the slide. "Leonid Vodokanal. We don't know much about Vodokanal's background. He was not in the army or KGB. No police record. He was a minor party official in the old Soviet Union. He's known to have a temper and to be heavy-handed with those who cross him. No real outstanding qualities. Somehow, he made it into Alexander's inner circle."

Jim changed the slide again. "Mikhail Kruzanshtern. Alexander's quartermaster. Ex-KGB. Served last three tours with Alexander. A very trusted companion. He's from the St.

Petersburg area. Mikhail seems to know everyone involved in any organized crime in northern Europe. He's Andreyev's chief negotiator. I've dealt with him on four occasions, and I've yet to get on his good side."

Jim stepped to the table where he placed both hands. Leaning forward just slightly, he looked at everyone. "Both Severny and Mikhail are missing. It is a good bet that if you find either one, you'll find Andreyev."

Jim took his seat. Bill stood and moved to the head of the table.

"Well, that's about it, boys and girls. David, it's up to you. Find 'em and kill 'em. If you fall on your sword on this one, we'll all have a rotten day."

Everyone looked at David.

"I'll be in Washington spending most of my time at the White House," Bill said. "The *Peterson's* been steaming at flank speed. She should be at the mouth of the Oslofjord by zero five hundred. We'll fly David and Steve to the airport in Oslo. David, you'll be secretly transferred to a helicopter, which'll fly you out to the *Peterson.* Jim, you're going to Stockholm. You'll make contact with our operatives there. In case you find the well is dry there, the jet we send will be on standby to fly you to Oslo. Catherine, we're going to fly you to Amsterdam. You'll catch a flight from London to Oslo as it stops there. Of course, the manifest will show you originating in London. You're due to arrive in Oslo around zero eight hundred. Check into your room, and then go to the port as quickly as possible. Ask the cab to take you to the boat launch. The *Peterson* will have a boat there to take you out to the ship."

Bill slowly looked at each person seated at the table. He took a deep breath. "God be with us."

FIVE

"TOO SNUG. GOT ONE OF THESE IN A DOUBLE-X?" JIM ASKED. HE struggled with the zipper on his flight suit.

"No, sir." A smile darted across the airman's face. "It's a G-suit. Keeps all your parts where they belong. You'll want it snug."

The door to the squadron ready room opened. An officer fully outfitted in his flight suit entered the room. The helmet in his hand was white with an ace of spades and a little red devil holding a pitchfork painted on the sides.

"Mr. Washington," he said extending his hand to greet Jim. "I'm Lieutenant Commander Jim Berry. I'm your pilot for the trip to Stockholm."

"Commander," Jim said as he stood and took Commander Berry's hand. "How long will it take us to get to Stockholm?"

"In a hurry, sir?"

"You bet!"

"It'll be a short trip. Normal speed, less than two hours. Stockholm's not far as the crow flies."

The crewman handed Jim a helmet. "Mr. Washington, if you'll follow me, sir," he said as he stepped out of the ready room.

The crewman led Jim through a maze of passageways and out to the elevator where an F-14 sat with the canopy open.

As the crewman helped Jim get strapped into the cockpit, Jim couldn't help but be overwhelmed by all the instruments. In front of him were small computer screens and an amazing array of buttons, lights, and switches. About eye level was a vertical sheet of Plexiglas with lines etched in several places. The crewman reached in and took a cord from Jim's helmet and plugged it into a socket. Then he plugged in a headset he was wearing. "Mr. Washington, we need to go over a few safety items. . . ."

The plane jolted as the ship's elevator started to move. It was a terrifying sight for Jim to look out over the water rushing by so many hundreds of feet below him. He swallowed hard.

I knew I shoulda took swimming lessons.

When the elevator got to the flight deck, Jim could see a whole swarm of activity. To his right was the stern of the ship. The massive cables he saw across the deck were used by planes for landing. Each plane had a tailhook that dropped to catch one of those cables.

Bet that's a rough stop. From a hundred miles an hour. . . . Whoo-ee. Glad I made the trip by helicopter.

To his left he could see the front of the flight deck. It was equipped with several catapults that were hissing steam.

"Red Devil one three, clear to cat, over."

"One three."

He felt the aircraft start to move as one of the tow trucks pulled it off to the left. Within a few moments they were in place. A small yellow utility truck raced up beside the aircraft. A crewman jumped out and hooked a rather large hose into the aircraft. After a few moments everyone on the deck stepped away, and one crewman gave the pilot a thumbs-up. Jim felt the vibration of the airplane's turbines as the pilot started the engines. The increasing whine rang in his ears and quickened his heart with anticipation. The cockpit came alive with lights. Soon, the loud whine turned into a roar. The crewmen on the deck raced over to unhook everything, and they drove the trucks away.

"One three, clear for takeoff. Contact air control on channel two."

"One three."

Jim had been given a briefing on how the catapult works. He was told to picture a big slingshot, one that would hopefully throw the aircraft off the end of the flight deck with enough speed for them to fly.

What happens if it fails? It's a big ship, and it's haulin'.

The pilot finished the checklist and gave a thumbs-up to the deck crew. In reply, the catapult officer began to circle his right hand above his head.

The engines thundered, but the plane didn't move. It just shook.

Seconds later, the pilot popped the catapult officer a salute. The CAT officer responded by dropping his hand from the circling motion and pointed directly toward the front of the ship.

Jim's whole body was slammed backward. It felt like he had just taken the long fall on the Great American Scream Machine at Six Flags Over Georgia. Fortunately it didn't last long. Soon it was replaced by the feeling that his stomach was coming up into his throat as the plane began a steep rise in altitude and a slight roll to the left. Below Jim could see the *Kennedy* get smaller as the plane began to make a wide circle to the left. Behind the carrier, on the port side, he spotted a destroyer and a helicopter.

"One three, clear to Stockholm. Zero three zero, flight level two five zero."

"One three."

As the plane settled on the new course, Jim sensed the speed increasing. His ears were giving him fits as the plane continued to climb. Suddenly the sound changed, and the roar of the engines seemed quite subdued. As Jim popped his jaw, he managed to clear one ear then the other. The sky was ablaze with stars.

"Whoo-ee. What a sight! Don't think I've ever seen so many stars," Jim said.

"Yeah, northern latitudes. You get a remarkable show."

"Is it always like this? Flying at night, I mean."

"No, well, maybe. Tell you the truth, I'm usually busy. Guess I don't stop to appreciate the view."

"It's amazing."

Jim sat quietly for several minutes as he took in the spectacle of nature's light show. Then the urgency of the mission crept back into his thoughts. "Commander Berry, I was told that my laptop could use the aircraft's communication equipment and that you can uplink to a satellite. Can I use it now?"

"Yes, sir. The modem's been hooked in. Configuration's set. It should work just as it would at home."

"Thanks."

Jim reached down and fetched the computer. Using his web browser, he entered the words *prostitution, Sweden* and clicked on "Search." Within moments, a page came up with general information about the legitimacy of prostitution in Sweden. About midway on the page was the bold heading "SPECIFIC INFORMATION ABOUT THE CITIES AND REGIONS." He put the cursor on Stockholm and clicked. Seconds later an information page came up with the following header:

Subject: Some sex services in Stockholm, Sweden
Date: 20 Aug 1995 03:450:12 GMT

The first part of the message gave a list of adult dancing clubs. About halfway down the page he began to read the following paragraph:

For a woman, find a street called Malmskillnadsgatan. In Stockholm it is an institution! You can satisfy any persuasion or idiosyncrasy . . .

The message went on to fully describe services and typical costs. There was also a note regarding adult salons around the city. They would also be a good place to arrange for services. That note was followed by several pages of shop names and addresses, along with subway stops.

Jim highlighted the whole list of salons and saved it to his clipboard. With a few clicks of the mouse, he started his e-mail and typed the following message:

Put operative in the Sergel Plaza Hotel.
Have 14,000 crowns delivered to me upon arrival.
Have agents check out the following for leads
ref: Choutov.

He pasted the list of adult shops to the message before he sent it off. Then he closed the laptop and put it away.

He decided to go through his briefing folder again, knowing he'd have to turn the folder over to the agency when he got to Stockholm. He didn't want to miss any details. Page after page, photo after photo. He spent the next hour looking and reading until his eyelids got so heavy he couldn't keep them open.

"Stockholm approach, this is United States Navy Red Devil One Three."

"Navy One Three, turn right to course zero eight zero. Squawk one three seven zero for ident," the voice responded in a heavy northern European accent.

"Navy One Three. Squawking one three seven zero."

"How much longer?" Jim asked.

"About ten minutes."

"Navy One Three, turn left to course zero two five."

"Navy One Three."

"Navy One Three, you're cleared to runway two niner north. Call your turn, over."

"Two niner north, call my turn."

Jim realized that the pilot had substantially slowed the aircraft. On the horizon he could make out the lights from the shore. As Jim looked out over the wings, they began to move out into their extended position. Within just a few minutes, the pilot turned and put the landing gear down.

"Stockholm approach, Navy One Three turning final."

"Roger, Navy One Three. You are cleared to land. Exit two niner at elevator two. Switch to ground control on frequency one one nine point seven for taxi instructions."

"Navy One Three. Exit two niner at elevator two. One one nine point seven for taxi instructions."

As the plane touched down, Jim began to feel apprehensive.

Near the end of the runway, he could see a yellow truck with a "follow me" sign and two airport security cars. Jim could also make out a brown SWAT-type vehicle. The plane began to taxi. The vehicles fell into a procession with the aircraft. Over the radio there was chatter between the tower and the pilot as instructions were relayed for the aircraft to proceed to a special hangar across the field from the terminal. It didn't take long. The aircraft turned into a brightly lit hangar and came to a halt. By the number of heavily armed guards, it was obvious that they had entered a secure hangar. The pilot shut down the turbines as the ground crew rolled two stairways up to the air- craft. Jim had taken off his helmet and released the seat har- ness. He reached down and took hold of the case with the computer and the files and handed them and the helmet to the ground crewman who had appeared to assist him.

"Welcome to Stockholm," the man said with a heavy accent.

"Thank you."

As Jim got down to the end of the stairway, a blond man extended his hand. "Welcome to Stockholm, Mr. Washington. I'm Paul Bowker, Stockholm station manager."

"Paul."

"We may have turned up a lead on your mark. He's appar- ently visited one of the shops you asked us to contact. Accord- ing to our source, we're not the first ones to inquire about your man."

"Russian intelligence?"

"Not sure. Could have been. There's no way the contact could be sure. Whoever is looking for Choutov asked for an introduction to the girl who serviced him."

"How long ago?"

"About two hours before our man made the contact. So it has to be around three to three and a half hours."

"What about the girl?"

"She's a redhead. Supposedly pretty. About five nine. From the description, she's not overly endowed, but she's into bondage and other weird things. We've rented a room for you in a hotel near the Mallmskillnadsgatan. The proprietor of the shop will arrange for her to come to your room. She'll be expecting seven thousand crowns."

"Reet! A thousand bucks!"

"Yeah," Paul said as he motioned for Jim to get into a nearby Volvo. "Guess that kinky stuff costs!"

"You bet. I've heard that you'd pay a thousand bucks for a great-looking class act in New York. Momma's gotta high opinion of herself."

"I doubt the New York high-class hookers are into this kind of stuff," Paul said.

Jim's expression soured as if he'd just bitten into a large lemon. "You're kidding!"

"Yeah. You can get anything you want on the Mallmskill-nadsgatan."

"I guess so. That Choutov has to be one sick puppy." Jim shook his head. "The thought makes my skin crawl."

After the two men got into the back seat of the car, Paul opened a briefcase and pulled out an envelope with money. "Here are the crowns you requested. Oh, and here's a message for you."

To: J. Washington
From: Mother

No active sightings Oslo. Boat registered Helsinki found on one of the islands of the Archipelago near Stockholm.
Assume Andreyev in your area.
##End of Message##

"Most every place you would want to go is accessible by the mass transit system," Paul said. "There's no timetable since trains come and go all the time."

He handed Jim a diagram of the city subway line. "There are three lines, Red, Green, and Blue. Here are the places where you change trains. I have marked the stops where the shops are located."

Then he handed him a map of the city. "Here are several contact points. The first is a tobacco shop across from the opera house here. You'll see the House of Parliament here and the Sweden House here. Notice the subway station on the street behind the tobacco shop . . . That's about it, sir. It's your show."

"Has there been any word on Andreyev?"

"None. We found his boat on one of the islands of the Archipelago. We have several operatives deep in the local underground. We'll hear something if he makes contact locally. You need to remember that this guy's well connected all over the Baltic. He doesn't need to contact any local mob bosses. Unless he's planning to move some kind of a large shipment of drugs. I'd say our better bet is to find Choutov."

"I don't like knowing that Andreyev's lurking in the shadows," Jim said as the car pulled up in front of a hotel. Both men jumped out, and the car sped away.

"Here's your room key," Paul said as he handed Jim a plastic coded key. "I'll be in the bar where I can keep an eye on the front door. You'd better go to the room. If we're lucky, our lady'll arrive soon."

With that they parted, and Jim went up the elevator to the third floor. His room was just across from the elevator. He opened the door and was greeted with the strong smell of scented candles. He could see a dim flickering light. Because of the room layout, only a small portion was visible from the door. To his left was the bathroom. Before entering a separate toilet and shower room, there was a vanity on one side and a large closet on the other. The closet formed a barrier between the bathroom area and the portion of the room where the bed was located.

Christoph Gluck's "The Dance of the Blessed Spirits" played softly.

Music's familiar. Someone's here.

Jim pulled his Heckler & Klock .40 caliber and attached a silencer. He eased to his left into the toilet area and checked behind the bathtub curtain, then the closet. He reached into his vest pocket for a small dentist's mirror and positioned it so he could see around the corner.

My, my, my.

Nobody else in the room. He put his .40 caliber away and stepped in.

"Do you come with the room?" He smiled.

The woman was young, probably twenty to twenty-five. She had creamy skin with a musk-rose flush on her cheeks and long lustrous golden hair. The shifting emerald lights of her eyes studied him intently. Around her neck was a black ribbon with a cameo in the middle.

Whoo-ee, righteous! Silk and satin.

Slowly her hands moved downward. Then she let out a long, audible sigh.

"I hear things about black men."

She stood, then slid gracefully over to Jim. Her hands explored his chest as she raised up on tiptoe, touching her lips to his. The caress of her lips sent a slight quiver up his spine. Her lips seared a path down his neck and behind his ear.

Focus Washington.

He drew back from her. "You're not the one I requested." He pushed her hands away.

She put her arms around his neck. "I'm sure you'll like me," she whispered.

Despite an intense yearning, he pushed her away.

Two candles were burning in the room. One was on a dresser on the far wall. The other one was located on the table beside the bed. Jim took her by the hand. Then he blew out the candle beside the bed and crawled across to the other side. Reaching out to her, he motioned for her to come across to him. She slid across the bed. He pulled out his .40 caliber with one hand as he reached up with the other to pull her down onto the floor beside him.

"Can you fake it?" he whispered. Jim stood up and took the pillows and placed them under the covers. Then he took the bedspread and arranged it so that it appeared as if someone had been rolling around in the bed. He sat back down on the floor and looked sternly at the girl.

"Sure, I fake one several times a day."

"Then just moan and carry on like you're having the best time of your life."

"What? You don't want me? Chocolate only?"

Jim raised the semiautomatic to her head. The tensing of his jaw betrayed his deep frustration. "Moan."

She began to moan in a most unconvincing manner.

"Look," he said as he spoke more calmly. "Just relax. I'm not gonna hurt you. I just need you to fake it. Anyone outside will think we're in the throes of wild passion. Understand?"

"I guess. Who's outside?"

"Please. Humor me."

She began to sound more convincing. It didn't take long. In less than two minutes, Jim heard the click of the door lock. "Louder," he whispered.

Jim could make out the silhouette of a man stepping into the room. The stranger began firing into the pillows on the bed. Jim was ready and returned two shots to the head. The stranger dropped.

Jim moved to the end of the bed and along the wall to the corner. He reached into his vest pocket and pulled out the dental mirror. He couldn't see anyone around the corner. He checked the bathroom, then returned to the bedroom. The girl sat on the bed with a look of horror on her face.

Jim walked toward the door of the adjoining room. In a smooth series of motions, he opened the door while dropping to a crouch. With his mirror, he looked into the other room. A woman was lying on the bed, and a man was on the floor. Neither was moving. He stood up and entered. Both individuals had been shot. Both had been dead long enough to turn blue around the lips.

He kept the girl in the other room in his line of sight as he quickly looked around. He didn't want her to escape before getting a chance to question her.

On the bed was a red-headed woman, fully dressed. The man on the floor had an earphone. Jim assumed he was an agency operative. He walked into the first room and over to the telephone. A man answered in Swedish.

"English please," Jim said.

In a few moments another man came on the line and in a heavy accent said, "Front desk, may I be assisting?"

"Yes, I need for you to page a Mr. Paul Bowker in the bar. Could you ask him to call me in room 305?"

"Mr. Paul Bowker in the bar. Room 305. Yah, sir, I can comply."

"Thank you."

Jim hung up the phone.

These Swedes speak pretty good. Wait a minute. How many Swedish working girls speak perfect English?

He walked back to the other room keeping her in view at all times.

She walked to the door where he stood. "What happened?" she asked.

Jim walked over to the bed. He raised the dead woman's head so the girl could see her face. "Recognize her?"

"No. Never seen her before."

"Who sent you to this room?"

"Stefan."

"Stefan's the proprietor of the shop?"

"Yeah."

The phone rang, and Jim went back into the other room to answer it. He grabbed her and dragged her with him. "Paul?"

"Yeah, Jim. What's up?"

"Get up here. Call for a cleaner."

"How many people?"

"Three."

"I'll be right up."

Jim hung up and turned his attention back to the girl. "Got a name?"

"Linda."

"Well, Linda, I think you and I should have a little conversation." Jim grabbed her around the throat with one hand and lifted her off the ground. He walked across the room while holding her by the neck. Then he threw her onto the bed. As she lay there gasping, he looked down on her. The veins in his temples stood out, and he clinched his teeth. Finally he spoke. "Who sent you?" His voice had no vestige of sympathy in its hardness. "The redhead in the other room is the girl I ordered."

"What are you talking about? Stefan said to come. I came. Now I want to leave! This is too much. You're too rough."

Jim reached down with his left hand and grabbed her arm and pulled her upward. With his right hand he slapped her.

"I don't have time, or patience. If you don't want me to break every single bone in your body, you'd better answer my questions!"

"I don't know who paid Stefan. I just got a call to come. So I came."

"How did you get in?"

"Asked a maid."

Jim slapped her again. Blood oozed from her nose as the woman let out a cry of agony.

"Wrong answer, sweetheart. Stefan didn't send you, and the maid didn't let you in. How'd you get in?"

The door burst open, and Paul entered with seven men. They quickly put the bodies in body bags and dumped them in hotel laundry carts. Three men moved the carts out as three other men went to work removing any evidence of a death. The one remaining man stood beside Paul. They were looking at Linda.

"Want to introduce us?" Paul said as he took out a handkerchief and handed it to the girl for her bleeding nose.

"Yeah, this is Linda."

The woman was still crying and holding her face.

"Guess what?"

"What?"

"She speaks perfect English."

"Perfect?"

"Yeah. Sounds like she just got off a plane from Des Moines."

"Well, Jim," Paul said as he walked over to the girl and began to gently clean the blood off of her face. "Either we got us an American in Stockholm, or, we have ourselves a Russian trained in English. Maybe from the infamous KGB language institute. Which do you think?"

"For a fact, Jack! I wouldn't bet on a sweet misguided girl from Des Moines."

"Well, Linda," Paul said in a serious tone, "I'm guessing Linda's not your name. Doesn't matter. I want you to meet a friend of mine. I've nicknamed him Boris. He's the kind of guy, well, let's just say he gives bad guys a bad name. Boris, meet Linda."

The man standing next to Paul pulled a rather large Bowie knife from a sheath under his coat. He stepped over to the girl and wiped the dull flat edge along her body up to her neck. In a quick jerky motion, he cut a slit in her dress on both shoulders. He quietly and slowly started to speak.

"Such pretty white skin. Wonder how much I'll have to cut off before you start begging to die?"

He flipped the knife blade over and cut a tiny portion of her neck. It was enough to cause her pain and a lot of blood. She cried out again. She was beginning to look awfully bloody.

"Let's start with the easy questions. What's your real name?" Boris said as Paul went into the bathroom to grab a hand towel. Paul brought it back and gave it to her to press against the wound.

She just stared at the men. It was hard to tell if she was in shock or just defiant.

He put the knife back into the sheath and then reached down into a gym bag and pulled out a long cylindrical object resembling a cattle prod. He touched it to her leg and then began to bring it up across her body. He touched it to her lips.

"I understand you claim to be into kinky stuff. Do you like to hurt, sweetheart?"

He pressed the trigger, and a bolt went through her body. She convulsed and then went limp, falling to the floor. Her eyes were open, and she appeared to be breathing. You could see a twitch in one hand, but otherwise she seemed incapable of moving.

Boris motioned to the other men in the room. They picked the girl up and laid her on her back on the bed. He continued to poke her with the wand as he painted an awful picture of what he would do if she didn't answer his questions. This went on for almost five minutes until she could regain control of her motor functions.

The two men raised her to a sitting position and then braced her legs and arms in such a way as to restrain her movement.

"Now, my dear, I can get really creative with this. In fact, I can make it so you'll feel pain like you've never felt it before. You're gonna answer my questions. Sooner or later. It'd be such a shame to ruin such a beautiful body." He paused and glared into her eyes without so much as a single blink. "Your name, sweetheart, your name."

"Dasha Dudareva."

Boris moved away as Paul motioned to the men on each side of her to release her.

"I'm glad you're willing to cooperate. I need to ask you some questions. I'm afraid the stakes are serious enough that I'll use any means necessary to get the information. Don't want to. I have to. Understand?"

She nodded.

"Dasha, are you a Russian intelligence operative?"

She nodded. "Former KGB."

"Who do you work for now?"

"Severny Iourtchak."

"How'd you get to Stockholm?"

"By boat. From Helsinki."

"Who was with you besides Severny?" Paul asked as Jim moved toward the door where he had left his computer case.

"Two other men and the boat's pilot. I didn't know them. They didn't speak to me."

Paul took out the file and pulled the picture of Choutov out and showed it to Dasha.

"Was this one of the men?"

"No."

He then took out the photograph of Andreyev and showed it to her.

"How about this man?"

She nodded. "Severny appeared to show—how do you say—deference toward him. He was someone important. But we didn't speak." Dasha's facial responses did not fluctuate. There were no body movements or movement of the eyes that might have suggested she was lying.

"Did you overhear any conversation between the two men?"

"No. They only conversed twice during the trip. Both times they went outside the compartment."

Paul pulled a photograph of Mikhail Kruzenshtern out and showed it to her.

"And this man?"

She nodded. "He stayed with the boat pilot most of the time. Only came down into the compartment to get coffee— maybe he got a sandwich too."

"Did he say anything you can remember?"

"No, not a thing. The only person who talked with me was Severny."

"What's your mission? What'd Severny tell you about the reason for your presence?"

"Severny said one of his lieutenants had sold out to the DEA. Planned to sting and arrest Severny. I had to find this traitor and eliminate him. I was to find out what the big Negro man knew."

"Then what?"

"Then kill him."

"How?"

"I have a spray in my bag."

"Well, it looks like your boyfriend had different ideas. What about the girl in the next room?"

"She was the lead. We followed her to this hotel. When she contacted the night maid, Severny killed them both and took the pass key. He entered the other room and killed the American. Then he set me up in here. He was supposed to be in the other room. I'll kill him! If I ever see him, I'll kill him!"

"Did he question the redhead?"

"No."

"Was anyone with you and Severny?"

"Two Swedes. I didn't know them."

"Did Severny say anything to either one that you can remember?" Paul asked.

"After he killed the American, he asked one of them a question. My Swedish, it's not so good. I did make out the word airport."

"Paul, what about the airports?" Jim asked.

"Two main facilities used for commercial purposes. We have both fairly well covered. The problem is that there are several private fields. If they use a chartered plane, they'll have to file a flight plan. Of course, nothing says they have to follow it."

Paul returned to questioning Dasha while Jim took out a pen and scribbled a note on a piece of paper.

To: Mother

Severny Iourtchak one step ahead of us. Got to Choutov's hooker first. Substituted own operative, ex-KGB for sanction on me. Assume Andreyev aware of our interest. Possible exit by air. Assume Choutov and Andreyev no longer in area. Sanction Girl? Orders?

Jim handed the note to one of the agents and told him to get it off immediately. Then he sat and listened to Paul question the girl for about five minutes.

Several minutes later the agent returned and handed Jim a reply. It read:

To: J. Washington
From: Mother

Proceed Oslo via F-14. Contact tobacco shop across from Engebret Cafe. Use the same coded greeting you were given for Stockholm. Assume cover compromised. Do not contact Papa Bear.

Do not sanction female. Transport Langley for debriefing. ##END OF MESSAGE##

"Ever been to America?" Jim asked Dasha.
"New York."
"Well, you're gonna get a chance to visit Virginia."
Jim motioned to Boris. He reached into his gym bag, pulled out a syringe, and moved over to Dasha. She pulled away, but as she did, Paul and the two other men grabbed her and held her. Boris injected the contents of the syringe, which began to take effect quickly. Moments later she was out cold. Paul instructed one of the other agents to get a laundry cart and an oxygen setup from the van. Meanwhile, one of the other agents tended to her wounds and wrapped her in blankets.
About four minutes later an agent came in the room with a laundry cart, body bag, and oxygen equipment. One of the men put an oxygen mask on her. Another grabbed a body bag.
The others lifted her and placed her in the bag with a small air tank and regulator. Then they put her body bag inside the laundry cart and covered it with towels and sheets.
"She'll be out for four to six hours," Boris said.
"Stuff her in the diplomatic bag. Get her off to Langley," Paul instructed as the two other cleaners began to move everything out of the room and down the hall to the service elevator.

Jim grabbed his coat. He and Paul quickly moved to the public elevator. Paul put his earphone back in and spoke into his lapel microphone.

"Bring the car around front."

Neither man spoke as the elevator descended to the first floor. The doors opened, and both men proceeded out of the hotel to the Volvo that was waiting. The car pulled away.

They drove two blocks and made a right turn. Just as the car was completing the turn, an explosion went off shattering the windshield. The car must have been hit by a rocket-launched grenade. Sliding, skidding, and on fire, it turned 180 degrees, and the rear bumper slammed into a light post. Then a spray of bullets followed. Paul slumped onto Jim. He was bleeding from a head and a shoulder wound. Blood was also starting to drip from his mouth. Jim checked for a pulse. There was none.

Jim pulled out his weapon and waited a moment. The gunfire quickly subsided. He stuck his head up and saw two figures disappear around a corner. Pushing Paul off of him, he opened the door and rolled out onto the ground checking to see if he was in a line of fire. Then he opened the front door, and the driver slumped out.

Jim could feel the blood pulsating at his temples.

What's going on?

He took a deep breath. Suddenly, bullets began to strike the car around him. Across the street Jim could make out a man firing from behind a car. Jim realized he was alone and didn't know how many men were shooting at him.

Not one of my better days!

He frantically looked around. There behind him was the entrance to a mass transit station.

In the distance the sound of emergency vehicles became audible. As they did, the man who had been firing at Jim jumped into the car he was using for cover. The car pulled away. Jim decided not to stick around. He didn't want to explain things to the Swedish authorities. He put his gun back in its holster and headed for the subway.

SIX

A LIGHT FOG ROLLED OVER THE WATER AS THE HELICOPTER TOUCHED down on the deck. David Egan was exhausted, but it was impossible to sleep with the thunder of the rotors pounding in his ears. He allowed the rotors to slow before exiting the aircraft.

Four bells sounded over the 1-MC followed by, "*Peterson* arriving." Then another bell.

"Good morning, Captain," the XO said as he rendered a salute.

"Good morning, Miles. What's the weather forecast?"

"Light fog. Should burn off in the next hour."

"Set the special sea and anchor detail. Have the first lieutenant set a fog watch until it burns off. Tell the OOD to proceed up the fjord at a slow speed."

"Aye, sir."

The XO walked toward the telephone in the hangar. David proceeded toward his cabin. "I'll be in my in-port cabin if you need me," David shouted so that Miles could hear him over the noise.

"Yes, sir."

Through the hanger and down the ladder.

How many pairs of shoes have I worn out on these decks?

The thought of giving up command was like losing a child. He opened the door of officers' country and was greeted by several officers in towels. They had just stepped out of the shower closet. He returned their greetings and went forward to the wardroom and entered. The six officers who were eating breakfast stood and greeted him.

Over the 1-MC the boatswain's pipe sounded attention. "Now secure from flight quarters. The smoking lamp is lighted in all authorized spaces."

Even though the word was not passed in officers' country, a main deck speaker was just outside of the wardroom porthole. All messages were clearly audible in the wardroom.

"Good morning, gentleman," David said as he motioned for them to keep their seats. "Please, continue your breakfast."

"Mornin' Captain, what can I get you?" the wardroom mess specialist said.

"Good morning. I'll have scrambled eggs, bacon, and toast. Oh, bring that to my in-port cabin with coffee."

"Yes, sir." The sailor turned and disappeared into the pantry.

"Gentlemen, if you'll excuse me," David said. He exited the wardroom.

He entered his cabin and set his briefcase on the couch. He removed the briefing file and put it in his safe. Then he went over to the phone and dialed the number of the officer of the deck.

"Bridge, officer of the deck."

"This is the captain, have Mr. Reese report to my in-port cabin."

While David was talking, the boatswain's pipe sounded attention outside of officers' country. "Now set the special sea and anchor detail. Post the fog watch."

"Yes, sir," the OOD said.

The pipe sounded attention. "Mr. Robert Reese, your presence is required in the commanding officer's in-port cabin."

David slumped onto the couch. Before he could fall asleep, there was a knock at his door.

"Enter," he shouted.

"Good morning, Captain. Here's your traffic," the messenger from radio said as he entered the room.

"Good morning. Just set it over there." David motioned toward the desk. The messenger did so and promptly left the room.

Given the rough weather the night before, David was running on a sleep deficit. He had caught a short nap on the flight from the *Kennedy* to Oslo. Other than that, he hadn't slept. The stress brought on a real headache. He got up, went into the head, and took two aspirin. As he was swallowing the pills, he heard another knock.

"Enter."

"Captain, Bob Reese."

"Good morning, Bob," he said as he walked out of the head. "How long have you been aboard?" He motioned for Bob to sit down.

"Oh, an hour and a half. Looks like the mission has begun to unravel in Stockholm."

"How so?"

"Andreyev's contacts traced Choutov to a shop where he had engaged the services of a young lady."

"Looks like our information's accurate."

"Our station chief arranged to have this same woman service Jim at a nearby hotel. Andreyev intercepted the girl and put a plant in Jim's room."

"Hmm."

"The plant turned out to be ex-KGB. Working for Severny Iourtchak."

David was staring directly at Bob with an intense look. Bob took a deep breath and continued. "Bad news. There was an attempted hit on Jim in the hotel room. Jim sanctioned the assassin."

"A hit? Iourtchak? How could Iourtchak know anything about Jim?"

"It gets worse. As Jim and the local station chief were leaving, their Volvo was destroyed by a rocket-launched grenade. Simultaneously, Andreyev managed to destroy the van with the cleaners. Severny's operative also. She was being transported to Langley. No one in the van survived."

"Jim? Is he okay?"

"Yeah. Almost took out the whole Stockholm field office though."

"Where's Jim?"

"On his way to Oslo."

"Did we find out anything useful?"

"Maybe. In debriefing of Severny's operative, we confirmed that Andreyev arrived in Stockholm. Apparently he and his men are planning an exit by air, but we don't know from which airfield. We're trying to cover all the bases."

David dialed the radio room on the ship's telephone.

"Radio, Milton speaking."

"Milton, this is the captain. Can you connect this phone to one of the radio frequencies?"

"You bet, sir. I'll have to key it for you in here."

"Good. Get me the secure channel with the *Kennedy.*"

"Aye, sir. It'll take a minute."

"Call me when you're ready."

"Aye, sir."

"Go on, Bob," he said as he hung up the phone.

"Jim asked a very interesting question by the way."

"What would that be?"

"If Andreyev and Choutov have a prearranged meeting, why is Andreyev following him around? You know, taking out anyone who inquires about Choutov? They started a minor war in Stockholm."

"How would you answer that question?"

"Well, two answers, I guess. With a number of secondary questions and possibilities."

"Go on. What are your two answers?"

"First, Andreyev and Choutov have a prearranged meeting. Andreyev is following Choutov and cleaning his trail. Given Choutov's past history, that's entirely a possibility."

"Okay. Doubt it, but go on."

"Second, they don't have a prearranged meeting. Andreyev is actually looking for Choutov. If it is the second option, the question is, why? Has Choutov gone into business for himself? Does Choutov actually have the weapon? Is it with him? Or, is it hidden?"

There was a knock at the door. "Enter," David said.

The door opened, and the wardroom mess specialist entered. "Here's your breakfast, Captain," he said. "Will there be anything else, sir?"

"Did you remember the Tabasco for my eggs?"

"Yes, sir."

"Thanks. That'll be all," David said as he got up and moved toward the table. The sailor promptly left the room.

"Do you mind if I eat as we talk?"

"Not at all. Please, eat."

"Have you had breakfast yet?"

"Yes. Please enjoy yours."

The phone rang. "Captain."

"Captain, this is Milton in radio. We're ready, sir. All you need to say is 'key'. I'll key the mike. When you say 'over or out', I'll unkey the mike."

"What's my call sign, and what's the *Kennedy's* call sign today?"

"Sir, the *Kennedy* is Alpha Sierra, and you're Tango Bravo."

"Key—Alpha Sierra, this is Tango Bravo, request you patch me to your air boss, over."

"Tango Bravo, Alpha Sierra. Wait one, out."

David sat with the earpiece of the phone next to his ear. Bob poured him a cup of coffee. "Thanks," David said. "What's your evaluation of the options you just laid out?"

"First, I doubt Andreyev is just cleaning up. That was a wholesale assault in Stockholm. It has every mark that he's frantically looking for Choutov."

"I agree."

"Here's my question. Is Andreyev looking for Choutov because the Stockholm stop was unscheduled and threw their plans off? Or, is Choutov somehow out of the fold and Andreyev is trying to chase him down?"

"Hmmm. At the very least, their plans have been interrupted. That may buy us a few hours. Maybe even a day."

"Tango Bravo, this is Alpha Sierra Air Boss, over."

"Key—Alpha Sierra, do you have an E-2 aloft, over?"

"Tango Bravo, affirmative, over."

"Key—Alpha Sierra, I need to know about all noncommercial aircraft that have taken off from airfields in and around Stockholm. I need to know if any have headed for Oslo, over."

"Tango Bravo, we can get you that data, over."

"Key—Alpha Sierra, Keep one intercept fighter on station near the mouth of the Oslofjord, out. . . . Thanks Milton."

"Yes, sir."

"Sorry, please continue," David said as he hung up the phone.

"You're right. The interruption may buy us some time. However, given the events in Stockholm, we can't expect Andreyev to linger. He's pulling in every favor—literally pulling out all the stops."

"Have you heard from Steve?"

"Yeah. His group's set up. Oh, we've brought in additional agents. They've been posted in several of the major hotels in the city center. They have pictures of all the major . . ."

"Don't you think they will stick to the secondary hotels?"

"Can't be sure. I'm banking on the hope that Choutov's perversions'll cause him to want to be near the action. That'll probably put him right near the city center."

"Let's hope you're right."

"On a different subject, have you met the new captain?"

"No."

"Want me to schedule a briefing?"

"Good idea. Tell him we'll meet here after we secure from the special sea detail. In fact, be sure to invite him to the bridge."

"He's already there." Bob stood. "Enjoy your breakfast," he said as he left.

David looked up at the clock.

It's getting late—better get to the bridge.

He swallowed down a few bites. Grabbing his *Peterson* ball cap and his cup of coffee, he departed for the bridge.

Attention was piped over the 1-MC. "Now secure the fog watch. Make all preparations to anchor."

"Captain's on the bridge," the boatswainmate sang out as he entered the bridge hatch.

"Good morning, Captain," Ted Sanders said. Ted was the special-sea-and-anchor OOD as well as the general quarters OOD.

"Good morning, Ted," David said as he crossed to his starboard bridge chair.

Ted walked over beside David and began his report. "Captain, we've secured the fog watch. I've increased speed so that we can make our anchor point by zero eight hundred. The starboard anchor is set and stoppered. The first lieutenant reports that the motor whale boat and your gig are ready. Also, the sea ladder is in place ready to lower."

"Very well."

David got up from his chair and walked out on the bridge wing. Looking aft he could see the deck crew setting up the quarterdeck at the point where the sea ladder was secured to the main deck.

He looked forward. On the forecastle the chief boatswainmate was standing with several crewmen near the anchor stopper. David noticed puddles of water all over the deck. He turned and walked back into the bridge.

"Ted, did we clamp down this morning?"

"No, sir. The deck crew was up early rigging the ladder."

"They look like they have things in hand. Get the decks clamped down before we anchor."

"Aye, sir."

Ted turned to the boatswainmate of the watch. The boatswainmate gave Ted a nod. The pipe shrilled attention over the 1-MC. "Sweepers, sweepers, man your brooms. Clamp down all exposed decks fore and aft, now sweepers."

A commander stepped onto the bridge from the port bridge wing and walked over toward David. He saluted.

David returned the salute and extended his hand in greeting.

"Captain, I'm Phillip Rowe, your relief."

"Phillip, welcome aboard. I hope Miles and the crew have been able to assist you. Did you get settled in alright?"

"Yes, sir. They've been quite helpful. I understand that we have some kind of a briefing after we anchor."

"I'll meet you in my in-port cabin."

"Will I find out why I've been pulled over here so quickly to take command?"

"You will."

"Good. I'll look forward to the meeting. You need to get on with the business at hand. With your permission, I'll just stand back and observe."

David nodded to Phillip and then turned toward the OOD. "Ted, I'll be with Mr. Reese. Send a messenger when we get close to the anchorage."

"Aye, sir."

"Captain's off the bridge," the boatswainmate sung out as David disappeared down into CIC.

He paused for a moment to greet the CIC watch and then proceeded out the hatch and down the passageway. For the next ten minutes he had Bob Reese give him a detailed briefing of the communications equipment.

The boatswain's pipe sounded attention over the 1-MC. "Commanding Officer, your presence is requested on the bridge."

"Can you pull together a briefing folder for Commander Rowe?" David asked as he got up and moved toward the door.

"Yes, sir. I'll have it for our meeting," Bob said.

"Captain's on the bridge," the boatswainmate sung out as David appeared.

He walked over to the chart table where the navigator was running a continuous plot. On each bridge wing he had two men calling out bearings to fixed points on the shore. The chief quartermaster was keeping a log of the bearings. The navigator used the bearings to draw intersecting lines on the chart, which would give a fix of the ship's position. He could then tell the OOD how far to the right or left of the center of the channel the ship was and how long until the next planned turn. David could see the anchorage point marked. Fortunately, it was near the small boat launch area. This meant it wouldn't take long to run back and forth from the shore.

"Turn on final bearing in forty-five seconds," the navigator sang out.

"Very well," Ted responded.

Ted was standing at the center line gyroscope repeater. It would be used with the jack-staff up on the bow to shoot a precise bearing. Once he made the turn, he would be able to see the range on the center of the channel. The ship was about to turn into a special channel used to anchor deep draft ships. The navigator started a ten-second countdown.

"Left full rudder, steady new course three four zero," Ted commanded.

"Aye, sir, my rudder is left standard . . ."

"Slow to five knots."

"Aye, sir, slow to five knots."

David walked over and stood beside Ted. He could see that the ship was slightly out of the center of the channel.

"Set new course three four three," Ted commanded.

"Aye, sir, new course three four three."

The navigator started calling out distances to the anchorage every fifteen to twenty seconds. This went on for several minutes.

"Clear the stopper, stand by the anchor," Ted said.

"Forecastle, bridge. Clear the stopper, stand by the anchor," the messenger shouted into the sound-powered headset.

"Forecastle, aye, sir."

"All stop!"

"All stop, aye—"

"Release anchor."

"Forecastle, bridge. Release anchor."

The senior boatswainmate on the forecastle took the sledge hammer he was holding and hit the brake on the stopper. This caused the stopper to fall off, allowing the anchor chain to run. The ship had very little forward motion.

"Anchor released, sir."

"Very well," Ted said. He headed for the starboard bridge wing.

"Anchor set, sir. No dragging."

The boatswainmate of the watch immediately blew a long, loud blast on a police whistle into the 1-MC. "Anchored, shift colors."

"Very well," Ted said.

David stepped out on the bridge wing.

"Very good, Ted. It's always good to impress a new captain with a precise anchoring. I'm sure that when Tom gets a final fix, you'll be right on the money."

"Thanks, Captain."

"I'm going to be in an important briefing in my in-port cabin. Tell the in-port watch to call the XO for anything short of sinking or fire."

"Yes, sir."

David walked back onto the bridge and over to the center hatch leading down to CIC. "I'll be in my in-port cabin," he said as he disappeared through the hatch.

"Captain's off the bridge."

As David came out of CIC, he called down the passage-way to the marine guard. "Tell Mr. Reese I'll be in my cabin."

"He's already there, sir."

David proceeded down two decks and aft toward his cabin. A marine guard had been posted outside the door. There were also two guards posted on the quarter deck just beyond the entrance to the in-port cabin.

"Good morning, Captain," the guard said as he opened the door for him.

David stepped in and saw that Bob had set up the briefing. The wardroom staff had supplied coffee and pastries. David went into the head to relieve himself.

He swallowed down more aspirin. When he came out, Commander Rowe was in the room. Bob went over to the door and ordered the marine guard not to admit anyone.

"Phillip, this briefing is top secret . . ." They talked for half an hour.

"I'll hold a separate briefing in the wardroom," David said. "I have a slight marital problem to discuss with the officers."

"Marital problem? I was under the impression that your wife was deceased."

"True. But a stunning woman is about to show up posing as my wife."

"Oh. Yes, I see. Do you wish for me to attend the briefing?"

"No, it won't be necessary. I think you ought to go with Bob and get familiar with the equipment we have aboard in the operations center. Plus, I'll be able to say good-bye to my officers. No chance for a hail and fairwell."

"I understand."

"Any questions, Phillip?" David asked.

"No. It all sounds very scary."

"Believe me, it is," Bob said. "Commander, if you'll follow me, I'll give you a short tour of the operations center."

As both men got up to leave, the boatswain's pipe sounded attention again. "Now hear this. The crew will assemble at quarters on the flight deck in thirty minutes for the change of command ceremonies. The uniform of the day is service dress blues."

The phone rang. It was the officer of the deck reporting that the watch had been shifted to the quarterdeck and that David's gig had been dispatched to pick up his wife.

"Have all officers assemble in the wardroom," David said to the OOD.

"Yes, sir."

The boatswainmate piped attention over all circuits including officers' country. "Now here this. All officers assemble in the wardroom. All officers assemble in the wardroom."

David walked into the head and ran some hot water into the basin. He proceeded to shave. He changed his uniform shirt and skivvy shirt. As he was tucking in his shirt tail, there was a knock on the door.

"Enter."

"Captain, the officers are assembled," the XO said sticking his head into the door.

David followed the XO to the wardroom. A marine opened the door as they approached and called out in a loud voice. "Attention on deck."

The officers all stood as David and Miles walked in.

"At ease. Seats, gentlemen," David commanded. "Let me begin by pointing out that this briefing is top secret . . ."

As soon as the briefing broke up, David returned to his in-port cabin. He headed straight for the couch and was asleep in a few moments.

The phone woke David.

"Captain," he said into the phone handset.

"Captain, Chief Johnson on the quarterdeck. The gig's approaching with your wife."

"Have the messenger escort her to the wardroom. Tell her I'll join her shortly."

Within thirty seconds of hanging up, the phone rang again. This time it was the XO reporting that preparations had been completed for the change of command.

"Good," David said.

He went to his desk and found the folder with his orders. There was a knock at the door, and the senior supply officer entered. He handed David a folder with the ship's inventory and the various forms necessary for the change of command.

"After the ceremony, I'll bring Commander Rowe here. You need to be here to make sure we sign all of these forms properly."

"Yes, sir."

The boatswain's pipe sounded attention and was followed by a prerecorded bugle. "All hands assemble at quarters on the flight deck."

David picked up his hat and headed for the wardroom.

Catherine and Phillip were seated and talking with each other when David entered. They were alone since the other officers had left to assemble at quarters with the crew.

"David," she said as she got up and walked across the room. She gave him a short kiss and then put her arm under his. "Are you ready, sweetheart?"

"Sure. Can you remember your way up to the flight deck?" He smiled.

"Oh, come on. You know how I get turned around on these ships. I'll follow you."

The three of them wound their way through officers' country and up the ladder to the hangar bay.

"Attention on deck," the XO called out as they appeared.

The crew immediately came to attention. The XO saluted David and then greeted Catherine.

He saluted Philip and then escorted Catherine to her chair behind the podium.

"Ship's company, parade rest," he ordered.

The rails of the flight deck had been outlined with signal flags. The crew was assembled in service dress blue.

"Where'd they come from?" David said nodding toward a band that was playing German march music.

"Embassy sent 'em," the XO said. They abruptly stopped their march and tried to play a rendition of "Anchors Away." It came out sounding somewhat like a cat fight.

"Couldn't we do better?" David whispered to the XO.

"Sorry, Captain."

Changes of commands are fairly routine affairs. Usually the old and the new commanding officers give short speeches followed by an inspection of the crew by both commanders. David was short with his speech, acknowledging some of the major accomplishments of the crew during his tenure and thanking them for their loyalty and service. Commander Rowe was also brief.

Following the inspection, the XO had the crew stand at parade rest as David read his orders from the Bureau of Naval Personnel. Then Phillip Rowe read his orders.

Phillip turned to face David. "I am prepared to relieve you, sir," he said loud enough to be heard by the crew.

The XO called the crew to attention.

David stood. "I am prepared to be relieved."

In a ceremonial fashion, the color guard paraded the American flag, the navy flag, and the ship's flag to a position in front of David. Salutes were exchanged, and a flag bearer handed David the ship's flag. He turned to Phillip who saluted. Then he handed Phillip the ship's flag.

"I relieve you, sir," Phillip said.

David took a step back and saluted Phillip. "I stand relieved."

Phillip gave the flag back to the color guard. They marched off to their preassigned position. Then Phillip told the crew to stand at ease.

"Before we see Captain Egan and his lovely wife off, we have one more little ceremony." He pulled out a promotion notice for David and read it aloud. The XO then handed Catherine a new dress blue jacket with full captain's stripes. She went over to David and waited for him to remove his coat. Then she helped him on with the new coat. As the crew applauded, she kissed him.

A hint of lemon was a welcome pause from the brackish odor of the port. David felt his neck warm.

"Congratulations, sweetheart," she said with a tilt of her head and a coy smile.

Several of the officers started calling on David to make a speech as the crew continued applauding with what seemed to be more intensity. It was hard to tell whether they were applauding for him or the kiss. He awkwardly approached the microphone.

"I wasn't expecting to make a speech. However, I do want to thank all of you for your part in this promotion. There's no doubt in my mind that the officers and crew of this ship played a significant role in helping me to achieve this milestone in my career. I thank you all from the bottom of my heart . . ."

When David concluded, the XO called the crew to attention. David, Phillip, and Catherine departed and headed back to the in-port cabin to sign the necessary paperwork. They all sat and made small talk for five minutes following the paper signing.

The shrill of the boatswainmate's pipe sounded attention over all circuits. "Now hear this, sideboys man the rail for honors."

Four bells were stuck over the 1-MC. "Captain, United States Navy, departing."

It was time for the outgoing captain to make a graceful exit. David and Catherine were escorted out to the quarterdeck. Four sailors and the chief boatswainmate had manned the side rail in front of the sea ladder. David turned to say goodbye to the XO and reminded him where to send his luggage. Then he said goodbye to Phillip. He and Catherine started toward the sea ladder. David saluted the officer of the deck.

"I have permission to go ashore."

The OOD returned his salute. "Very well, sir."

The chief boatswainmate raised his pipe and began to pipe the side. The sailors saluted as the couple walked between them. David stepped to the top of the sea ladder and turned aft to salute the colors. As he lowered his salute, the chief boatswain ended his piping of the side, and the messenger sounded one bell over the 1-MC.

David and Catherine went down the ladder and got into the captain's gig for the ten-minute boat trip to the shore landing.

"Permission to shove off, Captain," the coxswain asked.

"Permission granted," David said as he sat down next to Catherine.

He couldn't help but feel a real sense of loss. Every naval officer looks forward to the day when he will command his own ship. The *Peterson* had been an excellent ship with a great crew. David could say that he had enjoyed every day of this tour. As the boat pulled away, he stared. There was no doubt, he was going to miss her.

"Hey, why such a sad look, sailor?" Catherine asked as she nudged David.

"Forgive me. It's sad having to leave such a great lady."

David turned away from the ship and looked at Catherine. He began to focus on the reality of the day. The *Peterson* was in the past now. Here he was heading to shore for one of the most important assignments of his life with one of the most incredibly beautiful women he had ever had the pleasure to meet.

"Say, didn't your mother ever tell you not to kiss sailors?"

Catherine laughed. "Y'all were so serious, and with all the pomp and circumstance. Besides, wouldn't a wife kiss her husband when he's been promoted?"

"Just remember, it's been three years since I lost my wife. I've spent the last year and a half on sea duty. You don't want to give an old salt the wrong idea."

She put her arm inside his and looked up into his eyes with a smile. "Oh, I'll remember."

They didn't say much the rest of the way. David was intrigued by Catherine's response. However, it didn't take long for him to shift the focus of his thoughts from her to the mission. He began to ponder what Bob had reported to him when he returned to the *Peterson* from the *Kennedy*. Why was Andreyev carrying out a holy war in Stockholm? He knew the Russian Secret Service had put out orders to arrest him. Andreyev had to assume that the Americans were also looking for the weapon. Why would he turn on a neon sign saying, "Here I Am"? Was this a decoy? Are we sure that Choutov had actually engaged the prostitute or was that a plot to distract us?

It took just under ten minutes for the gig to reach the boat landing. David helped Catherine off. He shook hands with and said goodbye to the two boat crewmen and the coxswain.

"Inter Nor Hotel Bristol," David said to the taxi driver as he and Catherine entered a cab.

She slid to the center of the back seat. When David got in, she put her arm in his and snuggled up. David didn't know if this was Catherine's attempt to appear in public as husband and wife or if she was coming on to him. It really didn't matter. Having a good-looking woman hanging on to you is a fantasy for every man.

Feels good, even if it's only for show.

The car made its way the short distance to the city center. "What a quaint, pretty place," she said.

"Yah," the taxi driver responded in a heavy northern European accent. "We are having a mixture of old world, ah, how do you say, charm. Yah, and new modern progress. Oslo is being a very modern city. Many wonderful things to see. The university is being the home of many important museums. Yah, the Nobel Institute, the National Gallery, the Museum of Decorative Art, the Norwegian Folk Museum, Frogner Park, and the Munch Museum. If you are having interest in Viking heritage, I take you to the Kon-Tiki Museum. Yah, also the Akershus Fortress, the Royal Palace, and the Stortinget. We are having special package. I take you seeing all of these sights. A very reasonable fee."

"Thank you," David responded. "I'll take your name and number. We may want to do that several days from now."

The taxi stopped near the front of the hotel. A doorman opened the car door for Catherine and greeted her quite warmly. David got out on the other side of the car.

"Luggage?" the doorman asked.

"The ship should send it along in the next hour or two. Could you please have it brought to my room? Honey, what room?"

"Three one two," Catherine said.

"Of course. I am personally ensuring your luggage is being brought to your room. Welcome to the Hotel Bristol. Please to be having a very pleasant stay." He tipped his hat.

David paid the taxi driver and walked around the car to the doorman. He handed the doorman a large tip. "You'll take good care of my luggage when it arrives, won't you?"

"Yah. Dhank you."

David and Catherine entered the lobby. It was elegant. The hotel was located on one of the main streets of Oslo in the city center. It was world renowned for its old-world charm. The first floor was comprised of restaurants, lounges, and banquet rooms. David could not avoid sensing the prestigious ambience to the lobby. A striking winter garden with palms and graceful furniture was a haven of calm in the center of the room.

Steve was sitting in a high-back chair across from the elevator reading a magazine. David and Catherine walked to the front desk and asked for messages. There were none. Then they proceeded to the elevator. As they did, Steve got up and walked over beside them. When the door opened, the three of them entered the elevator. They were alone.

"You need to make contact at the Engebret Cafe at noon. We've put an outfit in your room just in case your luggage doesn't arrive in time. You'll have one of my teams as backup whenever you leave the room. We'll remain out of sight at all times. Catherine, you'll need to go along to keep the cover in tack," Steve said.

The doors opened on the third floor. Steve walked down the hall to room 310. David and Catherine proceeded to the next room, room 312. When they were inside, Steve opened the door from the adjoining room.

"Let me show you the communications setup," he said as he motioned for David to follow him into room 310.

Steve had set up a video uplink with Mother. David and Bob exchanged greetings. Bob gave David a short briefing on the tactical situation off Norway's coast. The British had their carrier and several destroyers in the area, and they were joining the task group. In addition, several American elements from the NATO exercise had been detached and assigned to the task group, including David's first ship, the *Spruance*.

"Finally," Steve said as he came to the end of his briefing. "We are also tied into the operative tracking system using this laptop. In reality, we are linked to the system on the *Peterson* through a modem connection. The modem ties into a cellular network, which is linked to a standard long-distance satellite and is received in Virginia. Langley retransmits over our system to the *Peterson*. Needless to say, it sometimes causes problems. However, it works in a pinch."

"Very impressive," David said.

"Remember, the visual communication uplink to Mother is up only when the satellite is up."

"Well, if you don't mind, I'm going to catch a nap before our little rendezvous at noon," David said as he went back into his room.

Catherine sat on the couch beside the bed. David slipped his coat, shirt, and tie off and hung them in the closet. He then sat down by Catherine and slipped his shoes off.

"How much sleep have you gotten?" he asked.

"Not as much as I would like. I did get to sleep on the flight here and then a few hours early this morning, so I'm OK."

"I'm going to try to catch a nap."

"No problem. I'll sit with Steve so you can darken the room."

She reached over to the telephone and dialed the front desk.

"Yes, this is Mrs. Egan in room three twelve. Could you ask the doorman to hold my husband's luggage until we call for it? He didn't get much sleep last night, and he is going to try to catch a nap. Yes, thank you."

David went over to the curtains and drew them closed. Then he got into bed. Catherine went to the front door of the room, hung out the "do not disturb" sign, and turned off the lamp. She walked over to the bed and sat down behind David. Then she reached over and began to massage his neck and upper back.

"I didn't realize I was so tense," he purred as she worked his muscles.

"Anyone would be tense in this situation." She leaned over. "Get some sleep; we'll just be in the next room," she whispered in his ear.

David snuggled a pillow. The image of Catherine at their first meeting came to mind. A slight smile appeared on his face as he drifted from consciousness.

SEVEN

"JUST SET THEM OVER THERE. THANK YOU," CATHERINE SAID AS she grabbed her purse to tip the bellboy. After he left, she walked to the window and opened the curtains.

"David, you'd better get up. Sorry to wake you. We don't have much time. I let you sleep as long as I could." He stirred and then slowly sat up.

"Your bags are over there," she said pointing across the room.

David got up. He fetched his shaving kit and went into the bathroom area. He used a washcloth to clean his upper body. After shaving and brushing his teeth, he replaced the shaving kit and took out a pair of pants and a shirt.

Catherine couldn't help but notice the definition of the anterior and posterior heads of his shoulder muscle and the horseshoe outline on his upper arm where the brachialis and triceps joined.

"I hope our contact has a lead," she said as he returned to the bathroom area.

"Let's just hope that Choutov's as perverted as the intelligence suggests. Maybe we'll get lucky and catch him before he hooks up with Andreyev."

David reappeared and went over to his luggage to find his shoes. Then he sat down on the bed and put his shoes and socks on.

"Ready, Mrs. Egan?" he asked with a teasing grin.

Her smile faded. "I've never done this spy stuff. Ready as I'm ever gonna be, I guess."

"OK then, let's do it."

They left the room and walked down the hall to the elevators in silence. While they were in the elevator, David did a last-minute check to see if he had everything. Then they continued to the lobby.

The center of the lobby was a spacious winter garden with palms and Chesterfield sofas. Off to one side of the room, a pianist was playing the Andantino from Mozart's Concerto No. 14 in E Flat Major. The soft melody filled the elegantly appointed lobby. Catherine couldn't help but sense the old-world charm. She put her arm under David's as they walked through the lobby. Her mouth curved into a smile. "What a wonderful place," she said. "I think I recognize what he's playing."

"Ah, yeah, it's very nice," he responded as he noticed the surroundings.

She looked over toward an enclave with the piano. Large palms formed a barrier, which obstructed the view from the lobby.

"Mozart, I think," David said. "The Andantino from one of his concertos. Can't remember which one."

"I'm impressed. You know classical music."

"My mother believed that everyone should play an instrument. I wanted to play football and baseball. As a compromise, I had to put up with piano."

"So you play the piano?"

"Play? Not well. Piano lessons gave me a foundation, I guess. It was when I went to sea that I really started to appreciate—"

"You have a piano on the ship?"

"No," he said smiling. "I do have a CD player. Besides, I haven't always been at sea."

"I realize that."

"One of the perks of intelligence work is being able to hear great symphony orchestras all over the world."

"I'd love to have that opportunity."

"Yeah, I couldn't play, but I could listen. The music became my stress-reduction therapy."

Her fingers wrapped around the fabric of his sleeve lightly caressing the muscle beneath. David looked at her hand. A faint smile appeared on his face.

The pianist finished with a bold flourish. He sighed as he looked down at the keyboard. Then lifting his head up and straightening his back, he took both hands and brushed his blond hair back. A smile came across his face as he turned toward a woman sitting in a chair beside the piano.

"It was wonderful," she proclaimed as she began to softly applaud.

He bowed his head. "Thank you."

For you, Grigori.

The pianist stood and turned to another man seated nearby. "Thank you for allowing me to play."

"It was a pleasure," the man responded.

"Come, my dear," the pianist said as he extended his arm to the woman.

She got up and put her arm under his. She gazed into his blue eyes. "I had no idea you had so many talents."

"My music, it is a tribute to my brother."

David and Catherine reached the front of the lobby.

"I am getting for you a taxi?" the doorman asked.

"No thanks, I think we'll walk. Can you direct me to the Engebret Cafe? I understand it's within walking distance," David said.

"Yah. Dhat's true," the doorman said pointing to his left. "See next street? Just beyond hotel?"

"Yes."

"Rosenkrantz Gate. There, ah, right to Karl Johans Gate. How do you say, ah, progress left. Past Stortinget. Two blocks past Stortinget, ah, Nedre Slortsgate. Progress right. Two blocks. Yah, you see Christiania Theater. Engebret Cafe is near the theater."

"That seems simple enough. Go there to next street. Left to the Stortinget. How far is that?"

"One block, ah big."

"Okay, one long block to Stortinget, then two more blocks. Right and two more blocks."

"Yah. Dhat's precise. Very popular for theater peoples. Ah, how do you say, too early in the day. True ambience. May I, uh, advocate our Bristol Grill. Yah, distinctive English design. Only restaurant in Oslo, food, ah, preparing with authentic charcoal grill."

"Sounds wonderful," David said. "We'll give it a try some other time. Right now we have other plans. Thanks for the recommendation."

"Yah. Being most welcoming, sir."

David took Catherine's hand as they crossed the street and proceeded toward the café. "Somehow it feels like I just stepped into an old movie," she said.

"Oh, how so?"

"Look around. What'd you notice about this city?"

"I'm not sure what you mean."

"The buildings, the layout, the shops."

"Well, there aren't many tall buildings, you know, like there are in New York or Atlanta. Most of them look old, well kept, but older."

"Right. It's kind of old world, wouldn't you say?"

"I guess it is."

"Look at all the arches. Every building seems to have 'em."

"Yeah, now that you mention it. It does feel like a scene from an old forties' movie."

"I'm surprised how warm it is here. At this time of the year I expected it to be much colder. I'm sure it was colder in England."

"Norway's got an interesting geography. The warm waters of the North Atlantic Drift are an extension of the Gulf Stream. Anyhow, they play a big part in the weather."

"Hmm."

"Oslo's in a major fjord, which tends to moderate the climate. Even in January, the mean temperature is around thirty degrees."

"Thirty degrees?"

"Yeah. But things change drastically as you go inland. There you'd find a subarctic climate."

"I hope we can wrap things up quickly. I'd like a chance to see some of Norway. I understand the scenery is super, really breathtaking . . . you know, some of God's best handiwork."

"Funny you should mention God's handiwork," David said.

"Why's that funny?"

"I'm sorry. Just thinking out loud."

"You've got me curious. What'd you mean?"

"Last year I read an article about alternate theories regarding the formation of the Great Lakes and the Grand Canyon and fjords. Actually, the bulk of the article dealt with theories about continental drift, shifting geological plates and that sort of thing, and it called into question the idea that the fjords were the result of erosion or ice age glacier flows."

"And?"

"Your mention of God. It caused me to think about the conflicts that scientists and religious thinkers have."

"What conflicts?"

David noticed a blank look on Catherine's face. He didn't know if what he was saying had puzzled her or if he offended her by being so presumptuous as to discuss scientific philosophy. After all, he didn't know her very well, and she was the Ph.D.

"Yeah." he said. "Mainstream scientific theory holds that the spectacular fjord landscape is a result of the last ice age.

You know, great glaciers over millions of years. However, an increasing number of geologists have suggested that the traditional views are flawed."

"I've heard of the glacier explanation. What's that got to do with religion?"

"This alternative theory speculates that a major shift in the crust of the earth occurs every forty to fifty thousand years. You know, the center of the earth is assumed to be liquid rock. Ice builds up on the two poles, and after forty or fifty thousand years, the ice causes the crust to shift rapidly."

"I've heard something about that. Saw something on TV. Maybe PBS. Go on."

"I'm just a dumb sailor. Certainly no expert on geology. But, if this alternative theory is correct, Norway would have been in a more moderate climate in the past. That invalidates the glacier theory."

"I know what you mean. I visited the Grand Canyon last year. Our tour guide gave us the old spiel about the Colorado River cutting the canyon. Seemed to me that we could measure the rate of erosion by water on that kind of rock and then figure how long such a thing would have taken. I remember thinking that the number would be outrageous. There must be some other explanation. You know, like a geological shift."

"It makes you wonder. I'm not that religious a man, but sometimes I wonder about the veracity of science."

"I don't follow. What'd you mean?"

"How much more do we really know? After all these years of scientific inquiry, have we really disproved the religious concept that a God created?"

"Oh my, a warrior philosopher," she said with a wink. "I thought I was well-read. Is all this reading another diversion to relieve stress?"

"Maybe." His eyes searched her face looking for a sign as to her genuine interest in the nature of their discussion. "I find that a number of disciplines of human thought tend to run in ruts intellectually, especially science."

Her eyebrows raised. "I guess I can buy that."

"In fact, scientists may be as arrogant about what they think they know as the so-called experts in the intelligence community."

She squinted as if she was very puzzled. "Intelligence community? How does that relate?"

"I need to stop thinking out loud," David said. "You don't talk about politics, religion, or philosophy in the wardroom. It's nice having someone intelligent enough to carry on a meaningful—well, you know—"

Catherine responded to his complement with a large grin. "No. Go on. I'm interested in what you're saying. Not sure how we got here, but I'm interested."

"When I was on the White House staff I tried at length to get senior intelligence types to realize that international terrorism required a whole new way of looking at international affairs. We tend to westernize our ideas of how and why people work."

"Ugly Americans?"

"Yeah, kinda. We make assumptions about law and the reasons people act based on centuries of western culture. It puts us at a great disadvantage in the evaluation of intelligence data because we're never willing to reexamine our basic premises."

She nodded her head, "Hmmm."

"For example, western culture looks at religious zealots in a peculiar way. We've seen a history of martyrs, and in some cases even wars, because individuals became very devoted to a belief. In western culture many zealots felt that an ultimate standard, God's law, was being violated. These individuals had a high view of law. The problem is, western religious devotion is not the same as Middle-Eastern Islamic religious devotion."

"And how are they different?"

"In the western model, sane zealots never think of killing large numbers of innocent people. Their view of the image of God residing within all humankind is an integral part of their whole makeup. Mass murder, terrorism, and serial killing are all considered to be perversions, maybe even signs of psychosis, and definitely not the result of true religious devotion. That's not the case when it comes to Islamic models."

"I don't know much about Islam. I've heard that Muslims think it's okay to deceive infidels . . . you know, anyone who's not a Muslim. Although, now that I think about it, someone once told me there's a difference between the two major sects."

"You hit the nail on the head. Their views of the faithful versus the infidel is what gives them justification for acts of terrorism. I think it became a celebrated belief during the crusades."

"Interesting, but not all are terrorists."

"True. The Sunnis tend to be more open to the west. Nonetheless, their theology allows for holy wars and righteous deception of the infidel."

"So, if political alliances change—"

"Our response to terrorism is based on a model of international affairs that is rigid and western. We look at nations like Syria, Libya, Iraq, and Iran and fashion our response dealing nation to nation. We treat the terrorist as an aberration. In reality, the terrorist is often the heroic model of true devotion."

"So, when the president and other world leaders call them cowards, it means nothing to them," she said.

"Exactly! They don't have a sense that they are violating some basic universal ethic. In terms of our response, we need to realize that terrorist groups are not extensions of these states; they're really sovereign entities themselves. They have alliances with these nations, but we're foolish to believe these nations control them in some covert manner. What we need is a declaration of war, a real congressional declaration . . . not against a national entity but against the terrorist groups themselves."

"War? Why war?"

"It'd free us to pursue them as we would any enemy. We could hunt them down. It'd also mean that we'd not have to extend the same civil liberties to combatants working in western countries that we would to noncombatant civilians."

"I'm not sure I buy your premise about religious devotion being the root of terrorism. It might explain the Arabs, but what about the IRA or Pol Pot or Idi Amin?" she asked.

"I suspect that if you looked at the philosophical view each of these movements had toward the sanctity of life, you'd find the same sort of thinking."

"Maybe. But war? I'm not sure that removing civil liberties is a good idea. History seems to show that whenever a crisis suggests such a thing, the long-term results are undesirable."

"When we were at war with the Germans, did we afford civil liberties to their forces?"

"At least we didn't kill POWs and that sort of thing," she said in an argumentative tone.

"That's not what I mean. We certainly didn't hold a trial before going into battle and killing their troops. You mentioned POWs. They didn't have the rights of habeas corpus or other civil liberties. If a court had issued a writ, the Defense Department would have told the court to mind its own business."

"Yeah, but we were fighting armies of other countries. It's not the same thing," she said.

David stopped and looked at her. "Here's the reality as I see it. Abu Nidal is a group of several hundred men and women who are devoted to destroying Israel and the United States. They're an army, an army at war with us. If we're not successful in our mission, they might succeed in reeking more carnage than Hitler could have ever accomplished. Even if we're successful this time, sooner or later they're going to get their hands on some kind of a weapon of mass destruction. And when they do, they'll use it."

"You have a point," she said.

"You bet," David said. "What's the difference between a group of terrorists or a whole country, like Russia, nuking New York City? You still get a big hole in the ground. If we thought that Russia was actually going to strike with a nuke, we'd go to war in a heartbeat. We spent forty years preparing to do just that."

They started walking. "I see your point. I guess I just don't see anyone getting away with blowing up an entire city," she said.

"It can happen."

"Maybe. On the other hand, we've managed to stop several potentially disastrous attempts against targets in the United States. Even the fact that we are on this mission shows that the intelligence community is on top of what is going on."

"You said, 'I don't see.' That's the essence of the problem. Kant rears his ugly head. We don't have a framework of understanding for such a heinous unprovoked event of mass destruction. As a result, we don't consider the evidence that might point to such a thing."

"Isn't that sort of a survivalist mentality? Remember all those bomb shelters in the sixties? And all the militias stockpiling water and weapons?"

"We never believed that the Russians really wanted a war. That's why the policy of mutual deterrence worked. It's different with terrorists. They've proven time and time again that they're willing to act. No, they want to act. We may have stopped them several times, but they've also seen some limited successes. What if the bomb at the Trade Center in New York hadn't been homemade? There's all kinds of garbage out there. Keep in mind, they're learning as they go. They're learning about our intelligence efforts as well as our weak points. They may be zealots, but they're not stupid."

David's passion and sense of urgency radiated a vitality that drew Catherine like a magnet. She wondered if his style of leadership with men was to inspire their socks off.

Maybe to scare 'em.

A momentary mischievous grin came upon her as she pictured David spouting philosophy as he tried to inspire a sailor.

"Why don't our leaders take this threat seriously?" she said.

David noticed the momentary pause in the conversation. Had she suddenly drifted off in space? Then, too, there was that unusual grin.

"Some do," he said. "Lugar and Nunn have talked about this sort of exposure at length. In fact, a number of the intelligence committee members of both the House and Senate are becoming more aware of what we face. But it's that emotive feeling that the rest of our leaders don't have, especially in the White House. They're not going to react until it shows up in some poll!"

"Egan, how'd we get into this deep discussion? You sure know how to show a girl a good time."

They crossed another street and stepped up onto the sidewalk in front of the café. David turned to face her. He gently pushed back a small amount of hair that had fallen in her face. "Forget about a good time for now," he said as he opened the door for her to enter.

The Engebret Cafe, named after Engebret Christoffersen who founded the restaurant in 1857, was located on a street corner adjacent to the Christiania Theater. The main floor was distinguished by a very high ceiling and elegant appointments in furniture and decorative art. The theater motif reflected its history and created a unique atmosphere. On a balcony covering about a third of the area, a small chamber group often played music in the afternoon and evening.

The tables reflected a traditional Norwegian custom of dressing the table. Beautiful table runners that had been handwoven with elaborate and colorful designs adorned each table. Cut flowers and unique wooden sculptured pieces of art were also on each table.

"Welcome. Two for lunch," the maître d' said in Norwegian.

"Do you speak English?" David said.

"English, yah. Welcome to Engebret Cafe. I may be seating you?" the maître d' asked.

"Please."

He showed them to a table and held the chair for Catherine. As he did, he began to give them a short history of the café. Obviously proud of the heritage, he mentioned the names of several actors and writers who had frequented the café over the years. The only name that David thought he recognized was the name Ibsen. He concluded his short history by handing them a menu in English and wishing them a good appetite.

"Thank you. Very interesting," David said as he took the menu. "We've something special to celebrate. Could you ask your wine steward to bring us a wine list?"

"But of course. I may be asking, ah, reason you are celebrating?"

"It's just a new job for me. And the chance for us to catch a long overdue vacation in your beautiful country," David said as he looked at Catherine with a grin.

"Congratulations for a new job. I am wishing you to be enjoying your time with us. Yah, Norsway. Many vonderful sights. Are you skiing?"

"Yes, I ski."

"Vonderful! Please to be seeing me when you are going. I will be directing you to, how do you say, tourist information center?"

"Thanks," David said.

"Here, your wine steward." Turning to him, the maître d' told the wine steward to speak English. He excused himself and returned to his station.

David looked up and said, "I understand that the Marchesi Antinori family is a premier wine-producing family. Do you have a selection of their wines?"

"Yah, an excellent line of wines. For over twenty-seven generations the family are producing, ah, best wines of the world. Please, I am apologizing. We are having a limited selection."

"I understand they have a classic Chianti made from the Sangiovese grape. It's renowned to give the wine a strong personality."

"Yah. Very true. They are producing from their Badia a Passignano Tenute. Please, I am being truly apologizing. We are not having it inside our cellars. Please, I am bringing special Italian wine list?"

"Please do."

He responded correctly to my mention of Sangiovese grapes.

The steward retired to the kitchen area as Catherine and David began to look over the menu. The waiter came with water and bread.

"Look, David, they've quite a selection of Norwegian and international specialties," Catherine said.

"Oh yes, madam, we have an excellent chef! Please take your time," the waiter said.

"Your English is very good," Catherine said. "Where'd you learn to speak so well?"

"St. Louis. Born and raised. I'm here on an exchange program at the Oslo University. I'll return in a moment to take your order." He turned and walked away. As he was leaving, the wine steward returned and handed David a new wine list.

"Our Italian wines."

David opened the wine list and saw a note inserted inside. It read:

Possible location of Choutov. Entered the Hotel Continental thirty minutes ago. Hotel is between the Royal Palace and the City Hall. You can walk there. Exit the café, turn right and start walking. Your backup will greet you in English by saying, "Good day, sir. I see you are visitor. May I assist you in any way?" Your response is, "Thank you, I'm looking for the Hotel Continental." He will respond, "It is a short walk, sir." He will then show you the way.

I will telephone the café and ask for you. Make an excuse.

It's only been a minute or two since he left. I doubt he typed the note in the back room. Must have been given to him to pass along.

David closed the wine list and passed it to Catherine.

She opened it and read the note. "Sweetheart, I really feel like something light. Since we plan to see the sights of Oslo, why don't we put off our celebration. We'll do it this evening."

"Sounds good." David was reluctant to withdraw his gaze from Catherine. With a sheepish grin, he cleared his throat and looked up at the wine steward. "I'm sorry. I believe we'll pass on the wine this afternoon."

"Not being a problem, sir. Please, to be enjoying your meal."

Several minutes later, the maître d' walked up to the table. "Mr. Egan?"

"Yes."

"You have a call. Please, to be taking it here or the booth?"

"In the booth, please."

David got up and followed him. The maître d' pointed to the phone. David went to the booth and faked a short conversation. Then he returned to the maître d'.

"I must go back to my hotel and retrieve a file to be faxed to my office. Please go ahead and serve my wife. I will get a sandwich from room service."

"Certainly. I am being sorry the meal is being interrupted."

David returned to the table and went through the motions of giving Catherine an excuse for leaving. In order to keep up the appearance of being married, he leaned toward her and brushed a gentle kiss across her forehead. To his surprise, she put her arms around his neck, and her lips barely touched his.

He savored the moment. It had been years since such yearnings had stirred. The last thing he wanted to do now was leave, but that was the story of his life.

The blasted needs of the navy.

He left the café. His thoughts drifted to the task at hand. Would he find Choutov?

Choutov. I wonder if Catherine flirted with him? Maybe they . . .

A momentary hint of anger was aroused out of jealousy. It quickly turned to suspicion.

EIGHT

DAVID AND HIS ESCORT STOPPED JUST INSIDE THE LOBBY OF THE Hotel Continental. Similar in style to his own hotel, the old-world charm was evident.

No piano music. Too bad.

A second CIA operative joined them. Without speaking the three men proceeded to the elevator.

"Second floor, please," the new agent said as the group entered the elevator car. David smiled at two hotel guests that were already on the elevator.

The door opened, and the three men exited.

"We've had the lobby and the room under surveillance for about an hour now," the new agent reported. They rounded a corner. In front of them was a man lying on the floor motionless. David and the two agents pulled their weapons out. The agent who had escorted David to the hotel turned to clear and protect the rear. David and the other agent eased up the hallway to the spot where the victim was lying in a pool of blood. Implanted in his right eye was a martial arts weapon known as a Bo Shuriken. His eyes were open, but he was obviously dead.

"He's our man."

"Didn't you become concerned when he didn't report in?" David said.

"He reported about half an hour ago."

"Half an hour? You don't do radio checks more often than each half hour?"

David cautiously moved close to the room where Choutov was reported to have taken a woman. The door was slightly ajar. He positioned himself beside the door for a two-man police style entry. When he nodded, the agent kicked the door open. The two entered. It was quiet. A woman dressed in a black leather thong was motionless on the bed. Her hands were bound to the headboard. David walked up and felt for a pulse. There was none.

He looked over her body. There were no wounds. She had a tiny tattoo of a rose on her ankle and her right shoulder was tattooed with a spiderweb. Both ears had multiple piercing with an assortment of jewelry. Her left nostril was pierced with one gold stud. The only marks on her were on her neck and wrists.

Why would any woman do this to her body? Drugs and prostitution. Look where it got her.

David reached for his cellular phone.

"Mother," Bob said.

"This is David. Choutov's been seen at the Hotel Continental. He killed a woman and probably an agent. Send cleaners to the second floor. Oh, check his file. Did he have any martial arts training?"

"Understood."

David shut off the phone and put it back into his jacket. "Did you have the fire escape covered?"

"He'd have to use the stairs to the lobby. I'd have seen him," the agent responded.

"He may still be in the building. You stay here and wait for the cleaners," David said as he hurried from the room toward the stairs.

The CIA agent in the hallway joined him. When they entered the stairwell, David told the other agent to go up. David went down. It was only one flight to the lobby. He tucked his gun away and entered. No sight of him. He walked across the lobby to the doorman and pulled out a small photograph of Choutov. "Have you seen this man?"

"Yah, I was obtaining for him a taxi. Ah, forty-five minutes before."

"Did he say where he was going?"

"No."

"Do you know the name of the taxi company? Can you write it down for me?" David asked as he pulled out a pen.

"Yah." The doorman took the pen and wrote a name on the back of the photograph.

"Thank you."

David started walking back toward the stairs. He pulled out his phone. Mother answered.

David read him the name of the taxi company and told him to call and see if he could get a lead on where the cab dropped Choutov. Then he went back up the stairs.

David reentered the room. The agent in the room held up a thin leather strap. "Found this on the floor," he said. "Why kill her?"

"Knowing this guy's history, I'd say it happened during the act."

"An accident?"

"Don't know with this guy. Her attire would suggest that she was a wild one. There is another possibility. Maybe he didn't kill her."

"Oh?"

"You say your man reported half an hour ago?"

"Yes, give or take five minutes."

"The doorman recalls putting Choutov in a taxi over forty-five minutes ago. I'd say someone else was here."

David noticed her handbag beside the bedside table. He picked it up, emptied the contents, and found money, gum, keys, and a small handgun. David threw the keys to one of the operatives in the room with him.

"Here, see if you can trace any of these keys. Oh, and take this gun and see if you can determine its owner. I need to know how Choutov contacted the victim."

About that time Steve and four other men rushed into the room. They quickly set about the job of removing all evidence of the crime. Steve examined the body.

"Perverted man, isn't he?" Steve said.

David removed his cellular phone.

"Mother."

"Bob, David. Got an answer yet?"

"Yeah. Choutov was delivered to the Akershus Castle."

"I'm going to check out the Akershus Castle. Choutov was dropped off there," David said.

"We've got a car out front," Steve said. "Use it. I need to call for the van anyhow."

David went as quickly as possible to the lobby and out to the car. "Akershus Castle," he said as the car door shut behind him.

David's driver, a local CIA operative, began to narrate a brief description of the castle's layout and history. It was built in 1299 but was rebuilt in a renaissance theme in the seventeenth century. David asked various questions regarding access and possible exits.

It'd be easy for Choutov to disappear from there. After almost an hour, it's unlikely he'd be anywhere around.

The car phone rang. The driver answered and then handed it to David. It was Bob Reese.

"What else can go wrong?" David said.

NINE

"I AM SORRY YOUR HUSBAND WAS LEAVING ABRUPTLY," THE WAITER said as he handed Catherine the leather folder containing her receipt and her American Express Card.

"Me too." After leaving a tip, she left.

The temperature was now in the upper forties, and Catherine felt a little bit of a chill. She turned up the collar on her coat and buttoned the top button as she began to walk.

I think I'll take a slightly different route back. It's such an elegant city.

She walked west along the Radhusgata until she came to the Rosenkrantz Gate. Recognizing the name of that street, she turned north for several blocks until she came to the large park bordered by the Stortinget on the east side and the National Theatret on the west. Instead of crossing the park, she turned west toward the theater. It was a light yellow, almost golden brick building with concrete and stone accents. The front of the building was distinguished by a stone pillar facade with large Greek-style pillars. Above the pillars the word NATIONALTHEATER was etched in the stone in large block letters as one single word.

Why not theatret?

She stared for a moment at the building.

She looked around at the other buildings on Karl Johans Gate, which bordered the park on the north. The Stortingsgata, along which she was walking, bordered the park on the south. None of the buildings were over four or five stories high. All were stone or brick. The aspect of the architecture she found most interesting was the extensive use of arches. Virtually every building had numerous arched windows. Wherever there was a brick or concrete facade on the building, it was usually arched.

Catherine gazed across the park to one of the hotels. The central entrance was a large jutting semicircular structure. The ground level had arched entrances all around the semicircle leading into the lobby. Above the entryways, which were at least fifteen feet high, was a series of large arched windows. Each window was around eight feet high and four or five feet wide. Above that was a series of smaller, more closely placed arched windows. As Catherine pondered the scenery, she remembered the trip she'd made to Germany as a teenager. The architecture looked very similar—very old world.

She crossed the street and started walking through the park. Suddenly, she realized that Steve had gone with David. Looking around and behind her, she wondered if an agent had been assigned to protect her. There were a number of people in the park and on the sidewalks in front of the stores. The streets were busy with modest traffic.

Oh well, there's safety in numbers.

She continued past a statue in the center of the park.

Just in case, I'll pick up my pace. Better to be in a shop or in the hotel.

There were several hotels and a number of shops on Karl Johans Gate. Catherine remembered noticing one particular building when she and David came out of the hotel on the way to the restaurant. It was near the corner of Rosenkrantz Gate and Karl Johans, beside the Grand Hotel. She caught a glimpse of one of the shop windows, which was filled with troll dolls of various sizes. They were similar to the ones she had noticed in the airport that morning. She was curious.

Why would a whole store be devoted to trolls? Must be something cultural.

Anyhow, she could pick up a couple of dolls as presents for her nieces.

Who knows when David will return?

Catherine didn't pay attention to the man seated on the park bench near the statue. As she walked within two feet of him, he buried his face in a newspaper. It was Leonid Vodokanal. After she passed, he stood and folded his paper and put it under his right arm. Yakov Krylov, an ex-KGB operative who had emigrated to Oslo, was standing under an arched entrance of one of the buildings watching Catherine and Leonid. He had a lapel microphone and radio attached to his coat. The tell-tale earpiece with plastic tube was in his left ear.

"Dmitry, the mark's moving," he said.

"Da. I see her."

Dmitry was sitting in a white BMW 325i parked near the corner of the Kingenberggata and the Stortingsgata. From his vantage point he could see the park and the hotel clearly. Leonid started to follow her and made sure to stay a comfortable distance behind her.

"Wait! She's passing the Rosenkrantz Gate. She's not returning to her hotel," Yakov said.

"Da. Let's see where she goes."

Catherine walked past the Nobel Hotel, crossed the Rosenkrantz Gate, and entered the shop.

"Did you see?"

"Da."

"Gives us three minutes," Yakov said as he started out of the hotel and toward the shop. Leonid was just behind him.

The front room of the shop was small and crowded with merchandise. Near the rear of the room on the right-hand side was a tight spiral metal staircase leading to a loft that covered the rear third of the main floor. Tapestries with Viking scenes adorned the walls. Trolls of every size and shape were all over the store. Catherine took a moment to take it all in.

So many trolls. My nieces would love this place.

Over in the corner, she spotted a small female troll with a colorful Scandinavian dress.

She's adorable.

"Please to be helping you," the shopkeeper said as she approached Catherine.

"Yes. Oh good, you speak English."

"English. Yah. Most do." She paused. "You are liking," she continued, nodding at the little troll that had caught Catherine's attention.

"Oh yes. My nieces would adore her. How much is she?"

"Three hundred thirty kroner."

Catherine quickly divided by six. Fifty dollars seemed expensive, but with the dress, maybe not.

"I'll take it. But I need to find another one."

"Yah, please. You are being comfortable," the shopkeeper said with a smile.

The only other patron in the shop opened the front door to leave. As she did, Yakov appeared at the door. He held the door for her and smiled saying 'good day' in Norwegian. He entered and began to look around as if he were also a patron. Within a minute, Leonid entered. As he shut the door, he locked it. While the shopkeeper was busy helping Catherine, he pulled the shades on the front windows and turned over the sign that said "closed" in both Norwegian and English.

Yakov made his way over to where the shopkeeper and Catherine were standing. He spoke to the shopkeeper in Norwegian.

"I'm looking for a present for a friend's daughter who lives in America."

"Oh Americana," the shopkeeper responded also speaking Norwegian. She's an American," she said nodding in Catherine's direction.

"Excuse please," Yakov said to Catherine speaking in English. "American?"

"Yes. I'm an American," Catherine said with a warm smile.

Leonid stepped behind a display of trolls, took a handkerchief, and doused it with chloroform. He lunged out and grabbed Catherine, clamping a handkerchief over her mouth.

While it startled her, she realized almost instantly what was going on. Catherine knew that as soon as she breathed it would be over. She reached up beside her head and behind her hoping to be able to grab an eye or something. As she did, she felt her earring against her wrist.

The earring!

She stopped trying to grab her assailant and grabbed the earring instead, pressing it between her fingers as hard as she could.

In the meantime, Yakov had pulled a Glock 9mm from under his coat and placed the barrel between the eyes of the shopkeeper. "Not a peep," he demanded in Norwegian. When Catherine lifted her right arm behind her head to reach for her attacker, it shifted her center of gravity just a bit. Leonid inadvertently stepped forward with his left foot to compensate. That placed his foot right between Catherine's legs. She was still squeezing the earring when she noticed his foot, and she jammed the heel of her pump as hard as she could into the top of it. He let out a loud yelp of pain and let go momentarily. She pulled away but wasn't quick enough. He caught a handful of hair with his left hand and pulled back, almost pulling her off her feet. Turning toward her, he struck the side of her head with a right hook. She was dazed.

He then picked up the handkerchief he'd dropped and put it over her face again. Within moments she was out cold.

TEN

Aboard the USS *Peterson*.

THE ACTIVATION OF THE EARRING SET OFF AN ALARM THAT MADE A loud shrill noise in the operations center aboard the *Peterson.*

"It's Catherine's beacon," the operator said as Bob looked over toward the tracking console.

"Do you have her implant squawking?" Bob said.

"Clear signal. Location's coming up on the main viewing screen."

Moments later a two-mile radius street map depicting the center of Oslo appeared on the main screen. All of the major buildings were noted. Flashing lights illuminated the location of David, Steve, and Catherine.

"Two hundred-yard view on Catherine," Bob ordered as he picked up the ship's telephone and dialed 222.

"Captain." The voice had a low-pitched, guttural quality with an edge of impatience. "Captain, Bob Reese. I need to launch SEAL team three."

"No problem. I'm on the bridge; I'll relay the order to the OOD."

"Thank you, sir."

Bob turned to the communication console operator. "Get David on the phone."

The shrill of the boatswain's pipe sounded attention over the 1-MC. "Flight quarters, flight quarters. Set condition Zebra aft of frame one five zero. Stand clear of all weather decks aft of frame two five zero. The smoking lamp is extinguished throughout the ship, now flight quarters."

David had left standing orders for a five-man SEAL team to be ready and waiting inside the helicopter whenever the operatives ashore were chasing leads. Two teams were set up to stand alternating six-hour watches. Since the *Peterson* was sitting at anchor, a team could be on scene in less than ten minutes.

Oslo. The shop next to the hotel.

As soon as Catherine went limp, Leonid moved over to the shopkeeper. She wrenched her head back and forth fighting his attempt to place the handkerchief over her mouth and nose. While the others braced her shoulders tightly, he grabbed a fist full of her hair. Suddenly he felt a sharp piercing pain in his hand, which quickly turned to intense pressure.

Blood flowed from her mouth.

Leonid didn't yell or attempt to wrench his hand free. He used his other hand to secure the handkerchief around her nose and mouth. She was out very quickly. They tied and gagged her.

Dmitry waited three minutes and then pulled out from his parking space. He drove around the square until he came to the front of the shop where he parked. He quickly got out and went around to open both car doors opposite the driver; then he jumped back behind the wheel, and waited.

The shop door opened. Leonid and Yakov held Catherine between them. They walked across the sidewalk and slung Catherine in the back seat. Yakov pushed her over behind the driver. Leonid went back to the shop and pulled the front door closed, making sure it was locked. Then he got in the front seat of the BMW, and the car sped away.

Back on the USS *Peterson*.

"What's the problem?" Bob demanded.

"It's the radio. We've got a bad frequency with the helicopter," the operations console operator said.

"Don't navy pilots believe in checking their equipment? Have the bridge relay the location."

"Captain Egan's on the cell line," another operator said as he gave Bob the phone.

"David, Bob. They've got Catherine."

"I can't believe this! What else can go wrong? . . . What happened?"

"Don't know. Just got her alarm."

"Are you tracking her?"

"Yeah. A shop on the Karl Johans Gate between the Rosenkrantz Gate and the Grand Hotel.

The SEALs have disembarked and are en route."

"On my way," David said.

The operations controller had changed the main-view screen to the camera aboard the helicopter. Each of the SEALs also had a small minicam attached to his body. When the console operator changed the view, he didn't notice that Catherine's position was changing.

The SEALs had a very short flight to the city center. The helicopter flew over the old fort and then down behind the royal palace heading toward the national theater. The pilot's plan was to fly over the theater and across the park. He would hover adjacent to the target building at the edge of the park. This would keep him from becoming entangled in the overhead wires near the streets, and he would not have to hover between the buildings. Only a few hundred yards lay between the edge of the park and the target building.

As the helicopter pulled up into a hover, the SEALs repelled from both sides. Using a quick-release brake harness, they appeared to be free-falling from the aircraft. They hit the brake just before impacting the ground and then quickly hit the release. It took less than two minutes to put all five on the ground. The helicopter lifted in altitude as the SEALs ran across to the shop.

Cars on the street slowed or stopped. Most of the pedestrian traffic stopped and watched. The children pointed and showed excitement as the adults stood quietly.

Using SWAT team procedures, they positioned themselves. One man kicked open the front door. Two others crashed through the windows on either side of the door. Two entered through the front door. The four men quickly swept the room and found the shopkeeper tied up and still out cold.

"Target not in sight. Area secure," the officer in charge of the team reported.

Aboard the USS *Peterson.*

"What's going on?" Bob said.

Everyone in the operations center focused intently on the scenes from the minicams. Suddenly the console operator with the satellite tracking system realized they had missed her. He frantically tried to locate her.

"What happened?" Bob said yelling.

"They must have moved just as we switched to the view cams."

"So, where is she now?"

"Can't say."

"What?" Bob glared at the console operator. His teeth were clinched tightly, and his face was reddening.

"We're not getting a track."

"Is the satellite down?" Bob snapped in a demanding tone.

"No, ah, just don't have a track. She could be in a tunnel, an underground garage, or the basement of a large building."

Bob's internal sense of fury almost choked him. He'd just lost their biological expert.

In Oslo.

David's car pulled up in front of the shop. He charged in.

"Where's Catherine?" David's voice was loud and demanding.

"Attention on deck," one of the SEALs called out as soon as he spotted David. Immediately the officer in charge ran up from back near the staircase. He and another member of the team had been untying the shopkeeper and trying to revive her.

"Captain Egan," the officer said as he snapped to attention and rendered a trenchant salute. Since David wasn't in uniform, he nodded in response.

"Report. Where's Catherine?"

"Sir. There's no sign of Doctor Evans or the terrorists. When we arrived we found the shop closed and the shades pulled. We found one woman tied up and unconscious."

"At ease."

The young officer and the SEAL standing beside him immediately assumed the position of parade rest.

"Reconnoiter the block and then return to the ship."

"Aye aye, sir."

The SEALs departed the store. David pulled out his cellular phone.

"Mother."

"This is David. What in the world's happening?"

"We've lost her signal. She's in a tunnel or the basement of a large building. Maybe a parking garage."

"How will I find her now?"

"Let's assume they haven't killed her. It's likely they've taken her to a hotel. If they take her up to a room, we may get her signal again."

"What do you mean, may?"

"Nothing's a hundred percent."

"It better be this time," David yelled. He took a breath and calmed down. "I'll go back to the room and wait for your call."

"I'll let you know as soon as we pick up a signal."

Twenty minutes later.

David answered his cellular phone. "Egan."

"David, Bob. We've got a track on her. She's in the Comfort Hotel Majorstuen. It's near the city center on the Bogstadveien."

David grabbed his map of Oslo. "Bogstadveien."

"Yeah, just down from the Royal Palace and the Vigeland Sculpture Park."

"Okay, I see it."

"She's on the ground floor. Looks like room 117."

"Got it. Steve and his crew are still cleaning up. Let's see—drop the SEAL team on the Sculpture Park and have them double-time it to the hotel. Is there a side entrance?"

"Yeah, west side of the building."

"Have the team leader put two men outside the window. The other three will meet me at the west side entrance. Oh, and have 'em bring an extra com set."

"Roger."

David hung up the phone and surveyed the room. He spotted a small letter opener on the desk. He got up and unplugged the lamp beside the bed. With a forceful pull he managed to separate the wire from the lamp. He coiled up the wire and put it in his pocket and then grabbed the letter opener. Before leaving the room, he collected several extra clips of ammunition.

It didn't take long to get anywhere in the city center. As the cab drove by the Sculpture Park, David saw the helicopter, nose down, make a quick approach. It suddenly drew nose up into a level hover.

We're probably driving the local authorities crazy.

This was the second time in less than an hour that a strange black helicopter had dropped five heavily armed men into the city center in broad daylight.

Bet the ambassador's about to wet his pants. He smiled.

Within three minutes the three SEALs joined David outside of the west entrance. The team leader handed David a com set.

"Orders, Captain?"

"Have the two men at the window tie off above the window. On my signal, one will use the line to crash through the window while the other provides cover. Make sure they understand that we will be coming in from the opposite wall through the door. Oh, and tell 'em not to shoot Catherine."

The SEAL team leader relayed the instructions as David and the others entered the hall. The hall was deserted except for a janitorial cleaning cart. David located the room and then looked for the electrical outlets in the hall.

"What am I going to do now?" he said quietly.

"Problem, sir?"

David pulled the lamp cord out of his pocket. "Not long enough," he said pointing to a wall outlet about fifteen feet away from the door to the room. He paused and looked around, and his eyes suddenly fixed on the janitor's cart. He signaled one of the SEALs to accompany him. They eased down the hall. A radio played in the room being cleaned. It was almost loud enough to drown out the sound of the vacuum cleaner. David motioned for the SEAL to stay near the door. David holstered his gun, pushed the door open, and stepped into the room.

"Excuse me," he said loud enough to be heard over the noise of the vacuum cleaner.

"Yah," the maid said as she switched off the machine.

"I'm here to inspect the vacuum cleaner. Is it UL approved?" David asked as he walked over to her.

The maid's facial expression changed to show her puzzlement at this odd intrusion. "UL, please UL?"

David pointed down toward something on the machine. As the maid bent slightly to look, David took his left hand and covered her mouth and pulled her up next to his body. Since she was just over five feet tall, her feet were pulled up off the floor. With his right hand he began to pinch her neck near the base hard enough to constrict the blood flow to her brain. She flailed around with her hands and kicked him in the shins with her heels. He watched her eyes closely. Soon she stopped struggling, and within moments her eyes rolled up as she fell unconscious.

The SEAL outside the room entered as soon as David grabbed the maid. When David lowered the maid to the ground, the SEAL grabbed a top sheet and began to tie her hands behind her back. David found a pillowcase and another sheet and made a gag. Next the two men lifted her to the bed. David unplugged the vacuum cleaner and removed the cord. The SEAL used another sheet to tie her feet to the bed.

Back in the hallway, David plugged the vacuum cord into the wall and then plugged the lamp cord into the female end of the vacuum cord. The two cords together were long enough to reach the door. Next, he took out the letter opener and inserted it into the electronic door lock. Then he handed the wire to the team leader. "You short out the lock and push the door open as you fall away to the side. I'll roll in."

The SEAL officer nodded.

"You two on either side of the door," David ordered.

The men nodded in response.

"Are you ready outside?" David asked using the com head-set.

"Ready."

"On your leader's mark," David said. He quickly removed his headset and everyone got into position.

Inside room 117, Catherine sat on the bed with her hands tied. Leonid had left her under the watchful care of Dmitry while he and Yakov rejoined Severny. The television was tuned to an episode of "Baywatch" dubbed in Norwegian. This time Dmitry wasn't interested in Pamela Anderson. He stared only at Catherine. His cold brown eyes narrowed and hardened.

Oh Lord, I'm in trouble. I wish he wouldn't look at me that way.

Dmitry abruptly got up from his chair while removing his belt. Then he sat down beside her on the bed. He took her hands and tied them to the backboard of the bed behind her head.

Oh God. Help me. Don't let him do this.

Dmitry gently stroked her face with the back of his hand. "You like Russian men?"

"Please don't," she said. Shivers ran up her spine, and her stomach gnawed. She could feel her eyes moisten.

"Oh," he said smiling. "I show you great ecstasy. Do not fear." He abruptly moved his face to hers, attempting to kiss her. She jerked her head away.

In frustration he shifted positions so that he straddled her. With both hands he grabbed the hair on the sides of her head. Holding her head steady, he once again pressed in to kiss her. In his excitement he pressed hard against her face. The hair from his moustache pricked her upper lip. He forced her lips open with his thrusting tongue. The smell was awful! Catherine didn't know what was worse: the odor of his unbathed skin and hair or the lack of dental hygiene combined with the hint of alcohol.

"Ouch, don't Russian men know how to touch a woman?"

Dmitry stopped and sat up momentarily like a little boy who has been chided by his teacher.

"I will be gentle," he said penitently as he lowered his head toward her face.

An idea occurred to her. When she was in elementary school, she could draw her tongue into the back of her throat far enough to gag. It was a very useful ability when she wanted to stay home from school.

As Dmitry began to force her mouth open again, she caught a strong whiff of his odor. This time she encouraged the gagging sensation, and she heaved. . . .

"Agh-h-h," Dmitry screamed as he abruptly jumped up from the bed. He began to cough and spit. Catherine had covered his mouth, head, and shoulders with her partially digested meal.

His face was red, and he began to scream obscenities in Russian. Then he crawled back onto the bed and straddled Catherine. Dmitry had ceased to be aroused, and now he was just angry. He grabbed her throat and began to choke her.

"Now you die for that stunt!"

Catherine gasped for air.

"Go! Go! Go!" the team leader said into the microphone as he touched the exposed wire to the letter opener. The surge shorted out the low voltage lock. He dropped the electrical wire and opened the door giving it a push as he fell out of the way. As soon as he did, David rolled off his left shoulder into the room. It looked somewhat like a somersault, but it left him on his feet in a crouched position.

One of the SEALs was outside with his feet planted on a stone lip above the window. He held a rope, and he had already taken a measured amount of slack. He pushed hard off the wall. His weight swung him into the window like a battering ram. With his head tucked behind his hands and his feet extended in front of him, he broke through the window with little damage from broken glass. The other SEAL would provide covering fire if needed. He crashed through the window at almost the same moment David rolled through the door.

The breaking glass startled Dmitry, and he immediately raised his head and turned toward the window. David had his Heckler & Kock .40 caliber at the ready as he completed his roll. He made sure Catherine was not in his line of fire and squeezed off three rounds. All three struck Dmitry in the back and shoulder. David quickly adjusted his aim and squeezed off another round. The round entered the back of his head at a glancing angle. The bullet exploded as it went through the skull. Tissue splattered against the wall and all over the bed. Dmitry fell to his left toward the window. His legs still straddled Catherine.

The rest of the SEAL team rushed in and swept the room as David rushed to Catherine. She was shaking. Her right eye stung from the spray of body fluids.

"Get him off of me! Get him off!"

David rolled Dmitry's body off her legs. Then he untied her hands. Catherine jumped out of the bed and ran to the bathroom.

"Secure, Captain," the team leader responded.

David nodded as he took out his cellular phone.

"David?"

"Yes. You saw and heard it all?"

"Yeah. You'd better get out of there! An agency car should be at the west side door now."

"OK," David said. He closed the phone. "Catherine, we've gotta go," he said loud enough for her to hear. Then he looked toward the team leader. "Call in the chopper. Secure the mission."

"Aye, sir."

Catherine appeared from the bathroom. She was still wiping away the blood and other offal. David walked up next to her. She looked up into his eyes and then started crying uncontrollably. David put his arms around her and pulled her in close. He let her cry for a moment.

When she calmed, they departed to a waiting car. The SEAL team made its way to the secondary LZ.

ELEVEN

December, 1972.

GRIGORI IOURTCHAK STRUTTED UP THE HALLWAY. HIS HEAD WAS elevated, and a radiant grin embellished his expression. He entered the luxury apartment building located several blocks from Red Square.

What a stupendous evening.

For the first time he had been the featured soloist with the Moscow Symphony. A cadre of government dignitaries attended the performance.

Soloist. Mama would have been so proud.

In the years since graduating from college, he had lived an almost charmed life. He and his brother had been recruited by the KGB. They were wonderful benefactors. Indeed, they had encouraged and even promoted Grigori's musical career. Their sponsorship brought many perks, especially the luxury apartment he shared with his old friend Ilya Choutov.

Ilya was technically in the army, but he was being supervised by the KGB. As a bright young biology graduate student, the KGB had also taken up the sponsorship of his career. After helping him achieve his Ph.D., they moved him into a well-funded virus research project. He excelled, and that brought him even greater favor among his benefactors.

What a duo.

Grigori and Ilya had been lifelong friends and grew up together in Leningrad. Grigori remembered a funny event from his boyhood. Ilya was trying to make homemade gunpowder while Grigori serenaded him with a traditional Russian folk song.

Both Ilya and Grigori were good students. When they completed secondary school, they were sent to the University in Moscow. They were like two free-spirited adventurers.

That first trip to Moscow. We had the whole train singing and dancing.

He, Ilya, and his twin brother, Severny.

Severny and Ilya. Always a slight tension. His mama noticed it when they were boys. She said it was just a little bit of jealousy.

Guess we sometimes aligned ourselves together. Left Severny the odd man out.

But, they were just children. Severny always acted like Ilya and Grigori shouldn't be so close.

Ah, not to worry. Everything turned out OK.

After college Severny became an active KGB agent and was sent to various language institutes and training camps. He did well. After years of intense training, he was sent to America to hone his language skills.

It has been years since we've been together.

With the concert season ending, Grigori was looking forward to going home for a week. Severny would be there. Ilya was taking time off and would join them in a few days.

Grigori was quietly singing as he inserted the key to open his apartment door.

Da. What a glorious day.

Lara Andreyev was seated on the couch. Her eyes were red. It was obvious that she'd been crying. Lara was an old friend from Leningrad who had attended the university with the others. They were all part of a small group of exceptional artisans and scientists who had become close friends. In the six years since graduating, Lara had returned to Leningrad. She married an older, established man named Alexander. He was a lower-level official in the party who had an administrative position with the KGB. He had a reputation for being cunning and was a bright rising star in the KGB. He treated Lara well.

None of us could understand why she married him. When I asked, she simply responded that we had all gone off to other pursuits. Guess she assumed that Alexander was the only man who wanted her. At least enough to pursue her. On the other hand, he was able to provide a comfortable living.

Life was hard in Soviet Russia, and being married to a party official meant a good apartment and plenty of food. The KGB had power.

Even with her large blue eyes bloodshot, Lara was still a beautiful creature.

Men still stop and stare at her.

She still had long, rich auburn hair. It was dark enough to pass as a shade of brown in dim lighting. Her smooth, flawless, creamy white skin, accented with cinnamon hues, gave a warm glowing highlight to her complexion. Grigori had always been impressed with Lara's lips. Full and well formed, they had a natural deep color. She once told him that she frequently used a colorless lip gloss rather than a traditional lip color. She could get away with it.

"Grigori. You finally made it," she said. "I thought we might miss our train. I didn't want to miss the last train to Leningrad."

"Da. I think every diplomat in Moscow thought they had to congratulate me. I thought I would never break free of them. Lara, are you upset?"

There was a long pause as Lara looked down toward her feet. Ilya walked into the room from the kitchen.

"Ah, Grigori," Ilya said with a big smile. "Welcome the conquering hero. You were brilliant, simply brilliant."

"Da, Grigori. I think it was the best concert you've ever given," Lara said as she raised her head and smiled.

"Please, please. You will give me a big head . . ." The three friends laughed and joked as Grigori finished his packing.

At the station.

Lara hugged Ilya. Her expression and manner showed both hurt and devotion. Grigori knew something was going on. He watched in silence.

Had the old flame been rekindled?

Nine years before, Lara had joined her old friends at the university. Grigori, Severny, and Ilya had been in school for a year. Grigori was happy to take Lara under his wing. At one point during the fall, he and Lara were alone in his small apartment. The latent attraction between the two began to blossom. She had acted so excited to have him kiss her.

I was pretty thrilled myself; so soft and innocent. Not like the others. What a stupid move.

The episode amounted to little more than a few minutes of kissing. Grigori didn't know at the moment how much emotion Lara attached to it. For the next several days she was beside herself with happiness.

Grigori, Severny, and Ilya lived in a cramped apartment close to the university. People came and went on a regular basis. The apartment seemed to always be the location for some kind of gathering. It was a wonder the three men ever got any work done. Several days after Grigori and Lara's first romantic encounter, she showed up at a party unannounced. Lara opened his bedroom doors only to find him with another girl.

She didn't speak a word to me for weeks.

Several months later, Lara and Ilya began to date and quickly became lovers. Ilya didn't have the chiseled, Nordic look, although he was not unattractive. One thing Grigori could say for him, he was devoted to her.

Guess that's what she needed.

In the succeeding years, Grigori became more and more attracted to her. But, out of love and honor to his good friend, he kept his feelings in check. The only person who ever knew of Grigori's secret love for Lara was his brother, Severny.

After they finished school, the love affair ended. They all went their separate ways. Now, for the first time in over three years, they were together again.

Grigori watched them intently. He could sense the embers of the old flame heating and igniting.

"Come on, you two," he said. "Lara, we better get aboard."

As she pulled away from Ilya, Grigori caught a glimpse of a tear. Meanwhile, Ilya stepped up to him and embraced him in a grand bear hug.

"Three days. I shall see you in three days, my friend," Ilya said.

"Da, three days. We shall enjoy ourselves. I'm really looking forward to it."

Grigori and Lara got on the train and took their seats. As the train pulled away from the station, Grigori could see another tear. She said nothing for more than a half hour. She just sat staring out the window.

"Lara, you seem upset. Is anything the matter?"

She looked at him with puffy eyes.

She looks distraught. Something very—

"Grigori, you are one of my oldest and dearest friends. Please, what I say must stay between us."

"Of course. You know I will always keep your confidence."

"Da. I could always trust you." She took a breath. "This is not my first trip to Moscow during the past few months."

"Oh? I did not know that. Why did you not . . ."

"Da, two months ago I ran into Ilya while I was visiting. You were away with the symphony."

"Go on."

"We, well, we resumed our romance from our university days." She burst into tears. Grigori put his arm around her to console and calm her.

"Oh, Grigori, I am trapped in a passionless marriage, and . . ."

"I sensed that something was going on. At least you know Ilya loves you. Is that so bad?"

The intensity of her sobbing increased. He took out a hand-kerchief and began to wipe her tears from her cheeks.

"Dear Lara. Nothing is so bad you can't tell me."

"It's not that simple. Alexander has become very powerful, very quickly. He loves to show me off in public. No doubt I have added some to his success. He would be furious! He would have us both shipped off to Siberia."

"Oh, no, no. Do not worry. He could not do that. There are things you don't know about Ilya and me. Alexander would not be able to touch us."

She's right. Maybe Alexander could. I don't know how valuable the Kremlin thinks Ilya is. They have a bad habit of shipping people off for undesirable conduct.

"Maybe not. But he could destroy my life."

"Maybe. Of course he doesn't have to know. You and Ilya can see each other occasionally. Besides, he is due to be posted in Europe. Unaccompanied."

"Grigori, oh, Grigori. It's not that simple. I am pregnant. It is Ilya's. Not Alexander's . . ."

TWELVE

1995. Somewhere between Moscow and Minsk.

"E XCUSE ME," THE RUSSIAN PORTER SAID. "MISS, YOU ASKED TO be awakened at seven." Tatyana Andreyeva slept through the night propped against a window. She stirred and smiled at the porter.

"Da, thank you."

"It is my pleasure, Miss. When you are ready, the dining car is serving breakfast."

Tatyana nodded in response as she rubbed her eyes and began to stretch. Her eyes hurt a little.

I wish I had a mirror. I bet my eyes are bloodshot. Several days of crying and little sleep'll do that.

She pulled out a pocket powder case with mirror and scrutinized her face.

Guess I do look a little like mama.

Tatyana's mother, Lara, died of breast cancer when Tatyana was sixteen. Tatyana worshiped her, although she had always been a little jealous of her good looks.

Mama was so stunning.

Her father, or at least the man she thought was her father, was a successful owner of a shipping company in St. Petersburg.

During the old Soviet regime, he was away often. Her mother told her it was the price of being an important government official.

When the iron curtain fell, he set up several businesses. While her family had always enjoyed a comfortable life compared to most Russians, his new position brought the family vast wealth—a large home, even servants. There were ample resources when the time came for her to go away to the university.

After the university she found a position as a rehearsal musician for the ballet in Moscow. It was a good first job.

Her talents were recognized, and she was offered a position playing for the house orchestra at the opera in Odessa. She planned to move in three weeks.

Odessa was now just a phantom of what could have been. Her world had imploded two days before with the arrival of a letter and a phone call.

I always wondered why Mama and Papa, ah, Alexander, were so formal toward each other. God, it's hard to remember them ever smiling or joking together. But he loved to be seen in public with her.

Her stepfather, Alexander, was almost sixty. Before the cancer was discovered, her mother looked twenty-eight even though she was forty-two years old. At home Alexander seemed withdrawn and dispassionate. Over the years his temper had become more and more dangerous. Fortunately for everyone in the house, his work kept him away most of the time.

It had all become painfully clear now.

He never showed me any real expression of love. Certainly not devotion.

He was never overly harsh with her, just distant and aloof. Throughout her life he seemed indifferent to what she was doing. He never came to any of her many recitals. Even when she competed to win a coveted placement at the conservatory in Moscow, Alexander was conspicuously absent.

Tatyana acquired her deep love for the piano early in life. Uncle Grigori, not really her actual uncle, was a friend of her mother's since the two were teenagers. He also had a passion for the piano. In fact, he studied at the same conservatory that she attended.

Grigori played for the Moscow Symphony and traveled extensively. When he wasn't in Moscow or off around the world, he frequently visited her home. In 1984, Alexander helped him get a position with the Madrid Symphony. Alexander was stationed in Europe for almost seven years, and she always wondered why he hadn't sent for the family.

I would have loved Paris.

In 1985 Uncle Grigori was killed in a shoot-out between some terrorists and the Spanish authorities. Her mother grieved for years.

Even though the last few days were emotionally devastating, they served to give Tatyana some understanding of her family. She learned that her mother was a bright and popular college student who loved the arts and firmly embraced the lofty ideals of socialism. While her mother had numerous good acquaintances, she developed an intense friendship with a small group of scholars who attended the university in Moscow with her.

Two of them came from her home region of St. Petersburg and would remain lifelong friends. One was Uncle Grigori, the other Uncle Ilya. Like Uncle Grigori, Uncle Ilya was a man she knew and adored. He never forgot her birthday, even when he was posted far away, and he always lavished presents upon her. He seemed to dote on her.

The letter, written in her mother's hand, was accompanied by a note from Uncle Ilya. Her mother, knowing death was upon her, wrote the letter and gave it to Ilya to deliver to Tatyana should he ever feel the situation demanded it. In the letter her mother explained that she and Ilya had become lovers during their time together at the university. Ilya went on for advanced studies while her mother returned home to eventually marry Alexander.

Several years after the marriage, her mother ran into Uncle Ilya in Moscow. The old flames were rekindled and Tatyana was conceived. Alexander never knew about the relationship, but he suspected. It lasted off and on for years after that. The marriage slowly evolved into a marriage of convenience.

The note from Ilya explained that Alexander was involved in high-level espionage. Sooner or later the Russian Secret Service would come after her and hold her hostage as leverage against Alexander. Once the government got its hands on her, she'd disappear. Ilya instructed her to take the first train to Minsk and to call from there. A message would be left at the central telegraph exchange detailing where to call. If she couldn't reach him, she was to proceed to Riga. From there she was to go to the commercial airport where a ticket to London would be waiting in her name. They would meet in London and then go on to America. He said he had something the Americans would desperately want. It was important enough that they would give them new identities.

The day Tatyana received the letter from Ilya, she got a frantic phone call from him. He said that his plan had been interrupted. She was to go from Riga to Stockholm. He would leave a ticket with SwissAir. She was to leave immediately. She couldn't tell anyone. "Just grab your passport and the clothes on your back and get out," he told her in an urgent tone. He gave her the name of a hotel in London. She was to meet him there.

Tatyana was still trying to understand how she felt about recent events and revelations. She was thrilled that the man she adored, her doting uncle, was really her father. The prospect of living together in America was exciting. She was also surprised that Alexander was engaged in international espionage.

An international spy? Well, he had been KGB.

Even though he had been somewhat aloof to her, he had been part of her life. What was to become of him? Of course it didn't matter. If Ilya felt she was in trouble, she'd better heed his warning.

Oslo.

Ilya Choutov looked at the picture of Lara and Tatyana. He always felt a little guilty when he had a romantic liaison, even though Lara had been dead for over three years. After falling in love with her in college, he swore he'd never marry anyone else.

Silly oath.

Lara was married to a Communist party official, and any scandal would have landed both of them in Siberia.

He knew Lara wouldn't leave her husband. When she became pregnant, she forced Ilya to agree never to reveal their secret. He'd have to be satisfied watching his daughter grow up in a detached relationship as a family friend. He agreed but only if Lara would continue to see him. For years after that, Lara made two or three trips a year to Moscow. Alexander was gone most of the time. From 1982 until 1989, Alexander was stationed in Europe.

In the mid-eighties, Ilya was posted to Paris, and the affair ceased. In the succeeding ten years they were never close, but they both carried their mutual passion in their hearts.

While in Paris Ilya began to see other women. He didn't want an emotionally charged relationship with anyone, and casual relationships were the only substitute.

Alexander was well-connected and was able to introduce Ilya to some real fringe women. Most were into very odd stuff. Ilya got something of a reputation during that time, although in truth, he really didn't care for that sort of thing, usually opting for more traditional relationships. Even so, the reputation stuck.

He knew that his associates at work laughed at him, but it didn't matter. His outstanding scientific brilliance was intimidating. They were not going to like him on any account.

As Ilya began to receive worldwide recognition as a biologist, he tended to distance himself more and more from his jealous associates.

There was a knock at the door. Ilya put his pictures away. "Who is there?"

"Nora. Yah, you are looking for a companion?"

Ilya pulled out his Glock 9mm and went to the door. He eased it open. The only person in the hallway was the girl. He opened the door and welcomed her in. She entered and took off her coat.

"Da. I am Russian. Do you speak English or French?" he asked in broken Norwegian.

"Oui, both," she replied in French.

She walked over to the radio and selected a punk rock station.

Ilya went and sat on the side of the bed. "French then. It's the language of love. We'll use French."

Nora began to dance to the music around a floor lamp. His eyes focused on her long legs as she wrapped them around the lamp pole. Her jet-black mane and heavy crimson lipstick contrasted with her mimelike complexion. Her hips pumped to the dark punk rock tune pulsating from the radio. Her lithe body slithered around the pole like a vampire on a quest for fresh meat. When she opened her mouth, her white fangs showed. He looked at her as if he were photographing her with his eyes. Even the spider web tattoo on her shoulder was exciting.

Ilya didn't hear the click of the door lock as he began to passionately press his lips to hers. She bit him.

"Ouch!"

Just as he hollered in pain, five Russian agents rushed into the room. Three wrestled Choutov and held chloroform over his mouth and nose until he passed out. One of them slipped a wire around her neck.

She writhed and struggled for air. Her fingernails cut into her neck as she tried to pry her fingers under the wire. In a matter of moments, her arms fell limp to her side, and her eyes rolled up.

THIRTEEN

CATHERINE WOKE UP IN THE CAR ON THE WAY BACK TO THE HOTEL. She buried her head in David's chest and sobbed most of the way. She managed to pull herself together by the time they reached the hotel.

"You need to lie down and rest for a while," he said.

"I'll be okay."

"Who's in charge here?" he said with a smile.

"Well, Commodore, if you're gonna pull rank—"

"I'll make it worthwhile."

"Now just how are you gonna do that?"

"Magic fingers," he said as he held up his hands and wiggled the fingers on both hands.

She crawled into the bed. He sat beside her and massaged her shoulders until she relaxed. In minutes she fell asleep. He slipped into the adjoining room.

His cellular phone interrupted his thoughts.

"David, Bob. You'd better get back here. We've got a situation developing."

"What?"

"Russians. They're trying to divert a SwissAir flight bound for Amsterdam. To Moscow."

"SwissAir?"

"Yeah. Flight originated in Stockholm and stopped in Oslo. Guess we missed—"

"That I don't need—we can't let them get—Are you sure Choutov's on that plane?"

"No, of course not, but the Russians aren't going to engage in international air piracy on a whim. The helo's on the way. It'll set down in the park near your hotel."

"You give the Russians too much credit. Anyway, tell the captain to get under way. Don't worry about breaking any speed laws getting down the fjord! It'll give our lazy diplomats something to do for a change."

Bob laughed. "Heck, David, the ambassador's already been here chewing the captain's butt about the helos and SEALs. The old man just about had an epileptic fit when I ordered you picked up just now. The ambassador probably saw the helo fly over his car on the way back to the embassy. Probably blowing a major head gasket about now."

"Just get under way. Forget the ambassador."

David made it to the lobby and out into the park in record time. He left one of Steve's men in the hotel room with Catherine. Two additional agents were posted in the hallway.

She'll be safe for now.

The flight was uneventful, the landing a little tricky. The channel allowed no room for maneuvering. Wind direction and speed made the helicopter landing uncomfortable because of the smidgen of clearance between the edge of the rotors on the helicopter and the deck house. Even in good conditions, landing on a destroyer is tricky.

Good thing they're naval aviators and not agency guys.

It didn't take long for David to make it to the 0-2 level. A marine posted outside of CIC called out as David appeared at the top of the ladder. "In here, Commodore."

Bob had already shifted from the operations room to the CIC. Tony Scapecchi was standing watch as the TAO and immediately got out of the command chair as David entered. David sat down and began to examine the tactical picture displayed before him.

"Report," David said.

"Commodore, Admiral Kuznetsov has launched two MIG 29 Fulcrums to intercept SwissAir 848, which is bound for Amsterdam. He followed the plane for several miles and then ordered it to accompany him to Moscow," Tony said.

"Moscow? A MIG doesn't have those kind of legs."

"Yes, sir. Anyhow, the SwissAir pilot declared an emergency and stalled for a while—until the Russians started getting a little testy. Just before you arrived, the pilot finally changed course. He slowed his speed, which made the Russians very angry."

"Bob. Any reason to believe Choutov's on that plane? Other than the obvious interest by the Russians?"

"Can't say there is."

David picked up the handset for the tactical net and keyed the mike. As he did, he picked up an authentication table that was sitting in front of his chair. "Alpha Sierra, this is Tango Bravo. I am prepared to authenticate, over."

"Tango Bravo, this is Alpha Sierra, authenticate Charlie Charlie Delta, over."

David looked up the response. "Alpha Sierra, this is Tango Bravo. I authenticate Alpha Foxtrot. Immediate Execute. Launch two intercepts. Target—Russian MIG 29s in company with SwissAir 848. Standby, execute. Out."

"Is that F-14 still on station at the mouth of the fjord?"

"Yes, sir. Under our air control."

"Get him out there!"

"Aye, sir." Tony relayed the order to the air controller. "Red Devil Six, *Peterson* control. Intercept MIG 29. Vector one one zero. Kick it in the butt, over."

"Red Devil Six."

"Weapons free if fired upon," David commanded. "Do not engage bogey."

"Red Devil Six, *Peterson* control. Bogey may be hostile. You may return fire. Do not engage unless fired upon, over."

"Red Devil Six."

David sat and watched the display as the F-14s left the carrier and joined Red Devil Six. Because of the relatively short distance, it didn't take long for the three planes to catch up with the others. David put on a headset and dialed into the air control frequency.

"Red Devil flight, *Peterson* air control, this is Commodore Egan. Who's the flight leader, over?"

"*Peterson*, Red Devil Two. This is Commander Tom Ellen, squadron skipper, over."

"Red Devil Two, have your RIO come up on this tack with me. I want you to contact the Russians and tell them that I've ordered the SwissAir flight to return to Oslo. We'll dial in the SwissAir frequency to talk to the airliner. Use the air distress frequency, over."

"Red Devil Two."

Tony reached over and switched David's frequency to the SwissAir channel. "SwissAir 848, this is Commodore Egan of the United States Navy, over."

"Commodore Egan, SwissAir 848. This is the pilot, over."

"SwissAir 848, I have dispatched three fighters to give you safe passage back to Oslo, over."

There was a long pause. "SwissAir 848, did you copy, over."

"Commodore Egan, SwissAir 848. Yes, I copied. I'm afraid I can't turn back. The Russian made it quite clear that if I did not stay on this course, he'd shoot me down. I have to think about my passengers, over."

"SwissAir 848, I understand your situation. However, I have the authority of my government to take any hostile action necessary to prevent you from entering Russian airspace. I can't—"

"Americans would not knowingly fire on a passenger airliner in international—"

"SWISSAIR 848! I will fire on you if you do not follow my orders. I have an aircraft carrier in your vicinity that will back up the fighters in your airspace."

As David was talking to the airliner, the Red Devil Skipper initiated a conversation with the Russians. "Russian MIG 29 flight, US Navy F-14 flight leader, over."

"Amer-ican F-14, this Russian flight leader. You interfere! Break off now or face hostile fire, over."

"Russian flight leader, you're facing down three navy top guns. You're involved in an act of international air piracy. Be assured, we are going to escort that civilian airliner back to Oslo, over."

"Not your affair! Break off now. I have orders to shoot! I happy to show arrogant Amer-ican butt of donkey how to fly!"

"Russian flight leader, we have orders to shoot you down if you take any hostile action. Disengage and return to your ship, now. We do not want an incident."

The SwissAir pilot began a slow turn toward the northwest. The Russian flight leader screamed at the SwissAir pilot to return to the original heading. Suddenly, one of the MIGs let go of a burst from the 30 mm cannon. The tracers streamed in front of the SwissAir flight. The Russian was screaming at the SwissAir pilot that this was his last chance. The SwissAir pilot started screaming at David over the radio.

David switched to the Red Devil control frequency. "Red Devil Two, *Peterson*. Weapons free, splash MIG flight, over."

"Red Devil Two. Splash MIG flight."

As soon as the order came, the RIO in Red Devil Six fired an air-to-air missile at the MIG in front of him. The missile impacted creating an enormous fireball. Red Devil Two peeled off to the left and Red Devil Four broke right. The second MIG started a high G steep climb knowing that the F-14 had trouble following that maneuver. Red Devil Six began to follow the MIG.

"Six, break off! Break Off!"

It was too late. Red Devil Six's engines flamed out, and the aircraft began to tumble. The pilot desperately tried to force the fighter into a spin.

"Punch out, six! Punch out!"

The crew members ejected, and a pair of chutes opened.

The remaining MIG maneuvered to a position behind Red Devil Four. Red Devil Two was on a course perpendicular to the MIG.

"Get 'em off my tail!" Red Devil Four shouted.

"Counter measures, break right! Break right!" Red Devil Two yelled over the radio.

Red Devil Four released the countermeasures, broke right, and started a dive. Red Devil Two fired his cannon at the MIG forcing it to take evasive action and to break off from the attack on the other F-14. Once again the MIG started a high G climb. The two F-14s maneuvered in such a way as to prevent the MIG from coming in on their tails. Red Devil Four was the first to get a lock on the MIG. He fired.

"*Peterson*, Red Devil Two. Splash MIG flight. Over."

A cacophony of applause, cheering, and whistling erupted in the CIC.

"Red Devil Two, Commodore Egan. Well done! Have Red Devil Four escort SwissAir 848 to Oslo. Tell 'em to take the long way home. I need to get set up on the ground before they land. You stay with your downed crew. *Spruance* is near your present position and has launched her helo for recovery. ETA five minutes, over."

"Red Devil Two."

"Bob, get the ambassador to run interference with the Norwegians. I'm afraid we're gonna violate their sovereignty again," David said. Then he dialed the captain's number.

"Captain."

"Phil, David Egan. Head back to port and turn out both SEAL teams. I want to be on the ground at the Oslo airport before that SwissAir flight arrives."

"Yes, sir."

FOURTEEN

HALF AN HOUR LATER, DAVID WAS MET BY A LOCAL CIA STATION
operative, the ambassador, and a Norwegian SWAT team
commander.

"Commodore Egan. So you're the jerk that's making everyone's life miserable!" the ambassador said.

"Not now, sir," David said in a stern but polite tone as he
turned toward the Norwegian. "Are you in charge?"

"Yah."

David pulled photographs of Choutov, Andreyev, and
Iourtchak out. "Please have your men gather around and
memorize these faces."

"Terrorists?" the Norwegian asked. David nodded in
response.

An agency station wagon pulled up to where the men were
standing. Catherine jumped out of the back seat wearing a yellow biological hazard suit.

"Gentlemen. Let me introduce you to Doctor Catherine
Evans of the Centers for Disease Control in Atlanta."

"Oh my—I hope this doesn't mean—" the ambassador
cleared his throat. "Doctor Evans, welcome to—"

"You asked if these men were terrorists. Yes, Mr. Ambassador, they are. And the weapon they have could wipe out all of Oslo."

David looked at the SWAT team leader. The SWAT leader swallowed hard.

"I have a group of navy SEALs with me. They're trained to handle this type of situation. With your permission, I'd like to have them disarm the terrorists with your SWAT team as backup, of course."

The SWAT team leader stared at the large biological hazards symbol on Catherine's suite. "Yah. Yah. Goot thought."

Another agency car pulled up, and Jim Washington got out. "David, what can I do?"

"Jim. Good, you're here. I may need you to identify any of Andreyev's operatives."

The SEALs and the SWAT team set up as Jim, Catherine, and the ambassador sat by the cars discussing the events that had transpired. As SwissAir 848 arrived, it was directed to the secluded area of the airport where the teams had set up. The door opened, and the SWAT team rolled a stairway up to the aircraft. The SEALs were ready to enter the aircraft.

The flight attendant motioned for them to board. They moved quickly and deployed throughout both cabins. Jim and David entered the aircraft. Jim walked down the aisle looking at every passenger. He pointed his .40 caliber at a man sitting next to the window. "Yakov Krylov."

David motioned to the SEALs, and they rushed up and forcibly removed Yakov from the aircraft. Jim continued looking. Two seats back he recognized another Russian. He pointed him out, and David had him removed also.

"Don't know his name," Jim said. "I remember him from St. Petersburg. Seem to recall that he's ex-KGB and an active Russian security agent; also on Andreyev's payroll."

The SWAT team and SEALs checked the plane, the cargo, and the luggage for any sign of the weapon. While they searched, David had the SEALs remove the two Russians to one of the helicopters. The SWAT team was preoccupied with searching the luggage. He ordered the helicopter to return to the ship. The ambassador saw the SEALs.

"You can't detain a foreign national on foreign soil," the ambassador demanded.

"Mr. Ambassador, please return to the embassy," David replied as he stared into the ambassador's eyes. This infuriated the ambassador even more.

"Who do you think you are?"

"Mr. Ambassador," he said in a loud voice. "Return to the embassy now."

David paused as he stared into the ambassador's eyes.

"Sir, I'm going to need you to run interference."

"By what authority do you presume to order me to do anything? I'll have you know that civilians are still in charge of the United States government! I'll have you court-martialed! You'll spend your twilight years in Leavenworth!"

"By now it should have dawned on you that I'm conducting covert operations with the full backing and assets of the United States Armed Forces. My authority comes from the president. Until he relieves me, all assets of the United States will carry out my orders including the Department of State."

"I never—"

"Ambassador. We're like a football team. I'm the quarterback, you're the pulling guard. Do I make myself clear?"

"Okay, Commodore," he said clenching his teeth. "I don't know how long you're gonna be in charge after I get on the phone with Washington."

"I understand, sir. Feel free to call the chairman of the Joint Chiefs or the National Security advisor."

"I don't answer to either—"

"Ambassador, we're wasting time. I have my orders from the president, and your boss doesn't have the authority to countermand them. Now, can we focus on the situation at hand?"

"Even if you do have the authority, there'll be a day of reckoning. In the meantime, what do I tell the Norwegians? They're already protesting your little flight into Oslo. They're sure to hear about Doctor Evans. When they hear that you absconded with their prisoners, they'll be furious. They're gonna want—"

"Tell them we're dealing with terrorists and can't give them further details at this time."

"Say what? That'll go over good."

"Best I can do. Now, please sir. I'll let you know as much as I can when the need for you to know arises. Please. Return to the embassy. Stall the Norwegians. Use diplomatic double talk. Make up a lie if necessary. Just buy us some time."

The ambassador stormed over to his car and drove off.

FIFTEEN

DAVID STOPPED IN THE LOBBY. CATHERINE WENT ON TO THE ROOM. The hotel served drinks and sandwiches in the lobby during the afternoon and evening. David stopped one of the waiters. "May I order something and have it sent to my room?"

"Yah. Room service is happy to be helping you. Please, what may I be serving you?"

"Yes, I'd like a roast beef on rye with hot mustard. Oh, and send up a bottle of the 'Chateau de Gaudou.'"

"Chateau de Gaudou" he said as he wrote it down. "Very goot, sir. I am havink our steward calling your room, ah, if we are not havink in stock."

David walked slowly toward the elevator while scanning the area. Several couples were enjoying the piano music and afternoon drinks.

No one looks suspicious.

He entered an empty elevator. As he stepped out of the car into the elegantly appointed hallway on his floor, an eerie tranquility engaged him. It reminded David of a funeral home.

Standing by the door to his room, he could hear a Vivaldi Concerto for Strings playing on the sound system. He stepped in.

Catherine was perched on the couch reading tourist brochures. She had removed her shoes. Wisps of hair framed her face. As David entered, she tilted her head to one side in an unconscious flirtatious acknowledgment of his presence.

"Welcome home, sweetheart." Her infectious smile set the tone.

"Glad to see you're in a good mood. You've had one heck of a day."

"Just glad my knight in shining armor showed up," she said softly but with a hint of teasing in the tone.

"What are you reading?"

She was partially reclining on the couch with her legs stretched out. The deep rich color of her generous lips, her extraordinary eyes, and her perky manner combined to provoke David's romantic interest. He wasn't sure if he ought to pursue it. With an inward sigh, he resolved to let the desire pass. He walked to the couch, and she repositioned her legs so he could sit down.

"Several brochures regarding Norway. Your comments on the landscape made me curious about this country. It's very scenic. Did you know that in the north there's an area known as the Finnmarksvidde? Has the largest glaciers in Europe."

"Didn't know that."

"You weren't kidding about the subarctic climate. There are also numerous fjords. The largest is the Sogna-fjorden."

"The what?"

"Sogna-fjorden. Says here that it's a hundred miles long. In some places the rock walls rise abruptly more than three thousand feet. Must be a breathtaking view."

"I'll bet."

"Okay, Mr. Science critic, how'd these fjords get formed if it wasn't from an ice-age glacier?"

"Don't know. That's the problem scientists have. They cease to be scientists and become theologians and philosophers when they offer anything but a hypothesis to answer those kinds of questions."

"You're being a little unfair to us eggheads. Science—well, it's after answers that are verifiable."

"Maybe."

"So, what's your hypothesis regarding the fjords?"

"Well, remember, I'm a naval officer and not a geologist. I don't know that I'm a proponent of the theory I was telling you about."

"Yeah, but you think it's plausible," she said in a playful tone.

"Yeah. Makes sense to us simpletons. Norway was mentioned in the article I read."

"They don't give simpletons destroyers to command. Go on. The article you read."

"If I recall correctly, the major coastal island groups are formed by the glaciated tops of ancient volcanic mountains. You know, now partially submerged."

"I saw a mention of that in one of these brochures," she said.

"According to my harebrained theory, a radical shift over a short time would cause volcanic mountains to sink under the ocean. It would also create rugged fjords. Even places like the Grand Canyon or the Great Lakes could appear as a result of that kind of cataclysmic event."

"Interesting. What other scientific theory do you question? You seem to discount major theories of geology. What about my field? Do you look down your nose at evolution?"

"You sound a little defensive. I don't mean to offend. Excuse me a second," he said as he pulled out the cellular phone.

"Mother," David heard Bob say.

"This is David. I think we'd better pool our assets and cover eating establishments near the city center. Our friend has already had his kicks for the day. He's not likely to surface until dinner."

"True, but he might just take his meal in his room."

PAUL T. McHENRY, III

"We can always redeploy later this evening. I just have a feeling that he's in one of the hotels nearby. How's the debrief going?"

"Dead end. Seems Yakov panicked after hearing that we rescued Catherine. Seemed terrified of Severny. Jumped a flight out of Oslo," Bob said.

"How'd Russian Intelligence get involved? Or, was he working for Andreyev?"

"Says they, that is, the Russian Intelligence Service, had a full-court press on. He was assigned to watch the airport. Saw Yakov and followed him. He thought he saw Severny also board the plane and reported that to Moscow. Doesn't add up."

"Go on," David said.

"He's on Andreyev's payroll. You'd think he'd look the other way."

"Your evaluation?"

"Andreyev's lost his clout with the remnant of KGB within the government. Could make him desperate."

"Let's hope so."

David unplugged the phone and looked at Catherine. "I'm sorry, you were saying?"

"I'm not defensive, I'm curious."

"Darwin made a number of observations. He discovered a principle, which led him to a conclusion that life has slowly evolved over time from basic life forms to ones that are more complex. What's that principle?"

"Duh, could it be natural selection?"

"Exactly." He chose to ignore the sarcasm. "Now, Darwin's premise holds that natural selection results in evolution. Problem. Entropy is also a verifiable principal that coexists with natural selection. Entropy is, in many ways, the exact opposite. Both exist. So the natural hypothetical conclusion should be equilibrium, not evolution."

Catherine was irritated by his deliberate, didactic manner. Although his argument made sense, she wasn't ready to concede the issue to a nonscientist with a nutty philosophy. She had always accepted evolutionary concepts as a matter of fact.

David continued. "Take mathematics as an example."

"Math?"

"Yeah, math and physics. Einstein and others developed exciting new theories. You know, quantum physics. In some ways a literal revolution in science. Any two lines will eventually intersect. But do we throw out thousands of years of geometry? Do you want to drive on a bridge built by an engineer who doesn't believe in Euclidean geometry?"

"Of course not. But how do you deal with the overwhelming amount of evidence that tends to support the evolutionary model? My whole field's based on it. We wouldn't have human-based insulin or any of a thousand advances in genetics if we didn't understand the process of mutations."

"True, but now you're into the difference between microevolution and macroevolution. You can mutate anything you want out of a species, manipulate the DNA and RNA until you produce things like insulin."

"That's my point."

"But you make a serious inductive leap of faith when you start talking about jumping from one species to another. There isn't any evidence to support that."

"Are you kidding? Of course there's evidence! What about Lucy? Every seventh grader is aware of Java man."

"Now you're moving from philosophy to a discussion of methods of evaluating empirical data," David said. "I've read that the museums of natural history no longer display the Java man because it's been demonstrated, you know, using DNA testing, that the skull bone fragment is that of a common ape. The leg was human. Notes from the excavation show that the discovery of the two bone fragments were as much as forty feet apart."

"You can't believe everything you read."

"True, but I think some very reputable scientists believe that the Java man conclusion should have been discounted from the beginning."

"There's more than just the Java man."

"I also understand that Lucy is falling victim to the same fate. Some scholars have debunked that initial conclusion and hold that Lucy was just an ape."

"I suppose you think we ought to teach creationism in schools." Her tone was condescending, and her mouth pulled into a sour grin.

"I told you before, I'm not really a religious man." He broke eye contact. She could see his jaw tensing and untensing. "Religion and science are two different disciplines," he continued. "I'm not opposed to children learning about historical Christianity or any other major religious beliefs. However, I am opposed to the rigid indoctrination that takes place in some science classes. Science is where a child should learn critical thinking, the scientific process."

"I agree. I'm not sure about teaching Christianity in school, historical or otherwise, but I agree with what you said about science."

"The question is not whether creationism should be taught, although it has no place in a biology or physics classroom. To me, the question is whether macroevolution should be taught. I think it would be appropriate to teach in a college-level philosophy of science class but not in a high school biology class."

"I have a doctorate in microbiology. I have to tell you, I've never heard such a simplistic philosophical challenge to commonly accepted scientific theory. You oversimplify."

"Probably. But what would you expect from a common sailor?" he said as he flashed a smile that seemed to disarm the intellectual tension.

She was actually relieved. At this point she really didn't want a disagreement to build between them, even if it was purely intellectual.

"Oh, I didn't get a chance to ask you," she said. "What happened after you left the restaurant? Get any leads?"

"No, we were one step behind him."

"Are you sure he was there?"

"No. He may have left his calling card. You know."

"Another dead prostitute?"

"Looks like she was strangled."

"Nice guy."

There was a knock at the door. David jumped up and pulled out his Heckler & Klock .40 and asked, "Who is it?"

"Room service."

"I didn't order anything," Catherine whispered.

"I did. Open the door and step back. I'll cover you."

Catherine opened the door. "Your order's here," she said as she invited the agent in the room. As he rolled the food cart into the room, Catherine noticed a bottle of wine.

What's he got on his mind?

"Do I need to sign for . . ." David started to ask.

"No, sir. We took care of it. As far as the hotel staff knows, you're in your old room," the agent said before he exited.

"What's this?" she asked.

"You wanted French wine. How could I not indulge the desire of such a beautiful woman? Besides, I never got lunch, so I ordered a sandwich for myself."

"What's this? Planning to mix business and pleasure?" she said with an arresting smile. There was an eagerness in her eyes.

His gaze was riveted on her face.

"Well, you know what they say," he said. "Work, work, work makes David a dull boy."

Catherine leaned into him and whispered into his ear. "We don't want David to be a dull boy."

"No, we wouldn't want that," he said.

Catherine raised her head and leaned up on her tiptoes. He bent to meet her. His lips tasted hers, gently, caressing her mouth more than kissing it. They both lingered, savoring every second.

Catherine slowly pulled away. "What kind of wine did you order?" she asked.

"It's a Cahors wine from the southwest region of France. Some people claim to detect the aromas of truffles, oak, and juniper," he replied as he uncorked the bottle.

"Truffles maybe," she said. "But I don't detect the oak or juniper."

The moment was shattered by a knock on the adjoining room door.

"Come in."

Steve entered. "The Bo Shuriken that killed our agent is very interesting."

"How so?" David cleared his throat and turned slightly away from Steve. He put his hand in the front pocket visible to Steve.

Romance interfering with the job just isn't worth it. My subordinates'll expect professionalism, not some James Bond wannabe.

David resolved not to let it get out of hand again.

"Well," Steve continued, "it's a weapon made of layered steel with special markings. It also had a residue of poison on it that appeared on the upper two-thirds of the shank, but no poison near the tip."

"Go on."

"An ancient martial arts discipline from the Togakaryu family. That's an ancient discipline that made extensive use of this type of weapon. The layered steel is a very old method of forging these tools. Only masters would bother to carry a weapon crafted in this fashion. They frequently poisoned the weapon but not the tip. By not poisoning the tip, they could avoid accidentally sticking themselves with the poison."

"A master?"

"A master. The Togakaryu discipline hails from a remote mountainous providence of Japan. It's the predecessor, by several hundred years, of the Tokugawa martial arts discipline, which predominated during Japan's Shogun period. The more ancient techniques commonly used thrown weapons, but thrown weapons require a master's skill to kill. By the time of the Shoguns, the art had evolved, and the discipline embraced by the Samurai focused more on swords as fundamental weapons. Nonetheless, there is one remote village in Japan where the ancient discipline is still practiced."

"So, our killer has much more than standard CIA or KGB martial arts training?"

"That's an understatement. One breakthrough. The Bo Shuriken did have a set of prints on it. It wasn't Choutov's. We have a wild card in the deck."

"Thanks," David said. Steve left the room.

David sat down on the couch. He took his shoes off and reclined his head on one of the couch pillows. Water was running in the bathroom. Except for a short nap in the morning, he really hadn't slept for several days now. As he closed his eyes, he began to rehash the events of the last several hours in his mind.

She's something . . .

Ten minutes later.

David was startled awake by the pounding on the adjoining room door.

"Come in."

"Leonid Vodokanal's been spotted by one of the agency operatives. He'll meet you downstairs. I'm spread thin, so I'll stay here with Catherine."

"Right. Have Mother put a SEAL team in the air in case they're needed. Better keep them out of the city unless I call for them."

"Got it," Steve said.

David put his shoes on, grabbed his coat, and headed for the lobby.

SIXTEEN

Meanwhile, across town . . .

LEONID WAS STARTLED BY THE SOUND OF A LOUD POUNDING ON THE door to his room. He pulled his Glock .40 caliber and crouched out of the line of fire from the door. "Da. Who is it?"

"Severny and Pavel. Open the door."

Leonid opened the door slightly and stepped back. "Come in."

Severny kicked the door, and it flew open. He stood perfectly still and stared at Leonid for several seconds.

"You screwed up!"

"No, Severny. We secured the woman. Our mission was a success. That arrogant Dmitry screwed up."

"The mission was a success? Come now, Leonid. Hardly a success."

"But Severny—"

"Sit! Tell me every detail, every blasted detail."

For the next ten minutes, Leonid related the story. Severny asked various questions to try to put the time sequence together in his mind.

"And you did not see the American helicopter?" Severny asked.

"No, Severny. We were gone. With the girl."

"Were you followed?"

"No. I am sure of it."

"Then tell me how the Americans found her so quickly? You were followed."

"No. I have done this before. I know when I have a tail."

"The American special forces land at the store. Half an hour later they land again at the hotel and rescue the girl. And you say you were not followed. You are an idiot."

"I do not—"

"Why did you come back here? Why did not you stay in the hotel room with Dmitry?"

"I do not know. Yakov was going to report to you. I did not think I was needed."

"Why did you leave in the first place? It does not take two people to report to me!" Severny's face turned red around his light eyebrows.

Front of the Inter Nor Hotel Bristol.

Finally a break.

If David could just get his hands on Vodokanal alive, he might be able to find Andreyev. He'd decided to put out an order to sanction Andreyev and Iourtchak on sight. It was apparent that they knew who the key American players were.

Got to isolate Choutov. If he knew who the buyers were, he could continue the deal himself. Nah. Highly unlikely Andreyev would be stupid enough to let him know.

If he sanctioned Andreyev and Choutov didn't know about the death, maybe he'd try to make the original rendezvous.

If he doesn't get spooked, he'll leave by air in the next twenty-four hours. Andreyev's been conducting a frontal assault to slow us down—time to fight fire with fire.

"Cümodore Egan, I'm Douglas Carrollton," the driver said as David approached an agency car. "We're shorthanded. I'm your driver."

David stopped and looked directly at Douglas. Something was wrong. He couldn't put his finger on it, but something just didn't feel right.

It's been ten years since my last actual field assignment. Used to be able to smell trouble.

"Let's go," David said as he started toward the car door.

No ear piece? A CIA driver's always in contact with his control.

David turned back toward Douglas who had already begun a backhanded karate blow designed to strike at and break the neck. Because of David's sudden movement, the blow missed its intended mark and landed on his back between the shoulders.

David was knocked toward the car. He instinctively planted his feet and began a round kick. His leg had the height to hit its mark, but his opponent was quick enough to use a forearm to deflect the kick. Then Douglas knocked the other leg out from under David. He fell hard on the pavement. Douglas raised his foot for another blow. David moved, and the blow landed on his inner adductor longus muscle several inches from his groin. David felt a sharp piercing pain followed by a burning sensation.

The doorman started blowing his whistle and several of the waiting taxi drivers got out of their taxis and ran toward the two men. Douglas saw them and turned away from David. He ran toward the Rosenkrantz Gate and disappeared around the corner heading toward the Karl Johans Gate.

David was dazed for a moment.

I'm too old and slow for this.

He began to run after his assailant. The run was more of a fast hobble. When he arrived at Karl Johans Gate and saw the crowd, he knew he'd lost Douglas.

Sooner or later it's my turn for a break. He took out his cellular phone.

"Mother."

"Bob, David. I just got bushwhacked outside the hotel. I have no idea what happened to my real driver. Give me directions to the hotel and get someone there to back me up."

"Driver? You were supposed to meet the agent watching the Victoria Hotel. It's only two blocks away."

"Whoever. He's probably history. How do I get to the hotel?"

"Just a minute."

"David, Bob. Do you know Karl Johans Gate?"

"Yeah, I'm standing on it now."

"Where exactly?"

"Karl Johans and Rosenkrant."

"Good. You're facing the park between the Stortinget and the National Theater."

"Yeah."

"Good. Cross the park. Stay on the Rosenkrantz Gate. One block. You'll see the Victoria Hotel. Room 415."

"Okay, Bob, get me some backup. I'm almost there now."

"You want me to pull Steve off Catherine's guard detail?"

"No! Get someone else."

"Wait ten minutes. I'll get Jim there."

"David," Jim said as he ran into the lobby.

"Here's the plan," David responded. "I've cased the place. It's an older style of building with large recessed doors to each room. When I saw you coming in the hotel, I called room service and placed an order. We'll hide out of sight in the door insets of a nearby room. Since Vodokanal didn't place an order with room service, he'll become very suspicious. I doubt he'll open the door right away. More than likely he'll have 'em leave the tray outside the door. Of course, curiosity will get to him, and eventually he'll open the door. We have to jump him when he finally steps into the hallway."

"Not much of a plan. Hang out in a cramped space until he opens the door, then go in guns blazing. Not sure I like that. We don't know how many men are in that room—or the other rooms. We could be in deep cow patties real quick."

"Did I say guns blazing? You misunderstood me. I want him alive."

"Now there's a blasted government order if I ever heard one. What ever happened to the good old days when you just shot the bad guys?"

"We'll have the element of surprise. And we need to know where Severny's located," David said.

"Yeah, maybe—Okay, let's do it."

David and Jim stepped off the elevator and turned down the hall. As they rounded the corner, Pavel recognized David and opened fire. Severny was almost to the far end of the hall near the fire escape when the shots rang out. He ran a few steps, then lunged, hitting the emergency quick-release bar on the door. The fire escape door flew open, and Severny rolled out. He quickly shut the metal door behind him and slid down the ladder of the fire escape.

David and Jim fell to the floor and rolled back to the corner. However, Pavel had hit Jim in the shoulder with a round. David stuck his .40 caliber around the corner and fired two rounds without looking. Then he quickly stuck his head around. Pavel was almost to the fire escape door. David took aim and squeezed off several more rounds.

Pavel fell to the floor.

"I thought you said not to shoot anyone," Jim said.

"So I did. Here, take the phone and call for help." He gave Jim his cellular phone.

As Jim made the call, David moved down the hall toward Pavel. A door opened, and David hollered for the guest to get back into his room. He carefully eased by room 415, making sure that no one else was waiting to open fire. Leonid was lying on the floor. He eased on past the room and down to where Pavel was located. He was dead.

He went back to the room to check on Leonid Vodokanal. He had a small knife stuck in his left eye. No pulse.

"We'd better get out of here," David said as he came out of the room. He helped Jim to the stairs and down to the lobby level. An outside fire door was located on the lobby level. David pushed the quick-release bar. He and Jim made it to an agency car just as the police arrived at the front door.

The car dropped David in front of his hotel and then sped away to get Jim back to the *Peterson* for medical help.

SEVENTEEN

DAVID WAS DEAD TO THE WORLD. HE HADN'T SLEPT FOR OVER twenty-four hours. Catherine got up from the couch and quietly went to the bathroom to freshen up. She had also fallen asleep after her day of excitement. Like David, she hadn't slept well for the past several days.

She returned and sat on the couch. He was sleeping so peacefully.

Doesn't snore.

The edges of her mouth turned up into a slight smile.

Strong, intelligent, and attractive—I could fall for this guy.

The problem was that the men she found attractive were men like David—strong, professional men who were self-assured and in charge of their environment.

Doubt he'd give up his career to change dirty diapers.

Her thoughts were interrupted by a knock on the adjoining door. Steve opened the door quietly, walked over, and sat beside her.

"The fingerprints on the Bo Shuriken belong to Severny Iourtchak," he said in a whisper.

"Bo what?"

"Shuriken. It's a martial arts throwing knife. Actually, it can be anything thrown. Usually they're specially made knives."

"Interesting. Sorry. Got you off track. I know very little about martial arts."

"No problem. Tell David we've got a lead on the prostitute. A number of 'em have a referral network that's frequently used by foreigners."

"You mean a pimp?"

"No, prostitution's legal in Norway. It's more like a network of hotel desk clerks, cab drivers, and the like."

"I've heard of networking in business. But, wow," she said.

Steve didn't change his expression.

He's all business.

"Tell David that several of the girls have put the word out for us on the streets. They'll be on the lookout for Choutov. If he goes looking for a good time again, we'll catch him."

"Glad you're so sure. Any word on Andreyev?"

"No, with Severny Iourtchak involved, assume that Andreyev is in Oslo. We're running out of time."

"I know. Seems like such a hit-or-miss way of finding someone. Are all spy missions?"

"Tomorrow morning, our ambassador's gonna approach the Norwegian government," he said. "He'll ask for their help in covering the airport and the ports. He's going crazy with all the protests from the Norwegians."

"Yeah, I caught a glimpse of the news. The helicopter incidents are being reported as joint NATO antiterrorist exercises?"

"Yeah," Steve replied with a grin. It was the first time Catherine had seen any emotion from him. "Don't ask me how the ambassador got them to agree to release that story."

"Hope it's not too late."

"The Russian Embassy's filed credentials with Norway for seven new staffers. We assume they're intelligence operatives. Oh, David might want to know that because of his little air war, most of the Russian Northern fleet is underway. The ships are all over the Baltic and the Skkagerrak. They're mad!"

"Do the Russians know anything we don't?"

"Who knows? They're denying the charge of air piracy."

"Doesn't sound good."

"The thing that's got everyone in Washington on edge is the lack of contact with the civilian leadership in Russia. Their ambassador's been recalled for consultations. Their president and foreign minister have been unavailable. All contact has been through people at the Ministry of Defense, and they're not happy campers right now."

"Could it escalate?

"For a fact! How's it feel to be a part of the team that started World War III?"

Catherine couldn't tell if Steve was trying to be humorous, or what.

"Oh, most important," he said, "you and David need to make contact again at the Engebret. You'd better go ahead and wake him."

As Steve left the room, Catherine walked over to the bed and sat down. She hated to wake him but called his name.

David opened his eyes.

"Welcome back to the world," she said. "I hate to wake you. We're supposed to make contact at the Engebret for dinner."

David got out of bed and walked toward the bathroom.

"Steve said that they identified the fingerprints on the Bo Shuriken," Catherine continued. "Belongs to Severny Iourtchak. Oh, and Russia has sent in seven new agents according to the local CIA station office."

"It'll be a shooting gallery out there," he said from the bathroom.

She heard the toilet flush followed by the sound of water running in the sink. "That's not the end of it. The whole Russian northern fleet has put to sea."

Catherine sat down on the couch and proceeded to put on her panty hose and shoes. David came back into the room drying his face. He walked over to his bags to fetch a set of clean clothes.

"Did Steve say anything else?"

"Yeah, they've identified a network that several of the working girls use for foreign referrals. The ladies have agreed to help."

"Probably won't be much help now. We may be out of time."

"Think positively. We'll get a break."

"Choutov's been reported with two of the girls in just under twenty-four hours. What a geek."

"You think he's a geek because he's a scientist?"

"Uh, no. Not necessarily."

"Is it that you think scientists are less virile than other men?"

"No. I just engaged my mouth before my brain." He furrowed his brow and cleared his throat. "Besides, I'm sure you'd know if he was macho or not."

"Now how would I know that?" she glared. "What are you trying to imply?"

"Well, you know. You seem to be enamored with him." He looked at her with a taunting expression that infuriated her.

"What?" She swallowed hard, trying hard to control her anger.

"At the briefing. You said he was brilliant."

"He is brilliant. That doesn't mean I've got the hots for him."

"Sorry. I just thought that the way you reacted to the mention of his name. Well, I thought he was someone, you know, that you were interested in."

"David," she said sternly, "let me assure you, I don't have a thing for Choutov. I heard him lecture, and I said hello at a reception. That's it! And frankly," she swallowed hard, "I resent your implication that I'm a traitor."

David could see the tears in her eyes.

Stupid idot. You really stuck your foot into it this time.

"I'm so sorry. I misunderstood your reaction. I, ah, didn't mean to imply you were a traitor. Just exploring the possibility that you'd, well, had a relationship with him."

Why'd I say such a stupid thing? They kidnapped and attempted to rape her. It's obvious she wasn't in league with 'em.

"Ah, what else did Steve say?"

"He said we're running out of time," she said in a grudging tone. "Andreyev's in Oslo."

"He's sure to find him soon if we don't."

"Maybe." Her tone was still cool, matter-of-fact. "You know, Choutov did make an unscheduled departure in Stockholm. I gotta believe they're off their game plan. Unless they had a contingency meeting site. Andreyev's gonna be looking for him just like we are."

Her scowl gave way to a doleful demeanor. Although her anger subsided, she was still hurt by David's comment. He had changed the subject without bringing the issue to a genuine closure. Could it be that she was so preoccupied with him that she'd misread everything?

Maybe he is genuinely suspicious? He is the senior American in charge of a delicate intelligence operation.

She would have never fallen for a superior in any other environment. In fact, she would have done quite the opposite. She knew that female agents often used romance in covert operations and that men got aroused without necessarily having genuine affection. Had she misread the spark that seemed to ignite between them?

"Both Choutov and Andreyev are ex-military," David said. "I doubt they'd have set up a plan without a rendezvous of some sort."

"Yeah. But in Oslo?" I doubt they had multiple contingency plans. No, Choutov's planning to make the original rendezvous."

"Maybe."

"If he's planning to fly to the original destination, that'll give him a few extra days to kill. Maybe he figures he'll have some fun."

"Assuming your theory is correct, Andreyev's been one step ahead of us. To complicate matters spooks from Israel and Russia are running around looking for this guy. If he gets wind that anyone is looking, he'll disappear."

"Oh, I hate to tell you," she said. "Steve said we're going to inform the Norwegians in the morning and solicit their help in covering the airports and harbors."

David's brow furrowed. She saw the veins in his neck and temples engorge. "That's just what I need," he growled.

David put his shoes on and grabbed his cellular phone.

"Bob, David. Get a message off to the White House. Ask 'em not to brief the Norwegians until the last possible moment. If Choutov gets wind anyone is looking for him, he'll disappear."

"OK."

He put his phone away. "You know, I never ate my sandwich. Oh well. It'll keep if we want a midnight snack."

He walked around to the closet and took out both of their coats.

"I'm scared. What if we miss him?" she said.

David put his arm around her shoulder and hugged her. "Think positively. Things have a way of working out for the best." He smiled and gave her a kiss on the cheek. "After all, I met you."

Confused by this tease, she turned to face him. The expression in his eyes seemed to plead for forgiveness. If David were genuinely suspicious, he certainly wouldn't engage in anything that approached romantic banter. If he's not really suspicious, then why would he imply a relationship with Choutov unless—

"That's true," she said with a coy tilt of her head.

"We'd better go," David said. "Duty calls."

EIGHTEEN

THE LOBBY WAS ALIVE WITH ACTIVITY, BUT NO PIANO MUSIC. Steve sat near the front door reading a paper. David and Catherine approached the door without acknowledging him. A new doorman greeted them. "Goot night. I am getting the taxi for you?"

"No thanks, we'll walk," David responded as they left the hotel.

They did not speak as they turned the corner and walked toward Karl Johns Gate. The streets were busy. Some of the shops were closing as the cafés and entertainment establishments bustled with business. The air was crisp. Catherine put her arm under David's but said nothing all the way past the Stortinget. As they turned onto the Nedre Slortsgate, she gazed up into David eyes.

"How'd your wife take to all this spy stuff?"

"What'd you mean?"

"You know, the danger, the intrigue, the women." She smiled.

David snickered. "You watch too much TV."

"Oh, come on. You're telling me she wasn't concerned?"

"I wouldn't think any more than any other navy wife. When I was on a mission as a SEAL, she didn't know about it. I usually couldn't tell her. When I worked for the White House . . ."

"I'm not talking about your safety, silly."

"Ah—"

"I'm talking about all the intrigue—the gorgeous Russian spies running around Washington," she said.

David smiled again and shuffled his feet a little as he looked down. "You mean there were gorgeous Russian women? I must have missed 'em."

It took only a few minutes to make the short walk. The street was active as theater patrons arrived. While it was several hours before the scheduled performance, it was not uncommon for people to gather in the café and other establishments near the city center.

Chamber music played on the balcony of the café. It was the first thing David and Catherine noticed as they entered. The room buzzed with activity as conversations flourished between patrons at different tables. The place exhibited more of the ambiance of a social club than a traditional restaurant.

"Welcome, Mr. and Mrs. Egan," the maître d' said. "Your reservation, we are having. A table is being ready shortly. Please to be seating, for moment."

The maître d' walked around a corner to check on the status of the table. He returned and led a group of four to their seats. Minutes later he called for David and Catherine to follow him to their table.

"I am, desiring your company, is permitting ah, enjoyment of the dining," he said as he seated Catherine and handed them menus.

"Yes, I've not eaten all day. I could eat a horse," David said.

"Sir! Please, we are not serving horse meat."

Catherine laughed. "No, it's just a silly American expression. It means he's hungry."

"Yah, yah. We hope you will be enjoying the food."

David smiled. "I'll enjoy."

"Yah, enjoy. The wine steward, he may be attending you shortly."

As the maître d' left, Catherine looked at David. "I find Oslo to be—" She paused and gazed toward the balcony as if she were searching for the perfect word. The lights from the chandeliers sparkled in her blue eyes. "Enchanting. It's unlike Atlanta, or any other city I've visited in the States. It's almost like I've stepped into some kind of a time warp. You know, back to a more refined, genteel era."

"Yeah, I kind 'a know what you're talking about. Never been in a refined era, though," he said with a grin.

"Oh, come on. You know what I mean. Haven't you been amazed at the cosmopolitan atmosphere throughout the city?"

"Yeah, I guess I know what you mean. I can't remember when I've been in a hotel lobby that plays classic piano concertos in the afternoon, or a restaurant with a chamber music group playing on the balcony. Kinda' nice to have music and still be able to hear myself think."

She smiled at his response. A waiter approached their table. "Please to be ordering?" David motioned to Catherine.

She pointed to Kjøttkaker on the menu. "What's this?"

"Yah, SHET-kah-kair. Yah, a meatball."

"Like Swedish meatballs?"

"Yah, similar."

"What are these vegetables?" she asked.

"AR-tuhr, unt peas. MUH-henna-tut PER-un-at, unt potatoes—stewed. KOHK-teh poh-TEH-tuhr, unt potatoes—boiled. SEEL-th-duh ah-GOR-ker, unt cucumbers, how you say, pickled."

"I'll have the, how'd you say it, SHET-kah-kair," she said.

"Yah, very goot."

"Give me the peas and boiled potatoes."

"Goot. Unt dessert?"

"I'm sorry, what are these?" she said pointing at the menu.

"Rice pudding. Norsway, Sveden, unt Denmark."

"Oh, well, the pudding from Norway, of course."

"Very goot. You are having, sir?"

"UH-vehn-shtehkt torshk with Finnish stewed potatoes and Danish pickled cucumbers."

"Goot. Unt desert?"

"FRUKT-suh-puh," David said.

"Very goot. You meal, ah, will be serving soon," the waiter said and then left the table.

"Showing off, huh. OK, what'd you order?"

"Baked cod. Cooked in milk and butter with parsley."

"And the dessert? I didn't see it when I looked at the menu."

"Fruit soup. It's got raisins, apricots, cherries, tapioca, and such. I hate rice pudding. The locals eat rice pudding coming out their ears."

"Oh?"

"Yeah. If I were going to get the rice pudding, I'd get the Swedish or Danish."

"Why's that?"

"The Norwegian has just a little sugar. The Swedish has raisins and lemon flavoring. The Danish has vanilla, almonds, and whipping cream."

"Wish you'd said something when I ordered. You've been to Norway before?" The expression on her face showed genuine interest.

"Several times through the years. Every fall for as long as I can remember, NATO's conducted a large North Atlantic joint operation. We tool around the ocean playing war for a few days a week and then make port calls."

"So they weren't just whistling Dixie with the old saying 'join the navy and see the world?'" she said in a casual, jesting way.

"Is that an old saying?"

She laughed gently.

"I'm sure they'll let you change your order," he said. As he did, the wine steward approached the table.

"Please, I am showing you unt Italian wine list?"

The steward demonstratively handed the list to David who opened it and looked inside.

No sighting of Choutov. One of our working girls is to meet
a customer at the Anker Hotel in two hours.

Man matching description of Severny Iourtchak may have
checked into the Norrona Hotel. Two blocks from the Bristol
at the corner of Akersgata. Full stakeout of all entrances.
Clerk would not give our agent the room number.

"Sweetheart, why don't you look at the list and see if there's
anything you wish."

David passed Catherine the list, and she read the note.

"Are you planning to have fish or beef?" she asked.

"Fish. Remember?"

"I'm having beef this evening. Why don't we let our expert
here select for us," she said as she passed the wine list to
David.

He opened it and removed the note. Then after closing it,
he gave the wine list back to the steward.

"Thank you, my good man, but I'll save myself for something back in our room."

"He's such a romantic," Catherine said smiling. The steward winced.

As the steward walked away, David pulled out a pen and
wrote a memo on the bottom of the note that had been in the
wine list. It read:

1. Have two of your men meet me in the lobby of the Anker
   Hotel in an hour and fifteen minutes. Take the woman
   into our confidence and put a wire on her.
2. I want you and a full complement of men to detain
   Iourtchak at the Norrona Hotel. Try not to kill him.
   Expect surprises. Take the desk clerk into custody and
   use any drug or means necessary to get the room number out of him.

David got up and kissed Catherine on the cheek. "Excuse
me a moment," he said.

He walked toward the rest rooms near the door. Steve sat waiting for a table. David stared straight at Steve as he walked up to and then past him. Steve got up, told the maître d' that he would be in the rest room and followed David into the men's room.

David noticed that the attendant was the only person in the room. He walked over to an empty stall and closed the door. Steve walked in and occupied the stall next to him. David reached down and held the note under the stall partition so that Steve could see it. He took it.

David flushed the toilet. As he came out of the stall, the attendant handed him a warm wet washcloth. David washed his hands, tipped the attendant, and left.

NINETEEN

STEVE WAITED A FEW MINUTES BEFORE HE LEFT THE BATHROOM. Then, he canceled his reservation with the maître d' and left the café, pulling a cellular phone from a coat pocket. He called Mother. Steve instructed Bob to have his team meet him at the Norrona Hotel and to have two men meet David as requested.

He continued to walk briskly toward the corner where he hailed a waiting cab.

"Norrona Hotel," he said as he got into the cab.

"Yes, sir. It's a very short ride."

"I'm in a hurry. I'll double your fare."

After five blocks, Steve threw the cabbie a twenty-dollar bill, told him to keep the change, and jumped out. He walked into the lobby and looked around for anyone wearing a Gideon lapel pin. A few patrons darted in and out from the lounge near the main doors. The bell captain sat facing the main doors with his head buried in a magazine. A large raised sitting area with ample indoor plants obscured the line of sight between the lounge and the main desk. One single man sat in a high-back chair across the room from the desk reading a magazine. Steve moved close enough to discern the nature of the man's lapel pin, then walked up beside the man.

"Have you seen a weather report today?" Steve asked.

The man put the magazine down. "Not for today, but it should be nice for the next few days."

"Good, I hate snow."

The man got up. "That's too bad; Norway is beautiful when it snows."

After a short pause, the man said, "Jon Rivera, Oslo station," as he stuck out his hand to greet Steve.

Steve shook his hand. "The code word is 'traveler.'"

Jon's smile left his face. Steve's demeanor was rigid.

"Is the clerk who identified Iourtchak on duty?" Steve asked.

"Yeah." Jon said pointing to the young blond man standing behind the main hotel check-in counter.

"Do you speak the language?"

"Yes, my grandparents still speak Norwegian at home."

Five of Steve's men entered the lobby. One took a seat in the sitting area, two sauntered over near the main desk, one lingered near the entrance to the lounge, and one took a position near the elevators just as the doors opened. A young couple stepped off and crossed the lobby laughing and chattering. They entered the lounge.

The agent nearest the elevator stepped in and removed a half-inch hydraulic cylinder with angling pads from his coat. He positioned it between the adjacent bulkhead and the OPEN DOOR button. Then he stepped out and pressed the button to call for the second elevator car.

"Walk with me to the counter," Steve said.

Steve and Jon walked across the room. As they stepped up to the hotel's main counter, the desk clerk looked up and greeted the new customers.

The second elevator car arrived, and the agent stepped in and pressed the button for the top floor.

"Elevator clear. Two minutes until the elevator returns to the lobby," Steve heard in his earpiece.

Steve pulled out a wad of kroner and counted out 7,000 kr in large bills. The clerk's eyes widened. Steve slid the money over to him.

"May I be of assistance?" the clerk said in Norwegian.

"English please," Jon said.

"Yah, English. Please, to be assisting?"

Steve slid him a picture of Severny. "This man's a guest. What room?"

"Ah, I am not being unt allowing."

Steve pulled the money back to him and picked it up. "Too bad! He's an old friend. I was really looking forward to seeing him again." Steve took out his wallet and started to put the money away.

"Pardon. Arrangements mebbe, ah, poss-i-ble."

"Tell you what," Steve said, "I'll add another thousand kroner." He took the money back out of his wallet and then counted out another 1,000 kr. Then he slid the money over to the clerk.

"One twenty three," the clerk said gawking at the money.

Steve took out a very small aerosol spray resembling a mace spray that women carry and cupped it in his hand. He sprayed the hotel clerk with desflurane while slightly angling his face away.

The clerk stepped back upon recognizing what was happening. His eyebrows shot up, and his eyes took on an expression of shock.

"What are you do-o-o-"

His pupils dilated. A glazed unfocused look spread across his face. His knees buckled and he slumped to the floor.

"Drag him into the back and tie him up," he told Jon. "Put on his jacket and man the desk."

Steve put a blank coded key in the key machine and typed 123. In the meantime, the agent near the elevators had moved to the doors leading into the hallway. The other agents started to move toward the hallway when the message "hallway fouled" came across their earpieces. They stopped where they were.

A middle-aged man walked out of the hallway and toward the front doors.

"Hallway clear."

The team quickly entered the hallway and closed the doors to the lobby. Steve motioned for two of the men to sweep each side of the hallway to clear the doors to rooms on either side of the hallway.

"Clear," one of the agents said.

Steve and the five agents moved to the door of room 123. One man crouched on each side of the door with his weapon raised. Another stepped back toward the doors to the lobby and peered through a small window in the door. One man stood in position to kick the door with a second standing right behind him. Steve inserted the key.

Across the hall two doors opened revealing the silenced muzzles of automatic weapons.

Blood sprayed the window of the door leading into the lobby. The sound of high caliber "cop-killer" rounds tearing flak jackets reverberated through the hallway.

TWENTY

A GEAR AND RATCHET WITHIN A WALL-MOUNTED CLOCK CLICKED WITH each full swing of the clock's pendulum. Each click reminded Jon how long the team had been away. He felt a bead of moisture run between his pecks until it touched his undershirt at the top of his abdomen.

"I say my good man, how much longer?" a reddish blond man in his late forties asked with a scowl.

Two other guests stood behind him waiting for service.

How do I know how to look up this arrogant Brit's bar bill?

"Yes, sir, it says here that you're an executive VIP guest. Good news," Jon smiled at the man. "That means your bar tab is on us tonight," Jon said looking past a blank computer screen.

The man's face broke into an effervescent grin. "Jolly good then." The man turned and strutted off.

"May I help you?" Jon asked the next person in line.

I wish they'd hurry up, before I have to give away the whole hotel.

People continued to come to the lobby desk for routine business. Since Jon didn't know a thing about the hotel's operations, the situation became increasingly awkward. Finally, he got a break from customers and decided to check on the team. He made a coded key for room 123.

As Jon entered the hallway, he saw the blood on the walls. He pulled out his Glock .40, inserted the key, and pushed the door open before jumping to a crouched stance behind the wall. He eased into the room and spotted a body. A quick scan revealed several others.

Oh my, they're the Americans.

He closed the door and ran back to the lobby where he called the CIA station watch officer and reported the incident.

Jon stood near the front door waiting on the cleaners. Five guests stood at the main counter, and one banged on the service bell.

"Young man," a woman shouted across the lobby in Norwegian. "Are you going to just stand there?"

"I'll be with you as soon as possible," Jon responded just as the CIA cleaners from the Oslo Station entered the hotel. Jon turned without speaking and walked briskly toward the room. The team fanned out in the lobby, and one by one, followed him toward the room.

"Go, watch the door to the hall from the lobby," one of the operatives said to Jon. "Don't let anyone in. If you see a guest open a door, tell him to return to his room. Police emergency."

The CIA team took the hotel janitorial cart into the room and dumped the contents on the floor. One radioed for the van to meet them at the side entrance. They threw the six bodies in the cart and put sheets over the top. One agent tried to push the cart but barely budged it. Two others jumped to help get it rolling out of the room and down the hall toward the exterior door opposite the lobby.

Halfway down the corridor, one of the bodies slipped off the cart. The agents scurried to retrieve it when the silence in the hallway was shattered by the voice of an elderly woman.

"Jorgen! Come quickly," she called out in Norwegian. "A man is hurt in the corridor."

Jon ran and positioned himself between the woman and the body.

"Please, return to your room. We have a serious police emergency, and it may not be safe for you to be out of your room until the authorities have secured the hotel."

"Oh my, this is awful," she said.

She stepped back into her room and closed the door. The agents quickly pushed the cart the rest of the way down the hallway to a van waiting just outside the door. Jon followed them, and they all got into the van with the bodies.

"Aren't you going to clean the scene?" Jon said.

"No time," one of the men answered. The van slipped off into the night.

Back at the Engebret Cafe.

David finished his last bite of fruktsuppe and then checked his watch. Catherine had been understandably quiet during dinner. Both of them had eaten hurriedly.

"Half an hour," David said. "You should return to the hotel. Get your weapons-handling equipment and be ready for my call."

"Do you think he'll have it in his room?"

"Fifty-fifty, I guess. Either there, or in a locker somewhere."

The waiter brought David his change. "Dhank you. Please dhat your dining unt excellent? Your meal, ah, acceptable?"

"Excellent, thank you."

"Goot. Please to return."

"Yes, I'm sure we will."

David took the folder from the waiter and left a handsome tip. After putting his coat on, he helped Catherine with hers.

While they were walking back to the hotel, the peace of the night was broken by the sound of several emergency vehicles. The street was still quite busy.

"Choutov can't have that much of an appetite," Catherine remarked. "Is it usual for a man to want two or three women in one day?"

"How would I know? I've never paid for it in my life! In fact, I've only been with my wife."

"I find that hard to believe," she said smiling.

David returned her smile. "Remember, I've been in command of a ship for a good part of the time since Rebecca died."

Catherine took his arm as they walked on.

"You know, it's strange," David said.

"What's strange?"

"I had the local station office pull the tails off the girls and put them on the restaurants. I didn't think this guy would go looking for another one so quickly."

"Duh, like do I hear an echo?" she responded as she lightly poked him in the ribs.

"Hey." They stopped just in front of the hotel. "Didn't know they had any valley girls in Atlanta."

Catherine put her arms around his neck and smiled as she gazed into his eyes. David reached up with his right hand and gently caressed her cheek with the back of his hand. There was a pause as they stood there looking at each other.

"Better get ready," he said.

Catherine nodded and put her arms down.

He continued. "Hopefully, I'll have a weapon ready for you to disarm very shortly."

Catherine smiled and then reached up to kiss David on his cheek. She pulled away before he could respond and entered the hotel.

As she entered the hotel, David watched her, savoring the sight. Then with a sigh, he turned and motioned for the doorman to hail him a taxi.

"Anker Hotel, please."

The ride was a short one. Along the route the cab drove past the Stortinget, a large cathedral-looking church, a huge civic arena, and a large modern, high-rise hotel.

An interesting blend of the old and new.

The cab pulled up to the front of the hotel. David was feeling uneasy. He really liked Catherine. He was sure that his earlier suspicions were unfounded, but he was still uneasy. It had been three years now since Rebecca's death. His sons had encouraged him to start dating. But, somehow the opportunity had never presented itself.

She's quite a . . .

His thoughts were interrupted as the cab arrived at the hotel. After paying the fare, he entered the lobby. He was looking for two men and a woman. He only saw a few older couples, so he sat down in a high-back chair near the door to wait. Looking at his watch, he realized he was a few minutes early.

While waiting, he began to reflect on the conversation with Catherine just minutes before. There had been no references in Choutov's file to any kind of psychopathic acts or tendencies. He certainly had a weakness for working women, but there was no mention of any dead ones. His weakness could be related to the fact that he was a loner. Psychopathic killers tend to be loners, but loners aren't necessarily psychopathic killers. If he had engaged a woman in Stockholm and then one again this morning, it would be really strange for him to be looking again so soon.

That's a perverted man. On the other hand, we're really not sure whether either girl had seen Choutov. Both were dead.

Two men and a woman approached. "Have you seen a weather report today?" one of the men asked.

"Not for today, but it should be nice for the next few days."

"Good, I hate snow."

"That's too bad. Norway is beautiful when it snows."

"Paul Simmons, this is Don Watson, Oslo station," the man said as he stuck out his hand to greet David. "Oh, this is Christina," he said motioning to the woman with them.

"Christina," David said, "thank you for helping us get this man. We believe he killed your friend this morning. He is a dangerous pervert."

"Yah. Please to tell. Mr. Simmons notified me, ah, not the police you are," she said. "Regards drugs?"

"No. Not drugs. But it's just as dangerous," David said. Then he looked at Paul. "Does she have a wire?"

Paul nodded. David took out a photograph of Choutov and showed it to her. "All we want you to do is verify that this man is in the room. Look closely. If he is in the room, all you need to do is signal us. You just say, 'I understand you like it rough.' Do you understand?"

"Yah. Verstand," she said.

"That'll be our signal. We'll come in as soon as you give the signal. Don't worry, you'll be safe," David said.

She nodded.

David turned to the others. "Paul, you're with me on entry. Don, you're rear guard. Oh, Paul, don't kill him if you can help it. He may not have the item in the room. Understand?"

"Understand."

The group proceeded to the elevators and up to the floor where the room was located. The hallway was deserted. The group walked down to the room where Paul and David crouched on either side of the door. Don stood several feet away facing back toward the elevator. The door to the room was ajar. Christina took a deep breath and knocked on the door.

"Who is it?" someone answered from inside.

"Christina."

"The door's open."

She opened the door and stepped in. Paul and David had not noticed that several men who had been hiding in adjacent rooms had stepped out into the hall. One silenced shot was fired in the hallway.

Don fell.

"Freeze, Commander Egan!"

Caught off guard and outnumbered, David and Paul checked their guns upward and raised their hands. Christina and one of the men in the room disarmed Paul and David while another group of men dragged Don into an adjoining room. Christina motioned for David and Paul to enter the room. As they entered, David put his hands down and activated the homing beacon on his belt.

"Put your hands back up," Christina said in a stern voice.

One of the Russians began to pat them down. He found the pens, the cellular phone, a coded room key, a cigarette case, and a concealed Smith & Wesson .38 Airweight on David; and an extra Sig Sauer 9mm on Paul. He left the pens in David's coat but took the cigarette case, room key, phone, and gun.

"Welcome, Commander. At last we meet."

David was shocked. The man speaking to him was Severny Iourtchak. "I believe you have me at a disadvantage, sir," David said.

"Now, Commander, don't trifle with me," Severny said without a hint of a European accent. "You know exactly who I am."

"Yeah, I know who you are."

"Of course you do. You would not have sent your Armageddon group to eliminate me." Severny paused for a moment and stared directly into David's eyes. Then he laughed. "Yes. I have been one step ahead of you all the way. Let me answer your obvious question. I am still alive. Your team is dead. Now I have you."

"Why have you spared me? A little personal revenge?"

"You remember. Good. But work first. Pleasure later. I need time. With your special team dead, your CIA will pull out all the stops to find you. Their distraction will give me time. Who knows? They may find you and rescue you before we kill you. We shall see."

"You're mistaken. They'll not be distracted into looking for me. They'll assume I'm dead."

"That is where Christina will provide us with one more service. She will report you alive."

At that point Severny nodded. Christina sat down in a chair. One of Severny's men put on a set of brass knuckles and slugged her twice in the face. Both hits cut her skin and left a large bruise. Then she tore her dress, and they took some blood from Don's wound and spotted her dress.

"That should do," Severny commented. "Christina, you know what to say?"

"Yah."

"Go," he said as he motioned for her to leave. "You see, Commander, they will know you are alive. Besides, I have one little pleasantry to attend to before I kill you."

"Oh?"

"Yes. Since your Rebecca is dead, I will have to console myself with your roommate," he said smirking. "I hear she is quite beautiful."

"You . . ." David shouted as he tried to get up.

Severny got up and walked out of the room. Two men grabbed David's arm and held it steady as a third pierced his skin with a hypodermic. He felt a slow burning sensation around the injection site. The men moved to repeat the process with Paul. David's vision blurred. He struggled to keep his eyes open.

"This horse better kill me, you scumbags," he heard Paul say. "If I ever get . . ."

David and Paul were unconscious in a matter of moments. The Russians picked them up and carried them to the service elevator at the end of the hallway.

Back at the Hotel Bristol.

There was a knock on the adjoining door, and without waiting for a response, Brian Thompson and two other agents walked in.

"We have to move you, Catherine," Brian said.

"What's the matter?"

"Mother has ordered us to move. Something went wrong. Steve and his team are dead. Two hotel attendants were found dead. If they got Steve, we've got to assume they know about this room. Anyhow, we're going to play it safe and move you."

The other agents began to gather David's belongings while Brian helped Catherine pull her things together. Before escorting Catherine from the room, the agents made a security sweep of the hallway to ensure no one was in the area. They opened a room at the end of the hallway. Brian and Catherine followed from the old room and into the new one.

"We've configured the hallway with cameras. If Andreyev finds out where we're located, he may try to take us out. We'll have our own ambush set up. Maybe we can get a lead on his location. In the meantime, you'll be safe here," Brian said.

"Have you heard from David?"

"No, he's not reported yet."

"I hope he's okay," she said as a feeling of apprehension overwhelmed her.

TWENTY-ONE

T HE BOAT LAZILY LOBBED BACK AND FORTH. OUTSIDE, THE SOUND OF
the bells on marker buoys clanged. In the distance a faint
foghorn sounded.

David awoke with a horrible headache. It took a moment
for him to become fully aware of his surroundings. He could
feel the sixty-cycle vibration and hum of machinery.

Metal deck. Vibration of machinery. Harbor noises.

For a moment he had the feeling that he was back on the
Peterson, waking from a night's slumber.

Too bad I'm not waking from a bad dream.

The room was dark except for a faint light coming from outside.

A porthole on a hatch. Good, I'm on a weather deck.

David's eyes were conditioned for the dark so he could see
in the room. His left hand was cuffed to a five-foot chain that
was attached to the metal frame of a bed. There were two
chairs and a table in the room.

*Constant slow roll, no changes in rhythm. Sound from
nearby navigational aids. No dock noises. Must be at anchor.
But where?*

David knew that in most busy ports merchant vessels would anchor in harbors. Port authorities would only bring a ship alongside a pier to load or off-load cargo. The faint light from the porthole indicated that it was still dark outside. David had no idea how long he had been out or what had happened to Paul.

The compartment was painted marine red lead. He surmised that the bed and chairs were probably not the normal fixtures since the bed was not bolted to the deck and there were no deck grommets to affix a tie for the chairs.

Must be on a merchant vessel of some kind.

He began to wonder if they were still in Oslo. Andreyev had thirteen vessels, and none were in the area.

Couldn't be one of his.

On the other hand, Andreyev was heavily involved in both shipping and fish processing and would have numerous contacts with access to ships.

The hatch opened, and two men stepped in. One of the men turned on the red interior light. He had dark hair, a full beard, was about five feet ten inches, very stocky, and he wore jeans, a flannel shirt, and a jacket without sleeves.

The second man had light brown hair, almost blond. He was six feet two inches, slender, clean shaven, and wore a suit with a designer shirt that had no collar or necktie. He had an automatic weapon in his hand.

The bearded man came up to the bed, unlocked the handcuffs, then walked to the door.

"Follow my associate," the taller man said with a heavy accent.

David got up and followed him out of the compartment onto the weather deck. Once outside, he could see that he was indeed on a standard tramp cargo vessel lying at anchor. He followed the man up several flights of an exterior ladder and in through a hatch onto a bridge. Seated in one of the bridge chairs was Alexander Andreyev. He turned toward David as the men entered.

"Commander, at last we meet."

"Alexander Andreyev. I see you made it to Oslo after all," David said.

"Please, join me in my cabin," Andreyev said as he got up and walked toward a hatch that led down a short passageway to the captain's cabin. The others followed.

The cabin was twenty-five feet by thirty feet, with a bed, a table with five chairs, a small couch, and a high-back chair. Andreyev sat in the high-back chair as he motioned to David to sit on the couch. The other two men remained standing.

"Still in Oslo, Alexander? It seems that you're having as much trouble finding Doctor Choutov as we've had."

"Only a minor setback. As we speak, Severny is locating our missing doctor. We should have him back soon. Then we'll be back on track."

"On track to destroy the world?"

"I love you Americans! You are so dramatist."

"Dramatic."

"Yes, dramatic. Do not worry. Our Arab friends will not destroy the world. Just a bunch of Jews in Israel." He broke into a malicious laugh.

"If your associates release that virus in any major city, it will spread throughout the industrialized world in a matter of days. You're not talking about a remote village in Africa or South—"

"Dramatic. Da, you entertain me."

"By the time officials realize what they're dealing with, it'll have spread in such a way as to defy any possibility of quarantine."

"You worry too much. Our Russian scientists have developed a new virus of weapons grade. Kills very quickly. Then virus dies. Few are infected beyond the target area."

"Alexander, we have two of the Russian scientists working for us who worked on your virus. Like any government bureaucracy, your scientists exaggerated the reports to Moscow to keep their funding. The reality is that Russia never created a controllable virus."

Alexander stood. He was red in the face, and he shook his fist at David.

"Nothing has changed," he said. "You arrogant Americans. Superior to everyone. You will not accept that Russian scientists are better than American ones."

As Alexander stormed toward the door, David replied. "Alexander, you've been high up in your government's intelligence community. You would know if corruption and false reporting were common or not. Can you afford to take the chance I'm right?"

Alexander stopped, turned, and answered David. "I shall enjoy killing you myself. Insolent American dog!" He looked at the man dressed in the suit. "Lock him up. I will deal with him later."

Following Andreyev's order, the two men escorted David back to his compartment and chained him to his bed.

On board the USS *Peterson*.

The *Peterson* made its way down the Oslofjord and into the harbor under the cover of night. The ship had received permission to enter port and to anchor in a spot about two thousand yards from where most of the merchant vessels were lying.

The navigator started calling out distances to the anchorage every fifteen to twenty seconds. This went on for several minutes.

"Clear the stopper, stand by the anchor," Ted commanded.

"Forecastle, bridge. Clear the stopper, stand by the anchor."

"Forecastle, aye, sir."

"All stop."

"All stop."

"Release anchor."

"Forecastle, bridge. Release anchor."

The senior boatswainmate on the forecastle took the sledgehammer he was holding and hit the brake on the stopper, which caused the stopper to fall off and allowed the anchor chain to run.

"Anchor released, sir."

"Very well," Ted responded as he headed for the starboard bridge wing.

"Anchor set, sir. No dragging."

The boatswainmate of the watch immediately blew a long blast on a police whistle into the 1-MC.

"Anchored."

"Very well," Ted said.

"OK, Ted, set flight quarters and pass the word that the briefing in the wardroom is now underway," the captain said as he got up out of his bridge chair. "I'll be in my in-port cabin. Keep the watch on the bridge."

"Aye, sir. Boats, set flight quarters, then pass the word that a special briefing will commence in the wardroom, all hands stay clear of officer's country."

"Aye, sir. Captain's off the bridge," the boatswainmate sang out.

The pipe sounded attention over the 1-MC. "The Special Operations team briefing is commencing in the wardroom. Personnel not involved stand clear of officers' country. Officers' country is now a secure area. Now hear this. Flight quarters, flight quarters . . ."

In the wardroom eight members of the SEAL team and eighteen marines had assembled. Bob Reese walked in with the officer in charge of the SEAL team and the marine platoon leader.

"Attention on deck," the marine guard sounded out as he opened the door to admit Bob and the officers.

"Be seated, gentlemen," Bob said. "Our objective is the rescue of Captain Egan from the freighter *Kargina* . . ."

After a thorough briefing, Bob concluded. "Can I count on you?"

"Sir, yes, sir," they thundered back as the group jumped to their feet at attention.

"OK, check your gear and get going."

The senior chief petty officer of the SEAL team and the gunnery sergeant of the marine platoon started moving the men out of the wardroom as the two officers huddled with Bob for a last-minute discussion. Following this short discussion, Bob headed back to his operations center, and the two officers rejoined their men.

Within five minutes the first helicopter of marines was airborne. The deck crew started rolling the helicopter gunship out of the hanger. The motor whale boat on the starboard side and the captain's gig on the port side were lowered into the water. The SEAL team disembarked the *Peterson* from the fantail.

All of the small boats started the three thousand–yard trip to the *Kargina* as the helicopter gunship turned up its rotors and launched.

The battery-powered motors on the rubber SEAL team boats were quiet but slow. They had trouble keeping up with the motor whaleboat, which was not exactly a speedboat. Running without lights, it would be easy to hide the two power boats between the ships at anchor. However, the rubber boats with the SEALs would be exposed for the last eight hundred yards. It was hoped that they could make it undetected.

As soon as the hatch to the compartment closed, David began to feel his pockets to see if he had any of his tools.

The pens.

He pulled out the black one and put a small amount of acid on the chain near the point where it attached to the metal frame of the bed. The acid worked quickly. He got up from the bed and walked over to the hatch. Looking out the porthole, he saw a guard sitting on a chair. David moved back to the bed. As he did, he pulled a small metal chair over beside him. He arranged the chain so that it would appear to still be attached to the bed. With his free hand he used the chair to smash against the bulkhead as he began to yell for the guard.

"Da. Ameri-con butt of donkey. Why yelling?"

"I need to take a pee."

"What this pee?"

"I need to urinate."

"Use bucket," the guard said as he pointed to a five-gallon bucket in the corner.

David stood up beside the bed. "I'm not that good. I can't hit that far." He pointed to the chain on his wrist.

The Russian mumbled obscenities in Russian as he went over and picked up the bucket. He brought it across the room and bent over to set it down.

"Urinate."

As the Russian stood up, David unleashed a forward kick that hit the Russian and stunned him. David struck a second blow with his forearm. The Russian recovered quickly and lunged toward him, but David managed a blow to the Russian's knee. He stepped behind the Russian, took the chain, and wrapped it around the man's neck.

The Russian fought hard hitting David's ribs just before David snapped his neck.

Lucky . . . I gotta spend more time in the dojo.

He examined the dead Russian for weapons. He found one Glock .40 caliber and several clips of ammunition.

The blackened faces of the SEALs couldn't mask the tension among them. The eyes of the older petty officers were stern, fixed on every detail of the operation, while the eyes of the younger men betrayed apprehension.

"First live mission, Jennings?"

"Yes, senior chief."

"Well, this one's gonna be a cakewalk, son."

"Gonna kick some Russian butt," another man chimed in.

Jennings forced a smile and responded to a high five from his teammate.

The two boats approached undetected. Lieutenant Hansen spotted an armed man sitting on the starboard side, half asleep.

That'll be the guard assigned to watch Captain Egan.

He decided to approach the starboard bow of the freighter and cut the motor. Using a single oar, the men sculled the boat along the freighter's water line to the stern section of the freighter.

A four-inch hose used to pump oil-polluted bilge water from the ship ran from the main deck down to a doughnut tied beside the ship. The doughnut was secured to the ship by two double-braided two-inch lines. It was perfect for the SEAL team to use. They would not have to fire a line and grappling hook onto the main deck in order to get aboard. Each member of the team had a headset with small transmitters and receivers.

"Senior Chief, we have lines in place to get aboard. Do not fire your grappling hooks. We will drop you a line," Lieutenant Hansen said in a whisper into the microphone.

"Aye, sir."

The SEALs tied the rubber boat off and then shimmied up the two lines. Once aboard, two SEALs took ropes and went to the port side. They tied them off so the other boat team could come aboard. Lieutenant Hansen took a dart air rifle and a mirror and went to the corner looking up the starboard side of the ship. Using the mirror, he looked around the corner. Instead of the guard, he saw Captain Egan moving quietly toward him. He stood and stepped around the corner where David could see him.

"Well, I see Mother sent the cavalry."

"Captain, if you will follow me, we'll get you out of here."

Gunfire erupted. Rounds ricocheted off the bulkhead. One of Andreyev's men had stepped outside for a cigarette and saw the SEALs boarding on the port side. He opened fire and hit one of them. Another SEAL returned fire and killed him.

"Run aft, Captain," the officer yelled.

Lieutenant Hansen ran to the port side and helped carry the wounded SEAL as two more SEALs ran to the starboard side to provide cover. David grabbed one of the ropes and started to let himself down to the boat below. One of the SEALs followed him as the other hastily rigged a harness to lower the injured man.

Suddenly there was another burst of gunfire. The team backed up against the rear bulkhead out of the line of fire. The problem was getting over the side.

"Mother, we need a guardian angel to cover our starboard side egress, over," the SEAL officer said into his microphone. Within thirty seconds, the helicopter gunship came up on the starboard side and started to lay down covering fire. As it did, the SEAL team made it to the side and lowered the injured man.

The door to the stateroom flew open. "Alexander, the Americans have boarded," the man said in Russian. "They are all over the main deck."

Alexander had heard the initial gunshots. He had assumed that David had somehow gotten loose.

"How could the Americans know Egan's location? And so quickly?"

"Tracking device," Alexander said.

Suddenly the noise of the guns from the helicopter gunship could be heard as well as the sound of the rounds hitting the metal bulkheads.

"Is our package stored below?" Alexander said.

"Da."

"Go below. Prepare to depart. Do not let the crew see you. Send them out to fight the Americans. Use the missile."

The man nodded as Alexander went to his closet and pulled out a heavy wet suit. He quickly changed and then pulled his trousers and coat back on over the wet suit. After putting his shoes back on, he departed his stateroom. He walked as quickly as possible down five decks to a passageway that ran the length of the ship. Running forward, he went through hatch after hatch as he made his way toward the midships section of the ship. The passageway allowed access to several large storage compartments. As Alexander opened one of the watertight hatches, he could see his three associates preparing a four-man scuba submarine for departure.

"Mother, we need the gig along the starboard side now," the SEAL officer said as they were leaving the ship. The rubber boat, which had been along the starboard side, had already departed taking David, the injured SEAL, and two other men. The rest were left holding onto the ropes beside the ship.

The gig stood eight hundred yards off. It moved in quickly and scooted into position under the dangling men. All the while the gunship hovered off the starboard side and opened fire on anything that moved on the ship. After retrieving the stranded SEALs, the boats raced toward the *Peterson*. The gig pulled alongside the rubber boat David was aboard. Both boats stopped. David and the injured SEAL transferred to the gig while some of the extra men got into the rubber boat. They tied the rubber boat to the stern of the gig.

There was a loud explosion, and the helicopter gunship burst into flames. Andreyev's men had fired a handheld missile bringing the aircraft down. Then two more missiles were fired. They were aimed at the *Peterson*. One stuck the side halfway between the waterline and the main deck. It exploded with a massive fireball but did not actually penetrate the skin of the ship. The second missile hit the superstructure and did manage to rip a hole in the much thinner aluminum there.

The gig was within a few hundred yards of the *Peterson* and within range to hear the general quarters alarm sound on the ship. As the gig pulled alongside the ship, there was a flurry of activity as the crew went to general quarters and attended to the fire caused by the missile.

The boat crew recovered and hooked the gig up to the boat davit. Suddenly another burst of light followed by ear-piercing thunder and the shock wave of an explosion as another missile struck below the main deck just aft of the amidships boat davit. The ship's crewmen recovered from the explosion, then raised the gig up out of the water and swung it into its cradle. A stretcher detail waited to take the injured man to sick bay.

While they were dealing with the injured man, David left and moved as quickly as possible to the CIC.

"What air assets do you have available?" David demanded as he entered the CIC. Tony Scapecchi immediately got up from the command chair allowing David to sit down. "One helicopter with six marines, one F-14 on cap station in international—"

"Have the helo with the marines stand off. Bring your F-14 in." David ordered. "Tell the captain to load armor piercing shells. Weapons free."

"Bridge, flag plot. Load armor piercing. Weapons free."

David sat down and listened as the attack continued. "Bob, get a message off to the White House. Our ambassador is going to have to explain this one. Let 'em know that Andreyev is on board that ship. Tell 'em that we responded to an overt hostile attack on a U.S. man-of-war. Give 'em a casualty report."

TWENTY-TWO

Bridge of the *Peterson*.

"CAPTAIN, WEPS REPORTS STAR BURST LOADED AFT, ONE ROUND phosphorus loaded forward. Armor piercing to follow."

"Very well. Aft mount one round, shoot."

"Aft mount one round, shoot," the messenger called out into his headset. Moments later a thunderous thud was felt all over the ship as the aft five-inch mount fired the starburst. The sky over the harbor lit up.

"Shot, one round expended, bore clear," the messenger reported.

"Bridge, gun plot, solution set in."

"Very well, forward mount one round, shoot," the captain ordered.

"Forward mount one round shoot."

The ship shook as the forward mount fired a phosphorus round. It hit the freighter. "That's good shooting. Right on the mark," the captain said as he observed the round through his binoculars.

"Shot, one round expended. Bore clear, sir."

"Forward mount, ten rounds, shoot," the captain ordered.

"Forward mount, ten rounds, shoot," the messenger said.

The forward mount pumped out ten rounds of armor piercing in quick succession. A timpani hum resonated in the midst of the vibrations.

"Shot, ten rounds expended. Bore clear, sir."

Seven of the rounds hit the freighter. Because the ship was at anchor, the force of the guns firing caused the *Peterson* to shift its position. Three of the shells fell several yards away from the freighter. The one phosphorus round caused a conflagration on the main deck.

Two large gashes marred the side of the freighter from the armor-piercing shells. Numerous smaller explosions and fires could be seen just inside the skin of the freighter.

CIC.

"Commodore, bridge reports hits. Target is burning."

"Very well, break off the F-14," David ordered.

"Helicopter reports several men abandoning ship, requests instructions."

"Pick 'em up. Don't let anyone escape," David said.

The air controller passed the order to the helicopter. Reports continued to flow as the freighter burned. David monitored the activity for five minutes.

"Commodore, the bridge reports the freighter breaking up," a messenger called out.

"Very well. Have the captain weigh anchor and get out of here. Bring the helo with the marines back. I'll need it to get me ashore," David said.

Bob picked up the phone to relay the order to the captain as the air controller relayed the order for the helicopter to return. David got up and headed for the hangar to meet the chopper.

By the time David arrived on the flight deck, the helicopter was unloading the marines. He ran and climbed aboard. The air crewman strapped him in and gave him a set of headphones.

"What's your pleasure, Captain?" the pilot asked.

"Go to the city center. Keep your eyes open for any police or other activity. Come as low as possible. When you find a clear space, I'll repel out."

"Aye, sir."

The aircraft turned up the RPM and lifted off the deck. David motioned to have the crewman help him with a repelling harness and gloves. The crewman also gave David goggles.

Aboard the freighter.

The ship was a tramp steamer fitted with a special door just below the waterline on the starboard side. The doors were large enough to permit a two-man submarine to enter and exit. Alexander used the submarine to run cocaine from the ship to shore undetected.

The secret doors on the hull of the ship opened to a large holding tank within the skin of the ship. A mechanical boom overlooked the tank with the submarine attached by a single six-inch cable. Alexander's three associates were lowering the submarine into the tank when the first armor-piercing round hit. The explosion shook the whole ship throwing the men to the ground. It jammed the wench on the boom, leaving the submarine dangling just inches above the water in the tank.

"Where are the tools?" Alexander yelled.

One of the men pointed. Alexander ran to the chest and tossed aside wrenches, sockets, and calipers until he found a small-caliber pipe cutter. He mounted the boom and scurried out to the wire cable. Attaching the pipe cutter, he tightened down as he spun the cutter around the cable. Around and around. Strands of the cable started to spring back as the pipe cutter sliced.

"Hacksaw," he yelled.

Alexander continued to use the pipe cutter as one of the other men ran for a hacksaw. The man returned to the boom where he shimmied out to hand Alexander the saw. By that time Alexander had cut into over two-thirds of the cable. He couldn't tighten the pipe cutter any further so he removed it from the cable and reached for the saw. Just as he started cutting with the saw, a second shell exploded in the aft section of the ship near the engineering compartment.

This explosion created tremendous stress along the length of the ship, and the hull began to sheer and tear just forward of the superstructure. The shock threw two men in the compartment up against a bulkhead breaking one's shoulder and the other's neck. The third man on the boom was knocked unconscious and fell into the tank. Alexander managed to hold onto both the cable and the hacksaw. As soon as he regained his balance, he continued to saw feverishly. Suddenly, there was a high-pitched twang, and the cable gave way sending the submarine plummeting into the tank. Similar to a bungee cord, the cable slapped the overhead with a loud crash. Alexander dropped off the boom into the tank seconds before the cable snapped back to the boom.

"Get the air tanks, and open the outside door," Alexander shouted.

"What about the others?" his companion yelled in response.

"Leave them; we don't have time. Get the tanks and open the doors, now!"

Alexander jumped into the tank with the sub. He powered it up and then removed the hoisting harness.

The outside hull doors opened, and water rushed into the holding tank. It didn't take long for the tank, usually partially filled, to fill completely. Alexander's associate lowered the air tanks into the water and then jumped in. Both men quickly donned the tanks and cleared their masks.

The freighter began to list to one side, but not enough to reduce the necessary clearance for the submarine to maneuver. The two men guided it through the open doors in the hull. At the maximum speed of four knots, the sub inched away from the ship as it descended to thirty feet near the bottom of the harbor. When it was about forty feet away the ship, the forward part of the freighter sheered completely from the aft portion with the superstructure.

Both sections began to sink. The turbulence shook the sub. However, the sub was far enough away that it did not get sucked in by the effect of the freighter breaking up and sinking.

It took a while to traverse the harbor to the pier area. Since it was dark outside and the Americans were busy picking up anyone who jumped off the ship, the sub and its occupants managed to get away undetected. In the darkness, the helicopter crews did not see the trail of bubbles from the air tanks.

Alexander maneuvered the sub so that it settled on the bottom, and the two men exited and swam the few feet to the pier. They grabbed the metal ladder bolted to the far end of the pier and dropped their air tanks off into the water.

The pier itself was empty, although a few people had gathered at the head of the pier, drawn by the noise of the attack on the freighter. They were watching the police and the military as they investigated the site where the freighter sank. Alexander and his associate Nikolai stayed near the warehouses on the pier and in the shadows. Without warning, a door opened within several feet of them, and a warehouse guard stepped out onto the pier. Alexander signaled Nikolai who then slipped behind the guard unnoticed. Nikolai twisted the guards neck and broke it before the guard could respond. Both men dragged the guard back through the door into the warehouse.

"See if you can find coats or clothes in that office over there," Alexander whispered.

As Nikolai moved toward the office, Alexander began to undress the guard. He removed his wet suit and put on the guard's clothes. The trousers were so big in the waist that he had to gather a fistful of fabric to keep them from falling off. The hem struck his leg midway between the shin and the ankle. Alexander took a piece of rope lying near him and made a belt. Then he slipped on the gun and the guard's coat. The shoes were a bit large, so he wadded up some paper and stuffed the toes.

Nikolai came out wearing rubber rain trousers and a guard's overcoat. "It will have to do."

The two men departed the warehouse and walked to the end of the pier past the other guards who were preoccupied with the sights. Alexander and Nikolai disappeared into the night.

TWENTY-THREE

THE PILOT HOVERED THE BOEING SEA KNIGHT OVER A PARK ADJACENT to Frederiks Gate across from Oslo University. A Bell Super Cobra circled the park perimeter while David repelled from the Sea Knight. When he touched the ground, he quickly slipped off the harness and goggles and tied them to the line. The aircrew recovered them. David returned the aircrewman's salute and slipped off into shadows.

The distance from his drop-off location to the Bristol was several city blocks. David took off at a quick pace. He hurried into the hotel spotting only a doorman and the desk clerk.

David fumbled through his pockets.

The key? Severny took it.

He stepped over to the front desk where the clerk seemed to recognize him.

"I seemed to have misplaced my key card," David said. "Is it possible to—"

"Yah," the clerk said, smiling. He made several entries into his computer and placed a blank card in the coding machine. "It will have a new security code," he said handing the key to David. "The old card will not be working."

"Can I get breakfast sent to my room?" David asked.

"Yah. Are you knowing what you wish to order?"

"Yeah."

"Please, to be taking your order?"

"Scrambled eggs, toast, coffee. Breakfast meats?"

"Yah, we are having vhat you wish."

"Bacon then. Oh, and send up a bottle of Tabasco sauce. Make it two orders. One for my wife."

"Yah."

On the fourth floor David inserted the key into the room lock. Several CIA agents jumped out from adjoining rooms with their guns leveled in a firing position.

"Freeze."

Not again!

David slid his hands into the air.

"It's Captain Egan," one of the men remarked. He and the others checked their guns upward as the agent moved toward David.

"Sorry, Captain. We've moved your room for security reasons. If you'll follow me."

The agent led David down the hallway to his new room. He handed him a new coded key and then returned to his station. David started to enter the room but stopped and turned to the agent.

"I've ordered breakfast from room service," David said. "Better put someone inside the old room—"

"We'll take care of it, sir."

One soft light glimmered in a corner of the room. Catherine, still fully clothed, lay on top of the bed. It was as if she had been waiting up and had nodded off. David removed his shoes and lay down on the couch trying not to wake her.

"David?" she asked in a groggy tone.

He sat up. She got out of bed and went over to the couch beside him. She put her arms around his neck and embraced him.

"Thank God you're alive." Tears sparkled in her eyes.

David put his arms around her and pulled her close into a tender hug. He gently began to kiss her face. He worked his way to her lips for a more passionate embrace.

"We heard that you had been taken. I was so afraid that you had been killed," she said. "What happened?"

"We were ambushed. The prostitute was one of Andreyev's girls, and she led us into a trap. Andreyev felt that if he had me alive, it would distract our effort and would give him more of an edge in locating Choutov. He knew who Steve and I were, and he seemed to be one step ahead of us all the way."

"How could he know all of that information?" she asked as she sat up and leaned her head against his arm.

"Exactly what I wondered. Most of our original team's dead. He almost got Jim shortly after he arrived in Stockholm."

"Do you think there's a mole or a leak?"

"Where? The list of people who know is so very limited."

"The White House, Congress?"

"You know, I don't care for that man we have in the White House, but I have to believe it's not there. There's no possible advantage for him. Regardless of the fact that I have no respect for him, I just can't believe that he would knowingly allow millions of people to die."

"Yeah, but what about his staff?"

"No, there's a time lag for intelligence gleaned from secondary sources. Andreyev acted within hours against Jim and within a day regarding us. He knew too much too quickly for it to be information gleaned from an aide with loose lips."

"Congress?"

"I know the chairmen of the House and Senate oversight committees. I've briefed them before myself, and I don't believe they'd share that kind of information with aides or anyone."

"Then who?"

"Don't hate me for saying this, but for a while I thought it might be you."

"Yeah, I gathered that from your comment earlier. Still think I'm a rat?"

"It may have just been a series of circumstances, you know. Maybe a leak in the local station."

"You didn't answer my question."

"No. Of course I don't think it's you," he said. "It's just that Alexander and Severny seemed to know who was involved from the beginning. The circle of players was so limited. You know. I hope you can—"

"I understand all that. I just want to be sure—you trust me now?"

"I do. It's obvious," David said with a soft smile and a tender tone.

She stared intensely at him.

"They would have never kidnapped you," he continued, "if you were in league with Choutov. I didn't think when I spoke before. And, well, I guess I just stuck my foot into it. You know, since we've met, I've come to, ah." He paused for a moment searching for just the right words.

She smiled and looked at him with a slight tilt of the head. "Come to what?"

"Let's just say I care what happens to you." He paused, looked into her eyes, and then touched her cheek with a gentle caress.

Catherine dropped her eyes, looked at his chest, and then slowly looked up to meet his eyes as she slid her arms around his neck. They embraced in a long, tender kiss.

A pang of concern nagged at David.

Now's not the time to lose control over my emotions. It's a bad time to fall in love.

He withdrew suddenly and nervously cleared his throat. "We shouldn't. We need to put this on hold. We can't afford to get wrapped up in each other now. If we focus on each other, it makes it harder to concentrate on the mission. I should be continually reviewing, evaluating, and reassessing every little detail and event that happens. My every waking thought should be focused on stopping these men."

He paused and looked away from her. "As it is," he continued, "I'm becoming emotionally engaged. I spend more and more time thinking about you. It colors my judgment at a time when I need to be alert enough to be able to see the one small opportunity and to seize control of the circumstances when that opportunity presents itself."

Catherine saw his point. She also began to feel a little guilty. She'd been given a lot of responsibility and trust by her superiors.

David's right.

She'd let herself become too dependent on him. The mission had drifted into the background. Conviction seized her like a young child caught using her mother's forbidden makeup. She knew her passion needed to be focused on her job—not on him.

"I should'a never told you how much I'm attracted to you," he said. "It's not fair to you, and we ought'a just cool our interest in each other for now."

"I guess you're right."

When we get our hands on the weapon, I'll have to devote my complete attention to that task. I'd think he was a jerk if he expected me to pay attention to him just because he'd finished his part of the mission.

"Did I tell you we've thrown 'em a curve?" he said.

"How so?" A sense of relief surged through her.

Glad he changed the subject.

"Andreyev's dead. At least I assume he's dead."

"Andreyev? How?"

"He attacked the *Peterson* with missiles."

"What? Missiles? Here in the harbor?"

"Yeah. I ordered the ship he was on destroyed. We picked up the survivors. He wasn't among them."

"Are you sure he's dead?"

"Do you mean, do we have a dead body? No. But we know he was aboard. No one escaped before the ship went down."

David stood and walked to the bathroom area. "It's almost daybreak," he said. He lathered up to shave.

An unusual sense of anxiety gripped Catherine. A flash-back memory of sitting with her sister and her nieces playing a game raced through her consciousness.

What if we don't . . .

"David, are we gonna get Choutov?"

Half-shaven, he stopped and stood staring at his face in the mirror.

God help us. I'm out of ideas, and I don't see any options.

He took a deep breath. "It's not looking so good. The pros-titute angle is exhausted. Our only hope may be to spot him trying to leave the country. That's not an easy prospect though. It still poses a number of problems."

"What kinda' problems?"

"Well, one problem is that it would be very easy for him to rent an aircraft and fly to Holland or Denmark or England. We just don't have the assets to cover all possibilities—even with the local authorities involved."

"Yeah. But why go to the trouble if you can just jump on a scheduled commercial flight?"

"That's what we're banking on. It's a big roll of the dice. You know, the idea that he doesn't know everyone in the world is after him. If he's not been tipped off, maybe, just maybe, he'll use a regular commercial flight. That and us getting lucky. We need some luck right now."

"What about other problems?"

"I guess the biggest is Severny. He's still out there looking for Choutov. And Severny's very well connected in this part of the world."

"What do you have in mind for today?"

"Well, first we'll have breakfast. I need to stay here and mind the store. At noon we'll make contact at the Engebret Cafe. I'll redeploy our assets to the airport. This afternoon I want you to go and help watch the departing international flights. Bob'll arrange to have the local field office set you up as some kind of inspecting supervisor doing a spot inspection of SwissAir counter employees. That'll allow you to stand around behind the counter looking for Choutov as you monitor the clerks at the counter."

"And you?"

He came in wiping his face with a hand towel and sat down on the couch. "I'll return here and set up a communications base. By noon the Norwegian government will be in on the operation. I destroyed a ship in their harbor. You gotta admit, the boys at State have their work cut out for them. It'll be hard to keep the locals out."

"Yeah, I hear you. Shooting down airplanes, sinking ships—must be a testosterone thing." She had a large grin.

Glad she can joke about it. If we don't succeed, State is going to hang me from the highest yardarm in the navy.

"I could use the extra manpower," he said. "We'll use their manpower to cover every hotel lobby in the city center area and most of the restaurants. They can also watch the streets and adult shops. Maybe we'll get lucky and he'll want a woman before he leaves."

"I hope so," Catherine said as she walked over to her luggage. She picked out a change of clothes. "I'm going to take a quick shower."

"Oh, I've been separated from my cellular phone. May I take yours?" he asked.

"Sure, it's in my handbag. I'll get it for you when I get out."

David sat down to relax. He began to think about other ways Choutov could get out of the country when he was interrupted by a knock at the door. He pulled out the Glock .40 caliber he'd taken off the Russian.

"Who is it?"

"Russ Baker, sir. Your room service tray is here."

"Thank you. Leave it at the door please."

"Yes, sir."

David waited for a minute until the agent returned to the decoy room. Then, he opened the door and pulled the cart into the room. Catherine walked out dressed in a bathrobe with a towel in a turbanlike crown.

"Breakfast is here. I hope you didn't mind my ordering for both of us," David said.

"No problem. I could eat anything, now."

David set the food onto the table, and they both sat down to eat. While they were eating, they heard a knock on the adjoining room door.

"Come in," David said.

Brian Thompson entered.

"Captain Egan, I'm Brian Thompson. I'm replacing Steve Hsieh."

"Good to meet you, Brian. Excuse me for not shaking your hand."

"That's quite all right. Captain, I've several men on this floor monitoring your old room. Do you want me to pull them off?"

"Absolutely. I want all hands covering the airports. In fact, why don't you go ahead and redeploy all the troops. I've asked for local assistance for the hotels and restaurants. Be back here at noon."

"And the working girls?"

"Did the local station office lose any men during the raid last night?" David asked.

"One."

"Do we have a real line on a referral network, or was that part of Severny's setup?" David asked.

"That's hard to say. Yes, there is a network of hotel clerks and taxi drivers and the like who refer inquiring minds to certain girls. However, while this is legal, recreational drugs, rackets, and those kinds of activities are still illegal. Local organized crime is always gonna be around. That's why Severny had no problem using the network for his plan."

"Go ahead and identify yourself to the new local station chief and take over that operation. Spread some money around and put the word out that we're paying a quarter of a million dollars to the person who leads us to Choutov."

"What about watching the girls?" Brian asked.

"Cease the surveillance on the girls. Keep a few men in reserve as a rapid reaction team. It's 7:30 in the morning. I doubt too many girls are on the streets before mid-afternoon."

"Yeah, but Choutov managed to find one in the morning yesterday."

"True, but he's gonna have to leave Oslo in the next twenty-four hours if he wants to make the original rendezvous in Spain. We only have so much in terms of manpower assets. Let's spread his picture around with the money. A quarter of a million is a huge payday for any desk clerk. If he goes for a hooker today, they're gonna be our best lead to finding out."

"Catherine, your SwissAir uniform is on the way over," Brian said. "Would you like me to get it for you so you can get dressed?"

"Thanks, Brian. If you'll just hang it there in the closet."

With that, Brian disappeared into the other room. He reappeared moments later with a laptop and radio equipment. He fixed a small satellite antenna in the window and plugged the antenna into the other electronics.

"Mother is on-line by secure satellite uplink. If you don't mind, please monitor this until I return?"

"No problem," David said.

Catherine finished eating and began to clear away her dishes. David finished his meal.

"You know, we haven't had much of an opportunity to talk since we've been together," she said as she sat on the couch.

"Oh, what would you like to talk about?"

"It seems we've been through so much together, you know. We've become partners and all. Yet I really don't know much about you," she said with a shy smile. "I thought we might relax and get to know a little bit about each other."

"What's there to know?" David said. He was thinking about how much he hated this kind of touchy-feely conversation, the kind that women so enjoy. "I am a forty-year-old widowed man who's midlife crisis is absorbed with running around with a beautiful woman trying to save the world." He smiled.

"Come on now, I'm serious. I want to know more about you."

"What do you want to know?"

Humor isn't gonna get me out of this conversation.

"Well, I know you can tell one classical piece of music from another—shows good breeding, or at least some sophistication."

"I'll have to tell my parents," he said with a jovial tone. "They'll appreciate the compliment."

She lowered her eyebrows and glared at him.

She's determined to have this conversation.

She softened her look and continued. "You're something of a philosopher with nutty ideas about science and evolution."

"Nutty?"

"Yeah, nutty."

"Well, I've been called worse. OK, what do you want to know about me?"

"Tell me about your wife. Rebecca was her name, wasn't it?"

"Yeah, Rebecca."

"How'd you two fall in love? What was she like?"

"I thought you wanted to know about me."

"I do. You can learn a lot about people by looking at the company they keep."

"I'm not sure I can give you a realistic picture. When you lose someone who's the center of your universe, you tend to forget any negatives. You know, you only hold onto the good memories," he said. "What about you? Tell me about some of your past loves."

"I asked first. Besides, don't you know that all us women are suckers for a good love story? That's why romance novels are so popular. I want to hear about how you two met and fell in love."

He took a dramatic breath, betraying his level of discomfort. "I was a junior. She was a freshman. I was part of Sigma Alpha Epsilon, and she was attending a rush party for one of the campus sororities. She was terrific. Somewhat reserved but a knockout."

"What'd you like best?"

"The thing that was most attractive, and she had a lot going for her, was her disarming smile. She just seemed so genuine, you know, in the midst of a lot of people who were pretty good at putting on a mask. I'm sure you know what I mean."

"I think so."

"We danced and we talked. I was hooked from the very beginning."

"Why? Was it looks?"

"Hmmm, yeah, a large part of it. Rebecca was certainly one of the better looking girls I'd ever dated. But she had a little more going for her. For one thing, she looked at you and showed a genuine interest in what you were saying. You know us guys, everything we say is profound."

Catherine chuckled.

"We ended up talking for hours that night—about everything. She was smart and laughed at my jokes, which is very important," he said with a wink. "She was stimulating."

"So you liked her for more than her looks?"

"Oh, yeah. Rebecca had a positive view on life and a relaxed manner about her. She was confident but not arrogant. And she was affirming.

"Affirming?"

"Yeah. In all the years I knew her, I can't remember her using slights toward someone. You know, to achieve a psychological advantage."

"She sounds too good to be true."

"I warned you. . . ."

"You're right, I'm sorry. I'm sure she was a very affirming person. It's only natural for you to remember her positive traits. Please, go on. What happened after your first meeting?"

"Well, I was smitten. I had dated some but hadn't found anyone that swept me off my feet, so to speak. The sorority girls seemed to be into looks and were somewhat status conscious. The non-Greeks tended to be hippies. All of 'em had to be smart to be there in the first place. But you didn't pick that up from a lot of the sorority sisters. Even though they acted like airheads, I tended to date the sorority chicks. It was natural."

"Cause they acted dumb and easy?"

"No," he said emphatically but with a smile. "I was in a fraternity. I wasn't into drugs. Anyhow, Rebecca was just different. I thought that the first night. So I asked her out for the next evening. We started dating, and I never saw anyone else after that."

"I was thinking about a comment you made last night. It led me to believe you hadn't had a whole lot of experience."

"Rebecca was the first person I ever connected with emotionally. After I met her, she was the only girl for me."

"How'd you stay faithful? Being a spy and all."

"I think you watch too much TV. Most intelligence work involves watching and evaluating. As a young SEAL officer, I was involved in only a few real covert operations. And they were all male parties. The rest of the time I did office-type work. I was no more or less subject to an affair than any other man who goes to an office every day."

"What about GRAPO? Didn't sound like that was a desk job."

"Well, there was some fieldwork, but intelligence work usually involves collecting information and evaluating it. Even that operation was fairly routine. I was helping the Spanish government round up terrorists. They did most of the grunt work."

"You have to forgive me," she said. "I'm new as the CDC's liaison to the CIA. I've never been on an operation before this one. I just assumed all field operations had drama and romance."

"No. We're not a bunch of 007s shooting up the bad guys and saving the day because of our ability to sweep gorgeous women off their feet." He smiled. "Now, it's your turn. Tell me about your love life."

Catherine blushed a bit and shifted positions. "Well, I really don't have much to tell. In high school I didn't start dating until I was a junior. At first most of the boys were part of our church youth group. Some pushed a little, but I managed to keep them at arm's length. In the summer between my junior and senior year, I started dating a popular guy from school. He really pushed, and I almost gave in."

"What kept you from giving in?"

"Two things really. First, I grew up in the First Baptist Church of Snellville, Georgia, outside of Atlanta. My father's a deacon. We were very faithful church members. I felt really guilty about the petting. I wanted to save myself. The second reason was that the guy made me angry."

"He made you angry?"

"Yeah! Homecoming was just before Thanksgiving. It was a real honor to have him as a boyfriend and date, or so he thought. He delivered an ultimatum. Put out or he'd take someone else to the homecoming."

"And?"

"Well, he took someone who was happy to put out for him. I stayed home crying."

"Sorry. That must have hurt a lot."

"More than you could imagine. But I think it was good for me in several ways."

"How so?"

"I paid more attention to school than boys from then on. I'd always done well, but now I wanted to be the best, and I made it. That carried on to Georgia Tech and set me on my way toward my Masters and Ph.D. Also, I felt good about myself. I hadn't given in to that kind of pressure. I think it helped me in all my future relationships. I learned that there is always someone who's gonna seek out an emotional weakness and try to take advantage of it. I think that helped me in a lot of ways not to let others just run over me."

"It's curious that you learned a lesson from your disappointment. Some women would have become bitter, maybe even begin to distrust men."

"Oh, I was bitter for a while. But it ended. Since then, I met a lot of nice guys and some real skunks. But you know, I realized that guys came with varied emotional packaging, just like women. Everyone's a player in life's games. What I wanted was to find a man that played on my team—someone who affirmed, maybe even led, but looked out for my welfare."

"Did you ever find this guy?"

"I'm not sure yet" she said coyly. David started to blush.

"What happened after high school?"

"Georgia Tech. I was a biology major. Everything was precise. In the middle of my freshman year, I met a sophomore philosopher."

"Philosophy major? At Georgia Tech?"

"Actually, his degree program was public policy, or some such thing. Now that you mention it, I don't know why he chose Tech. Maybe he was realistic enough to know how hard it would be to support yourself in the humanities."

"That'd make sense."

"He was a romantic. He wrote poetry and he loved music. He seemed to love life. He was so different from all the other men I knew in my classes. They all seemed so serious and technically minded." She smiled. "Aren't too many philosophers at Tech, after all. Anyhow, it was what I call my hippie year. We dated for a while, and just before the summer break we went a little too far."

"And?"

"Well, all summer I felt guilty. My strong religious upbringing, you know. We had planned to get together for a trip to Florida, but something came up and he couldn't make it. I called him and wrote him, and he returned some of my letters. He called me once. I had a feeling that something had changed in our relationship, but it really wasn't clear until we got back to school in the fall."

"What happened?"

"I realized that as long as I wanted to add to his existential enjoyment of life, our relationship was OK, but he wasn't interested in what made me tick. If I wanted to walk barefoot in the rain, or listen to him spout poetry, or listen to his nutty philosophy, he was great. But he had no interest in going with me to anything that might be scientific, and he was really intolerant any time I defended science or scientific pursuits in discussions."

"Nutty philosophy, huh. Seems you used that term to describe some of my thoughts."

"Now who's getting defensive?" she said. "Besides, your nutty philosophy made some sense. I just don't think you appreciate how much empirical evidence there is to support natural selection. Of course, if your theory about the earth's crust shifting on its core every forty or fifty thousand years is true, we scientists are going to look like those middle-age scholars who were sure the earth was flat. And you, my dear, nutty, warrior philosopher, you're gonna look like Copernicus."

"Well, I hope so. Better Copernicus than Don Quixote."

Catherine giggled. Her giggle set him to chuckling at his own joke.

"I'm not sure my geological theory has anything to do with evolution," he said. "But I digress. I don't want to get off onto my nutty philosophies. Please, go on. What happened to him?"

"We had a rocky fall semester. At one point before the Thanksgiving break, he let me know that he really believed in free love. He wanted to make it with someone else, but he wanted to continue to see me too. He felt we needed to do away with the shackles of archaic moral norms and the outdated concepts of monogamy. I realized he was just another jerk, another emotional taker. He simply had a fancy intellectual packaging for it. So I told him where to put his philosophy."

"Wow, two strikes," David said. "I guess we guys weren't doing so good?"

"I suppose. But I really didn't impute it to all men. I dated some and had a couple other boyfriends in college. But I focused on my schoolwork and spent most of my time with my studies. I just didn't let anything get serious."

"What happened after you graduated? I would imagine that with your looks you always had plenty of opportunity."

"Now you're flattering me," she said with a wink. "I've had occasional romances over the years but only one other love. I met him after my first year in the Master's program. He was a marketing representative for a computer company. We met at a party through a mutual friend. We dated off and on for a long while. Then one day he professed his love to me and asked me to marry him. I found him charming and intelligent. He was good looking and had a positive self-image, and he seemed like the faithful type. He went to church and came from a churchgoing family. His parents had been married over thirty years, as had mine. I felt like he had the kind of Christian values to become a stable, loving husband. I agreed. That was in September, and we planned a June wedding."

"What happened? Did you get married?" David asked.

"No. In January, he got killed on Interstate 85 heading into the city." Tears welled up in her eyes.

David got up and pulled his chair around beside hers. He put his arm around her and gently pulled her close to him in a hug. She began to cry quietly. For a few minutes neither spoke as she cried. Then she reached out and took a cloth napkin from the table and dried her eyes.

"Well, I haven't cried like that for years."

"I understand. I still find myself crying once in a while when I think about Rebecca. It's hard to lose someone you love. At least you had a real love. You'll find that again."

Catherine got up and put her arms around his neck and kissed him gently on the cheek. She smiled and then walked over to the bathroom and pulled on a pair of sweatpants and a sweater.

"You seem to have had a strong church background. How do you square your Christian beliefs with your views of creation and evolution?" David asked. "Don't you think there is an underlying assumption in the scientific community that one of these days we'll answer enough questions so that we won't need a God to believe in? That's what the rationalists have been espousing for years."

Catherine came out from the bathroom area and sat down on the couch. "I can tell you like deep metaphysical discussions," she said with a smile.

"Occupational hazard for nutty philosophers."

"Actually, I avoid thinking about the question," she said. "From time to time I have some doubts, but I just focus on other things."

"I do that sometimes. The questions still come back. Don't the questions nag at you? How do you know? Is God real or just an idea? Sometimes it bugs me."

"No. The questions come and go, but they don't nag at me. When I was nine, I answered an invitation in church to receive Christ as my Savior, and I was baptized. I was told then and all my life from that point that if I accepted Christ, I'd be saved and couldn't lose that. I've always looked back to that time."

"So, you're a good faithful Baptist? Go to church every Sunday?"

"Well . . . no, not always faithful. I'm what a lot of people call a 'backslidden Baptist.'"

"But you believe you're going to heaven and all of that stuff?"

"Yeah."

"And it doesn't matter how you live?"

"No, it's not based on what we do, if we accept Christ."

"So, you've taken out a great big cosmic fire insurance policy by responding to an invitation. Now you can basically live any way you want. Not a bad deal."

"Well, no. You can't live any way you want."

"Why not? If your salvation is based on responding to an invitation and you can't lose your salvation, then what prevents you from living any way you want? According to your premise, you're going to heaven anyhow."

"You're twisting what I mean to say. No you can't go around killing people and the like and expect to get into heaven."

"But you can be 'backslidden,' as you call it, and get into heaven?"

"Well, yes, there's always forgiveness."

"Oh, so now we have greater and lesser sins. If you kill, that's a big one, but if you cheat or steal or have an affair, that's a lesser one. If you only do the lesser ones, you can ask forgiveness at the last minute and it's all OK. Doesn't that sound like the Roman Catholic concepts of sin and penitence?"

By this time Catherine's faced turned red. Her lips thinned out, and she appeared to be clenching her teeth. David realized he had pushed her a little too hard. After all, this was the belief system she'd grown up accepting, and she was comfortable with it. No one likes to have his or her basic beliefs challenged.

"No," she said in a stern tone. "It's not at all like that!"

She's angry.

She defiantly folded her arms across her chest.

"Your beliefs are similar to Rebecca's," David said to defuse and soften the situation.

She stared at him. A long moment of silence passed between them.

"Oh," she finally responded. "I thought you said that you weren't religious. I assumed that Rebecca was of a similar mind. Was she a Christian?"

"Yes. Several years before she died, I was stationed at the White House. We lived in Annapolis, Maryland. She got involved in a Presbyterian Church there and ended up joining it."

"I always heard that Presbyterians were kind of liberal. You know, about the Bible."

"Yeah," he said. "I didn't know much about 'em until she got involved in that church. I guess Presbyterian churches are not all alike. The church she became involved in believed the Bible completely. The preacher believed that it was accurate, or as he called it, 'inerrant.'"

"Did you get involved?" Her countenance softened some. A raised eyebrow betrayed her interest.

"Sometimes. I was kind of busy and often away, but I went with her most Sunday mornings when I was home. My two boys were active in the youth group. I appreciated the church if for no other reason than that. I liked the preacher and the people there."

"You said that her beliefs were similar to mine?"

"She also believed that salvation was obtained by a belief in Christ. These people believed that the essence of salvation was trusting in the message that God became man, that is, Christ, and that he died for sins. Salvation was achieved when Christ died. Salvation's given as a gift. You know, something you can't earn. Like you, she believed that once you received this gift, it couldn't be lost."

"That sounds a lot like what Baptists teach," she said in a puzzled tone. "I always heard that Presbyterians were like, well, Catholics. You know, that baptism and being in the church saved you. How were her beliefs different from mine?"

"Well, I read up on some of this theology after she died. The pastor was very compassionate. He spent a lot of time talking with me over several months. We still write each other once or twice a year. I'm not sure how much of what he said she believed about Presbyterian beliefs."

"I understand. What did he say about their beliefs that were different from mine?"

"First, they believed that salvation happened on the cross. It doesn't come by answering an invitation. Although most people do answer an invitation."

"Now there's some fancy theological double-talk."

"Maybe," he said. "But it does hang together logically."

"Go on. I'm curious. How?"

"Well, Presbyterians are Calvinistic. They believe that men and women are spiritually dead. Men won't accept this message of salvation until the Holy Spirit makes a person alive. When this supernatural birth occurs, men and women see their sin and turn in repentance and faith and accept Christ. In other words, people don't get saved by accepting the invitation; their acceptance of the invitation is just a reaction to something that's already happened."

"Some Christians believe that you come to Christ by accepting an invitation to believe in Christ," she said.

"There is one slight difference. Does this supernatural act of being born again, as some people like to call it, happen before or after the acceptance of the offer of salvation?"

"Why after," she said.

"Not according to Calvinists. They say that the supernatural act of the Holy Spirit happens before. The emotional response of accepting an invitation occurs because a man or woman suddenly becomes alive spiritually and thereby sees his or her sin and wants to repent. In fact, they go a step further. Some of them even say that an individual doesn't have to make an actual verbal profession of faith since the work of salvation occurred on the cross. Their salvation is based on what Christ did and not the act of professing one's faith."

"I guess I've never really thought about when the precise moment of being born again occurs. So how are they different in regard to losing salvation?"

"Here it's a little fuzzy to me. Like you, they believe that once you become a Christian you can't lose your salvation. But they also have this view that you're changed supernaturally and start acting and growing in holiness because you can't help it. They don't believe that a Christian can keep on sinning for any length of time. When a Christian starts sinning, the new person inside makes 'em so uncomfortable that they turn back. Short-term backsliders, you might say."

"I don't think I've ever heard that term before."

David grinned. "I just made it up."

"Now you're a warrior theologian?" She smiled back at him.

"Their belief system is all tied up in the concept that God did this work of salvation from beginning to end. He decided everything before the foundation of the world. Then, he became a man and died. As the Holy Spirit, he now brings people to faith."

"So, how did you respond to this?"

"Well, after Rebecca died, I wanted to believe in God and heaven. You know, that she'd be there and that I'd someday join her.

"I can understand that."

"The problem was that you had to make this leap of faith. You had to believe that there was a God, that Jesus was the Christ, and that he died for you. All I had to do was trust in what he did on that cross."

"Why do you call it a leap of faith?"

"Maybe that's the wrong term. I mean that the faith itself was a gift. I didn't have it. And I knew it. I wanted to accept, but, deep down, I just couldn't. According to the pastor, all my good works and church attendance wouldn't earn me the faith. The faith was a gift. I just didn't accept all of this."

"So what did the minister say when you told him this?" she asked.

"It was kind of an existential response. He said that if I truly wanted to know God, God would find me. He went on to say that I didn't really believe deep down that I needed God. Until I really understood my need, I couldn't appreciate the way God has provided for my need. According to him, God meets each person at some personal place in their lives. Rebecca's death may be just the beginning of my quest."

"What'd you think about his answer?"

"It left me empty, even a bit angry at God. I wanted to be sure that Rebecca and I would one day be reunited. There was no way I could make that happen. I hate to think I didn't get a chance because I wasn't part of some group called the 'elect.'"

"Yeah, I've never understood that election doctrine, although I know it's mentioned in several places in the New Testament. Our pastor used to tell us that he didn't understand all its implications but he believed it because it was there. He always breezed over it when he was preaching and came to it in the Bible."

"This pastor talked a lot about Martin Luther's conversion experience," David said. "He pointed me to a book Luther wrote called *The Bondage of the Will*."

"Did you ever read the book?"

"No, but I did purchase it," he said with a slight smile. "One day I'll get around to reading it. This mission has stimulated my interest in religion again. I guess it's the prospect of millions of people dying that causes one to become a little reflective."

"A little reflective!"

"OK, a whole lot reflective."

"Black Tiger, this is Mother, over."

David walked over to the radio and answered. "Mother, this is David Egan. I'm minding the store for now."

"David, meet the desk clerk at the Hotel Continental near the city center. He may have information regarding our doctor. Jim will join you in your lobby, over."

"Understood, out."

"Well, sweetheart, back to the salt mines," David said.

Catherine walked up and put her arms around him and then hugged him. She didn't lean in or in any way offer more than a hug.

"You be careful this time. I couldn't stand it last time when I thought you were dead," she said with a genuine look of concern on her face.

"I'm flattered that you feel that way," David said as he gave her a reassuring hug.

"Well, I'm a sucker for nutty philosophers," she said with a wink. She sat down on the couch as he went across the room to pick up his coat.

I could fall hard for this one. David opened the door. *Maybe I already have.*

TWENTY-FOUR

Oslo. Inter Nor Hotel Bristol.

SEVERNY IOURTACHAK SAT IN HIS HOTEL ROOM WAITING FOR A response from associates in the Oslo underground. Earlier that morning, he had given them photographs of Choutov and asked them to make the rounds of hotels, cabs, bartenders, hookers, and anyone who might have seen Choutov. Offering anyone a large monetary reward for information, he also promised the leaders of the local drug syndicate a substantial stake in a large drug buy if they came up with the information. By the time the Americans began to circulate their large offer, every thug in Oslo was beating the streets circulating Choutov's photograph. With the Americans offering a cool quarter of a million, a hotel clerk or bartender stood the chance of making a fortune by passing the information to both sides.

What the Americans, and Severny, did not know was that the Russians had been circulating Choutov's photograph two days earlier. Shortly after the incident with the airliner and the MIGs, the Russians received a tip from a local hotel clerk regarding Choutov. The Russian Intelligence Service intercepted Choutov and had him in custody at the Russian embassy.

In their usually heavy-handed manner, the Russians were torturing Choutov to get him to tell them where the virus was hidden. They searched his room and found no sign of it. Choutov resisted beatings, electrical shock, mutilations, and even sodium pentothal. They had stronger drugs, but they feared damaging his memory. After hours of torture, Choutov passed out, and the Russians decided to let him rest. They were confident they would break him in time.

It was dinnertime. Severny was confident that he would soon have Choutov and the weapon in hand. He left his room and went down to the library bar where he ordered a sandwich. One of his men came in and sat down beside him. The man's eyebrows furrowed, causing deep ruts in his forehead. He fidgeted with an ink pen in his right hand.

"I think we have a lead on Choutov," the man reported in Russian.

"Good."

"He was staying in the same hotel where the woman died yesterday."

"Is he still there?"

"No," he said, then cleared his voice. "He did not check out. However, a diplomat from the Russian embassy paid for his room and asked to have his belongings delivered to the embassy. That happened this morning."

"Why has it taken so long to find this out?"

"The clerk who gave us this information did not come on duty until late this afternoon. He remembered Choutov from when he checked in. As soon as he saw his picture, he went to check and see if Choutov was still there. He found that the doctor had checked out and the bill had been paid by the embassy. There was also a note that his personal belongings had been delivered per the embassy's request."

"That is not good news. We must act quickly. I doubt he had the weapon in his room. They will not move him from the embassy until they have found the location of the weapon," Severny said.

"That sounds logical."

"Where is Mikhail Kruzanshtern?"

"In his room, I believe."

"Have him meet me in ten minutes in my room. Tell him I want a layout of the Russian Embassy." The man left. Severny finished his meal and returned to his room. Ten minutes later, Mikhail, Alexei, and Anatoly joined Severny to map out a plan of action.

TWENTY-FIVE

S EVERNY CONTINUED TO STUDY THE PLANS. WHAT WERE THE POSSIBLE ways that the plan could unravel? Was he was missing anything? He went over every detail, including the strengths and weaknesses of each man involved in the plan. Satisfied that he had covered all the angles, he slumped into a chair.

Ilya Choutov. I took your bull as a child. I watched my brother's heart break as he longed for Lara. But no, he was too much of a friend to make a play for her. It's payback. . . .

The fire blazed in the huge fireplace casting an amber hue through the room. Several dim standing lamps provided additional light. The heavy velvet curtains were pulled to overlap, and the window shutters were closed to help keep the heat in the room. Even with the fire and the radiator going, the large rooms of the old Leningrad homes couldn't keep the heat. The floors always seemed damp and cold.

I too shall have my reward. Alexander is stationed in Paris, and Grigori is dead. She needs a man. She needs to know she is alive.

"Have you heard from Alexander?" Severny asked as Lara entered the room with their drinks.

"No. We do not speak much anymore."

"Ilya?"

A look of pain crossed her face. "No. He has become too important. He no longer thinks our love is worth risking Alexander's wrath."

"You must not be too hard on him. After all, your husband is the third most powerful man in the whole country. Can you blame him for fearing Alexander?"

"No."

"You must look to the future. You must take a new lover. A dozen new lovers." Severny smiled.

"Oh, I do not know if I ever will. I have made such a mess of my life."

"It is wrong for such a beautiful woman to have so little joy. You deserve so much better." Severny gently touched her cheek.

"Severny, you and Grigori have always been such good friends."

Severny put his arm around her shoulder and began to gently massage the back of her neck. "You know we both loved you since we were children? Grigori and I would sometimes fight over who would marry you."

"You are kidding."

"No. We would. Once, when we were eight, we took sticks and had a sword fight to the death. The winner got your hand in marriage."

Lara smiled. "To the death? Well, who won?"

Severny moved in quickly and pressed his lips to hers in a firm embrace. He held her tightly as she pushed against him.

"No, Severny. This is wrong. We are friends," she said pushing away.

He removed his shirt. The dancing light from the fireplace highlighted his chest and shoulders. Each muscle was substantial, yet lean; an obvious result of weight training modified by a rigorous martial arts routine.

"Da. And now we can be lovers."

Severny grabbed the drink Lara had brought in earlier, and flopped down on the couch. Lara laid on the floor quietly sobbing.

"Stop your whimpering."

"How could you do this? We were friends. I thought—"

"Nyet. Friends? Nyet, nyet!"

"But those years at the university? We—"

"We, nyet. It was you, Grigori, and Ilya."

"Is that what all this is about?"

"Shut up. You begin to bore me."

"Alexander's going to kill you for this."

Severny broke into a contemptuous laugh. "That old fool. He is not going to kill me. He is afraid of me. If he were to put out a hit order, I would know it before it left his office, and he knows it. A thousand charging horses could not save him. I am the world's best assassin."

"Ilya. He still loves me, I know it. When he finds—"

"Nyet." Severny broke into gales of laughter. "Ilya?" he howled. Lara's sobbing grew with the intensity of Severny's amusement.

"Loves you?" he said as he calmed down. "The wimp won't even touch you out of fear of Alexander. You think he is going to take on a trained assassin?"

She glared at him. "Then I will kill you!"

Severny chuckled. "No, my dear. You will not kill me. You will do whatever I want. Otherwise, your dear estranged husband will learn of your affair with Ilya. And Tatyana."

"He told you. He promised he—"

"Brothers have no secrets."

"You cannot—"

"Da. I can. And I will. Unless you do as I say."

She turned her head away as the tears began to flow again. "Do not hurt Tatyana. I will do as you want."

"Da, you will. Do not concern yourself with telling Ilya. One day I will tell him—"

TWENTY-SIX

MIKHAIL WAS BUSY. HE ASSEMBLED TWO SMALL BACKPACKS WITH plastic explosives and a radio-controlled detonator. Then he connected a multiple port regulator to several bottles of compressed nitrous oxide and compressed helium and fed the output line into the air-conditioning system. He set the flow regulator mix with just enough helium to enhance the normal absorption rate of the nitrous oxide. Next he checked each gas mask to ensure each one had a full canister of air.

"Severny told me to check and see if you need any help," Anatoly said as he entered the room.

"Da. Good, I see you are back and changed. Gather weapons and ammunition for each of us. Put them in those black nylon bags, and take them down to the van. Then meet back in Severny's room."

As Anatoly was preparing the weapons, Alexei entered.

"Mikhail, is there anything I can do to help?"

"Da, while I change, take those two duffel bags on the bed and that bottle of gas down to the van. Meet back in Severny's room."

Both men did as Mikhail asked. When Mikhail finished changing his clothes, he came out and opened a trunk. He removed four radio communication headsets, put new batteries in each, and then put them in a black nylon bag. Then, he took out four sets of night goggles and put them into the bag. He closed the rest of his luggage and set it beside the bed ready for a hotel porter. He turned off the light and proceeded down the hall to Severny's room.

"Were you seen?" Severny asked.

"No," Anatoly responded. "We took the service elevator to the basement. I have locked it out of service on this floor."

"Good, let's do it."

The four men exited the room and took the service elevator without stopping until the basement.

A hotel maid stood waiting for the elevator.

"This is for hotel staff use," she said in Norwegian. "We ask our guests to use the better main elevators over there."

"Thank you," Anatoly said. "We'll remember that."

They walked to the van and pulled out of the parking area unnoticed. Two blocks down the street, they saw a man similar in build to Choutov.

"Pull up," Severny ordered as he rolled down his window. The van pulled up beside the man who smiled politely. "Do you speak English?" Severny asked.

"Yah, I can help you," the man said.

"Great, I'm trying to find this street," Severny said pointing to a map. Then he opened the door and stepped out. "Can you help me find this?"

"Yah."

The man stepped over to the side of the van beside Severny. A side door opened and Anatoly smiled at the man.

The man returned the smile. "Goot night."

"Da. Goot night." Anatoly raised a silenced weapon and shot the man in the head. Severny pushed the man, and the body fell inside the van. Mikhail and Anatoly dragged him in as Severny shut the sliding van door. He jumped in and Alexei drove off.

The van stopped one-half block from the front of the embassy. Mikhail and Anatoly got out dressed in their Russian military uniforms. Anatoly carried a nylon bag with weapons and the plastic explosive. Mikhail carried a bag with knockout gas and two gas masks and two sets of night-vision goggles. The van pulled away as Mikhail put his headset on to listen for the signal.

Severny and Alexei pulled the van into the alley behind the building and got out. Each put on a gas mask and radio headgear. The night goggles were in a pouchlike belt, which they would wear around their waists. Both had silenced automatics carried in a side holster and an uzi on a shoulder strap. They maneuvered toward the door along the edge of the building. The door opened, and one of the kitchen boys appeared dragging a huge trash can. Severny pointed to the door, and Alexei moved to catch it before it closed. Severny snuck up behind the boy with the trash and placed a single blow to break his neck. The boy fell limp to the ground.

Severny and Alexei entered the kitchen unnoticed. The kitchen was a long room divided by a work and storage island. On one wall were several deep sinks and on the opposite wall a large industrial grill. At the far end of the kitchen was a walk-in freezer.

The kitchen crew was busy cleaning up, and the industrial dishwasher was making a loud racket. Severny and Alexei separated. One man was washing a pot in the deep sink, and another was cleaning the grease off the grill. Severny took out a Bo-Shuriken.

The man washing the pots turned toward the intruders. Severny threw the blade, striking the man in the right eye. The blade penetrated to the brain. The victim slumped and then let go of the pot in his hand as he fell to the floor.

Alexei worked his way across the room to cover the door that led into the dining room. Severny slipped around the center island unnoticed by the second man. He took a ninja dragon star laced in poison and threw it. It sliced precisely across the victim's throat and cut his artery. The man startled, then gasped for breath, and fell as he passed out.

Severny pointed to the walk-in freezer. Alexei took his cue, moved over, and looked in. He signaled Severny that there was one man in the walk-in. Severny walked over to the door leading out of the kitchen into the dining area. He looked through the window and saw that the room was clear. Then he turned to Alexei and gave him the all clear. Alexei opened the door and fired three rounds into the kitchen crewman's head.

"Kitchen secure, go," Severny said into his radio headset.

Out front, Mikhail answered. He took off his headset and put it into the nylon bag. The two men walked briskly to the embassy front door and opened it. Inside the foyer, a Russian guard snapped to attention and saluted. Mikhail returned the salute and stood waiting for the guard to open the interior door to admit him. Anatoly followed him into the room but stopped in the entryway and asked the guard about the local restaurants.

The receptionist stiffened her back and saluted Mikhail.

"Welcome to Oslo, Major. May I assist you?"

"I'm from Moscow. I'm here to interrogate Doctor Choutov," Mikhail said.

"May I see your orders? I was not told to expect you, sir."

"Certainly," Mikhail said as he reached into the nylon bag and pulled out a silenced Smith & Wesson .40. He shot the receptionist twice in the head.

Anatoly pulled his pistol out of his bag and shot the guard. He locked the front door and pulled the guard out of sight. Both men put on headsets and gas masks. Mikhail spoke into his radio.

"Front entrance secure," he said. "Entering mechanical room."

Then each man strapped a pouch with the night-vision goggles around his waist. It was just a few steps down the hall to the stairs and around the corner to the mechanical room. Mikhail signaled to Anatoly to guard the stairs.

In the back, Alexei moved through the dining room and down a hallway to the warehouse loading dock. As he opened the door leading to the area, he heard a man call out in Russian.

"Who is there? Freeze. I will fire."

Alexei dropped to the floor and fired several shots hitting the roving guard in the shoulder and upper leg. The guard returned several rounds as he fell and then dragged himself behind a set of stacked boxes.

"Trouble," Alexei said. "I'm pinned by the roving guard."

The noise of the guard's unsilenced weapon could be heard all over the embassy.

"Put on your mask and wait," Severny replied. "Mikhail, we need that gas, now."

"Gas released. Wait three minutes before moving," Mikhail said.

Mikhail and Anatoly could hear men running on the stairs. The running stopped at the landing that opened to the front hall from where the receptionist desk would be visible.

"Intruders," one of them yelled. They continued more cautiously down the stairs to the ground floor. At the bottom, the steps turned toward the dining room. Anatoly took aim and hit one of them in the back. He dropped and rolled out of the line of fire of the second man. Unfortunately, he was still exposed to the landing and the upper half of the stairs. A third man descending opened fire and hit him in the chest.

"I got him," the third Russian yelled to his companions. "Go and secure the back entrance. I'll cover the front." The man at the bottom of the stairs dashed through the dining room and toward the back hall.

The embassy guard passed the kitchen door. Severny slid the door open and fired two rounds into his head.

By this time, the gas had taken effect near the mechanical room. The Russian guard still on the stairs passed out shortly after reaching bottom. Mikhail came out of the mechanical room under the stairs and fired two rounds. Because the warehouse area was the farthest away from the mechanical room, the roving guard there had not yet been subdued.

"I'm going to start my search of the first floor," Severny said into his headset. "Alexei, kill the lights as soon as your guard passes out. Mikhail and Anatoly, go ahead and begin your search. We don't have much time."

"Anatoly is dead," Mikhail said.

"OK, you and I will have to get the third floor. Go ahead and search the second floor. Alexei, get Choutov's double and drag him to the foot of the stairs. Then get Anatoly's body back into the van," Severny said.

Both Severny and Mikhail started going room by room. A minute and a half passed. Alexei got up and moved carefully over to where the guard was. He put his silenced pistol up to the man's head and pulled the trigger. He ran and opened the overhead door. Following that, he darted to the circuit breaker panel and pulled the main breaker off. Everything went dark.

Severny and Mikhail immediately pulled out their night goggles and continued to search as Alexei went for the van.

"I have him on the second floor," Mikhail said. "He has taken a fairly rough beating, and he is missing several fingers."

"Where are you?" Severny asked.

"From the stairs, turn right. I'm the fourth door on the right."

Severny ran to the room. The two men carried Choutov out and down the hall. They met Alexei at the head of the stairs. He had carried the double slung over his shoulder in a fireman's carry.

"Fourth door on the right," Severny said. "Do you have the lighter fluid?"

"Da."

Severny and Mikhail carried Choutov down to the first floor.

"Can you carry him from here?" Mikhail asked. "I need to place the charges."

"Da. Help me get him up."

Mikhail set the plastic explosives in opposite ends of the building and turned the radio detonators on. When he returned, Alexei met him in the dining room.

"Let's get out of here," Mikhail said. The two men ran to the van in the loading area.

The van pulled away. About two blocks down the street, Mikhail set off the explosives.

"See if you can revive Choutov," Severny said.

Mikhail examined Choutov and decided not to neutralize the effects of the gas. He turned to Severny. "We cannot use the drug. He has been through hell, and in his weakened state, it will kill him before he can tell us where the weapon is located."

"OK, let us charm him. He is our best buddy. He is safe. Got it?"

"How strong do we have to get him in order to use the drug?" Alexei asked.

"That is hard to say. A good meal, some sleep, possibly an antibiotic for his wounds. He might bounce back to health in a few hours," Mikhail said.

"Good thought, Alexei. Mikhail, what medicinals do you have to treat him with?" Severny asked.

"I can clean up these wounds. If we could get any broad spectrum antibiotic, that would help prevent—"

"I do not care about his fingers. What do we have to do so that he will not go off the deep end with the drugs before we get what we need?" Severny demanded.

"Food and sleep. Make him feel emotionally secure," Mikhail said.

"Then that is what we will do. OK, there is the hotel. We will take him up the service elevator. When I stop by the door, you two get him out and into the elevator. I will park the van and follow you up later," Severny said as he pulled into the basement-level parking area.

On cue the two men took Choutov and entered the elevator. Severny drove off.

Mikhail quickly checked the hallway. All clear. It was a short trip from the elevator to their room.

"Go down and order soup, bread, and some citrus fruit," Mikhail told Alexei.

Mikhail put Choutov on the bed and began to dress his wounds. He decided not to revive him from the gas since he needed as much sleep as possible.

Five minutes later.

Severny arrived in the room. "I sent Alexei for some food," Mikhail reported.

"Good. Wake him up."

"We should wait."

"Wait? No, wake him up."

"Now look here, do you have a blockage in your ears? I told you, push now and you will lose. I did not come this far to have some bloody eager blunderer wreck it now."

Severny's face turned red, and he clinched his fist as if ready to strike.

A quartermaster, a gopher telling me what to do. Who does he think he is?

"Do not even think about it," Mikhail said looking him straight in the eye. "Without me you do not have a doctor. If I even think you are contemplating doing something to me, I will put you away with a disease that will cause you more pain than you ever imagined was possible. Do I make myself clear?"

Severny was dumbfounded.

Where did he all of a sudden get all this boldness?

"Now, cover him up. I am going to sleep also. I figure that you are not going to make a move toward me until you have the information. So now is as good a time as any to sleep," Mikhail said.

"What do we do with the food you just ordered?"

"It will keep. We can reheat the soup in the coffeepot. Just put it aside. Wake me when the doctor stirs. He should be asleep for several hours," Mikhail said as he turned to go to the adjoining room.

Severny hit the coffee table in front of the couch in anger. It shattered.

I will show him. No one talks to me like that and lives to tell about it.

TWENTY-SEVEN

THE NORWEGIAN GOVERNMENT MINISTERS WERE OPERATING IN panic mode. A civilian ship had been attacked and sunk in the harbor by the American Navy. The Russian embassy had been destroyed by a bomb. This peaceful nation was now the center of international speculation and intrigue. International media had descended on Oslo like an occupying army. The Norwegian prime minister was definitely having a bad day, and it had just begun. His staff had never seen him so upset and angry.

"What you're telling me, Mr. Ambassador, is that you are conducting your own bloody little private war in our peace-loving country," the Norwegian prime minister said in perfect English.

The prime minister had grown up in a diplomatic family and had lived in England and the United States. He had attended several years of college in Boston, so his command of the language was superb.

"Basically, we have to surrender our sovereignty and stand back while you do what you bloody well please. Is that what you're telling me?"

"No, Mr. Prime Minister," the American ambassador said. "The United States would never ask you to surrender your sovereignty."

"What do you call it then?" The prime minister leaned forward waving his finger. "Do you think you borrowed our sovereignty?"

"We only ask that you see the urgency of the situation. Your people, our people, indeed the whole world could suffer the loss of hundreds of millions of casualties because of this—"

"Hundreds of millions. A bit overstated, wouldn't you say? Maybe there is a crisis, but our law enforcement is just as good as the American CIA or FBI."

"Your excellent law enforcement officials simply do not have the time to take over this task. But your assistance in locating Doctor Choutov would be of tremendous help. And no, hundreds of millions is not an overstatement."

"What happens when you find the weapon? How do I guarantee the safety of my people? Why shouldn't I let your Doctor Choutov escape and then close off our borders to foreign travel?"

"Now, sir, please be reasonable. You know you can't insulate yourself from this virus. Besides, you couldn't live with the death of most of humankind on your head. Please, we must act with cool heads, and we must act quickly."

"I suppose I have no bloody choice. What about containment? We know nothing about this sort of virus."

"Don't worry. We have an expert microbiologist from the Centers for Disease Control here in Oslo now. Doctor Evans has worked on the type of virus we're facing, and she'll be ready to secure the weapon and transport it out of Norway without incident. What's important is to get the weapon in her hands."

"I have no choice, it appears. What do you want?"

The American ambassador handed him a photograph of Choutov. "We need as many men as possible to check hotels, restaurants, taxis, and the like for this man. They're free to tell these people that the United States will offer a quarter of a million U.S. dollars to anyone who gives us the lead that culminates in Choutov's capture."

"That's quite a sum of money."

"Yes, and if your government will agree, we will offer any policeman who secures that information fifty thousand dollars. We want Choutov, and we want him in the next twelve hours."

"We can't allow you to reward policemen. I'm sorry. However, I know they will do their duty in an exemplary manner. With all this money, you may have a lot of false sightings to deal with."

"True, but it only takes one real sighting to accomplish our mission."

"It will be done."

"Great. I'll have one of our operatives contact your office within the hour to coordinate the details. I hate to cut our meeting short, sir, but I do have very pressing concerns back at the embassy, and I know you'll want to get the ball rolling from this end," the ambassador said as he stood and offered his hand to the prime minister.

"Yah, I mean yes. I'll talk with you later," the prime minister responded as he stood and shook the ambassador's hand.

As the American ambassador left the government building he was swarmed by reporters.

"Mr. Ambassador, can we get a comment on the attack last night?"

"Mr. Ambassador, did we conduct an assault on the Russian Embassy?"

"Mr. Ambassador, is it true that the American government is offering staggering rewards for certain individuals?"

"Mr. Ambassador, there are reports that the Russian fleet is about to engage NATO. Are we on the verge of war? . . ."

"If you ladies and gentlemen will step back and give me room, I'll give you a statement," the ambassador yelled. "Please, step back."

The mob of reporters began to comply.

"Thank you. Yesterday, NATO forces averted an act of air piracy. Three F-14's from the USS *Kennedy* shot down two MIG's that were attempting to divert a SwissAir flight 848 from Oslo to Paris. The F-14's were retaliating to hostile fire at the SwissAir jet. Russia denies any knowledge of the incident. Again last night, NATO forces returned fire on a Russian merchant vessel in the port of Oslo in an act of self-defense. The vessel under fire was an American destroyer, the USS *Peterson*. A rogue element within the Russian intelligence fired three missiles at our ship. I can't elaborate further on the port incident.

"Later, sometime after midnight," he continued, "the Russian embassy was destroyed by what we believe is the same rogue element comprised of former KGB operatives that fired on our ship. Due to ongoing security concerns, the Norwegian government will not be able to make any public comments for now. The president has ordered a government-related news blackout. No reporters will be allowed on, or near, any military units in Northern Europe until the matter has been resolved. The only source of information will be the White House press secretary. I know you all have a lot of questions, but I'm sorry to tell you that I can't answer them at this time. Thank you."

Following this statement, the ambassador made his way to a waiting car.

"There you have it," the American network anchorman said speaking to a camera. "The American ambassador has confirmed that war clouds are indeed gathering over this peace-loving region of the world. Now we turn to Connie Robertson, at the White House. Connie, what do your sources tell us about these incidents? I understand that the Russian president has not been heard from. Could pro-military Communists be reasserting themselves in some kind of coup? Is this some kind of demonstration to help the Russian president in the polls? I understand he's trailing the Communists over the issue of Russian nationalism."

TWENTY-EIGHT

DAVID EDGED OFF THE ELEVATOR. HE FELT RELIEVED TO SEE JIM leaning against a pillar. They planned to check up on a lead with the desk clerk at the Hotel Continental. Catherine would be departing for the airport once Brian returned.

"Jim, good to see you in one piece."

"Captain, it's good to be in one piece. I heard you had an interesting night."

"Yeah, one I'd like to forget."

"What's up?"

"The desk clerk at the Hotel Continental has a lead on the doctor."

"Let's hope we get him and wind this up," Jim said as he opened the door for David.

"May I procure the taxi?" the doorman asked.

"No, thank you," David said.

"Will we have anyone with us as backup?" Jim asked.

"No, we're stretched thin. Time's running out."

David and Jim walked over to Karl Johans Gate, then west toward the National Theater. They crossed the park that was

257

situated between Karl Johans Gate and the Stortingsgata. The hardwood trees in the park had lost all of their leaves. However, a number of evergreens gave color to the landscape. Pansies still adorned the flower beds. The Continental Hotel was just across from the theater on the Stortingsgata. The two-block walk took just a few minutes.

"What about the weapon? Do you think he'll have it with him?" Jim asked.

"I doubt it, but if we get the doctor before Severny does, we should be able to recover it. It's probably hidden in a public locker of some sort."

For the rest of the short walk to the hotel, the two men did not speak. Jim checked his .40 caliber and returned it to its holster, then followed David through the revolving doors and into the lobby.

"Do you have a Peter on duty?" David asked a clerk.

"Yah, Peter is my name. May I be assisting you?"

David pulled a photo of Choutov from his coat and showed it to the desk clerk. "We're looking for this man. We understand you may have some information about him."

"Please, the Americans, ah, you offer the reward?"

"Yes, if we capture him alive using your information, you'll get the reward," David said.

"How may I know? I am receiving the kroner? No! The kroner first."

Jim stepped up to the counter and opened his coat to reveal the Heckler & Klock .40. "I'll make you a deal. You give us the information, and if it's good information, you'll get your money. You don't give me that information right now, I'll splatter what little brains you may have on that—"

"Here's what I'll do for you," David said. "Here's a thousand U.S. down payment." He took out a roll of hundred-dollar bills and began to count them out. "You give us what we want, you'll get the rest. My associate won't have to splatter your brains on the wall. How does that sound?"

"How may I be assured of your return?"

"You can't be assured. But you'll be at least a thousand dollars richer. And alive."

"What if he's not alive? You find him dead?"

"Our deal is for information that leads us to capture him alive. Here's what I do. If we find him dead, we'll let you keep the thousand dollars. Now what's it going to be?"

"The man you are finding checked out yesterday. Bill was being paid by Russian embassy. His bags were being sent to the embassy. I am hearing that the embassy was being destroyed during the night. It is being our agreement, I am keeping the money."

"Yes, you can keep the money," David said.

He stepped away from the desk and pulled out his cellular phone.

"Mother," Bob said.

"Bob, the hotel clerk says Choutov checked out yesterday and moved to the Russian embassy. Can you get me in touch with the chief investigator? I need to find out if Choutov died in that explosion."

"I'll get right back to you. Leave your phone on in the receive mode. I doubt Severny will be tracking it."

David and Jim got into a taxi. David told the driver to take them to the Russian Embassy.

"But sir, the embassy, ah, was destroyed during the night," the driver said.

"We know," David said. The cab pulled away.

"Are we up the proverbial creek?" Jim asked.

"I doubt the embassy just exploded on its own. My guess is that Russian intelligence got to Choutov and Andreyev's henchman, then Severny found out and carried out an assault on the embassy."

"So, I guess the question is, did Severny find Choutov or not?"

"That's the sixty-four-thousand-dollar question. I assume he did. Why blow up the embassy if not?"

"Why blow up the embassy at all?"

"My hunch is that they'll find an unidentifiable male body about Choutov's size in the debris."

"Trying to throw us off?"

"You bet," David said.

"But destroy the embassy? A little bit of overkill, don't you think?"

"Severny's no dunce. He's trying to create confusion. You gotta assume the Norwegian government is frothing at the mouth. With all the media involved, our president must be under a lot of pressure to back off. Actually, I am surprised we haven't gotten a cease and desist order."

"Yeah, sending helicopters into Oslo armed with uniformed men and shooting down MIGs certainly hasn't helped. I'll bet he wet in his briefs when you sunk the freighter." Jim chuckled.

"Maybe."

As the cab pulled up to the curb near the embassy, the cellular phone rang.

"Captain Egan."

"David, it's Mother. You're set. Just ask for the chief investigator on the scene. They're still going through the rubble."

"Thanks. Oh, do the Norwegians know yet?"

"Yeah, we couldn't keep them out of the loop with you conducting military assaults in their harbor. Our ambassador spoke to the prime minister early this morning. David, you've caused the largest media event since the Gulf War. Everyone in the media has jumped to the conclusion that the Communists have taken over in Russia and we're on the brink of World War III. You'll be happy to know that the White House has decided to hang tough—no comments to the press. My sources tell me that the boys at State are seething."

"Thanks," David said. He put the phone away and handed the driver a wad of kroner. Then the two men got out of the cab and walked over to a small group of uniformed officers.

"We're with the United States Government. We were told to ask for the chief investigator. Can you direct us to him?" David asked the officers.

"Yah, follow me," one answered. He led them into the rub-ble where they approached several men in street clothes.

"Sir, these men, the American government," the officer said in Norwegian.

One of the plainclothesmen nodded and turned toward Jim and David. "I was obtaining a personal telephone call from the prime minister—not five minutes ago. I am to answer your questions. We are giving you all assistance as you require, but I am not being told why. Do not like," the man said.

"I understand. You're a professional with a job to do. It's hard to work with outsiders interfering. Please, this situation is of utmost importance to your country and to mine. That's why you got a personal call from the head of your government. I can't tell you why; I can only ask you to trust that your gov-ernment is very concerned," David said.

"My government cannot be expecting me to do my job, ah, without information. What may you be needing to know?" the inspector asked.

"What happened? How? Have you identified all the bodies yet?" David asked.

"Last night two, ah, how you say, plastique?"

"Yeah, your English is very good. Plastique explosives?"

"Yah, explosives. The charges were being arranged, ah, managed to consume whole building. Yah, almost half a block. Everything, destroyed."

"Victims?"

"Yah, we are thinking we recovered bodies. One we are finding near the steps. Dying out of bullet. Another we are finding, ah, loading dock. Yah, also bullet. A kitchen helper we are finding outside. Ah, broken neck. One culinary is being dead from, ah, piercing, no, puncture. Screwdriver."

"Yes, I understand. A puncture wound like a screwdriver."

"Yah. No! No screwdriver. Object is being eleven centime-ters. Entering the eye, ah, toward the brain. Other culinary is being dead from throat, ah, neck blood vessels being cut by sharp object. Oh, finding evidence, poison being in the body on those two. Finding third culinary, being in freezer. Dying, out of bullet. All others dying out of explosion. And fire," the chief inspector said.

"Have you identified all the bodies?"

"Yah, but one. Finding one body badly burned. Little flesh is being with the body. Not knowing identity. Victim is wearing handcuffs.

"How badly were the other bodies burned?"

"Little burns present. Everyone is being recognized."

"Is there a reason? Were chemicals stored nearby? Did a gas line run into a nearby room?"

"No. I have not to be thinking, ah, this question. There was none."

"Please ask your lab to check for any residue of a flammable material on or near the body and report that back to your prime minister's office. Did you find anything else out of the ordinary?"

"Yah, one thing. Small gas cylinder, unt re-gu-la-tor is being in the mechanical closet. Is being evaluation now."

"Thank you," David said. "You've been very helpful. I'll let you get back to your work."

As David and Jim walked away, David took out his phone.

"Mother," Bob answered.

"This is David. It looks like Severny Iourtchak has our doctor. Dispatch a helicopter to pick me up at the airport. Jim will take over here on the ground. Get hold of the Norwegian government. We need to shut down all air traffic leaving Norway."

"That may take some time. Our ambassador didn't discuss that this morning, and I'm sure their aviation officials are not just going to shut it down without the prime minister's direct order," Bob said.

"Do what you can. Go ahead and order our forces to turn back all noncommercial traffic. We'll just have to hope they've not gotten through our people at the terminal. In the meantime, get me back to the ship. Oh, can you call for two cabs to pick Jim and me up in front of the Russian Embassy?"

"I'll call right away."

David turned to Jim and gave him the telephone. Then he pulled the coded key for his room from his pocket and handed it to him.

"I'm going back to the *Peterson* to assume operational control of shutting off air flights leaving from Norway. I want everyone pulled to the airport to survey passengers leaving on commercial flights. It may be hours before we get the consent of the Norwegians to shut down international travel. Take the key and telephone. The com equipment is back in the room," David said.

"You're sure Choutov's alive?"

"Sure? No. But it's reasonable to assume that someone entered the Russian embassy quietly through the kitchen. One cook was killed by an eleven-centimeter spike to the eye. He was likely killed by a practitioner of Bo Shuriken Do. The poison, and the placement of the spike, are characteristic of the art Ninjajitsu. Only someone who knew what he was doing would throw the Bo Shuriken to the eye," David said.

"I don't know much about that art. Why the eye?"

"An eleven-centimeter spike is less than $4 1/2$ inches long. In other words, about the size of a ten-penny nail. To kill, it must penetrate to the brain or go directly into the heart. Often these weapons are poisoned to help kill. The eye is about the only place you can throw a weapon like that and be sure it penetrates the brain."

"The two cooks are a stretch. Anything else that leads you to believe that Choutov is still alive?"

"Between the cooks and the plastic explosive, we can surmise that there was an assault on the embassy. I'll bet the gas bottle will test out to be a knockout agent of some kind. In addition, we have bodies all over the place that are burned but recognizable. We've one body where the flesh was burned off. No fuel source nearby that would intensify the heat. I'll bet they find residue of some type of flammable liquid. My assumption is that the body was a plant to throw us off."

"That seems like a lot of overkill. Why would they risk having the police enter into looking for them?"

"I dare say that the best police SWAT team in the world would have trouble taking Severny Iourtchak into custody. He's not worried about police. Plus, look at all the confusion an incident like this causes. It's easy to slip away when there is mass confusion and destruction."

Two cabs pulled up to where Jim and David were waiting. As the two men were getting into separate cabs, David yelled over to Jim. "Catherine's going to the SwissAir counter. Watch out for her."

Jim nodded in response, and then both men got into their cabs and proceeded to their separate destinations.

TWENTY-NINE

Inter Nor Bristol Hotel.

THERE WAS A LOUD THUD AS THE DOOR TO THE HOTEL ROOM slammed against the doorstop. Severny was startled awake. Alexander and Nickolai were standing just inside the room.

"I see you have captured Doctor Choutov. Do you have the weapon?" Alexander asked.

"No," Severny responded. "He has been out all night since we brought him back from the embassy. Mikhail says he must sleep to regain strength in case we have to take extreme measures.

"Not necessary. He is my friend. He has no reason not to cooperate. Wake him."

"Mikhail. Come in here," Severny shouted so he could be heard in the adjoining room. "Alexander, what happened to your prisoners? Our plan was—"

"Americans attacked the ship," Alexander said. "I was barely able to get away alive."

"Escaped. You let Egan escape?" Severny said with clinched fists.

"I'm pleased you're so concerned for my safety, Severny."

Mikhail appeared in the door as Severny sat seething. "Alexander, you're still with us," Mikhail said.

"Wake Ilya," was the reply.

Mikhail went back into the adjoining room. He reappeared in a few moments with a vial of ammonia and put it under Choutov's nose. Choutov began to stir.

"Where am I?" Choutov said as he woke up.

"Among friends, my dear Ilya," Andreyev said. "We thought we lost you to the Russian Intelligence. I see they treated you in their customary fashion."

"My hand and arm ache so bad," Choutov said.

"I will get you a painkiller," Mikhail said as he got up.

"Why did you have me put off in Stockholm?"

"The Russian intelligence became aware of what we were doing and came after me," Andreyev said. "I knew that they would certainly go after any of my ships in the region. So, I ordered the Master to put you off. I knew you would eventually make the rendezvous."

Mikhail walked back into the room with a pill and a glass of water. "Here, take this," he said. "It should bring some relief in ten or fifteen minutes."

"Why are you here? Not at the rendezvous?" Choutov asked after taking the pills.

"We knew that the Americans and the Russian intelligence were aware of our ship. And the port call to Stockholm. We wanted to get to you before they did."

"I wish you had been successful," Choutov said with a smirk.

"Da, we just missed you in Stockholm. We ended up in a firefight with the CIA. They were pursuing you aggressively. As you can see, the Russian intelligence was also tracking you. When they captured you, we knew we had to get you back," Andreyev said.

"I am glad you did. I do not know how much more I could take."

"Da, I understand. Ilya, we need to get out of Oslo as soon as possible. I am sure the Americans will try to close the borders. Where is the weapon?"

"In a locker at the airport."

"Where is the key?"

"I cut a small slit into the fabric covering the box springs in my room. I taped the key to a coil near the left side head of the box springs."

At this Andreyev looked at Alexi and Mikhail. "You two go. Get that key." Then he turned to Nikolai. "The Oslo Domkirke is six blocks down the Karl Johans Gate. Go and set an explosion with a remote control. We will detonate it as we leave. Good for a diversion."

"The cathedral is large. It would take some planning to destroy the building," Nikolai said.

"No! No! Dunderhead. I just want fire, smoke, and panicking people. We just need to slip past the local authorities. In Lillestrøm we have contacts who can help us out of Norway."

"Da," he said and left.

"Ilya, we have food here for you," Severny said as he got up. "You can reheat the soup in the coffeepot over there."

Andreyev followed Severny into the adjoining room as Choutov got up and started to prepare his soup. Andreyev closed the door.

"What are we going to do with him?" Severny asked. "He's a walking liability."

"Nothing. He is a friend."

"He is no friend. He eats your food and slept with your wife. A dog under your table, and you call him a friend."

Alexander's face turned red. He stared intensely as he grinded his teeth.

"You did not know your good friend was sleeping with your wife?" Severny started to laugh. "You old fool."

"Watch your mouth, Severny. I may not have been close to Lara, but I will not have you insulting her memory. Besides, I know more than you think."

"Then why do call him your—"

"First, we are going to retrieve the weapon. You will arrange transportation north. The Americans expect us to leave by air. We will fool them by doubling back to Russia."

"Russia?"

"Da, I believe we can strike a deal with Moscow for money and immunity."

"Immunity? What are you talking about? We can't renege on our contract."

"We must," Andreyev said. "The Americans say that the weapon we have is not as stable as our scientists claimed. The virus is not controllable. If it is unleashed, it—"

"Horse dung! American propaganda."

"It could kill millions. I am in this for money. Not to kill tens of thousands of my own countrymen. Nyet, it is best we deal and get it back safely into a lab."

"Come on Alexander, what would you expect the Americans to tell you? You cannot believe them. We know what our scientists have said. All we are going to see is a few thousand less Jews."

"Can we take the chance? We make good money from drugs and prostitution. We can strike a deal that would virtually remove the threat of police intervention into our business. If it were a nuclear weapon, I would agree with you. Kill all the Jews for all I care. This is much more deadly. We will deal," Andreyev said as he got up to open the door to the other room.

Severny reached for the Bo Shuriken he had sheathed out of sight. "Are you absolutely sure? You can't trust the Americans."

Andreyev turned to respond. Severny threw the spike and hit Andreyev dead center in the left eye. Andreyev slumped, then dropped to the floor.

"Your reward for letting my brother's killer escape," he said.

Severny quickly pulled Andreyev's body into the toilet area and rolled him into the bathtub.

"Where is Alexander?" Choutov asked as Severny entered the room.

"He has gone downstairs to a travel office to arrange for tickets. We must get away as soon as possible. By the way, which locker does the key fit?"

"Just off from the baggage return area. There is a bank of lockers. It fits the one in the third row from the top, number twelve. That's my lucky number, number twelve."

Severny moved behind Choutov. "Number twelve's your lucky number, huh?"

"You bet. Number twelve."

"Ilya, did I ever tell you about Lara?"

Choutov turned to face him. His face turned red. "What about Lara?" His pitch rose in intensity.

Severny laughed. "She could not get enough."

Choutov jumped up with fists ready to strike. "You lying scion of a whore."

Severny shot him between the eyes. Choutov fell to the floor. A rush of exhilaration pulsed through Severny.

He dragged the body into the toilet area and dumped it into the bathtub. Then he returned to the room, cleaned up the blood, and sat down to watch the news as he waited for Mikhail and Alexei to return. They arrived about twenty minutes later.

"We have it," Alexei said.

"Where are Alexander and Ilya?" Mikhail asked.

"In the other room," Severny said. He continued looking directly at Alexei. "Go and bring the service elevator up and lock it out of service."

Alexei turned and left the room.

"Do you have the key?" Severny said.

"Right here," Mikhail said opening his right hand.

"Good. Alexander would like to see you in the next room."

Mikhail walked into the adjoining room. It was empty. He reached for his gun and turned. However, Severny anticipated his move. He hit him directly in the heart with another throwing knife. Mikhail slumped to the floor, dead.

"That will teach you to defy me."

Severny turned and walked back into the adjoining room. Moments later Alexei entered from the hallway. "I have the elevator."

"Did anyone see you?"

"No."

"OK, get the others," Severny said.

Alexei walked by Severny heading toward the door of the adjoining room. Severny took out his silenced Smith & Wesson .40 and shot him twice.

Severny walked back into the other room where he took the key for the locker from Mikhail's hand. He took a bottle of dark hair dye from a makeup case and rubbed it into his hair and used a toothbrush to color his eyebrows. Since the dye needed to set for half an hour, he sat down in the other room to watch the news.

Severny turned the television off and picked up the phone. "Could you give me the number of the travel agency in the lobby? Thank you."

He dialed the new number. "Yes, I need to find out about any available flights leaving within the hour heading south toward London or the Netherlands. What do you have available?"

"The only flight I have is the continuation of a SwissAir flight to London. It departs in an hour and twenty minutes from now. Can you make that flight in time?"

"Yes, I believe so. Have the tickets ready for me; I will pick them up in the next fifteen minutes."

"We can assign you a seat and go ahead and give you a boarding pass. Will you need to check any luggage?"

"Yes, I do have one bag to check."

"In that case, you will be cutting it short. You need to check your bag at least half an hour before the flight leaves. Do you still want this flight, sir?"

"Yes, I will make it."

"We have two first-class seats and several coach seats available."

"First class," Severny said.

"The first class seats are aisle seats. Is that acceptable?"

"Yes."

"May I have your name, sir?"

"Jonathan Edwards."

"What passport do you have?"

"United States."

"How will you be paying, sir?"

"Visa."

"May I have the card number?"

"4271, 3820, 8374, 2826."

"And the expiration date?"

"Eight of ninety six."

"Thank you, Mr. Edwards. I have you confirmed on Swiss-Air flight 776 into London's Heathrow Airport. I'll have your tickets ready."

"Thank you," Severny said and then hung up. He waited ten minutes, then rinsed his hair and eyebrows. Following that, he took a blow dryer and styled his hair.

Severny knew that Mikhail had a virtual armory in the adjoining room. He searched through several bags.

Good. I knew you would have plastique explosives and detonators.

He opened the back of a nearby laptop computer and took out the power supply. Next he forced his way into the power supply, removing some of the electrical components. He carefully inserted a very small radio receiver. Then he spread the plastique around the edge of the motherboard and inserted a small detonator into it. With two wires he connected the plastique to the radio receiver. He put the power supply back and closed up the laptop.

He began to search until he found a handheld detonator.

Good old Mikhail. A detonator disguised as a pager.

Before leaving St. Petersburg, Alexander had ordered Mikhail to bring several parachutes. They were to be used as a backup. Severny located a parachute and put it into a small bag. Then he left the room with the computer and the parachute. He went down to the lobby and across to the adjacent shops where the travel agency was located. After receiving his tickets, he hailed a cab and told the driver to take him to the airport.

As they approached the airport facility, the driver asked Severny what airline he planned to use.

"Take me to the arriving flights concourse. I need to go to the baggage claim area," Severny said.

He paid the driver and then entered the facility.

Where are the lockers? Da. There.

The key worked. Severny spotted a large suitcase. He pulled it out and opened it. Inside was a second leather case. Severny took the leather case out and replaced it with the parachute he brought from the hotel. Then he opened the leather case. Inside were three metal cylinders about the size of a one-liter soda bottle. Severny took the three cylinders and put them in a nylon handbag he had in the side pocket of the computer case.

The metal cylinders contained glass liners. Each cylinder consisted of two pieces screwed together. Severny noticed that one cylinder was not closed flush along the seam. He gave it a hard twist.

I hope the threads are not misaligned.

After closing the suitcase, he proceeded toward the Swiss-Air ticket counter in the main concourse.

Catherine's back was toward the ticket counter as she watched the passengers who were heading for the departure concourse. SwissAir had been selected for her cover because the ticket counter was located next to the hallway leading to the international departure concourse.

Her anxiety was building. She hadn't seen another CIA operative for over an hour.

What am I gonna do if I spot him? I can call Mother. No, I can't. David took the cellular phone.

The airport was becoming increasingly busy. It was getting harder and harder for her to see every passenger who passed by her counter toward the concourse.

Three flights are due to leave within the next half hour. Over twenty flights in the following two hours.

"Do you have baggage to check, sir?" the SwissAir ticket agent asked Severny.

"This one," he said as he placed the bag on the scale.

"You already have your boarding pass. Here is your baggage claim check," she said as she stapled the receipt to the ticket envelope. "Your plane's on time. You'll depart from gate C-5 in about twenty-five minutes. Thank you for choosing SwissAir."

Catherine had been sweeping her focus in a 180-degree arc attempting a momentary look at each male passenger. She focused for a moment on Severny.

Looks somewhat familiar.

She continued to scan the passengers looking for Choutov.

"Thank you," Severny said as he retrieved his ticket envelope.

He walked in front of Catherine and on toward the departure concourse. Again, she focused on him for a moment.

He looks familiar.

She continued to scan other passengers. Something was bothering her.

Where have I seen that man?

Severny stepped up to the security checkpoint and emptied his pockets. He put the detonator disguised as a pager on the tray with his change. The security personnel passed it through without scanning. Then he opened his laptop carrying case and handed the guard the computer.

"I don't want to mess up the hard drive," he said with a smile.

The officer opened the top of the computer. After looking at the keyboard, he told Severny to put the case on the x-ray conveyer, and the guard passed the computer through without checking further. Severny walked through the metal detector, gathered his belongings, and headed for his gate.

At gate C-5, he found a chair. Ten minutes passed.

"May I have your attention, please. The continuation of SwissAir flight 776 to London's Heathrow Airport will now begin boarding. Please have your boarding pass available for the attendant as you board. All carry-on luggage must be stowed under the seats or in the overhead compartment above you. If you cannot stow your luggage properly, our attendant at the check-in desk can check the item for you. We will now board all first-class passengers and passengers with infants or special requirements."

Severny boarded the aircraft and took his seat. He placed the computer bag under the seat in front of him.

Hair color. He's changed his hair color.
She looked around frantically searching for an agent.
I haven't seen an agent for an hour.
Her eyes fixed on a large wall clock over one of the main doors leading into the ticketing area.
Flight's about to leave. I've got to stop him. He's got the virus. Ten minutes.
But who could she call? If she called the embassy, it would take more than ten minutes to notify Bob. Then, he'd need time to contact an agent in the airport.
There's no time to call anyone.
Employees have their own security entrance to the departure concourse, so she quickly passed through the security check.
Oh no! They've already boarded.
Noticing the door still open, she ran down the gangway to the plane.
"Wait," she called out just as the senior flight attendant was about to close the door to the aircraft. "Oh my, I'm glad I caught you," Catherine said panting. "I'm supposed to do a spot inspection in London. I would have been in deep trouble if I had missed this flight."
"We're full. You'll have to use the jump seat on the rear bulkhead," the senior flight attendant said.
"No problem."
Catherine turned to walk to the rear of the aircraft.
Oh Lord, help. There he is.

THIRTY

THE SHRILL OF THE PIPE SOUNDED ATTENTION OVER THE 1-MC. "Mail call. All division representatives lay to the post office. Now, mail call."

"What's the status, Bob?" David asked as he entered the compartment.

"No word, yet. Jim's checking out another lead."

"Oh. What lead?"

"One of the location station operatives had shown pictures of Choutov, Andreyev, and Iourtchak to several desk clerks in hotels day before yesterday. When the police were showing Choutov's photograph around today, one of the clerks in your hotel remembered seeing Choutov's photograph two days before with the others. In the meantime, he believed Iourtchak was a guest and had been seen in one of the hotel restaurants."

"A guest?"

"Yea. The clerk put it all together and asked if we were still looking for any of the three men. He also asked about the reward."

"What instructions did you give Jim?"

"I told him to offer to pay ten thousand dollars for Iourtchak," Bob said.

"And?"

"Well, we're waiting for Jim to check it out. I hope to hear from him anytime now."

"Is the captain on the bridge?"

"I believe so."

David picked up the telephone and dialed 222. It rang simultaneously on the bridge, in the captain's two cabins, and behind his chair in the wardroom.

"Captain."

"Captain, David Egan. I need to take over your CIC. I also need some of your better personnel to man combat. Could I impose on you for that assistance?"

"Certainly, Commodore. The *Peterson* and her crew are at your full disposal."

"Thank you. I'll be shifting my control within the next half hour. Oh, could you have one of your IC men run several sound power lines from the operations center to the CIC? I need to be in touch with Bob at all times."

"Consider it done."

"Thanks."

Within moments the boatswain pipe sounded attention over the 1-MC. "Electrical officer, 222."

"Okay, Bob, give me a tactical overview," David said as he looked over a large-scale chart of the area.

"We're here just a little over twenty-five miles from the entrance to the Oslofjord. The *Kennedy* is here, almost midway between the southern tip of Norway and the northern part of Denmark. The Brits have the Arch Royal here, just inside the Baltic. She has two destroyer pickets with her. They've been deployed here and here in the Baltic. The *Spruance* is here between us and the *Kennedy*."

"What's my call sign for today?"

"You are Tango Tango."

"What aircraft do we have up?"

"*Peterson, Spruance,* and *Kennedy* are each controlling one F-14 CAP. Likewise, each of the three Brits has a Harrier up on station."

"E-2?"

"No, not at this time," Bob said.

"What's the *Kennedy's* call sign? Throw me those authentication tables," David said pointing to a table near Bob.

"The *Kennedy* is Alpha November."

David picked up the radio handset and keyed it. "Alpha November, this is Tango Tango, I am prepared to authenticate, over.

"Tango Tango, this is Alpha November. Authenticate Delta Delta Delta Charlie, over."

David looked up Delta Delta Delta Charlie and responded. "This is Tango Tango, I authenticate November Foxtrot. Immediate Execute. Launch E-2. Out."

"Bob, what's the status on shutting down commercial air traffic?"

"We have a problem."

"Oh?"

"Yeah, the state department's pitching a royal fit about not being included in the loop. This morning the White House communicated directly with the ambassador in Norway. Cut out the secretary of state and the rest of the crowd over at state. With the attack of a freighter in the harbor being all over the world news, the secretary of state has been pitching a royal fit about defense and CIA conducting operations without their knowledge. There have been meetings at the White House all morning. The media is like a pack of wolves that just got the scent of fresh meat. Your little fireworks show last night set Washington on its ear."

"What does the state department know?"

"I don't know if the president has decided to bring anyone else in the loop. However, the White House has not responded to our request to have the ambassador request a civil aviation shutdown. It could be that State is opposed to it and is fighting it. It could also be that this sort of thing is likely to hit the world news in a big way. The White House could be having trouble making a decision."

"Maybe we should contact the first lady." Several men in the immediate vicinity snorted in an attempt to suppress laughter. "She could get 'em off their rumps."

"Maybe you're right," Bob said.

"Do you have the commercial airline international departure schedule for today?"

"Yeah. Just a moment, it's here somewhere," Bob looked through papers on a clipboard near him.

"Here you go," he said as he handed David the schedule.

"Okay, we've three flights leaving in the next hour. SwissAir to London, Scandinavian Air to Rotterdam, and Sabena Belgian World Air to Brussels. Rotterdam? Isn't that where Andreyev's freighter ended up?"

"Yeah, it is."

"Okay, get an agent on that flight and get some agents to check every passenger boarding the flight, including all carry-on luggage. Have 'em pull all the checked baggage off and go through it."

"What about the other flights?"

"We don't have the manpower. In the two hours following the departure of these three flights, there are twenty-two departures. The airport is going to be full of passengers. We can only afford to pull a few men off for this one flight."

"Should I contact Washington again?"

"No, I'm just going to shut down the air traffic myself."

"Well, if we're not successful, I guess you already fell on your sword last night," Bob said with a smile.

"Yeah, what's a little international air interruption compared to blowing up civilian ships in friendly harbors?"

The door to the room opened, and a marine lance corporal stepped in. "Commodore, the captain sends his regards. CIC's manned and ready for your team, sir."

"Thank you, corporal. Bob, I want you on a sound-powered headset with the CIC officer. That way I can be assured of getting your messages. We'll have two other lines. Put your net control on one and Oslo ground team on the other."

David shifted to the CIC where he took position in the center chair. "Let me have your attention," he said in a loud voice.

"All right, pipe down. Give your attention to the commodore," the senior chief operations specialist hollered in an even louder voice.

"Thanks, Chief. Men, I can't give you the details as to why, but we're involved in a very serious situation today that may impact millions of people in the world. I may have to give orders that are very unusual. They may be orders you're not going to like or want to follow. One such order may be to shoot down an identified civilian airliner."

There was a look of amazement and one or two barely audible groans.

"My authority comes directly from the president. I'll not give such an order unless I have to. It's essential that if I give such orders you relay them without hesitation or question. Am I clear?"

There were a few nods and a few affirmative answers.

"Yes, sir. You can count on us, sir. We'll do our jobs without hesitation," the senior chief sounded off in a loud voice.

"OK. Let's get back to work."

"E-2's airborne," the air controller called out.

Good. Now, I can see all the air traffic in the whole region.

"Do we have the commercial air control for Oslo patched in here?" David asked the watch officer.

"Yes, sir. This speaker," he said pointing to several speakers in the overhead. "And this handset."

David got up and went to the handset. He picked it up and then hesitated a moment. He keyed it and began to speak. "Oslo Air Control, this is Commodore Egan aboard the USS *Peterson*, over."

"Oslo Air Control."

"Oslo, would you put your senior official in charge on the radio please, over."

"Wait one, Oslo out."

Two or three minutes later the speaker blared.

"USS *Peterson*, Oslo Air Control. I am the watch supervisor, over."

"This is Commodore Egan. We have a very dangerous international incident underway. We're going to have to ask you to ground all international air traffic in one hour and fifteen minutes, over."

"Commodore, that is being a request, ah, no authority to give. What is nature of your situation? Over."

"Oslo, I understand that you don't have the authority. However, I must take this action. Your prime minister, and he alone, is aware of the situation. You must check with him. In the meantime, you must suspend all international travel in one hour and fifteen minutes, over."

"USS *Peterson*, Oslo. I cannot. Without authority. I may be happy to inquire. I will not stop international travel, ah, receiving authority, over."

"Oslo, let me encourage you. Do you see the six aircraft I have off your coast and over Sweden? Over."

"USS *Peterson*, yah, we have a track, over."

"Oslo, I'm going to double that number. In one hour and fifteen minutes those aircraft will forcibly turn back any, and all, international flights, over."

"USS *Peterson*, you cannot be doing that. Against international law, over."

"Oslo, I don't know if you realize it or not, but I AM the international police. And I'm going to turn back those aircraft. May I suggest that you personally call or drive over and demand to see your prime minister. Get the authority you need. I don't want to have to flex my muscle against a friend like Norway, over."

"USS *Peterson*, I am doing as you suggest. I hope, ah, you are knowing what you are doing. Your president and your media are hearing about this newest affront to our sovereignty, out."

"All right!"

"Kickin' it, Commodore."

"Yeahh!"

"Pipe down! Tend to your stations sailors," the senior chief yelled.

"Chief, do I have a task group designation?" David asked.

"Yes, sir, you do. Let me see, your task group designation is 24.2321.5."

David sat back down. He picked up a nearby clipboard, turned an old message over, and began to write out a new message.

TO:　　　　　All United States Military Commanders and Forces in Northern and Central Europe.

FROM:　　　Commander TASK GROUP 24.2321.5.

SUBJECT:　OPERATIONAL CONTROL.

AUTHORITY: JCS, Code Named: Antidote.

I hereby assume operational authority over all US Naval and Air Force Units in Northern and Central Europe. All units are to go to a ready alert status. Stand by for scramble orders.

Respond on the following frequencies:

"Chief."

"Yes, sir."

"Fill in the appropriate frequencies and then get this to radio. Have 'em send it Flash."

"Aye aye, sir."

"Commodore, I've relieved the CIC watch," Tony reported.

"Tony. It's good to see you."

"Thanks, Captain, ah, Commodore."

"Get a message off to the HMS *Arch Royal* and ask her to get three more Harriers airborne in forty-five minutes. Ask them to put all six on station near the Swedish and Norwegian borders."

"Aye, sir. Do we have Swedish flyover permission?"

"I assume so," David said. "The three Harriers up now are over Sweden. If we don't, it doesn't really matter. One more protest will just give our boys at State something to do."

David asked one of the petty officers which radio handset was dedicated to the tactical net. David picked up the authentication tables and keyed the tactical net handset.

"Alpha November, this is Tango Tango. I am prepared to authenticate, over."

"Tango Tango, this is Alpha November. Authenticate Foxtrot, Lima, Foxtrot, November, over."

"This is Tango Tango. I authenticate Tango Sierra. Immediate execute. Launch three additional F-14s in forty-five minutes. Assign to *Peterson*, *Spruance*, and *Kennedy* as additional CAP. Stand by, execute, out."

"Message for the bridge," David said to the bridge talker. "Take position in the mouth of the Oslofjord."

"Bridge, flag plot. Take position in the mouth of the Oslofjord."

"Bridge acknowledges mouth of the Oslofjord, sir."

"Very well," David said as he crawled back into the command chair.

This is going to be a long hour. We could use a break right about now.

THIRTY-ONE

One hour later in Oslo.

"YES, CHIEF INSPECTOR, I'M THE AMERICAN LIAISON FOR THE operation," Jim said over the phone. "What can I do for you?"

"Please to be coming to the Hotel Bristol. Center of the city. We have been finding your Doctor Choutov."

"I'm in the hotel on the third floor. I'll meet you in the lobby. I am a tall black man. You shouldn't have trouble picking me out."

Jim hung up the phone and ran to the elevator and took it down to the lobby. As he stepped out of the elevator, a policeman in uniform stepped up to him. "Sir. Chief inspector is asking you to be coming with me."

The room buzzed with police activity. "That being Chief Inspector Christman," the officer said as he pointed.

On the floor the police had laid out the bodies found in the two rooms. Jim recognized Choutov and Andreyev.

"I thought he was dead. What is his body doing here?" Jim muttered aloud.

"I'm sorry, what did you say?" the chief inspector said.

Pointing to Andreyev, Jim responded, "That is Alexander Andreyev. He's the local mob boss in St. Petersburg and the supposed brains behind this whole affair. We thought we had taken him out on the freighter in the harbor. I am surprised to see him here. Dead."

"Yah, your Doctor Choutov with him."

"Chief Inspector, did you find any heavy containers that could contain a small biological weapon?"

"Oh, that is being all this hush-hush? Appearance?"

"It could be any shape. Glass contained in some type of metal. Possibly in a suitcase or overnight bag."

"No, we are finding nothing. Clothes, guns, personal items."

"Severny!"

"Please?" the chief inspector asked.

"Did you find any other bodies?"

"No."

"Severny Iourtchak's not here. Inspector, it looks like Andreyev's right-hand man has pulled off a palace coup. Can you get me to the airport quickly?"

"Yes."

Jim pulled out his cellular phone.

"Mother," Bob said.

"Mother, Jim. We've located Choutov and Andreyev dead in a room in the Hotel Bristol. There's no sign of the weapon or Iourtchak. I'm heading to the airport now."

"Did I hear you right? You said Choutov and Andreyev?"

"You heard right. Somehow Andreyev lived through the assault on the freighter just to be done in by his own man."

"You believe Severny has the weapon?"

"Looks that way. I doubt the Russians could have possibly recovered quickly enough to find it. No, Severny's a snake. I'm sure he has the weapon."

"OK. We'll fax pictures of Severny to the SwissAir ticket counter. Catherine's there. By the way, David is shutting down all air traffic. The last flight we were allowing out has already departed. There's going to be a lot of confusion in the airport, so tell everyone to be on their toes. This jerk won't hesitate to take out a hundred innocent people in a firefight."

"We'll do our best," Jim said. They got into a police vehicle as he was putting the phone back into his pocket. "SwissAir departures, please," he said.

It only took fifteen or twenty minutes, but it seemed like hours to Jim. As they pulled up, Jim ran into the terminal and up to the SwissAir ticket counter. Catherine was nowhere to be found.

"Pardon me, please," he said as he pushed his way up to a ticket clerk. "I am looking for the woman who was here to do a spot inspection of your procedures. Is she around?" Jim asked.

"No, sir. She was leaving. Abruptly. Forty minutes ago."

"Do you know where she went?"

"Toward the gates, sir."

Jim pulled out the telephone as he headed toward the SwissAir departure concourse.

"Mother," Bob responded.

"This is Jim. We have a problem. Catherine left the ticket counter forty minutes ago."

"She didn't check in with us! OK, I'm going to try to get the Norwegians to seal off the airport. We'll get a fix on Catherine's transponder and get back to you. In the meantime, you get Severny's picture out. We'll tell all the operatives to meet you at the entrance to the terminal near SwissAir."

THIRTY-TWO

CATHERINE SAW SEVERNY READING A MAGAZINE.
Good. He's not paying attention. He knows Jim and David; they're operatives. I doubt the Russian intelligence has my picture.

She turned her head away and walked past him to the rear of the aircraft where she took her seat. Her heart was racing, and she could feel the sweat about to break out around her hairline.

"Excuse me," Catherine said to the attendant in the back. "Is there a telephone I can use on board?"

"You pulling an inspection on us, aren't you? Trying to trip me up," the flight attendant said. "You know the phone can't be used until we are at our cruising altitude and the pilot has cleared the use of electronic equipment."

"Yes, uh—keep up the good work."

She decided that she would not try to explain.

He's not likely to do anything rash before we take off; I'll just wait until we are airborne.

Suddenly, she began to feel panicked.

I don't know how to call Bob. For crying out loud! You can't just dial 911.

Catherine heard the blood pulsing through her temples with each heartbeat. Her breaths were increasingly short and more frequent. Who would she call? The White House, or CIA? How was she going to explain to an international operator why she was calling the White House from an airplane over the North Atlantic? Acid boiled up into her throat.

The plane jolted as the aircraft began to move away from the terminal. The lights flashed off and on, and the ventilation changed abruptly.

Oh God. If ever I've needed you, it's now. I'm here, and I don't know what to do. Oh Lord, I may be the only hope of stopping this guy. I've never been in a real fight. This guy's a professional killer. Oh Lord, please don't hold my sin or lack of faith against me now. Help! Please Lord, help.

The crew began the safety lecture. Catherine finished praying and began to consider her options. It seemed that contacting someone and obtaining help would be the best option. The people sent to help could meet the plane in London and neutralize Severny without endangering the passengers.

Who do I call?

She decided she would ask the operator to put her through to the office of the CIA director. That would get her through to a watch officer. She could tell him who she was, give him the code name of the mission, and tell him who knew about the mission.

Maybe I can convince him to pass the message along quickly. At least the CIA has a duty officer.

If she tried the White House, she'd likely get the secret service detail. They'd be less inclined to believe her since they deal with so many crackpot calls.

People are afraid of the CIA and the IRS.

"Good afternoon, ladies and gentlemen. This is your captain. I want to welcome those who have joined us in Oslo for the continuation of our flight to London's Heathrow Airport. We expect to get final clearance for takeoff from the tower at any moment. I'll be talking with you once we're airborne and have reached our cruising altitude. In the meantime, please pay attention to the safety instructions our crew will give you. Sit back and enjoy the flight."

A minute or two later the aircraft started to move. The pilot turned onto the runway and stopped momentarily. The engines began to roar. The plane started to roll. As the roar grew louder, the vibration in the aircraft intensified. Slow at first, then faster, and faster it rolled. Suddenly the front of the aircraft lifted up. Catherine felt a jolt as the rear wheels left the runway.

God, I'm in your hands.

Tears ran down her face. She reached for a handkerchief.

Get hold of yourself.

As the aircraft continued its sharp ascent, Catherine recalled a Bible passage she'd read and heard over and over again through most of her life.

Who shall separate us from the love of Christ? Shall trouble or hardship or persecution or famine or nakedness or danger or sword? No, in all these things we are more than conquerors through him who loved us. For I am convinced that neither death nor life, neither angels nor demons, neither the present nor the future, nor any powers, neither height nor depth, nor anything else in all creation, will be able to separate us from the love of God that is in Christ Jesus our Lord.

A strange settling came over her persona. Her heart rate slowed, and she ceased sweating.

Focus on the mission. I've got to focus on the mission. There's no time to wallow in fear or self-doubt. There's no one else here to do this. If God can use a boy with a slingshot, it'd be a piece of cake for him to use a poison dart.

Since she was no longer sweating, she started to put her handkerchief away. As she did, she brushed against her coat and felt something inside.

The Mont Blanc pens. I remembered to put those pens in my pocket.

In her other pocket was the cigarette case. Then she touched her right ear.

I was warned that diamonds are a girl's best friend.

Back on the USS *Peterson.*

Bob appeared in the CIC and walked over to David. "We have a problem," he said.

"What else could go wrong?"

"Jim's reported that Catherine's missing. We've tried to get a fix on her using her transponder. I'm afraid that atmospherics and sun activity have screwed things up."

"Not again. You lost her again?"

"We don't know if she's in the airport or if she's on one of the three aircraft that left within the past forty minutes."

"Tony, get me a fix on the three civilian airliners that left Oslo within the past forty minutes. Bob, get agents to each of the three airports to meet those planes. At least now we know who we are looking for. Oh, and tell them to be on their toes. It wouldn't be unlike Severny to alter his appearance in some way. I doubt he's had time for plastic surgery, but hair, mustaches, and beards are all very easy to alter. Tell them to focus on eyes, nose, and facial shape. Stop every man his size and make sure it's not Severny."

David felt a rush of emotional pain as the idea that Catherine might be in danger settled in.

I wish I'd never sent her to that airport. She's not trained. Certainly no match for a killer like Severny. She was assigned to this mission to handle the weapon. I might wind up getting her killed.

David was fighting to hold back his emotions. He took out a handkerchief and faked a cough so he could wipe his eyes.

"Commodore, the tracks are up on the status board, sir," Tony reported.

The London flight was heading southwest toward the tip of Denmark. Its probable track would take it out over the North Atlantic and south to England. The other two aircraft that had left before the London flight were already over land. The flight to Brussels was very close to its destination.

"Tell Mr. Reese to hurry. The Brussels flight is close to its destination," David yelled.

"Special Ops, flag plot. The commodore says that the Brussels flight is almost to its destination." There was a pause. "Alright, I understand. Commodore, all three airports are ready and have full SWAT teams standing by."

David got up out of his command chair and walked over to the tactical net radio handset. He keyed it. "Alpha November, this is Tango Tango. I am prepared to authenticate, over."

"Tango Tango, this is Alpha November. Authenticate Alpha, Bravo, Charlie, Alpha over."

"This is Tango Tango. I authenticate Oscar Alpha. Immediate execute. Launch two fighter intercepts. Assigned intercept is SwissAir flight seven seven six. Seven degrees east longitude, fifty-seven-and-a-half north latitude. Intercept to use *Peterson* air intercept frequency after launch. Standby, execute. Out."

David moved back to his chair.

"Tony, switch the CAP aircraft to an alternate frequency. Get a second controller up devoted to the intercept. Oh, and put the air intercept on this frequency," he said pointing to a speaker right over his head.

"Aye, sir."

"Ask Mr. Reese if they have a track on Dr. Evans yet."

"Special Ops, flag plot. Have you located Dr. Evans?"

"No, Commodore, no joy with the satellite."

If Severny got away on one of the three flights, things could get tricky. David sat considering the various scenarios that could play out. As he did, his mind began to drift toward Catherine. He replayed the images of that first day in Oslo. How fun she had been.

Smart, confident, feminine, sexy, with the face of an angel.

He thought about how she had reacted after he escaped from the freighter. She hadn't come right out and said that she had fallen in love with him, but it seemed that way. Now, as he thought about possibly losing her, he realized that he had fallen for her.

I need to tell her. I need to know how she feels. God, if you're there, please keep her safe.

"*Peterson*, Red Devil leader, over," the speaker blared above David's head.

"Red Devil, this is *Peterson* Air Intercept Control, over."

"*Peterson*, we're airborne and following your track to bogey designated Bravo Charlie. Time to intercept, twenty minutes. What are your orders? Over."

"Tell 'em to come in behind the airliner in their blind. Shadow 'em several miles back."

"Red Devil, this is *Peterson*. Approach their blind. Shadow several miles back, over."

"Red Devil."

THIRTY-THREE

"LADIES AND GENTLEMEN, THE CAPTAIN HAS TURNED OFF THE SEAT belt sign. You are free to move about the cabin as needed. However, we suggest that while seated you keep your seat belts on. Remember, there is no smoking on this flight. Also, the use of laptop computers or other electronic devices is not permitted until the captain has cleared their use. Electronic devices can interfere with the aircraft's navigational systems, so please refrain from using them until the captain has given the go-ahead. If there is anything we can do to make your flight more comfortable, please press your call button. We'll be serving complementary beverages in just a few minutes. Thank you."

The senior flight attendant pulled the curtain into the first-class cabin closed. Severny got up from his seat with his computer case and walked forward to the first-class pantry.

"May I get something for you, sir?" the flight attendant asked with a polite smile.

"I would like to show you something," Severny said. He pulled the laptop out.

"The captain has not—"

"I know." He took a small screwdriver out of the bag and loosened the screws, thus exposing the inside of the computer.

"Do you see this?" he said as he pointed to the plastic around the motherboard.

"Yes," she said with a puzzled look on her face.

"This is plastique explosive," he said while displaying a devious grin. "These wires lead to this small radio. If the wires are disconnected, the bomb detonates."

He replaced the back panel and the screws. The flight attendant took a step back, and a look of sheer terror came across her face.

"See this button on this pager."

"Yes," she said in a frightened tone.

"If I let go, the bomb goes off. Now, put your hands behind your head with your fingers laced."

She hesitated.

"You're not ready to die, are you?" he said heckling her.

She complied. He then reached into his computer bag and pulled out a roll of duct tape. He took the tape and wrapped it around the waist of the flight attendant and around the laptop so that the computer was held in place on her stomach just under her breast.

"Now, put your hands down and call the captain for me."

"Captain," her voice cracked. "This is Elisa. A man has just strapped a bomb onto me and wants to talk to you," she said. Then she handed the phone to Severny.

"Is this the captain?"

"Yes."

"Captain, I have enough plastic explosive to blow this aircraft out of the sky, and it is now attached to your flight attendant. I am holding a pressure detonator. If you try to overpower me and I release it, the bomb will explode. Do you understand?"

"Yes, I understand. What do you want?"

"What direction and course are you on?"

"We are heading south southwest on course two zero zero."

"Alter course to two one zero. Tell me when you cross zero degrees longitude. Do you understand?"

"Yes, two one zero. Tell you when we reach zero degrees longitude."

As the captain was talking, the navigator brought up the international air distress frequency.

"Mayday, mayday, this is SwissAir seven seven six. I have an emergency, over."

"*Peterson*, Red Devil, I'm picking up a mayday from bogey Bravo Charlie. Do you want me to respond, over."

"Negative," David called out.

"Red Devil, that's a negative, over."

"Red Devil."

"Tony, get the international air distress frequency up on this speaker over here," David said as he pointed to an unused speaker near his chair.

"Aye, sir."

"Mayday, mayday, this is SwissAir flight seven seven six. I have an emergency, over."

"SwissAir seven seven six, this is Alborg tower. What is your emergency, over."

"Alborg, this is SwissAir seven seven six, hijacking in progress, over."

"Ah, SwissAir seven seven six, we understand you're being hijacked. What is your position, over."

"Six and one half degrees east longitude and fifty-seven degrees north latitude. Course two one zero, over."

"SwissAir seven seven six, we're tracking three aircraft in your area. One is squawking, the other two are not. I assume they're military aircraft of some type. Do you have contact with the other aircraft in your area?"

"Alborg, no, we don't see them on radar or visually. They must be behind us, over."

"SwissAir, what instructions have you been given, over."

"Alborg, we've been ordered to change course from two zero zero to two one zero and to report passing zero degrees longitude, over."

"Standby, SwissAir seven seven six."

In the first-class cabin, one of the passengers was fidgeting and becoming upset because the flight attendant had not answered his call button. "Excuse me, Miss," he finally called out from his seat.

Severny poked his head out from the pantry and looked at the man. "She's tied up at the moment," he said. Then he turned back to the flight attendant and put a finger in front of his lips to tell her to keep quiet.

Not to be kept from his drink, the man got out of his seat and headed for the pantry. "Now look here, I paid good money for first class, ah, what's going on?"

Severny lunged for a sharp knife the flight attendant had been using to cut lemons and limes. In a fluid movement he turned and hurled the knife right into the heart of the man. Two of the women passengers in first class saw the knife hit and screamed as the man turned toward them and fell dead in the aisle. This brought one of the flight attendants from coach running forward to see what was going on.

Severny pulled the flight attendant with the bomb into the aisle. He demanded that the flight attendant from coach pull the curtain open so all of the passengers could see. Reaching for the plane's intercom, he keyed the microphone.

"Ladies and gentlemen, let me have your attention," he said.

By this time, a number of passengers had become distraught.

"Sit down and shut up everyone," he demanded.

Most of the people who were up and moving around quickly found a seat. Several parents frantically tried to calm their crying children.

Severny stepped back into the pantry and searched through several of the small drawers. He frantically searched half the drawers until he opened one with a small assortment of utility knives. He took two with six-inch blades and placed them in his pocket. Then he stepped back into the aisle.

"Do you people see this man in the aisle?" he demanded over the intercom. "He's dead from a precisely thrown knife. I don't need practice. Whoever speaks next will be my next target. Sit down and shut up."

The third flight attendant in the rear of the aircraft stepped into the coach pantry and called the flight deck.

"Captain, this is Gisela in coach."

"We know about the bomb, Gisela."

"Yes, sir. He's killed one of the passengers in first class."

"OK, try to keep the passengers calm. Tell him I would like to talk to him. Ask him to call me on the phone from first class. Remember Gisela, you need to project a calm manner. The passengers will be calmed by the way you act and respond."

"I understand, Captain," she said. Then she stepped out into the aisle.

"Sir," she called out. "The captain requests that you contact him. You can use the phone in the pantry beside you."

"You tell the bloody captain to fly the plane. I will talk to him when I'm good and ready. Tell him I don't want to hear from him or any other flight officer until he reports the crossing of the Greenwich meridian."

The flight attendant stepped back into the pantry and called the flight deck. "Captain, Gisela. He says that he doesn't want to talk to you or any of the flight officers until you report crossing the Greenwich meridian."

"All right, Gisela. He has to have some destination in mind. You need to keep the passengers calm."

"Yes, sir. Oh, sir, we have a supervisor who boarded at the last moment. Would you like to talk to her?"

"No, just have her help you keep the passengers calm. We'll sort this out as we go."

Catherine was horrified.

Now what do I do? I can't get to the phone now. If I tell the captain about the weapon, it'd only serve to upset him. On the other hand, he's the captain, and his aircraft has been hijacked. He should at least know why.

Catherine got up and moved to the rear pantry.

"The captain has asked that you help us keep the passengers calm," Gisela said.

Catherine went to pick up the intercom.

Gisela tried to stop her. "They're busy on the flight deck, and the captain doesn't want to talk to you right now. I already asked him. He told me to tell you to help keep the passengers calm."

"Well then, get out there and calm them down."

"Yes, ma'am," Gisela responded in a curt manner.

Catherine pressed the flight deck button on the intercom phone.

"Captain."

"Captain, this is Doctor Catherine Evans. I am with the American Centers for Disease Control in Atlanta. I'm also working for the American CIA on a very serious mission that involves this aircraft."

"Alright, Dr. Evans, you've got my attention. Does this involve our present crisis?"

"Yes, Captain, I'm afraid it does. The man who has hijacked your aircraft is named Severny Iourtchak. He's an ex-KGB operative who is now part of the mob in St. Petersburg. He has captured a biological weapon that contains a special strain of the Ebola virus. Are you familiar with Ebola?"

"Yes, isn't that the virus that comes out of rain forest and spreads rapidly?"

"Yes, sir. He's made arrangements to sell the virus to a group of Mideast terrorists who plan to wipe out Israel with it. They're under the mistaken assumption that the virus is controllable. It's not. If they unleash it, with modern air travel, it'll likely spread throughout the world in a matter of days. Millions would die before it could be contained."

There was silence.

"Captain. Are you there? Did you hear what I said?"

"Yes, Dr. Evans. What a bloody mess. What do we do?"

"I need somehow to get word to the people I work for. We need to surround the aircraft when we land so he can't get the weapon away. Even if it means sacrificing ourselves and the passengers, we have to prevent him from removing the weapon from the aircraft."

"So the people you work for don't know of his presence aboard this plane?"

"No, I didn't have time to report before the plane left the terminal."

"Then those two military aircraft behind us are not yours?"

"What military aircraft?"

"Ground control in Denmark has reported two aircraft on our tail that are not squawking an identification code. Jet aircraft that don't squawk are military."

"Can you talk to them?"

"We have been talking to ground control on the international air distress frequency. If they are monitoring it, they should be able to hear us."

"Try talking to them. Ask them to relay the following message to the USS *Peterson*. 'Mother, this is Dr. Evans. Reference code name: Antidote. Iourtchak on board. Has hijacked aircraft. Please advise.' Did you get that, Captain?"

"Yes. I'll get back to you."

As Catherine hung up the intercom phone, she wondered why the military aircraft were there. She remembered an old news report about a bank robbery where the thief parachuted out of a commercial airliner.

Oh no! I didn't consider that they can't let us get over land.

The captain switched his radio setting over from cockpit to the air distress frequency.

"Military aircraft behind SwissAir seven seven six, this is the captain of SwissAir seven seven six. Please respond, over."

He waited a minute and then tried again. He waited another minute and tried again. "Military aircraft behind SwissAir seven seven six, I don't know if you can hear me or not. I am going to say this in case you're listening. I have a message for you to relay to the USS *Peterson*. It's addressed to Mother from Dr. Catherine Evans. It's regarding operation code named Antidote. The message is as follows: Iourtchak on board. He has hijacked the aircraft. Please advise, over."

David could hear the SwissAir captain trying to raise the two interceptors.

"*Peterson*, Red Devil. Do you want us to respond to the bogey? Over."

David shook his head no.

"Red Devil, *Peterson*. That's a negative, over."

"Red Devil."

David could feel the tears starting to well up so he coughed and jumped up from his chair and exited the CIC. The only person in the passageway was the marine guard sixty feet down the passageway near the door to the operations center. David turned his head away from him and dried his eyes.

What kind of a God would take my wife Rebecca and then let me fall for a woman I have to kill? What kind of a capricious game are you playing? How could you do this!

Tears began to flow. As he thought about giving the order to shoot the plane down, his stomach began to knot.

All those innocent people.

Suddenly he was feeling very sick. He turned, and almost running, went past the guard and out a rear hatch onto the weather deck behind the O-3 level. He moved quickly to the leeward side and threw up.

"I didn't join the navy to kill innocent people. That's it. No more. I'll resign my commission before I ever accept another intelligence mission," he screamed into the wind. "Never again. Never!"

David wept uncontrollably.

"Dr. Evans?"

"Yes, call me Catherine."

"I'm sorry, Catherine, the military aircraft don't answer. Either they're not monitoring the air distress frequency or they're choosing to ignore us."

"Well, Captain, it looks like we're alone on this one. And this man is among the most highly trained killers the old Soviet Union was able to produce. The only thing we have going for us is that he doesn't know who I am or that we know who he is and why he's doing this."

"Yes, if what you say is true, what are we going to do? If he's the trained killer you depict, I doubt we can overpower him."

"Maybe. Maybe not. We do have the element of surprise, and I have one little trick we might be able to use."

"Should we do that? Shouldn't we wait and let the authorities capture him when we land?"

"Captain, I assure you, those aircraft are not there as friendly escorts. Right now a decision is being made whether it is better to shoot us down and lose several hundred lives or to let us land and risk millions of lives if Severny gets away."

"Certainly they could surround us and prevent his escape."

"Captain, are you sure Severny doesn't have a parachute somewhere on board this plane?"

"Well, not certain, but—"

If I were an expert like him, I would have an alternate plan for my escape. After all, his objective is not to die. He's a professional. He didn't take this aircraft without a plan. He's out for money, not to die for some cause."

"I see your point. So you think they may shoot us down?"

"I'd probably give that order, and so would you. After all, Captain, it's hundreds of lives versus millions. We haven't much time. What instructions has he given you?"

"He had us change course ten degrees. I'm to report to him when we cross the Greenwich meridian."

"Where does this take us?"

"Out into the North Atlantic. We were originally scheduled to turn more to the south to intersect London. I assume he's planning to also turn south at some point. But I have no idea as to the destination."

"OK, we have one chance. I have to get close enough to touch him. I need a distraction for that. Instead of calling him to report crossing the meridian, I want you to come out into the cabin and try to talk him into giving up. Try to negotiate. Call me first and give me time to work my way up to him before you come off the flight deck."

"And then what?"

"I have a cigarette case that'll stun him if I can touch him. We'll restrain him while he's stunned."

"What about the detonator?"

"What do you mean?"

"He has a bloody pressure detonator. He told us that if he's overpowered the bomb will explode as soon as his hand lets go of that bloody detonator."

"Can't stun him. Hmmm. Okay, I have an ink pen that fires a dart with a nerve agent. It kills very quickly. If you're focused, you should be able to reach for his hand and the detonator as soon as the dart strikes him. Keep the pressure on his fingers. He'll fall dead almost immediately."

"That's not much better than the bloody stun gun! What happens if I can't grab his fingers?"

"Well, I guess we die ten or fifteen minutes sooner than we would if we don't try."

"Thanks for the bloody reassurance."

"Make sure you're on the side where he's holding the detonator when I fire the dart. He's likely to reach his other hand up to the impact area, and then he'll begin to turn. You have to catch the hand with the detonator as he turns. By the time he can react to your grabbing him, he should be disoriented. All you have to do is hold on for a few moments until he's dead. Just hold onto his hand and the detonator for dear life."

"I don't like this plan. I'm a bloody pilot, not a martial arts expert." He paused. "OK, I'll let you know when we pass the meridian."

THIRTY-FOUR

"DAVID. ARE YOU ALRIGHT?" BOB ASKED AS HE STEPPED OUT ONTO the O-3 level weather deck.

David had stopped crying although his face was slightly discolored around the eyes.

"Yeah."

"CIC reported that you had left without telling anyone where you'd be."

"I had to get out for a moment. I've never faced having to order the death of innocent civilians. It made me feel a little queasy, and I didn't want to lose my lunch in front of the troops."

"So you're going to order the airliner shot down?"

"I have no choice."

"We could always surround the plane when it gets on the ground. We may be able to resolve the situation without killing everyone. Catherine's on that plane. She may be able to do something."

"Bob, Severny didn't just hijack that plane as a fluke. He has a plan. He could have just sat there and flown to London without bringing attention to himself. He has no idea who Catherine is."

"Your point?"

"If I'd planned it, I'd put the weapon and a parachute into a bag and check it. At some point over land, I could use the crew access to the luggage compartment and retrieve the weapon and the parachute. It's been done before."

"I didn't think of that," Bob said. "So you can't take the chance of letting the plane cross over land?"

"Not as I see it."

"Well, you don't have to give the order right away," Bob said.

"What do you mean?"

"They're out over the water. Looks like Severny is planning to bypass London. Until they change course and head for land, you don't have to give the order. Catherine's aboard. She's a very clever woman."

"Severny's the best the KGB ever produced. Catherine's no match for him. Besides, those carrier-based planes have short legs."

"I doubt with airport security that she still has either gun. May have her cigarette case and the Mont Blanc pens. Severny doesn't know her, so she'll have the element of surprise. Also, you can have the F-14s relieved by fighters from England."

"Well, she may not be trained, but she is pretty sharp, and she may get lucky. Let's hope she can pull a rabbit out of her hat before Severny turns toward land."

"She will."

"I've been out here long enough. I'd better get back to the CIC."

David took his chair in the CIC. The track showed that the airline was still heading southwest toward England.

"Assign Bogey Bravo Charlie to missiles," David ordered.

"Aye, sir. Red Devil, this is *Peterson*. Assign Bogey Bravo Charlie to missiles, over."

"Red Devil."

"*Peterson*, Red Devil. I'm locked on with missiles. Awaiting weapons free, over."

"Red Devil, *Peterson*. Remain locked on. Hold your fire, over."

"Red Devil."

Catherine wiped the sweat from her forehead. She sensed that she was starting to hyperventilate again. She focused on the red light on the coffeemaker and took a long deep breath. She held it for a moment and then slowly exhaled.

A little better.

She took several more cleansing breaths.

Lord, I've gotta calm down.

She had to urinate so badly that her bladder was about to burst. She stepped across from the pantry to the toilet. After finishing and flushing, she stood and looked at herself in the mirror for a few moments. She slipped her hand into her coat pocket and pulled out the cigarette case, removed the cigarette with the prussic acid, and returned the case to her pocket. Then she left the toilet, slipping the cigarette into the side pocket of her jacket. She went back to the pantry to wait on the captain.

Lord, please make this work. Don't let him get away with this. Give me confidence and a steady hand.

Her praying was interrupted by the phone. "Captain?"

"Yes. We've passed Greenwich meridian. We're getting close to England. I hope those jet jocks aren't trigger happy."

"Okay, give me two minutes to work my way up the aisle to first class. Then make your entrance."

Catherine hung the phone up and took a deep breath.

This is it.

She left the pantry. Within two steps, her toe caught the edge of a handbag protruding from under one of the seats causing her to stumble into the back of one of the seats.

"Excuse me," she said and scurried back to the pantry for several more cleansing breaths.

I've got to get up there before the captain steps off the flight deck.

She took another deep breath, gritted her teeth, and left the pantry.

"Miss!" one of the older female passengers called while grabbing her arm. "Are we going to die?" The woman began to sob uncontrollably.

Catherine stopped and tenderly hugged her. "No. Don't you worry."

Catherine continued up the aisle.

Severny sat in an aisle seat on the first row of first class. She walked right past him and then turned back to face him.

"Would you like something to drink?"

"No, if I want something, I'll ask for it."

The door to the flight deck opened, and the captain stepped out. Severny bolted from his chair and thrust himself within inches of the captain's face. "I thought I told you I didn't want to see any of you from the flight deck back here," Severny thundered. Then he hit the captain in the stomach with a hard blow.

The captain gasped as he bent over in pain. "I just came out to tell you that we've passed the Greenwich meridian."

"Oh, well, next time call," Severny said with a sardonic laugh.

The captain stood back into an upright position. Catherine reached into her vest pocket and took out the burgundy pen. She took aim at Severny's neck.

The captain stared beyond Severny instead of looking right at him. Severny noticed his gaze and began a quick turn as Catherine pressed the firing mechanism on the pen. The pen popped, and the dart whizzed by Severny's neck and lodged in the bulkhead.

With the noise of the pop, Severny instinctively began a round kick. He came across and struck Catherine knocking her to the floor. According to plan, when Catherine fired, the captain lunged for Severny's hand. He missed grabbing him. Severny recovered his balance from the round kick and executed a short side kick to send the captain flying against the bulkhead. Then he turned to Catherine who was still on the floor. He reached down and put his rather large hand around her throat and lifted her up off her feet and slammed her back against the bulkhead.

"So, we have a hero I see. Too bloody bad. Such a waste. I would rather enjoy the company of such a beautiful woman."

With a sadistic grin he began to squeeze her throat cutting off her air. Catherine began to flail around. She grabbed his arm with her left hand and tried to pull his hand away. With her right hand she reached into her coat vest pocket and grabbed the cigarette with the knockout gas. She held her breath and fired it in his face.

He gasped. His anger increased, and he began to squeeze his hand.

He's gonna crush my throat.

Seconds seemed like hours. She started to see black spots and was beginning to lose focus.

Got to hold on. Just a few more seconds.

He released his grip on her neck. She fell to the floor gasping for a breath. He stumbled back and began to fall.

The detonator! Catherine was having trouble focusing. She lunged for his hand. As she moved through the air, he released the detonator, and it fell to the ground before she could reach his hand.

He was bluffing. That lousy jerk was bluffing. Thank God.

"When will that SwissAir flight have dry feet?" David asked.

"Less than five minutes, sir."

David swallowed hard and hit his fist on his chair. "Catherine, forgive me," he whispered to himself.

"Air Intercept, tell Red Devil leader he has weapons free."

"Aye, sir."

Just as the intercept operator responded to David, the distress frequency started to crackle with a message.

"Belay my last air control," David shouted.

"Red Devil, disregard my last, hold missiles. Acknowledge."

"Red Devil. Understand, hold weapons."

Over the air intercept circuit David overheard the navigator and the tower in Amsterdam talking.

"Amsterdam, this is SwissAir seven seven six. We have subdued the hijacker. I repeat, we have subdued the hijacker."

Everyone in CIC started cheering and clapping. David stood. Tears filled his eyes.

"Unassign missiles," he ordered.

"Red Devil, *Peterson*. Unassign missiles."

"Red Devil." The response was in an excited tone of voice.

"Order the interceptors to take them into London."

"Aye, sir. Red Devil, this is *Peterson*. Contact SwissAir seven seven six and tell them to accompany you to London."

"Red Devil."

With that order the two interceptors kicked up the speed and came alongside the airliner where the flight crew could see them. The Red Devil leader came up on the air distress frequency.

"SwissAir seven seven six, this is United States Navy Red Devil Four, I understand you've had some excitement today."

"Red Devil Four, this is the copilot of SwissAir seven seven six. Yes, we have. Our pilot has been injured."

"SwissAir seven seven six, you are requested to accompany us to London."

"I understand, follow you to London. SwissAir seven seven six, out."

David reached down to the ship's telephone system and dialed 222.

"Captain."

"Captain, David Egan. Please set flight quarters. I need to get to the *Kennedy* as soon as possible."

"Yes, sir."

Moments later the boatswain's pipe sounded over the 1-MC. "Flight quarters, flight quarters, now set flight quarters. Set condition zebra aft of frame one five zero. The smoking lamp is extinguished throughout the ship. Now flight quarters."

David ran from the CIC to the special operations room.

"Bob, report this to the White House. I'm going to take the helicopter over to the *Kennedy*. Have them standby with an aircraft to get me to London," David said.

All of the passengers were clapping and cheering. Catherine smiled in response as she offered a silent prayer of thanks.

Forgive me for ever doubting your presence, Lord. Thank you for answering my prayer and giving me the presence of mind to do this. Thank you, Lord.

She prayed as she waved at the passengers.

"Thank you all very much," she said. "Thank you. Thank you."

The passengers began to settle down. Catherine slumped into one of the first-class chairs. She watched the flight crew as they used nylon straps to bind Severny.

He'd have to be Houdini to get out of that. What a day!

EPILOGUE

DAVID MADE IT TO THE *KENNEDY* JUST AS THE WEATHER GAVE OUT. The fleet faced a storm with gale force winds. Flight operations were canceled for the next six to ten hours. He took the opportunity to sleep, something he'd been short on over the past few days.

He didn't make it to London until the next day. By the time he arrived, it had been almost twenty hours since Catherine had touched down in London with the weapon. A British marine officer greeted David as he arrived.

Across the field he saw a makeshift compound of tents. On one of the taxi elevators, a large yellow and international orange tent had been constructed over a SwissAir 747. A fenced perimeter had been constructed around the tent compound and airplane. It was being guarded by the British Marines. They were dressed in full chemical/biological protective clothing. Near the large tent containing the aircraft, David noted a large olive canvas tent. The roof panels had large red crosses on white circle backgrounds. It was obviously a field hospital.

About a hundred yards from the edge of the perimeter fence, he saw several trailers that had been joined together into a makeshift building. The Jeep drove across the runways and stopped in front of this makeshift building. The British marine escorted David into a large room.

It was filled with personnel manning a staggering array of electronic equipment, most of which looked like communications equipment. Some were military, some civilian. Near the back, David saw Admiral Bill Hopkins with two U.S. naval officers and two civilians. He recognized one of the civilians. It was William Sherrington, the president's national security adviser.

"David," Bill said in a loud tone motioning him to join the group. As David approached, the men stood to greet him. "Good job, son. I knew if there was anyone who could pull a rabbit out of the hat, it was you," Bill said as he beamed with pride and enthusiasm.

"Yes, fine work," Bill Sherrington said as he extended his hand to greet him.

"Thanks. I'm afraid most of the credit goes to my partner. She's the one who rescued our bacon."

"True, true," Bill said. "Believe me, she's going to get more credit than she'll want. The nation needs heroes, and anyhow, its good to see you. Oh, let me introduce the others. This is Doctor Kase Pinckney. Kase is Catherine's superior at the CDC."

"Commodore," Kase said. "Thanks for taking good care of our girl."

"This is Doctor Bill Pioneer. And this is Doctor Randy Krumel." The two officers extended their hands and exchanged pleasantries with David. Both officers were commanders, and both wore medical insignias.

"Where's Catherine?" David asked.

Bill took a deep breath. David instantly knew something serious was wrong. "She's quarantined. David, some of the passengers have begun to show the early stages of hemorrhagic fever. We have them quarantined inside the compound."

David felt a sharp stabbing pain in the pit of his stomach. He was overwhelmed with a rush of grief and concern. "Is Catherine," he started to say with a crack in his voice.

"She's shown no symptoms up to this point," Doctor Krumel chimed in. "The exposure may have been limited to two or three of the passengers."

There was a moment of dead silence as David stared off at a distance. Finally, he focused on Doctor Krumel. "Ah, I don't understand. Why two or three?"

Kase Pinckney jumped in to answer. "The containers with the virus were brought into the passenger cabin. One was defective. It leaked. The virus got onto the case that Severny Iourtchak used to transport the containers. We surmise that one of the passengers moved the case at some point. If he got it on his hands, it would be easy to spread to the face. The other passenger with actual symptoms was in the same row."

"I thought this stuff was airborne? You know, all that protective gear," David responded.

"We really don't know if it can spread without a medium. Ah, by that I mean truly airborne. Blood, bodily fluids, dust, a sneeze, even a casual touch would certainly be possible methods of transmission."

"So, what you're saying is that you're not sure if any of the other passengers will come down with the fever?"

"Yes. That's a fair assumption, David," Doctor Krumel responded. "We've isolated the sick ones in the field hospital. The others are in the other tents."

"When will you know?" David asked.

"Soon," Doctor Krumel said. "The incubation is quite rapid. Hours in some cases. I'd say that if they don't show signs in oh, say forty-eight hours at the most, then they're likely out of the woods."

"Can I see or talk to Catherine?" David asked.

"We were going to run a land line in so the folks could call home," Admiral Hopkins responded. "You can talk to her then."

"When do you think they can leave?" David asked.

"Another five, six days tops," Doctor Krumel responded.

"What about the virus?" David asked. "Is it contained?"

"You bet," Bill responded. "We took one of the containers back to Atlanta, and we destroyed the rest of it."

As the men sat down and continued to discuss the events of the past few days, David couldn't help but think about Catherine. In a few days she'll be out of quarantine and there will be nothing standing in the way of their pursuing a relationship. A small smile crossed his lips.

"Captain. Are you still with us? Want to let us in on what you're grinning about?"

Two weeks later. The White House Rose Garden.

Twenty minutes behind schedule, the president stepped to the podium. "Good morning, ladies and gentlemen. I want to thank you all for being here this morning. I would like to extend a special greeting to our distinguished guests. First, the king of Norway. Thank you for coming. The prime minister of Israel. Mr. Prime Minister . . .

". . . We are gathered here this morning to honor the valor of a truly great American. Doctor Catherine Evans was responsible for subduing a very dangerous killer who hijacked an airliner in an attempt to transfer the Ebola virus to terrorist buyers. Because of her actions, we now have the virus safely under lock and key at the CDC in Atlanta. Doctor Evans, in a tense, frightening, and life-threatening situation, stepped into the breach and literally rescued hundreds of thousands, maybe even millions of people from certain destruction. Her valor and coolheadedness under pressure are deeply appreciated by the citizens of this nation and the nations of the world. It is my honor to award her our nation's highest honor for valor. It is the civilian equivalent to the Medal of Honor."

He turned to face Catherine. "Doctor Catherine Evans, on behalf of the Congress and the people of the United States of America, it is my distinct honor, and privilege, to present you with this Medal of Freedom."

The crowd stood and roared in applause as Catherine stood. The president draped the medal around her neck and then shook her hand. As the crowd continued to applaud, Catherine shook hands with all of the officials near her. The applause continued for several minutes until the president stepped back to the podium and motioned for the audience to sit down.

"Doctor Evans," he said inviting her to take the microphone.

Catherine had tears in her eyes, and her makeup was slightly smudged as she approached the microphone. "Thank you, Mr. President," she said shyly with a slight crack in the first two words. She cleared her voice and continued. "Thank you, Mr. President, distinguished guests. I want humbly to thank you for this very high honor."

By this time, those in the audience had resumed their seats and everyone was listening intently to what Catherine had to say.

"A little over a week ago, when the White House informed me that I was to receive this honor, I was a little bit surprised. I didn't feel particularly heroic. Certainly there had been numerous highjackings in the past, and I don't believe anyone was ever singled out and focused upon with the intensity that I've seen these last two weeks. I realize that the potential danger to the world is what focused such public interest in my case. But you have to realize, what I did was no more a danger to me than what hundreds of others do each day across this country. So it is with great humility that I accept this honor this morning. I know we need symbols in our society, and God has chosen me to bear this one as an encouragement to all Americans."

She cleared her throat again. Then she took a deep breath before continuing. "Over the past two weeks I have been astonished—no—flabbergasted would be a better term, by the media coverage I've received regarding this incident. Last week a political cartoon appeared in my hometown newspaper that depicted me as a nineties' kind of female James Bond. This past Saturday one of the New York papers ran a cartoon depicting me looking like a female Sly Stalone and dubbed me Ramba."

The crowd chuckled momentarily.

"I think Hollywood has given us an idea that heroes are somehow superendowed, fearless individuals with super-human strength and bravery. However, the truth is, real-life heroes are ordinary human beings who are thrust into extra-ordinary situations where they have to act in a way that may endanger their own welfare. As a rule, these ordinary humans have genuine fears and apprehensions. They have to overcome these fears in order to accomplish the task dictated by the sit-uation. Often, they take action because they have no other choice.

"When I was told that I was about to receive this medal, I took some time to look into what former recipients of medals for valor had said about their experience. It was interesting that among all the Medal of Honor recipients that I looked into, not one was a Rambo. I read what six different men said upon receiving their medals, and to a man, there wasn't a sin-gle Hollywood-style hero. Each man did what he felt needed to be done. Each man related that he experienced great fear. Each man had to overcome his personal demons and do what needed to be done.

"I have often thought that one of the more gruesome ways to die would be to burn to death. I know that firemen have a great fear and respect for fire. They tend to treat it like a living creature. And yet, every day firemen put their lives at risk to run into burning buildings rescuing people. Why? Because it needs to be done. They're ordinary humans doing an extraor-dinary job. And firemen aren't the only people who perform heroic deeds day in and day out. There are many individuals who will never be recognized by a ceremony like this one.

"I experienced tremendous fear aboard that aircraft. In fact, I cried and was panic-stricken. I assure you, there was no Jane Bond or Ramba aboard SwissAir seven seven six. In fact, I was so overcome with fear that I was unable to think or act.

316

Fortunately, due to my good old-fashioned Christian upbringing, I was able recall a key Bible verse at precisely the time I was completely overcome with fear. God gave me a peace in my spirit when he told me that I was more than a conqueror, that I had nothing to fear. He was in control. It's that settling in my spirit that allowed me to focus and do what needed to be done.

"I understand that the seriousness of the Ebola virus focused world attention on my situation. As I've already stated, I also understand that a society needs symbols. While I don't think my actions were any more significant than those performed day in and day out by many others, I understand the need of a nation to bestow medals and to honor some as heroes. In light of that, I humbly accept this award. I hope that all Americans who have ever risked life or limb to serve others will feel that they are sharing this award with me."

She waited for the applause to die down.

"In conclusion," she slipped into her exaggerated Southern drawl, and a slight smile tipped the edge of her mouth. "I just want to thank y'all once again for honoring me as you have. God bless you and may his peace shine in each one of your lives."

That evening in Alexandria, Virginia.
Daughters of the American Revolution Gala.

The dinner and speeches had taken hours, and Catherine was happy to see that part of the evening come to an end. David had been called away from London prior to her being released from the quarantine, and since then the events and schedules had kept them apart. In fact, the first time she'd been able to talk to him face to face had been in the White House just prior to the ceremony.

The music was playing. Few of the guests were taking advantage of the dance floor. Most milled about in small groups engaged in idle chatter. Catherine made her way across the room to a small group of four men. She smiled and slid her arm under David's. The men politely acknowledged her presence.

"Would you gentlemen mind terribly if I were to steal the commodore from you for a while? We've not had an opportunity to, how do you say it in the military, debrief?" There were a few smiles and chuckles.

"Whooo, David. Sounds like you've got orders, son," one of the men responded.

David took Catherine into his arms. The very air around her seemed energized. His gaze was soft as a caress. Her heart danced with excitement. For several numbers they glided across the dance floor attuned only to each other. Finally, David noted that a waiter was standing near his table. He took Catherine by the hand and led her to the table.

"What's this?" she asked with playful toss of the head and a smile that went from ear to ear.

"Why, it's a Cahors Chateau de Gaudou. I knew you liked the truffles." David said. The gleam in his eyes contained a sensuous flame.

Catherine snuggled close to David. She stood on her tiptoes and kissed him on the neck.

"I think I'll always like truffles," she said.